PO

Road to nowhere
FIC ROB 150977

Robertson, Paul J.
New Madrid County Library/Portageville Headquarters

W9-AGT-332

Road to Nowhere

ROAD TO

NOWHERE

BETHANY HOUSE PUBLISHERS

Minneapolis, Minnesota

NEW MADRID COUNTY LIBRARY
309 E. Main St.
Portageville, MO 63873

Road to Nowhere
Copyright © 2008
Paul Robertson

Cover design by Paul Higdon

All rights reserved. No part of this publication may be reproduced, stored in a retrieval system, or transmitted in any form or by any means—electronic, mechanical, photocopying, recording, or otherwise—without the prior permission of the publisher. The only exception is brief quotations in printed reviews.

Published by Bethany House Publishers
11400 Hampshire Avenue South
Bloomington, Minnesota 55438

Bethany House Publishers is a division of
Baker Publishing Group, Grand Rapids, Michigan.

Printed in the United States of America

Library of Congress Cataloging-in-Publication Data

Robertson, Paul J., 1957-
    Road to nowhere / Paul Robertson.
        p. cm.
    ISBN 978-0-7642-0325-1 (alk. paper)
    1. Murder—Fiction. 2. North Carolina—Fiction. I. Title.
    PS3618.O3173R6   2008
    813'.6—dc22

                                                          2007036381

A community is a commonality—we are the people who know the same streets; the rain falls and the sun shines on us all together; the decisions we each make affect us all; and we believe and hope differently, but together.

When there is tragedy, we all feel it together. My prayers and blessings go out over my home of Blacksburg, Virginia.

And Lisa, thank you. Only you know how much.

. . . said to Him, "What is truth?"

. . . then handed Him over to them . . .

January

January 2, Monday

Time to start. Bang the fool gavel.

"Come to order." Dead quiet anyway. "Go ahead, Patsy."

"Mrs. Brown?"

"Here."

"Mr. Esterhouse?"

"Here," Joe said, and he hated that he was. Wicked, evil business.

"Miss? . . . Gulotsky?"

"Please. Just Eliza. I am here."

"Mr. Harris?"

"Here."

"Mr. McCoy?"

"Right here."

"Everyone's here, Joe."

"Thank you, Patsy," he said. "Jefferson County North Carolina Board of Supervisors is now in session."

So many names over the years. Thirty, maybe, or forty. It wouldn't be easy to remember them all. "Motion to accept last month's minutes?"

"I'll move that we accept last month's minutes."

"I'll second that."

He didn't even listen to who said which. It was usually Louise Brown, then Randy McCoy. Now that the meeting was started, he just wanted to be done.

"Motion and second," he said. "Go ahead, Patsy."

"Mrs. Brown?"

"Yes."

"Mr. Esterhouse?"

"Yes."

". . . Miss . . . Eliza?"

"Just Eliza. I vote no."

"You what?" Wade Harris said, beside her. "You're voting against the minutes?"

"Well, she wasn't even here last month." That was Louise, from the other end of the table. "It's her first meeting."

"Go on, Patsy," Joe said.

"Mr. Harris?"

"I vote yes. For Pete's sake."

"Mr. McCoy?"

"Yes. Sure."

"Four in favor, one opposed," Patsy said.

"Motion carries," Joe said. "Minutes are accepted." Just be done, that was all. "Next is receiving public comment." He raised his voice to talk to the audience. "Any of you have anything you'd like to say to us?"

Nothing. There were only three people sitting in the rows of chairs. The newspaper reporter was sleeping in his corner, and the two others were each there for a reason of their own, and not this.

Those three. Five board members. Patsy, the clerk, at her desk, and Lyle, the county manager, quivering beside her. Just ten people in the whole big fancy room.

And not Mort. Joe couldn't bring himself to look to his left, past Wade Harris, where Mort Walker should have been. Where Mort had been for thirty-two years.

It didn't seem worth it anymore and he was tired of it. There was no purpose to the bickering and anger. Tonight there'd be plenty of that. He looked down at the pages on the table in front of him, a letter as wicked and full of trouble as anything he'd ever seen.

He set his other papers on top of it.

"We'll get on with the agenda. Everyone's got a copy?"

"Left mine at home."

That was Wade Harris. The man could just barely be bothered to come to the meetings. And likely as not, he had some hand in the letter and its trouble.

Patsy handed Wade a copy of the agenda.

"First item," Joe said. "Contract to pave five miles of Marker Highway. Winning bid was Smoky Mountain Paving. We need a motion to award the contract."

"I'll move."

"Second." Louise and Randy again.

"Motion and second. Any discussion?"

"Wait." Wade again, of course. "Which road?"

"Marker Highway," Randy McCoy said. "From Wardsville to past the interstate."

"What happened to Gold River Highway? I thought that was next."

"That's next on the list. It's not funded yet."

"So when does Gold River Highway get paved?" Wade asked.

"Whenever it gets funded," Randy said.

"Any more discussion?" Joe asked. The little there'd been had been more than enough. He didn't know Wade enough to trust him, and he didn't much care to know him better anyway. And tonight he was trusting him even less.

"Voting to award the contract," he said. He wanted the meeting to be over, more than he ever had. "Go ahead, Patsy."

"Mrs. Brown?"

"Yes."

"Mr. Esterhouse?"

"Yes."

"Eliza?"

"I vote no."

"Mr. Harris?"

"What if we all vote no?" Wade asked.

Randy answered, "I'll be voting yes."

"I mean, what if the board votes no?" Wade said. "The road doesn't get paved?"

"Lyle," Joe said, and Lyle startled. The poor county manager was as jumpy as a rabbit, anyway. "Explain what happens if we don't award the contract."

"Uh . . . Joe, when we sent out the request for bids, we said the contract would be awarded to the qualified low bidder. If you don't award it, they could bring a lawsuit."

"So why do we even vote?" Wade asked.

"The county can't enter into a contract without the supervisors voting," Lyle said.

"So we have to vote, but we have to vote yes. Whatever. I vote yes."

"Mr. McCoy?" Patsy said.

"Yes," Randy said.

"Four in favor, one opposed."

"The motion passes," Joe said.

Why was she voting that way? Every vote she'd be reminding him that Mort wasn't here.

The reporter was awake and scribbling.

Keep going. "Next item." There'd be more bickering about this one, too. "Nomination to a county board. Mr. Stephen Carter has agreed to serve on the Planning Commission, to fill the open seat." Joe checked his watch again. He'd give them five minutes for their squabble. "You see his qualifications. Is there a motion to appoint him?"

Wade Harris stifled a yawn. "I move we appoint him."

Louise. "I'll second."

"Motion and second," Joe said. "Any discussion?"

"Joe." Randy McCoy was shaking his head. "I'm not sure about it. Mr. Carter certainly seems to be a nice man, and real smart, and I appreciate his willingness. But I just think someone should live here in the county for a while before we appoint him to the Planning Commission."

Carter himself was in the audience. "How long have you lived here, Mr. Carter?" Joe asked.

"Five years, sir."

"How long do you think he should have to live here?" Wade asked.

Randy frowned. "Well, maybe longer than that. Especially if he doesn't live right here in town."

Wade frowned back at him. "Now, that's your real problem, isn't it? He doesn't live right here in town. Your problem is that he lives in Gold Valley." He held up five fingers. "We've got five places on the Planning Commission. One's empty, that we're filling, and one's Duane Fowler, and he lives in Marker." He folded down two fingers. "And the other three are Ed Fiddler, who's your next-door neighbor, and Humphrey King, who's your cousin, and you." He pointed right at Randy. "Well, I think it's about time there was someone from Gold Valley on the commission. It's as much a part of the county as Wardsville."

Joe just watched and waited.

With Mort and Louise on the board, there'd been three of them with a lick of sense and they'd get done what they needed. Without Mort it would be different. But even just the two of them would most often be enough. It would be tonight for appointing Carter.

"Now, Wade," Randy was saying, "it's not that he lives there in Gold Valley, which I know is part of the county, that's not what I'm saying. I'm only worried that, if he hasn't lived here but a couple years . . ."

"Five years."

". . . that he might not really have a good feel for how people do things here."

Joe checked his watch. He knew Randy plenty well and didn't trust him, either. Three more minutes.

And after this, they'd take up the letter.

Wade was getting hot. "And since I've only lived here four years, what's that supposed to mean exactly? None of the rest of you has ever lived in Gold Valley for a week, and it's as much a part of the county as Wardsville. In Raleigh the Planning Commission was divided by districts so everyone had a representative. . . ."

"You aren't in Raleigh anymore, Wade," Randy said.

"You don't need to remind me. It is *really obvious*. . . ."

"And you really don't need to remind us about Gold Valley being part of the county, because like I just said—"

"As long as we just pay our taxes and shut up—"

That was enough. Joe tapped his gavel. "As there is no further dis-cussion, I think we're ready to vote." He'd have given them two more minutes if they'd stayed civil.

Louise patted Randy's arm. "It's only fair," she said.

The reporter wasn't even looking up, just writing. He'd have his article finished before the meeting was. Always sat in the back corner.

"Go ahead, Patsy," Joe said.

"Mrs. Brown?"

"Yes."

"Mr. Esterhouse?"

"Yes."

"Eliza?"

"I vote no."

"Mr. Harris?"

"Yes, yes, yes. Yes!"

"Mr. McCoy?"

"Well . . . yes. But I still don't think he's necessarily the best person."

"We couldn't find anyone else, anyway," Louise said. "Thank you, Mr. Carter. We really do appreciate that you're willing."

"I'm glad to, Mrs. Brown."

"That's four in favor, one opposed," Patsy said.

"Motion carries," Joe said. Louise was right. Taken two months to find someone willing. "Next item."

This was the one.

If he'd felt like it, and if he'd had time, he'd have called someone in Raleigh to ask a couple of questions. Or he might have just ignored the letter and never said a thing about it. But there was a chance good might come of it. It was likely evil already had.

He took the letter out from his pile, as wicked evil as anything he'd ever seen.

It was about a road.

There was no trouble like there was with a road. A whole year of strife in one letter from Raleigh, and that would be for any road. This one would be worse.

" 'North Carolina Department of Transportation has announced a limited one-time grant program to complete highway projects meeting certain criteria.' " He was reading the first page. " 'The program is intended for high-priority projects of long standing.' " He glanced at Wade, but the man looked as ignorant as ever. "We would need to vote to apply."

"I'll move," Louise said.

Randy was frowning. "What project would we be applying for?"

"I'm sorry," Louise said. "Does that have to be in the motion?"

"It does," Joe said. "There's a pile of rules. We only have one project on the county plan that qualifies."

"What would that be?" Wade asked.

Joe leaned back and said the words. "To bring Gold River Highway over the mountain into Wardsville."

And that did it.

Everyone acted up together, even Louise. Even Patsy and Lyle. Right away there was a hubbub and people sitting up straight and the few of them in the room sounding more like twenty, like a chicken coop with a snake at the door. And that's what it was, anyway.

"Where did you get that?"

It was the reporter, from the audience, shouting over everyone else. Joe tapped his gavel.

"We need that road," Wade said.

"Read it again," the reporter called.

"Patsy will make copies after the meeting," Joe said.

"Good gravy," Randy said. "You don't mean they actually might build it?"

"Why not?" Wade said, turning on Randy.

"Well, that's not what I'm saying," Randy was saying, "not that it shouldn't, it's just that I don't think we've ever really expected it. Joe, wasn't that on the plan even before you were on the board?"

"No, it wasn't." Even Gold River Highway wasn't that old. He could remember the hand-drawn maps and the engineer up from Asheville presenting them. "It was added in 1967."

"Lot has changed in thirty-nine years," Randy said.

"You bet it has," Wade said. "Like four hundred houses built in Gold Valley. I'll second that motion."

"Her motion didn't count," the reporter said.

"I don't think it did," Louise said.

"Then I'll do it," Wade said. "I move that we apply for this grant, whatever it is, to get Gold River Highway put over the mountain."

"Second?" Joe said.

"I'll second," Louise said.

"Now we can discuss it."

The reporter had moved up to the front row.

"What's to discuss?" Wade said. "That road is the most important project in Jefferson County."

"Well, now, I think we should discuss it," Randy said. "Like I said, a lot has changed in thirty-nine years. You know, that road would come over Ayawisgi Mountain right into Hemlock Street, and there's a lot of houses in there, too."

"Does it have to come in right there?" Louise asked.

"We've been over it on the Planning Commission a dozen times. The only place it can get over the mountain is through the gap, along where the dirt road is now, and right into Hemlock. The high school's on one side and the furniture factory's on the other side. That's the only place it can go."

"That's where it should go," Wade said.

"That is a residential neighborhood," Randy said, "and it's no place for a big highway."

"But that's where the road needs to go, for Pete's sake." Wade was practically yelling. "That's the point! So people in Gold Valley can get to the school and the factory and into town at all without having to go all the way out to the interstate."

"I don't think any of the city people with their vacation houses in Gold Valley are wanting to get to the furniture factory, or even the high school," Randy said.

"The furniture trucks might want a better way out to the interstate than right through Wardsville." If Wade had been surprised by all this, he was sure recovering fast. "And I've got a daughter at the high school who rides a bus forty minutes each way. Look, this has been the plan all along. And all that development in Gold Valley has been based on the plan."

"Maybe it's the plan, but nobody ever expected it to happen."

"That's what a plan is, Randy." Wade was about as exasperated as a man could be. "A plan is what you're expecting to happen. Everybody in Gold Valley sure has been expecting it."

"Joe," Louise said, giving people a chance to calm down, "I thought the state didn't have any money for new roads this year."

"It says there's twenty-five million dollars here in this program."

"Twenty-five million?" Randy said. "That's nothing."

"It's enough to build Gold River Highway," Wade said.

"But every county in the state is competing for it. Our share wouldn't be enough to put in a traffic light."

"We can still apply," Wade said.

"Is there a deadline, Joe?"

"February first."

"That's three weeks," Randy said. "We don't even have time."

"Four weeks," Wade said. "And how long does it take to vote on a resolution? Two minutes?"

"But there'll be forms to fill out and engineering drawings to be made. We couldn't do all that in three weeks."

"We only need the resolution," Joe said. "If we get approved, the state will do the planning."

"Is this the only vote we'd have?" Louise asked.

"What's the timetable?" It was the reporter again.

Joe ignored him. "We'd vote again. What we're doing now is not the final vote. If our application is approved, we'd vote again when we saw the plans."

"Yeah, what is the timetable, anyway?" Wade asked.

Joe found the page of the letter. " 'Application, February first.' "

"Wait a minute." The fool reporter again. He'd dropped his notebook and was on the floor getting it. "Okay, go ahead."

"Announcement of projects approved, April board meeting," Joe said. "Presentation of engineering concept drawings, July board meeting. Public comment period following. Final county board approval by

January first of next year. Detailed engineering and putting out for bids, approximately one more year. Construction begins after that." He handed the page to Wade. "If we were approved, we'd vote in December. They'd start work about a year and a half later."

"There is no way we'll get accepted," Randy said. "Now, in my opinion, I don't think we should apply if we're not even going to be approved. Those folks in Raleigh have plenty to do as it is without going through a bunch of papers from us way out here that don't have any chance of being accepted anyway."

Wade was staring at him, full flabbergasted.

"Are you flat crazy?" he finally said.

Joe tapped his gavel. "Any more discussion?"

Louise had a question. "Joe, why only four weeks? I've never heard of such a short deadline."

"The letter came back in October."

"Nobody saw it?" she asked.

"It came to Mort," Joe said. Then he had to wait a minute. "He was the county contact for the Department of Transportation. It was out at his house. I only saw it yesterday." He glanced out at the audience, at the one person who hadn't yet said a word. "I think we'll vote now. Go ahead, Patsy."

"Wait a minute!"

Joe was already plenty angry without the fool reporter interrupting every two minutes. "The board is not accepting public comment," he said.

"You can't just vote!" the reporter said. "Nobody even knows what you're doing!"

"There's no requirement to schedule public hearings before we apply. Go ahead."

"Mrs. Brown?" Patsy said.

"Joe, you're sure we'd vote again if it's approved?" Louise said.

"That's what it says."

"Well . . . I'd want to think more about it. But to apply, I'll say yes."

"Mr. Esterhouse?"

"Yes."

"Eliza?"

"I vote no."

"Mr. Harris?"

"Yes, so it passes. Good."

"Mr. McCoy?"

"Well, it's already passed, so it doesn't matter."

Patsy waited. "Are you abstaining?"

"What? Oh. Well, I really don't think we should apply, and even more I don't think we should build a road, but I hate to vote no and seem contrary when something's already passed."

"What are you voting?" Wade asked.

"I suppose I'll say yes, since it doesn't matter anyway. But I know it won't get approved."

"That's four in favor, one opposed," Patsy said.

"Motion carries," Joe said. "Lyle, you'll make sure someone in the office fills in the forms?"

"I will, Joe." Lyle would probably do it himself. He was about all the engineering staff the county had. Patsy would check it over to make sure it was done right.

"And if it does get approved, somehow," Randy was saying, "I think a lot of people will have a lot to say about it."

"You bet they will," Wade said.

"There will be time for public comment," Joe said. "Everybody will have plenty of opportunity to say their piece."

"But it won't get accepted," Randy said. "So it doesn't really matter."

They'd know soon enough. Joe put the papers back in the envelope and handed it to Lyle. He might still call Raleigh, or he might just wait. There was nothing he could do to head off the fight they'd surely just started.

Roads were a mess, and this one would be like nothing any of them had ever seen. The reporter would stir it up even worse. That's what the man thrived on. He already had another page filled with his scrawls.

And it wasn't just that people here in the county could fight with each other. This would have people outside fighting, too. That made Wade worth watching.

Or maybe it wasn't worth anything, not anymore. Just let the lot of them have their way and do what they wanted.

He was still hating being here. Because now was time for the last item, and the hardest one. Not hard for the others—just for him, and maybe for Louise. "Final item. Proposal to put up a suitable monument in the flower bed outside the courthouse in honor of Morton Walker and his service to the county."

Silence. For this, not one of them dared to say anything. None of them had any right to say a word, even Louise. For thirty-two years Mort had been on this board, a better man than these two schoolchildren arguing over every blame thing.

Everyone in the county had known him, and not a one would have even run against him for respect of what an upright man he was. Not a one, but her.

Who knew how the idea had got into her head ten years ago. She'd run in every election she could since then, and never gotten more than a dozen votes. She'd run last November against Mort, an insult to the whole county, but nothing to even take notice of.

Then Mort had died three days before the election.

Joe forced himself to look to his left, past Wade, and there she was, sitting where Mort should have been sitting right now. She'd gotten her usual ten votes in the election, but there was no else who'd got any, because Mort, his friend, was dead.

He hated it.

"Go ahead, Patsy."

"Mrs. Brown?"

"Yes. Of course."

"Mr. Esterhouse?"

"Yes."

"Eliza?"

He didn't want to hear her even speak. What right did she, of all people, have to be here voting on this, of all things?

"I vote no."

Silence, again.

"Keep going," Joe said.

"Mr. Harris?"

"Yes."

"Mr. McCoy?"

"Yes."

"Four in favor, one opposed," Patsy said.

"Motion carries," Joe said. "Any other business?"

He waited just long enough for it to be a wait. "This meeting is adjourned." He stood and walked to his right, behind Randy and Louise.

"Joe?" That was Minnie Walker. The one other person in the audience. "Thank you. Mort would appreciate it."

"The least we could do."

"I hope that letter doesn't cause any trouble. I'd have brought it before but I kept forgetting."

"It doesn't make a difference," he said.

He tried to leave the room before anyone would say anything else, but Wade Harris was talking to Louise. He tried not to hear it but he did.

"Mort would have voted for the road," Wade was saying. "Bad luck he died right when he did."

Not even eight-thirty. That was one thing about old Joe being chairman, he kept the meetings short. Wade popped the Yukon into drive and started around the block.

What a joke. Everything around there was a joke. That loony tune Board of Supervisors was a joke, the town of Wardsville was a joke.

Just look at the buildings. Another plank of siding had fallen off the drugstore. Smack downtown, right beside the courthouse. Didn't that look dandy? At least the place was still open. Half of them weren't. What a shabby heap the town was, piled next to the river and straggling up the mountainside. The county was too cheap to put up even one streetlight, but the full moon shining on the snow was plenty bright to see it all. And top it all off, it was bitter cold.

He was behind the courthouse now. That was one building that would last a while—solid granite head to toe, and decked out like a wedding cake with arches and pillars and gables and a dome half the size of old Mount Ayawisgi.

Louise was standing in the back doorway, with about four coats on and a big white hat over her big white hair. He rolled down his window.

"Hey, you want a ride to your car?"

"Thanks, Wade, but I'm just looking for Eliza."

"So, what's her problem?" Wade said. "She said ten words the whole night, and they were all 'I vote no.' That's what we have to look forward to for four years?"

"It was her first meeting, and nobody said a single thing to her except you being mean."

"You were expecting Joe to give her a kiss? He looked like he was going to slug her there at the end."

"And you and Randy carrying on," she said. "You're all terrible. She was probably scared to death."

"Not her. Hey, weren't we supposed to swear her in or something?"

"Patsy said she refuses to take oaths. So Joe said to skip it."

"Whatever." He glanced up the street. For Pete's sake. . . . "Hey Louise, here she comes."

And there she came, all right, Eliza Gulotsky, looking like an unmade bed. Her hair straight out in every direction, and whatever she was wearing for a coat looking more like a ratty old quilt.

In his mirror he saw Louise coming out to meet her, and then he had a chance to think about the real bombshell.

Gold River Highway, and that was no joke. Where in the world did that come from? He'd have to call Charlie.

But first the Big Decision. Which way to get home? Option A, drive south three miles down Marker Highway to the interstate, drive twelve miles north, around the mountain, to the Gold Valley exit, and drive five miles back south on Gold River Highway to his house. Option B, one mile north on Hemlock through Mountain View and past Randy and all his cousins, two miles on Ayawisgi Road over the mountain to the south end of Gold River Highway, and north one more mile home.

Four miles or twenty miles, and the twenty would be faster because Ayawisgi was the mountain road that cars had nightmares about. *Dirt road* made it sound better than it was. Washboard dust or foot deep mud, and about twenty hairpins—the only good thing about it was the views, and those were looking out over sheer drops without guardrails. Someday, someone was going over one of those cliffs.

There it was up there, old Ayawisgi itself, shining under the moon. Nobody even knew what the name meant. It looked like a big pile of snow looming over the town, right in the way of everything and no use to anybody.

Except . . . people want to live in the mountains, and Ayawisgi was one big mountain, and that's why he was here. Somebody had to sell the people their big, beautiful, expensive mountain homes.

Gold River Highway! He was still dialing through the possibilities. Putting Gold River Highway over the mountain would make those houses a lot more accessible, and a lot more expensive.

What a wondrous thing a road was. Wardsville might be dilapidated and Gold Valley might be more speculation than reality, but a road would change everything. Wardsville would be worth developing, and Gold Valley would explode. This was big bucks. Real big bucks. And he had to make that call to Charlie in Raleigh.

That meant option A, the interstate, because cell phones were out of luck on the mountain, except at the very top. He pointed the Yukon south.

"It is *too cold!*" Louise set herself right down in front of the television. Byron was watching some basketball game. "I don't think I've *ever* been so cold." She hadn't even taken off her coats.

"Fix yourself some hot cocoa," he said. Just the thought of it made her tingle.

"I think I will."

"And while you're at it . . ."

She jumped right back up and marched into the kitchen. And stopped. Goodness sakes!

"You couldn't have even put the food away?"

"Forgot."

That Byron. To think she'd put up with him for forty years. "Then I'm going to be a while." Angie said they should get a dishwasher, but

23

Louise could wash dishes just fine, and she enjoyed doing it. She put some milk on the stove to heat. "Eliza Gulotsky was there tonight."

"It's a disgrace," Byron said. The television room was just across the hall from the kitchen and most of their talking was through the two doorways.

"Oh, it isn't! It's sad about Mort, but besides that there's no harm her being there. And I told her to come in to the salon and visit." She had the sink filled with soapy hot water and she put her hands deep down into it and just stood and felt the warm go all through her.

"What'd she say?"

"She said it would be splendid. That was what she said." Louise put the plates and cups in the drainer and took a good stiff scrubber from under the sink to do the pots. She had to concentrate. Everything had dried on, but it was her own fault, leaving it for Byron. He wouldn't have known where to start!

But there hadn't been a minute to spare and Joe couldn't abide anyone being late.

Wade turned onto the bridge, downtown Wardsville arrayed in all its glory behind him along the Fort Ashe River. It was almost quaint in the moonlight. Just as long as a person didn't look too close. *Quaint* and *derelict* were about three steps apart, and this place had already taken two of them.

What they needed was a good flood to get rid of a few buildings and clean off the rest.

At the far end was mighty King Food with its seven, count them, seven aisles of groceries. Cornelia drove all the way to Asheville instead of setting foot in that dump.

Time to call Raleigh. "I want to talk to Charlie." Right after the Fort Ashe bridge, the road got in range of a cell tower for a mile.

He'd covered half of it before he finally heard, "Charlie Ryder."

"Hey, boss, it's Wade. I was at the supervisors' meeting tonight and something came up."

"Zoning again?"

"No. A road. The road from Gold Valley over the mountain into Wardsville."

No answer.

"Charlie, are you there?" It was dead. This was too hard. No use trying in these hills—he needed to be on the interstate if he was going to have a phone conversation. So he got himself to the interstate, and didn't waste time doing it.

But he still had enough time to think. Charlie always had some deal up his sleeve. Usually too many deals. The more Wade thought about Gold River Highway, the more it was starting to look like a setup.

Right when he hit the ramp, his phone rang.

"What road did you say?" Charlie said.

Yeah, and hello to you, too. "Gold River Highway into Wardsville. Brand-new paved highway."

"They said that at the meeting?"

"It's some special funding from the state," Wade said. "It's just a chance, though, not a sure thing."

"I want that road."

"I know, Charlie." Like talking to a three-year-old. "That's why I called. Do you know anything about it?"

There was static. "I couldn't hear you," Charlie was saying.

"I'm just saying, if you're going to fix something in Raleigh, you could let me know first."

"You just take care of it at your end," Charlie said. "I could start two hundred houses up there the minute that road is announced."

"I know. But we don't have the money yet. We're just asking Raleigh for it."

"I'll take care of Raleigh."

"It'll still have to be approved here, too."

"Then approve it."

"It's not easy. We have to vote on it. The Board of Supervisors."

"Aren't you a supervisor or something?"

"One of five."

"Then fix it with the others, who are they, anyway?"

"That's why it would have been nice to have a little warning. Just a minute." He set the phone down to pass a truck. And take a deep breath. "Okay, here it goes. I represent Gold Valley. That's one yes vote. Randy McCoy represents Wardsville. He'll vote against it because it'll come right down into his neighborhood."

"Does it have to?"

"That's what they say."

"So forget him for now. Who else?"

"Joe Esterhouse is a tobacco farmer, and his district is all the farms around Marker. He doesn't care, he'll vote for it. Louise Brown will probably vote for it. Her district is southeast—it's called Coble."

"That's enough votes?"

"Maybe. When all the people in Mountain View in Wardsville start unloading on her, she could change her mind. She's pretty touchy-feely."

"Who's the fifth?"

"Eliza Gulotsky. Nutcase, certified. She just got elected as the at-large member and it was her first meeting. She'll vote no. Unless maybe it's a full moon or her tea leaves tell something different."

"Then work on the other lady."

"And besides, Joe the farmer, he's eighty. He'll vote yes if he lives long enough, but the guy could keel over tomorrow. That's what happened to Mort, the other geezer. He was the guy before Eliza. They found him in his barn, heart attack or stroke or something. Too bad, he would have voted for the road."

"Get that lady's vote," Charlie said. "Is there any way to persuade her?"

"I've already thought about it, Charlie. I don't think so. It would probably backfire."

"Well, do whatever you need to, a deal or cash or anything. Five thousand would be nothing."

"I'll see what I can do. Hey, bribe me. I'd take five thousand."

"I already own you, Wade."

You don't— Wade bit off his answer, just barely. "Look, Charlie, tell you what. After the vote, I'm coming back to Raleigh."

"You're moving back?"

"Cornelia's a sport, but we've both had enough. Four years."

"We'll talk about it later."

"Yeah. Once the road's built you won't need me to sell houses up here. Everybody in the office there will want to. You can take your pick."

"Then get the road built."

"I will."

Somehow.

The milk was hot, so Louise put it in two mugs with some cocoa and marshmallows. She gave Byron his and settled herself back into her big soft chair, and there they were, two big marshmallows themselves.

It was just a little room and filled with cute things, and she loved it. New houses didn't have shiny varnished paneling like this, or the red linoleum in the kitchen that looked like a brick floor. It was all so cozy.

The basketball game was ending on the television.

"And you'll never guess what we voted on tonight," she said. "They might go ahead and put through Gold River Highway over the mountain."

"Believe it when I see it."

"Well, sure. It probably won't happen. But you should have seen Randy and Wade, like cats and dogs."

"I see plenty of that every day at the furniture factory," Byron said. "And I can read it in the newspaper if I want to, and I won't want to."

"I'll want to see what Luke puts in his newspaper," Louise said. "He sure got excited about the road."

The news had come on. She stared and listened for a minute. "Oh, turn it off. I don't want to hear that."

It seemed like every night it was the same pictures and the same story. "He'll be all right," Byron said.

"I still worry. And Angie does, too."

"Matt can take care of himself."

"I don't like him being there . . . wherever that is."

"Baghdad. In a big army base."

"Angie says we should get a computer so he could send us e-mails. He sends her one every day."

"She's his mother. And who'd show you how to use a computer?" That was about the last thing Byron would spend money on.

"I could learn," she said. "The girls at the salon could show me. They send e-mails."

"It's a bunch of nonsense. They had computers at the furniture factory and they never worked right."

She was up again, taking the mugs, and she patted his shiny bald head. "I think *you're* the one who doesn't work right, you old stick-in-the-mud."

"It's the computers. When Jeremy left, nobody took care of them."

"Well, can't Mr. Coates find someone else who likes computers?"

"He wouldn't want to. It was Jeremy that put them in. Mr. Coates never trusted computers. That's part of why the two of them fell out, Jeremy always wanting to change things around and Mr. Coates not wanting any of it. When Jeremy left, Mr. Coates took them all out."

"Those two. It's a shame they can't get along."

"No one can fight like a father and his son," Byron said. "And those computers were one more bone between them."

She was tired of fighting. "There are too many bones, and mine are tired. *I'm* getting ready for bed."

January 3, Tuesday

Randy McCoy was having a somewhat unpleasant morning.

"Now look, Everett," he was saying, but it wasn't much use, as the gentleman was not listening.

"You voted *for* it?"

"It wasn't exactly that I voted for it . . ."

"It says right here that you did." Everett Colony slapped the newspaper with the back of his hand, and Randy knew just how the poor thing felt.

"It was just a first vote," Randy said. "It had already passed, and you know I don't like voting against everyone else."

Dr. Colony was only getting angrier. "Then why are you on the board? If that road comes through Mountain View, it'll destroy the place."

"There's no cause for alarm. It was just one vote, to apply to get the funds, and there's not much chance of that happening."

Randy was hunched up over his desk, the way he usually was when a constituent had come to his office to express his or her views, because it seemed to lessen the impact of the blows. Not real blows, it hadn't come to that—yet, of course.

He'd always leaned back when he was selling insurance, but this old wooden chair was none too stable. Once he'd been elected to the board and started getting to hear so many people's opinions, he'd worked out that having his elbows up on the desk made him feel more steady.

"That road better not happen."

"I really don't think it will, Everett." It would not be good for Everett to have a heart attack or a stroke right at this minute since he was the main doctor here in town and it was a long way to the hospital in Asheville. "Every county in the state's going to be grabbing at that money, and we were late off the starting line anyway."

"That's not what it says in here." Everett was waving the newspaper around, wild enough that Randy had to keep his eye on it and be ready to duck. "It talks about this 'secret midnight vote in an empty courthouse for an unpopular road that could disrupt the entire county.' "

"I read that myself, Everett. And you'd have to ask Luke Goddard what he's talking about in that article, because I don't think that's the meeting I was in."

"Will they widen Hemlock Street? That would take half my front yard."

"I really don't know."

Everett slammed the paper on the desk. "Everybody knows that road will never happen, and we're counting on it not happening."

"Now, it has been on the plans, you know, and people knew that." Randy braced his elbows a little harder against the desk and his head against his hands.

Everett about exploded. "Don't you tell me about some fifty-year-old plan! If you can't stop it, there must be somebody else who will. And there are plenty of other people to buy insurance from, too."

150977

NEW MADRID COUNTY LIBRARY
309 E. Main St.
Portageville MO 63873

"I know that, Everett, and I'm very appreciative of your patronage and support all these years. Let's just not worry about it yet. And if it does happen, well, at least the trucks from the furniture factory could use it and not come through Mountain View."

The desk shook from Everett's fist. Randy had got his elbows off it just in time, or he'd have lost a couple teeth, and that would have been just as bad, because Richard Colony, the dentist, was Everett's brother and they lived just across Hemlock Street from each other.

"Hey, Corny, we got some cream cheese?" For all they spent on food, there was nothing to eat. Wade closed the refrigerator and tried the pantry. Sometimes Lauren had granola bars. "What's for supper tonight, anyway?" No dice with the granola. Back to plan A, the bagel. He tried the refrigerator again. "How about some jelly?" He closed the refrigerator again.

Cornelia was standing in the doorway, watching him. "Yes, lasagna, strawberry. Are you still here?" She had on a nice thick ski sweater and blue jeans.

"Yeah, and I'm late. I got a family from Greensboro at the office in twenty minutes."

"Why don't you just sell them our house."

"No, they want something small, for a summer place." Wait a minute. Sell them what? He looked at her closser. "Hey, I told Charlie I was done here. If that road happens, this house'll be worth thirty thousand more, and we can sell it and get something nice back in Raleigh." Maybe forty thousand more. High ceilings, stone fireplace, nice ski lodge feel. Put in that road and year-round people would start looking at Gold Valley. Not just weekenders.

She didn't answer. There was a photo album on the table and he picked it up. "What'd you get this out for?"

"I was just thinking about it."

He opened the first page and for a minute forgot about everything else. There they were, the two of them, ten minutes married. Cornelia was fresh and glowing in her white dress, twenty-five years old, twenty-four years ago.

"Hey, look at you here." He looked at her, the real Corny, the middle-aged mother of two grown-up girls, standing beside him, and then back at the beauty in the picture. "You know, I didn't remember. You were almost as gorgeous back then as you are now."

"Oh, Wade." But she smiled.

"Yeah, and tell you what. This summer. We should go on a trip. Maybe France, but this time just for us, not on business."

"We don't need to."

"I think we should. For our anniversary, this fall. It'll be twenty-five, right? Okay, I got to go. What's for supper?"

"Lasagna."

"That's right. Hey, I'll be there."

"Good morning, Patsy. Thought I'd stop by and see if there'd been any mail come in."

Randy was really just needing a breath or two after his meeting with Everett, and the courthouse was only around the corner from his office.

"You can have this one that came in certified."

Randy glanced at the return address, a law firm in Texas, and that was all he needed. "Trinkle farm."

"There've been a lot of those in the last few months," Patsy said.

"There's a lot of Trinkles. Where do we even send the tax bill to?"

"Every address I can get. Texas, Michigan, California, Georgia. Every cousin. I even send one to those lawyers."

"When was the last time they ever paid?"

"I've never seen a payment in the five years I've been working here."

"We'll have to get a lawyer and foreclose eventually." He opened the letter and there it was, a whole long five pages of legal gobbledygook. "I guess we'll need a lawyer just to make this out." He tucked the letter into his pocket. "I'll put this with the others, and sometime we'll have to see what they're all about. It's usually just copies we get whenever one of them sues another over who owns the deed, and not anything we ever have to worry about. And there's enough I do have to worry about."

Patsy nodded and sighed. "I saw the newspaper this morning."

"That's exactly what I mean. For goodness' sake, that Luke Goddard is one to make trouble."

January 11, Wednesday

Louise opened the big appointment book. It was always fun to see who'd be coming in.

She had just started looking down the columns when Rebecca and Stephanie came through the front door together. Rebecca was in a pout and that meant she'd been arguing with her mother already this morning, but Stephanie was happy.

"Good morning, girls," Louise said, and went back to the appointment book. Rebecca had a perm to do first thing. "Becky, dear, you've got Grace Gallaudet in ten minutes."

Louise had her own morning mostly open, and that would be fine to catch up on the bookkeeping. She walked back past the four chairs and the big mirrors to her desk in the back corner, where she could keep an eye on the shop and the girls, and started opening the mail.

It was still as cold as it could be, and it had been all week. Not a bit of the snow from the weekend had melted. She turned up the thermostat. She didn't want the ladies shivering when they came in.

Grace was there just at nine and Louise chatted with her a minute to make up for Rebecca not wanting to. And that was where she was standing when the door opened and everybody—Rebecca and Stephanie, Grace Gallaudet, and Louise herself—turned to just gawk.

"Eliza! You came!"

She stood there for just a moment, looking at the salon and the salon looking at her. She was a sight to behold. She was tall, or it was more that she was thin, or not thin but like a tree, her arms lifted up like branches and her hair spread out wild. Her magnificent hair!

"Of course I came!"

Eliza's hands were still in the air and it seemed just right for them to be. Then she brought them together up against her cheek, so filled with excitement, like the salon was such a wonderful new place to see.

"Thank you so much for your invitation," she said, just as grand as a queen would say it.

Louise ran right over to her—she couldn't help it! "I'm so glad you did." And she was even more taken as she got up close. "And what a beautiful coat! I wanted to see it after the meeting, but I couldn't in the dark."

"Thank you."

It was so beautiful. It was pieced and quilted, every color and pattern and shape and size there was, but altogether just wonderful, like a spring flower garden. "Did you make it?"

"I did."

"I've never seen such a thing!" And here, up close, she could also finally see Eliza herself.

Her face was thin, buried under the mound of hair, older than she looked from a distance. But the wrinkles looked more like they came from laughing and crying and feeling than from age.

And that hair! It was about the thickest that Louise had seen, mostly gray but streaked with pure black in places and pure white in other places, and long enough to be more than halfway to her waist if it were hanging straight. It wasn't, though. It puffed and teased and curled itself out in every direction, like a thundercloud.

"Well, just sit for a minute and get warm. I know you're not meaning to have anything done."

"Oh . . ." She smiled, a little surprised schoolgirl smile. "I hadn't even thought."

Louise put her hand up to the cloud and touched it softly. "I'm not even sure what I'd do."

"I'd be thrilled to find out!" Eliza said. "It would be splendid." And then a look, one side to the other, and her shoulders hunched up a little, like she was telling a secret. "But not extravagant. I wouldn't have money."

"Don't you worry about that. And I don't know what I'd do with it all." She had her hands in it, feeling the texture. "I'll have to think about it. I just really don't know." She didn't, either. But she would. "And Eliza, I know we weren't very friendly at your first meeting, but I want to welcome you to the board."

"Thank you."

"You'll have to put up with Joe. And with Randy and Wade and their wrangling. The most important thing is not to mind anything that anyone says, because they'll say just anything. And I know it might be scary to vote about things you don't understand."

Eliza smiled. "Voting isn't frightening to me." She smiled more. "Not much is."

"Just use your common sense and that's good enough. Most things we all vote yes."

"When I vote, I listen."

What could that mean? "What do you listen to?"

"If I hear, I'll vote yes. When it's time."

"When you hear?"

"I do hear!"

Louise had to stop and think. "Hear what?"

Eliza sighed. "And we just follow."

Louise sighed right along with her. "Dear, I don't know what you're going to make of us for four years, and I sure don't know what to make of you."

January 14, Saturday

The sun wasn't up, and Randy didn't feel much awake, either. This was taking a chance but he didn't see a better way, and he might as well get up at six o'clock on a frigid Saturday morning. The only other thing to be doing was sleeping in a warm bed, and he'd have missed the opportunity to scrape ice off his windshield, too, in that nice howling arctic wind with all those little bits of sleet in it.

But here he was sneaking into Marker at not even seven o'clock. And there was his destination, the Imperial Diner, bright fluorescent glare from inside the plate glass shining on all those pickups rowed up outside. Right in the middle was the one he was looking for. At least he was not suffering fully in vain. Randy walked on in, just as if he had a right to be there, and he did anyway, the place was a public restaurant.

This was where the farmers of Marker often found themselves early on a Saturday morning, and if Joe Esterhouse wasn't a farmer, no one was. Joe saw him right away, so there was no sense for Randy acting like he was there for any reason but to talk to him.

He strolled over to Joe's table and put himself in an empty chair. Joe was finishing a conversation, and Randy had a moment to consider that he was probably the youngest person in the room, maybe by ten or fifteen years. Some of the farmers might have been older than the tablecloth in front of him.

"Good morning." The waitress was about his age. He gave her as big a smile as he could with his cheeks frozen solid.

"I'll just have eggs over easy, and coffee."

"Regular or decaf?"

"Honey, just look at me."

She did. "I've seen worse."

Joe was watching him. He would be understanding that this was serious, that Randy was showing respect by coming out here at this time of the morning.

"Morning," Randy said. "I want to talk a minute."

And Joe might just feel obliged to give him an answer.

"Go ahead."

Randy lowered his voice a bit. "This road we talked about Monday night. Gold River Highway."

Joe was just still, a weathered granite statue, watching him. A person would never think he was eighty, not even seventy, but he could also have been as old as the mountains.

"It's not very likely to happen, now, is it?" Randy said.

"You've had some folks asking?"

"I wouldn't say they were asking anything. I'd say they were expressing their opinions, which they held very strongly."

"I expect they did." Joe's voice was about as rough and hard as anything else about him. His white hair cut short made him look like the marine he'd been sixty years ago.

"So," Randy said, "I'd like to set their minds at ease, and it would be a big help if I could tell them that you didn't think we'd ever get that money."

Joe was taking his time to answer, and the look in his eye was that he was deciding how much to say. Randy waited.

"We'll get the money. You might as well count on it."

"Now, why in the world would they give it to us? There must be hundreds of other projects, and no reason at all that we should get picked over them."

But Joe wasn't going to argue. "Then I guess we'll wait and see."

Randy had not driven through the blizzard to argue, either, but to humbly supplicate, and he did so now.

"If you think we'll be approved, then I'll believe you, even if it doesn't seem reasonable. But are you just sort of thinking it's possible or are you really sure?"

Joe Esterhouse turned to stare through the foggy window at the dark outside, like he did a lot of looking into dark black places. The glass shook back at him from the cold wind against it trying to get in.

"We'll get the money. Sure as the sun'll rise."

February

February 6, Monday

Wade checked his watch. Three, two, one—bang went Joe's gavel.

"Come to order." The geezer was looking a little better this time. Last month the guy looked about ready to croak. Now he was just grouchy like usual. "Go ahead, Patsy," Joe said.

Wade checked out the audience.

Five chairs were filled in the front row, side by side, and the natives were looking restless. Somebody had something on their mind.

"Everyone's present, Joe," Patsy said.

For once, the newspaper guy wasn't asleep. Luke Goddard. He wrote the entire paper, three times a week. Wade read it none times a week.

"Thank you, Patsy. Jefferson County North Carolina Board of Supervisors is now in session. Motion to accept last month's minutes?" Someday he'd have to jump in and second before Randy could. That might even make it into the news. "Motion and second," Joe said. "Any discussion? Go ahead, Patsy."

On with the charade.

"Mrs. Brown?"

"Yes."

"Mr. Esterhouse?"

"Yes."

"Ms. Gulotsky?"

"I vote no."

"Mr. Harris?"

"Wait a minute." This was ridiculous. He turned to his left. "Are you ever going to vote yes for anything?"

This time he looked at her close. Somehow she wasn't what he'd expected. She was about ten years older than he'd guessed, and not how he figured a crazy would look.

"At the right time," she said.

"For Pete's sake." He turned back to Patsy. "I find last month's minutes worthy. Yes."

"Mr. McCoy?"

"Yes."

"Four in favor, one opposed," Patsy said.

"Motion carries," Joe said. "Minutes are accepted. Next is receiving public comment."

Looked like there was going to be some. A guy from the audience was already coming up to the podium, and he looked familiar.

"Please state your name and address for the record," Joe said.

"Dr. Everett Colony." Sure, that was it. Corny knew him from PTA at the high school. "712 Hemlock Street in Wardsville." And here it came.

"I wish to make a statement concerning this ill-advised plan to put a major road through the Mountain View neighborhood."

The board settled into their diatribe positions. Louise was looking all concerned, and Randy was pretending to, and Joe didn't move. On the left, Eliza Gulotsky's eyes were as big as saucers. Luke Goddard had moved to right behind Colony's chair, and he was as serious as if he were reporting Pearl Harbor.

"I can only presume that our Board of Supervisors was unaware of what they were voting for last month," the good doctor was saying. "I request that you immediately withdraw your application to the state for the construction of Gold River Highway over Ayawisgi Mountain. There is not a person in Wardsville who wants this road, and the damage it would do to Hemlock Street and Mountain View would be immeasurable. . . ."

The words poured forth.

". . . this colossal waste of taxpayer money is indefensible . . ."

How long did one person get for their comments, anyway?

". . . it will destroy a matchless vista and wreak havoc on the mountain wilderness we have all enjoyed for generations . . ."

Baloney. Wade checked his watch: four minutes, and counting. Well, it looked like he'd had his back turned and Randy had stolen a base. Ten months of this was going to wear them all down. Or at least, it would be enough to wear down Louise. She was already looking frayed.

". . . Hemlock Street is already burdened with a constant stream of trucks from the furniture factory . . ."

Blah, blah, blah.

". . . will serve no purpose, connecting Wardsville with an empty valley, and will remain an unused, expensive, empty scar . . ."

Yak, yak, yak.

". . . bringing hundreds and hundreds of cars through a once-peaceful neighborhood—"

"Wait a minute," Wade said. There was usually no point arguing with the public, but this was flat crazy. "So how is this road bringing hundreds of cars if it's an unused and empty scar?"

"Excuse me?" the man said. Joe shifted in his chair, the first time he'd moved, and now it was Randy's eyes as big as saucers.

"If there are no cars, there won't be any traffic bothering Mountain View. And if there are cars using it, then the road's no waste."

Dr. Everett Colony hit the roof.

"You wait a minute!" His face was hot red and his voice was red hot. "Your job is to listen to the people who vote and pay taxes. We're telling you we don't want this road, and you had better kill it as fast as you can."

Oh yeah? Any little pretense that this was going to be a polite discussion had melted in that blast. Wade didn't take heat like that from anybody.

"The voters and taxpayers in Gold Valley—"

"Gold Valley has no right to put a highway right through the middle of Wardsville, and they should just keep out of this." And Dr. Colony was not finished. "And we don't need a slick salesman from Raleigh who only got himself elected to line his own pockets—"

There was a crack like a gunshot and every eye was on Joe Esterhouse and his gavel.

"I'll thank everyone for their *civil* comments," he said. "And I'll point out the funding for this project has not yet been approved. Now we're going to proceed with our business."

Wade was taking deep breaths. What a hit job! Okay, then Randy McCoy was going to see how two could play this game, and pockets in Raleigh were a lot deeper than pockets in Wardsville.

Colony was sitting down, and Luke Goddard was leaning forward, whispering to him. He'd probably have to buy a newspaper whenever it came out next. Or maybe he could just imagine what it was going to say.

The meeting went on and Joe went through his agenda and Wade fumed. He stared up at all the curlicues and corkscrews in the ceiling woodwork just to keep his eyes from connecting with the audience. There was a place up in the corner between the ceiling and the walls where a sheet of plywood was nailed up over part of a mural. He was trying to figure why it was there, or what would be under it. It was painted to match the walls—

"Mr. Harris?" It was Patsy.

"Huh? What?"

"Are you voting?"

"On what?" He looked at his agenda.

"It's to put more parking meters on Main Street," Louise said.

Wade turned to Randy. "How are you voting?"

Randy scrunched back in his chair. "It's not my turn yet."

"What will you vote?"

"Well, yes."

Wade turned to Patsy. "Then put me down for a big fat no."

"Mr. McCoy?" she said after a little pause.

"Um . . . well, yes."

"Three in favor, two opposed."

"The motion passes," Joe said.

Wade looked through his agenda. There were three more items to vote on. He wasn't sure that what was left of his temper was going to hold.

"Next item," Joe said. "Report from the Planning Commission on flood control."

That sounded mind-numbing enough to cool everyone down.

Someone new had come to the podium. It took a second to remember that it was the guy they'd put on the Planning Commission. Whatever his name was. Stephen Carter.

"Good evening." he said, and he held out a wad of papers to them, one by one. "Um . . . I haven't presented anything to you before, and I'm not sure how it's done."

"Of course you haven't done it before," Joe said. "We only appointed you last month. How'd you get roped into this? Usually it's the chairman that presents reports."

"I am the chairman."

Wade laughed out loud. He was on edge, and the whole Jefferson County absurdity of it just got to him.

Joe ignored him. "How'd you get to be chairman?"

"No one else wanted to be."

Louise had to laugh at that and even Joe smiled. That blew the tension like a popped balloon. Wade turned back to Randy. "You mean, after all that fuss you made last month about not wanting him on the Planning Commission, you went and made him chairman?"

"Well, now, I didn't say I didn't want him," Randy said, in true Randy-speak. "Just that I had some concerns."

"But you voted him chairman?"

"You see, Humphrey King had been before and he wanted someone else to take a turn, and Ed Fiddler's real busy at the bank now that he's vice-president, and Duane Fowler wasn't there, and I can't because I'm on this board, too—"

"Never mind," Wade said. Bunch of hypocrites. "Go ahead and give your report."

"Yes." Carter straightened his papers. The man was probably thirty-five. Or maybe not yet—he was nervous, but he still had a competent feel that made him seem older, and thin hair and thick glasses, too. He paused, then set the papers down and looked right at Joe.

"The state wants every county to update the flood emergency sections of their comprehensive plans. Jefferson County doesn't have a flood section in their plan, so the Planning Commission has to write one. I've looked at other county's plans and state flood plain maps and put together a draft. However, the Board of Supervisors needs to approve adding sections to the comprehensive plan."

"Hasn't it only been a week since your first meeting?" Louise asked.

"Yes, ma'am."

"Ed Fiddler thought we should have it for tonight," Randy said.

Louise was shaking her head. "Honey, those people will run you ragged if you let them. Now, don't just give in to them like that."

"I don't mind," he said. Now that he was talking, he had presence. Like he'd made lots of presentations, and to more important people than the Jefferson County North Carolina Board of Supervisors. "I'm a civil engineer, Mrs. Brown. This is what I do."

"I'd say you were being real civil," she said.

That had given Wade a chance to look through his copy, and he was seeing something real interesting.

"What's this on page six?"

Carter didn't even pick up his own papers to look. "That's the part about accessibility into the town of Wardsville in the event of a flood. If the Fort Ashe River floods and damages the bridge, there's no access into town from the south and west. I'm sure you all know what would happen if the bridge went out."

"You either need to go all the way to the bridge at Coble," Wade said, "or over the mountain on the dirt road into Gold Valley."

"Exactly," Carter said. "The comprehensive plan shows Gold River Highway being completed, and that–"

"Oh, no you don't." Everett Colony was erupting again. "Who got this man on the Planning Commission? You're not from the county."

Crack went the gavel again. "This board appointed Mr. Carter," Joe said, "and he is a resident of the county." His voice would have intimidated a flood.

"You're trying to sneak this road in under some unrelated planning section," Colony said, and he was not intimidated. "This is outrageous."

Wade was biting his lip. Just don't get into it again.

"The board is not accepting public comment at this time," Joe said in a voice that would have frozen the flood solid, and this time even Colony sat down. "Is there a motion to add a section to the comprehensive plan concerning flood planning?"

"I'll move that," Wade said.

"I'll second," Louise said.

"Any discussion?"

"Now, Joe." Randy was squirming. The whole audience had their eyes on him, and the reporter had his pencil at the ready. "Am I understanding that the state says we have to put this section in?"

"Lyle," Joe said to the county manager, "you have any comments on that?"

The guy turned white. "Well, Joe, uh." Then red. "That depends. Or actually, uh—"

Carter cut in. Mercifully. "It's part of the basic requirements for state funding."

"My point," Randy said, "is whether this means we're making any kind of commitment to Gold River Highway. That's all I'm asking."

Joe shook his head. "We're not committing to build that road."

"But we're saying that we're counting on it in case of a flood."

"Do you have a better plan?" Wade asked. "What should we do if that bridge gets washed away?"

"Well, I don't think it will. It looks pretty strong to me, and I don't see it going anywhere."

"The last flood washed it right out," Louise said.

"That was thirty years ago," Randy said. "And they built this new bridge to stay put. I don't think we need to even talk about it washing away in this report."

"That's up to the Planning Commission," Wade said. "We're just letting them put in a section on flooding. You're on the commission— you can decide what to put in it." He waved the report. "Didn't you even look at this after you told him to write it?"

"There hasn't been much time." Randy's friends were glaring at him. "We'll talk about it at the next commission meeting."

"Go ahead, Patsy," Joe said.

"Mrs. Brown?"

"Yes."

"Mr. Esterhouse?"

"Yes."

"Ms. Gulotsky?"

"I vote no."

"Mr. Harris?"

"Yes. Absolutely."

"Mr. McCoy?"

"Well, it's already passed, and we can talk about it later, and we need to because Raleigh says so. So I'll say yes."

Everett Colony stood, his mouth clamped shut, and walked out of the room.

"Four in favor, one opposed," Patsy said after the echoes from the slammed door subsided.

"Motion carries." Joe said. Apparently he'd had enough, too. "We'll leave the last two items for next month. Meeting adjourned."

The deep, ancient black of night; her way curved and climbed in the forest shadows. Away from the false light of the hard streets and straight buildings, here the road respected the land and only went where it was allowed by the hills and trees, not going through but around and between and among.

Beneath and above her, and everything, was the mountain.

The quiet battering of the motor was the only sound. Zach left it running as he stopped in the clearing, but he darkened the headlights to give as little offense as he could to the night.

"Do you need anything?" he said as she opened the car door.

"No." It was cold, but still. "Thank you so much, Zach."

"We'll check in. Good night, Eliza."

He waited until she had her door open; then the headlights came on again and the car turned. Inside the old cabin, she watched the trees cover the light and sound of the car, and at last it was gone.

She stirred the embers of the fire. It came to flickering life, and with a match she lit two lamps on the table.

What a strange place that had been. How strange to have been there. Anger; force against force, will against will. One's purpose against another's.

In the small circle that each person drew around their own life, they saw so little. Few saw the great forces that ruled from their strongholds and dominated the small women and men living beneath. But the great conflicts were often fought using small lives.

The Warrior.

As she braided her hair, she considered her own presence on the council. It was for a greater purpose than her own that she was a member of it. She understood little of what was said, and the decisions they made were about such strange things.

What a strange place!

But the Warrior was mighty. It was his words she was listening for. She had heard his great and angry voice tonight in the angry voices of men. There were great powers involving themselves in the small world.

The Warrior. Ancient, and known by the ancient people who had lived here in ancient times. If he was not known now, he was still as mighty.

He had opened the place on the council for her. He would do anything else he chose.

"Outright bunch of schoolchildren." Home and sitting in the kitchen, Joe was feeling slightly less aggravated.

"Drink your milk." Rose had it on the table in front of him.

"That bunch from Mountain View are about the worst at it. Don't give a lick about anyone but themselves."

"They're worried about the road."

"People worry about too many things, and there's no sense to most of it."

"But they don't know that. When would anyone see what the road looks like?"

"We'll hear in April it's been approved, and we'll see plans in July." Joe sniffed the milk and set it back down. "Vote in December."

"Are you going to drink that or not?"

"I'm going to drink it."

"Is there something wrong with it?"

He drank a bit. It was the road that smelled. "It's not the milk."

"You're not letting people's complaining bother you?"

"No, there's always people complaining. It's the road itself. There's never trouble about anything like there is about a road. Especially this one."

"What if the state doesn't approve it?"

"They will."

She didn't question that. "And the five of you?"

"Might come down to Louise."

But it wasn't just the road, either. Rose had her eye on him.

"So what's really bothering you, Joe?"

"Mort."

"I'm sorry he's gone."

"It's more than being sorry."

"What about him?"

"Just a thought, and I don't care for it."

"About Mort or about the road?"

"Both."

"Both," she said, and that made her think. "What do you mean?"

Once Minnie had brought him that letter, it'd been nagging at him.

"In fifty years, I've never seen a letter like that one from Raleigh. I've never seen such a list of rules for qualifying. To get the money, the project had to have been in the plans for at least twenty years. That's what it said—projects of at least twenty years' standing. Only county roads, no state or U.S. routes. It had to be a new road, not an improvement to an existing road, but it had to be a connection between existing dead-end roads. Now what is all that supposed to mean?"

"You know better than anyone what to expect from them in Raleigh."

"I thought I did. How many roads in North Carolina are matching all those rules?"

"It's a big state," Rose said.

"They might just as well have said it was for Gold River Highway."

"Then what does that have to do with Mort?"

He hated to say it. "If Mort was alive, the road would have been voted in. Now that's he dead, it just might not."

"I don't believe that's the reason."

"Wish I didn't. There's always someone behind a road. This one's worse than the usual. There's like to be someone just as bad against it." He was sure of it, and he said it. "It's evil, Rose. It's more than politics. It's true evil."

"True good can stand against that."

"Joe looks so tired anymore," Louise said. She was sitting in the bed, thinking.

"Know how he feels," Byron said. "Put the light out."

"I will. He's been on that board for more than forty years."

"Enough to wear anybody out."

"I don't even remember how long," she said. Now she was thinking.

February 10, Friday

They were half way up Ayawisgi, looking north toward Fiddler Mountain. The snow was real thick; way down was Gold River, slicing between the white mountains like a knife—they could even make out the rapids.

Wade had the door to the model open but the customers had their eyes stuck. Wade pointed left, west. "That's the national park way out there. Sure looks nice in the winter when the weather's clear." Everyone's breath was little cloud puffs.

"It's just beautiful." That was the wife. Wade still wasn't sure if they were real or just window shopping.

"Come on in," he said. "Same view from inside, but a lot warmer."

Randy took a deep breath. Everett was really a reasonable man, and he always had been. He was just forceful. And he didn't hesitate when he had something to say. And—

"Mr. McCoy? Dr. Colony can see you."

47

He followed the young lady down the hall to the office in back.

Everett had a file open and was scratching notes on the first page.

"Thank you for seeing me, Everett. I just wanted to take make sure you were understanding that vote the other night."

Everett finished his writing and Randy was looking straight into his eyes. "I understand," he said.

"That wasn't about the road. It was completely different."

"No one's fooling me. Wade Harris and his crew back in Raleigh are pulling their strings." He closed his folder. "They're behind this flood plan."

"Now, that's why I came to explain. That's just a normal thing, Everett. We're always getting papers like that from departments in Raleigh. I'll take care of it at the next Planning Commission meeting."

"When is that?"

"We only meet every other month, and just when we have to, so it'll be March, or later. But I don't think it has a thing to do with the road. You can really believe me on this."

"I'll believe what I want to believe." He stood up from his desk with the folder in his hand and pointed it right at Randy. "Those people will do whatever it takes to force that road into Mountain View, and I'll do whatever it takes to keep that road out."

"Who's buying houses like these?" the husband asked. Wade had done the tour, the wife was just about sold and the husband was leaning.

"It's mostly people like you buying the cabins, couples wanting a vacation place in the mountains. The larger houses are more year-round people, retired or a few who work in Asheville. You have the quiet here, and the view, and the prices are reasonable." He started the finance spiel.

They acted okay with the numbers, but Wade was only giving it maybe a thirty percent shot. There was still the big hurdle to get over.

"And where is the grocery store?" the lady asked.

That was it. Wade smiled. "Well, now."

There were a couple strategies to try. He'd had a lot of practice experimenting with them, figuring which one worked best for which customers. Except that none of them worked for anyone.

"One big reason people like Gold Valley so much is it's not being real developed." This wasn't going to work, but it was the best he had. "Some people go into Wardsville to the nice little local grocery there. And some people drive on down to Asheville."

"How close is Wardsville?"

"You go out to the interstate and about ten miles, and then right into town. It's a cute little place."

"Ten miles?" Just that exact tone in her voice.

"That's after you get to the interstate," the husband said.

Move fast. Wade led them over to the big front window.

"Just look out here. Sure, you don't see any stores. But I'd say most people don't want to." The sun was reflecting off Fiddler Mountain and the whole thing was sparkling like Disneyland. The sky was baby blue and not a cloud in it, and Gold River looked like liquid silver through the bare black toothpick trees. "And for a second home for weekends and quiet vacations, you find out the shopping ends up not being so important."

But that was looking real hard for her to imagine. "Well . . . but . . ." She was sinking quick.

At least they didn't care about schools. That was death.

"We'll think about it," the man said, starting toward the door.

January and February were real thin months, and Wade was ready for desperate measures. "And let me mention that Gold River Highway, that we came up here on, is going to be extended right over the mountain into Wardsville. The town's only about three miles from right here in a straight line." Nothing wrong with saying that. It was on the plan.

"When would that happen?" the man asked.

"We're working on that right now." The law said he couldn't outright lie to them. "Last I heard, it might be about two years." That was the truth. He had heard it. "And that's going to push prices of everything in the valley here way up."

"Two years . . ." The wife was looking at the book again. Then back at her husband. "And then he says prices will go up."

"We'll think about it," the man said, and Wade took a deep, satisfied breath. They were the same words as before, but with a slightly different tone and a completely different meaning.

And Wade hadn't told any lies. Except calling Wardsville cute.

Louise locked the salon door. There was still some sunset left out over the courthouse, and she stood to look at it.

It was just lovely, a little pink and orange and a few clouds. And stars off in the other direction where the sky was black, and the mountain right up in them.

She made herself think about that road. She could see where it would come over Mount Ayawisgi. It had been a while since she'd been over in Mountain View, and she decided it might be worth a peek.

She turned onto Hemlock and passed King Food, and then up the hill by Memorial Park, past the library, and there was Mountain View.

It wasn't that big of a neighborhood, just about five blocks along Hemlock and three or four blocks on either side, but so fancy. The houses away from Hemlock weren't as large, but people still took such good care of them.

Of course, it wasn't the easiest place to live. She and Byron were just as happy to be where they were, on Coble Highway, where people didn't have to keep their yard perfect and neighbors didn't mind a few extra Christmas decorations or all the clutter of little statues and birdbaths she liked in her garden. There was a lot of looking down on each other in Mountain View, and having to please each other.

She came back out at the far end of Hemlock by the high school. The parking lot was mostly empty at this time of the evening, but across the street and down a little, the furniture factory still had some cars. They must have had some good orders recently to be running an evening shift.

And down past the factory, Hemlock just petered out into that dirt road. Goodness sakes. It was hard to imagine what that would look like.

Somebody was down there, tall and thin and in a black suit. She drove up close.

"Roger!"

Roger Gallaudet was looking every inch like a funeral home director, even just standing beside his car at the end of the pavement.

"Hello, Louise."

"I came to see what it would look like to have a road up here."

Roger nodded. "That's why I'm here myself. I suppose lots of people are thinking about it."

"Don't you live up here?"

"Right behind Everett Colony."

"Then you know what he thinks." Louise was not looking forward to the next year of board meetings.

"I do." Roger was still staring up the mountain. "I think I'll go have a talk with him."

"I won't get mixed up with that!" She gave him a big good-night smile and turned her car around and started back toward town. Hemlock was lined with trees through Mountain View, old oaks and maples, and even a few hemlocks.

Well, Randy and Everett Colony and all of them shouldn't have to worry a bit about widening Hemlock. There wouldn't be room, with all the old big trees right up by the street and leaning over it. Especially the biggest ones, right in front of Everett's house.

Oh, look at the sky! What a color it was, an impossible dark white mix of blue and red, and gray cloud smudges like old paint on weathered wood, and the knife-sharp silhouette of the mountain like torn black paper.

The trees were silent as the sky, watching. The whole mountainside of them, standing rigid and black, held their arms up to it.

Eliza joined them as the mountain, the sky, all of life together changed from day to night, through every moment between light and dark.

They had all talked about a road at the meeting. She couldn't imagine it, or where it would be; it was too disturbing to even understand. But she knew the Warrior would not allow it.

February 13, Monday

"Charlie."

"What?"

Wade was staring out his window. Dead day, not a client, not even a call. Might as well call the boss and make it worse.

"Hey. I've been thinking. You have the timeline for completions this summer?"

The voice in his ear was annoyed. "It hasn't changed since Christmas."

"Maybe it should. I think we'll be overbuilt by October, by maybe twenty or thirty houses."

"We need to sell eighty houses this year, so that's how many I'm building."

It was always the same. "Jump in a lake, Charlie. Nobody wants a house twenty miles from a grocery store." Wade was fuming, like he was most of the time when he was on the phone with Charlie Ryder. He took his three deep breaths.

Charlie was talking before breath number two. "I'd build a grocery store. What was the problem with that? I don't remember. The land by the interstate is zoned commercial, right? Didn't we try to buy it?"

"Yeah, when I first moved up here. The whole place around the Gold River Highway exit is zoned commercial. But it's all messed up who owns it. It's called the Trinkle farm and there's a bunch of heirs, and they're all out of state, and they're all suing each other over who owns it."

"Yeah. Now I remember. Can't we get someplace else rezoned?"

"There's no place big enough and flat enough, and the board wouldn't rezone anything else anyway."

"Go ahead and try," Charlie said.

"You try. I've got enough to do."

"Like what? You haven't sold anything in two weeks."

Three deep breaths wasn't going to do it, so Wade didn't even try. "I'll quit, Charlie. In a heartbeat."

"No, don't quit. Just sell the houses."

He didn't get to answer. The front door was open and a man was standing in it, letting in cold air.

Wade punched the button on the phone and Charlie was gone. "Be right with you," he shouted, and he grabbed a sales package and hiked out to the main room.

They called it the Lodge, high stone walls and a big fireplace, with his office back in the corner. The place would be the community center once there were enough residents to qualify Gold Valley as a community.

The man was still taking it in, door wide open, and Wade stopped cold when he saw who it was.

Maybe something good could come out of this. But he doubted it.

"Hi there, I'm Wade Harris." He held out his hand. "And you're from the newspaper, aren't you?"

"Luke Goddard." He did shake Wade's hand, and he had to come inside and let the door close to do it. "Wardsville Guardian." He was forty-something and already sort of bald. The hair that was there needed a trim.

"Thought so," Wade said. "Seen you at the board meetings."

"I've seen you there, too." Whiny voice. "I came out to see your operation, Wade, and ask you about it."

"Look around. And ask away." Wade followed him to the map.

"You all started off four years ago?"

"Seven years. Broke ground April of ninety-nine. I've been here four years."

"There's that Trinkle farm." He was pointing at the empty white space around the interstate. All around it were the colored sections that were part of the development plans.

"That's it."

"Sort of the hole in the middle of your doughnut."

"Maybe it'll be the filling someday."

"Yeah. Sure it will. Once those Trinkle cousins work out their differences." He winked at Wade. "They've got a reputation, you know."

"Don't know that much about them."

"Oh, you don't? Nasty bunch. Hermann Trinkle was ornery as all get out, and he passed it on. Now you got twenty Trinkle cousins or more, not a one hardly on speaking terms with another, and they all claim they own some part of that farm. I think you should give up on any idea of ever filling that doughnut, Wade."

"None of them are getting anything out of it now."

"I think any of them would rather get nothing than have any of the others get something."

"They couldn't be that bad, Mr. Goddard," Wade said.

"They are! I know it." He shrugged. "Or maybe they will work something out. That's apt to be worse than just leaving the farm as it is. I can't even think what they might come up with, but I'd know to stay away from it. And that—" Goddard traced his finger across the map— "that's Gold River Highway."

"That's it so far." He was keeping his answers short and neutral.

"Do you really think it'll go all the way?" He moved his finger past the edge of the board.

"I really think it should."

"Lots of people against it. You'll have to read my report after the January board meeting."

Might as well be blunt. "Sorry. I don't read the Wardsville paper."

"Oh, you don't?"

"I didn't like the things you've said about me the last two years."

"Just stating the facts."

"I could give you some facts."

"I'd be glad to hear them. Wade, the *Guardian* is an impartial news organization."

"Okay. There are four hundred houses in Gold Valley."

"How many are year-round residents?"

"I don't know."

"It's about a third, isn't it?"

"They all pay taxes year-round," Wade said, "and they pay twice as much per house as the rest of the county."

"You're saying people are richer here than the rest of the county?"

There was probably no way to win this. "The county appraises the houses for a lot more. I don't know that people here have any more money."

Goddard was writing it down. "Now, if Gold River Highway was built, you'd probably make a lot of money yourself."

Definitely no way to win. "I think a lot of people would make money, including the businesses in Wardsville. That's what roads do."

"Wade, isn't it kind of improper for you to be voting on the road?"

"Absolutely not."

"Well, that's interesting." He was suddenly already walking out. "Thanks so much for your time. I think I'll drive around some and see these big houses for myself."

"Mr. Goddard . . ."

"Everybody calls me Luke."

"I really believe it's the best thing for the whole county."

He stopped with the door open. "But if the best thing for the whole county was different than the best thing for Gold Valley, which one would you vote?"

Think fast. "I don't think they've ever been different."

A big smile opened up on Luke's face. "That's a good answer, Wade! I like that. I'll quote you!"

"Don't get me in trouble."

"Don't you worry! And have a nice day."

February 14, Tuesday

Louise was doodling, and why shouldn't she? The bills were paid for the month and the mail was all done and there were five appointments even before lunchtime. Becky was humming something happy. Maybe that was why everything seemed so bright. And the phone was ringing, too.

"Wardsville Beauty," she said. "Happy Valentine's Day!"

"Louise? It's Wade Harris."

"Good morning, Wade." Because it was.

"Yeah, good morning. Hey, Louise, I want to ask you something. Gold River Highway. I wondered what you were thinking about it."

"Oh, that?" The door opened, and the first two appointments for the morning walked in. "Aren't we waiting for something before we have to decide?"

"The funding from the state."

"That's right. Well, it'll be months before we hear anything."

"April."

"Then I guess I'll start thinking about it then. Wade, you know how those things are. Everybody gets all in a tizzy."

"But what would you vote when you do start thinking about it?"

She gave the phone her biggest smile. "Wade, I have no idea."

"Okay. Never mind. Louise, I want that road. If it ever comes up, don't decide anything without talking to me."

"I'll be glad to. I know it's important to you and everybody in Gold Valley. You should talk to Joe. He might know more about it."

"Yeah, I was going to call him next."

She frowned at the phone. "I don't think you should call him."

"But you said I should."

"You should talk to him, just not on the phone."

"What do you mean? He has a phone. Doesn't he?"

"Of course he does, but you won't get two words out of him on it. Call and ask if you can come out to see him. Then he might even give you a few whole sentences. And maybe you'll get to meet Rose."

February 15, Wednesday

Dirt road. Louise had said once you got on the dirt road, it was on the right after about a mile. All Wade could see was a bunch of fields and fences. The mountains were off at a distance from there but he could still see them.

Some of the fields were dirt just like the road, some had leftover rows of stuff, and some were just grass or weeds. It must make sense why they were all different, but he couldn't figure it out—this whole part of the county was a foreign country. Barns, sheds, tractors, and parts of tractors splattered all around farmhouses or just anywhere. Cows staring at anything going past. Farmers staring at him the same way. It was almost hard to tell them apart. Maybe when there weren't cars, the cows and farmers just stared at each other.

Then it was there in front of him, a big old white house with a worn-out gray barn behind it and as many outbuildings as any farm he'd seen. No tractors in sight. Red pickup parked on the lawn by the side door. Wade pulled up next to it.

He walked around to the front porch.

No doorbell. He looked, but nothing. The farmhouse was a hundred fifty years old. Maybe it didn't have electricity.

No, there were electric wires coming in from the pole.

It didn't look a hundred years, maybe just fifty. Nice white paint on the wood siding, probably less than three years ago. Painting this place must be a job—two stories of hand-cut wood planks. Real stone foundation, too. That would cost a bundle nowadays, if anybody could even do it, and it wouldn't pass inspection anyway.

Most of it wouldn't pass inspection if it was built today, but this house had stood for more than a century, and the stuff they built today wouldn't last half that. He stood back to look at it better.

Just a big cube with a front porch. No gables—the roof went up to a point. It would have been ugly but for the two huge oaks framing it, one in front and one off the corner. Massive trees. Probably already old back when the house was first built.

He knocked.

Nice flower beds, too. They'd be pretty in a couple months.

The door opened to a dark hall straight through and light coming in a window in back. And a person.

"Hello?" she said. Same voice as on the phone, and he would have recognized her from it. This would be the legendary Rose Esterhouse—tall, almost eye to eye with him, and straight as a level. Straight as her husband. "Mr. Harris?"

Maybe he could get a picture of her and Joe standing in front of the house. With a pitchfork. "Yes, ma'am. Wade Harris."

"Pleased to meet you." Plain dress of something dark, and an apron. Pure white hair in a bun. "Come in, Mr. Harris. Joe's outside, but he'll be in soon."

"Thank you." He followed her down the hall. On the right he had a glimpse of the front room. Rocking chair and sofa and stuffed chair, fireplace and rug, end tables. Grandfather clock. All of it old, old, old, and pictures everywhere. On the left was the dining room.

The wood floor. He couldn't tell in the dark, but it felt like real floorboards as they walked down the hall.

Bedroom on the right, grand four-poster bed with a blue and white quilt, like delft china. A big Bible open on a desk under the window.

They turned left into the kitchen.

He could sell tours to this place. That woodstove, complete with ancient coffeepot, was the real thing, from who knew when, and it was cranking. It was seventy-five degrees in there. And the fireplace, same stone as the foundation. Huge—just look at that thing! No fire in it, might not have been since the woodstove was put in, but that was where the cooking had been done back in the beginning.

There was a real stove, too, an electric one, that was maybe only forty years old. The cabinets were handmade and they were amazing. Somebody had known how to carve. They made him think of a—a what? A cuckoo clock. Not real ornate, sort of German. They'd be worth big, big bucks to a collector.

And the floor . . . not a nail, and not slotted. All pegs, all big wide planks. Big wood table that must have weighed a ton. Wallpaper that was . . . roses. Sure, her name was Rose.

Compare this to the Smoky Mountain Country Theme décor they offered in Gold Valley and that stuff looked like even cheaper plastic than it was. Even his own kitchen looked cheap next to this, and it had good quality stuff in it.

Open ceiling, exposed rafters. If this house were on a paved road, it'd go for half a million.

"Just sit down, Mr. Harris. I'll see where Joe's got to."

He sat. He could have sat there all day.

"And would you like something to drink?"

"Oh, no thank you. I'm fine."

"Then I'll be right back."

She opened the screen door and disappeared into the sunshine. Wade stared and kept seeing new things. Deep wood shelves packed with canning jars that were filled with everything—green beans, applesauce, beets, jams, whatever it all was. A refrigerator that was the same vintage as the electric stove. It looked like a '57 Chevrolet.

It was all real.

He kept thinking that. He wouldn't have even known what *real* was, except that now he'd seen it and he still didn't know what it was he was seeing.

There must be stuff like this back in Raleigh. He'd just never seen it. Maybe it was all gone, anyway, sold off to collectors and replaced by Carolina Colonial kitchens with Chair Rails and Dark Oak Floor. Who knew how to can their own vegetables, anyway? Or even grow them?

No, there was nothing like this in Raleigh. Nothing real like this.

Rose was back. "He's in the barn. He'll be a few minutes."

"I'm not in any hurry."

"Just make yourself at home." She had her back to him, standing at the stove. "You're from Raleigh, aren't you, Mr. Harris?"

Yes, he was from Raleigh. Completely from Raleigh.

"Yes, ma'am." The *ma'am* came out by itself. This lady was as real as the kitchen, and she commanded respect. She was making conversation to be polite, but she sounded as casual as a congressional hearing. "We moved here four years ago."

"You have a daughter in the high school."

Was there a period or a question mark at the end of that sentence? He took it as a question. "That's Lauren. Meredith is at college."

"Two girls."

That was definitely a period, for the sentence and the conversation. Her back was still turned. She wasn't hostile, just a no-nonsense hardworking farm wife.

Okay. He would not be intimidated.

His job was to make friends. Nobody bought a house from someone they didn't like. So maybe Joe and Rose weren't in the market for a nice weekend cabin in Gold Valley, but it could still be good exercise for him to get a smile out of one of those stone faces.

Pick a subject. Family? Her life story? No, way too personal. Have to step a lot further back.

"Have you been to Raleigh, Mrs. Esterhouse?"

"Not in a while."

It's probably changed a lot. No, she wouldn't care. *We'd like to move back sometime.* Not that, either. He had to get a hook somehow.

"Cities like that change so fast. Nothing ever stays the same."

There. Now she could say she liked it around here where things didn't change, or that she'd like some more changes. *Take it, Rose.*

"Gold River Highway would be a big change."

But she'd turned around to say it, and there was a little smile. And now Wade was stuck. What was he supposed to say to that?

"Well, that's what I wanted to talk to Joe about."

"I expect." She took her pot off the stove. It was cast iron. Did she know they had aluminum pots now? That thing would weigh ten pounds, and the handle was as hot as the rest of it. She probably knew all about the new stuff, and she preferred hers. "Now, are you sure you wouldn't like something, Mr. Harris?"

Regain control of the conversation. He glanced over at the woodstove again. "Is that coffee in the pot there?"

"Joe likes his coffee strong," Rose said. "I can make you some fresh if you like."

"No, thanks. I'd give that a try, if it's all right."

She took down a white mug from a hook over the sink and set it in front of him. She filled it from the pot.

The acrid steam hit him, and it felt like the cast iron pot had.

"There's milk or sugar."

"Black is fine."

Probably been sitting there on the hot stove since daybreak. It was a wonder there was any water left in it at all. He held the cup up close to his mouth and inhaled enough to get a few drops of the coffee itself.

He'd had straight-up horseradish that wasn't this bitter.

He tried an actual sip. After a cup of this stuff, he'd be out there plowing fields himself, probably with his bare hands.

The conversation was on indefinite hold while he gave full attention to this jet fuel. Taste was not the point—this coffee was a kick in the pants to get a person out the door to work.

After a couple minutes, though, he was about ready to try talking again. And she'd brought the subject up. "What do people around here think of the new road?"

"Around here it won't matter so much."

"I guess not. You're pretty far from Wardsville."

The door wheezed and Joe Esterhouse himself was finally with them. Overalls, flannel shirt, hands black. He nodded at Wade. "Morning. Be right with you." Then he was gone into the hall.

"Working on the tractors," Rose said.

Wade took one more swallow. The last third of the cup looked pretty swampy, and he decided that discretion would be the better part of valor. He took one more long swallow of the room instead, and then Joe was back with clean hands and it was time for business.

Fool tractor. It still wasn't right. And he wouldn't get back at it till tomorrow.

"What's on your mind?" he asked, even if he already knew. Only one reason Wade Harris would drive all the way down here.

"Joe, I need your help."

"I'll help if I can." Rose put some coffee on the table for him.

"It's the road, Gold River Highway. I don't know if anyone understands what it means for Gold Valley."

"I might not."

"That place could explode, and it's the road that's holding it back. There could be a thousand more houses in there, and I mean big ones. Million dollar houses. There'd be tax revenue and development. It'd put Jefferson County on the map."

That was all the man ever thought about. "Already on the map, last I looked."

"Okay, whatever. That's not really my point. I know how everyone feels about it. But now, here's the thing, and this is where I really need your help. My boss is a guy in Raleigh, Charlie Ryder. He's got developments all up and down the mountains. He has lots of friends in the legislature.

"I looked at that letter from Raleigh, Joe. I can't make out what most of it means, but I can tell there's something fishy about it. So now I'm in a hornet's nest, with Randy and all his friends screaming at me on one side, and Charlie screaming at me on the other side, and I'm just getting jerked around and I don't know what's going on. And I don't like it."

Salesmen and city folk, always the same. "How can I help you with that?"

"You'll level with me, Joe. You don't play games. Is this road deal rigged? Do you know?"

"There's never trouble like there is with a road." It hadn't changed in fifty years. Joe felt the tiredness coming down. A bunch of trouble and he didn't care anymore. But Wade was in it and he was asking for help. "Yes. It's rigged. I'd been thinking you were part of it."

"No. The first I heard of it was the meeting last month. Can you find out who's behind it? You must know somebody there in Raleigh."

"Most of the people I knew are gone, long ago."

"Oh well. At least tell me this, Joe. I know it's a ways off, but if . . . when the vote comes up, how are you leaning?"

"People have been counting on it. Wouldn't be right to change now."

"Okay. Great. I appreciate your time."

That seemed to be enough for Wade. He stared around the kitchen for a minute or so and said his good-bye, and Rose showed him out. And then she was back, sitting across the table from him.

"I'd say you know a few people in Raleigh."

"I suppose I do."

"And you've had your own thoughts about the road."

He didn't answer her.

"Then you must be giving up on it all," she said.

"Comes a time when it doesn't seem to make a difference anymore. It's too hard to fight."

February 21, Tuesday

Louise was fiddling in the kitchen. She had no idea what to fix for supper, and Byron was going to be home any minute. The man liked his dinner prompt.

Well, she did, too.

The sun was coming right in the window, like it did this time of year. Angie said she should put up some blinds, but Louise couldn't abide it. They cluttered up the window, and that was the one place in the kitchen she wanted big and open. There was plenty of clutter everywhere else. She didn't know what she'd do if Byron hadn't put up shelves on the wall for all her little things.

She picked up one that was about her favorite—a little castle with snow, like a fairy tale. She had a sticker on the bottom and she'd written "Christmas 1995 from Matt to Grandma" on it. That nine-year-old boy and his big hugs and he'd spent his own money.

What she wouldn't give for one of his hugs right now. She made herself get back to supper before she started thinking about guns and wars and where he was now.

And there was Byron, slamming the door and dropping his coat on the chair and his lunchbox on top of it. She knew that's what he was doing, anyway even if she couldn't see him from the kitchen.

"What's supper?"

"I don't know yet," she said.

Now he was settling into his chair, and the television came on. There was some roast left over and some chicken casserole that he liked.

"I think I'll warm up the casserole from Monday." She turned on the oven and put the dish in. The microwave was faster but she liked a hot casserole dish.

There, that was taken care of.

She went out to the front room to hang Byron's coat in the closet and get his lunchbox to put away. He had the news on and she sat next to him to watch, but he wasn't watching. He was just staring at the wall.

"Something happen at the factory today?"

"They had a meeting. Called everybody up front and Mr. Coates said he was giving us some news."

"Well, what was it? New orders?" She'd never seen Byron looking so glum. Surely . . . "He isn't closing the factory?"

"No. Well, not yet. But he's selling it."

"He's selling the factory?"

"Some big company down in High Point."

"Now, Byron, that doesn't mean anything's closing. They wouldn't just buy the factory so they could close it."

"They might. One way to get rid of competition."

"Fiddlesticks."

"It'll mean bosses coming in from outside that don't know how we do things, and making changes."

Louise could smell the chicken, so it was time to get to work on the table. "What about Jeremy?"

"Well, sure, since they fought, everyone's been guessing that he'd never take over. But nobody thought it would come to this."

"What else would Mr. Coates do? He must be ready to retire."

"Never acted like it."

"It might all be for the best, you know."

"Well, then I might be ready to retire."

"I hope not!" Louise jumped up to get supper on the table. "What would I do with you all day? I don't have any idea."

"Might be about time to retire. I wouldn't want to see things be all changed around."

"Just don't worry until you have something real to worry about."

But she was worrying. That man was all the world to her, and change was hard on him.

And there'd be a lot of other people worrying, too.

First that road and now this—why did they have to happen at the same time?

"Sue Ann, why did I do it?" He didn't feel like even moving. Kyle had put up a fire in the fireplace, and for that Randy would be eternally grateful. And now all he could do was just sit and imagine the further and endless persecution he would suffer.

"You had to vote yes at that meeting. It was just like you said." Sue Ann was such a comfort, always saying just what he needed to hear.

"I'm wondering more about why I wanted to be on this board. After four years, you'd think I'd learn. But I went and got myself elected again last November and now I've got another four years. What was I thinking?"

"You were thinking you could do some good."

"Then I was sorely mistaken. Everett Colony was in my office for forty minutes this afternoon and I don't believe I spoke a dozen words." He rubbed his head. "I think I'll take an aspirin."

"I'll get it for you."

"Thank you. Where are Kyle and Kelly?"

"They're at the high school. They went over for a club meeting and they'll stay for the basketball game."

For a moment the picture of a high school gymnasium came to his mind, filled to overflowing with hundreds of fans all screaming at the top of their lungs. His head throbbed.

"Here's your aspirin and some water."

"That's just perfect," he said, "and now I believe I'll sit here and enjoy the quiet."

"Let me know whenever you'd like your dinner."

"I'll do that." Randy opened his eyes to watch the fire, which was very soothing. A few more minutes and it seemed that maybe the aspirin was helping, too. Dinner was even starting to appeal to him a bit.

He looked over toward the dining room, and wasn't that sweet. Sue Ann had their two places set with her mother's china. She must have been thinking they'd be just the two of them with the children out for the night, and she'd probably made up a nice supper.

"Here I come, dear. I think I'm about recovered and I'm suddenly real hungry."

"I have a roast for you."

"I don't want to keep it waiting."

But it wouldn't have been a real dinner without the telephone ringing, and so it did. Randy sat down next to it and picked it up.

"Randy McCoy, can I help you?"

"Randy, it's Louise."

That probably wouldn't be too bad. "Well, good evening. What can I do for you?"

"I just heard some news and I thought I'd pass it on around the board. Byron says that Roland Coates told them all today that he was selling the furniture factory."

"Selling it? Good gravy." One little throb in his temple reminded him that his headache might be gone for the moment, but it was not far away. "What's that going to mean?"

"Well, I don't know. It might not mean anything at all. And, now, I've only heard it through Byron. I don't think that counts for being official."

"If they shut it down, there's a hundred fifty people out of work, and half the school budget gone."

"No one's said they're going to close the factory," Louise said.

"Well, if they don't, that means no end to the traffic and trucks through Mountain View."

"It's one way or the other, Randy."

"I guess it has to be. What will the neighbors think?"

"What's that supposed to mean?" Wade set the phone down. "That was Louise. The plant in Wardsville, the furniture place. The guy is selling it."

Cornelia had two steaming crocks of onion soup on the table. "So?"

"So? This is New York selling the Statue of Liberty."

"Whoever buys it, maybe they'll clean it up. Why is it way back there by the high school, anyway?"

"I think it was there first, before they built the school. I don't know. It won't matter to us." He shrugged. "I guess."

"No one in Gold Valley works there."

"No. All people from Wardsville and Marker and Coble." The soup had cooled off enough to eat. "But it's all one county. I told you the newspaper guy came to the office?"

"Last week."

"So I bought a copy to read."

"How bad was it?"

"Worse than I figured. I'm pushing the road for my own profit and I don't care about anyone else."

Cornelia gave him a big sympathetic smile. "That's not true."

"I guess not. Hey, I forget. Where was Lauren tonight?"

"At school. At a basketball game."

"How's she getting home?"

"Friends."

Kids? On those roads? "I'll get her." He started shoveling soup. Corny watched him.

"And Meredith called," she said.

Why did she ever call? "She needs money?"

"Not this time. She'll be home next month for spring break."

"Great. And the soup was, too." Wade had started toward the closet for his coat, but then he stopped. "We should do something."

"What?"

"I don't know. Something fun. I'll think about it."

A game in the high school gym on a cold February night was just about as good as anything ever got. Randy and Sue Ann waited at the door just a minute before they went on, listening to the crowd.

Then they were in the sound instead of just hearing it, like being under water instead of just seeing it, and that warm heavy feeling came down on Randy like it always did. He could have been a teenager again whenever he was in there, out on the wood floor and the basketball rough and hard in his hand and running the drills and warming up, he and Ed Fiddler and Jeremy Coates and the others, and Sue Ann leading the cheers.

Now it was Kyle playing, and Kenny Fiddler, and Kelly was leading cheers, looking for all the world like her mother.

They sat right under the Cherokee Warrior painted on the wall, and just in time. The referee tipped the ball and the boys were off. It was back and forth real quick to start, and both teams put up points in the first minute. Randy was watching for a few things to see how the Cherokees were playing—how much they were passing, how close they were getting in under the basket—and it was looking pretty good. They'd really been working on that passing especially. The defense wasn't clicking quite the same way, though, and Hoarde County was getting their shots in, too. There'd be a lot of points if it kept up like this. And that was fine.

Kyle wasn't as tall as most of them—and all of them were so tall these days, not like twenty-five years ago, when it was shooting that counted and not much else. Now they'd have to get in close and pass, or else try for the three-pointers. But Kyle was a good strong boy and didn't let anyone push him around. Some games he scored more from the free-throw line than from anywhere else.

Jefferson County was up by a few when the buzzer ended the half. Randy leaned back when the teams ran off to the locker rooms, and the whole gymnasium quieted down, and everyone started out to the concessions. It made him feel like the air going out of a balloon.

"Should we get a Coca-Cola?" he asked like he always did, and he and Sue Ann squeezed down to the floor and out into the hall.

"How's your headache?" she asked.

"I don't think I even remembered I had it."

They got their sodas. Gordon Hite was there in his sheriff uniform, and Randy talked to him about the Cherokees' defense while Sue Ann talked to Artis.

Then Gordon lowered his voice a little, even though it was plenty noisy in the hall. "You heard about the furniture factory?"

"Louise Brown called me," Randy said. "She said Roland Coates told everybody there today."

"That's all we need," Gordon said. "It was going to happen, though. Roland wasn't going to pass it on to Jeremy, not after the blowup they had last year."

"It'll be the end of an era. Three generations they've had that factory."

"Do you think they'll close it?"

"I sure hope they don't." At the back of his neck there was a little twinge, and Randy wondered if anyone at the concession stand might have an aspirin. "Why would they?"

"We'll hope for the best," Gordon said. "But I was thinking about the budget and how maybe we could use another deputy this year, and if the factory closes, that's going to mean hard times all around."

"It would be, but I think we'll manage, and I don't think we'll worry about it yet."

The game was ready to start again and the bleachers were filling up. Randy and Sue Ann went back in and got themselves settled. The teams came running out onto the floor and the fans started whooping. The boys ran their warm-ups, big doughnut eights back and forth and around, pass, pass, pass, shoot.

"Randy!"

He turned around, and right behind him was Everett Colony.

"Why, Everett. Nice to see you."

"What's this about the furniture factory closing?" Everett had his usual scowl but seemed fairly equable.

"It's not closing, at least that I know about. Just Roland Coates is selling."

"That factory's been making life unbearable for years with trucks and traffic up and down Hemlock. I wouldn't mind if it closed."

Randy had his eye on the referee, holding up the ball in the center of the court.

"Well now, Everett, those trucks would have a better way to get out to the interstate," he said, and waited a few seconds until just the right moment, "if Gold River Highway got put through."

The referee tipped the ball and the crowd went deafening loud. Everett was saying something but Randy could only put his hands up to show that he couldn't hear, and then he turned back around to watch.

It wasn't a bit difficult to not think about the road or the factory. The game started going a little downhill and Hoarde County got up on top, but not by far, and it was into the fourth quarter before Randy did look back to see if Everett was still there, but he wasn't.

The Cherokees were fighting hard and Kyle got them tied with two points from the foul line. Then it was back and forth, back and forth, right up to the last minute. Everyone was on their feet when the clock ran out with three more points on the home side of the scoreboard than on the visitor side. Even if it had been the other way, it wouldn't have hardly made a difference when the teams were both playing their hearts out like that.

Then the whole crowd started moving toward the doors like so much molasses. Randy and Sue Ann waited for the bleachers to clear some.

"Randy!"

He took a breath and turned around. "Good evening again, Everett."

It did not appear that Everett had enjoyed the game at all, as he was just as agitated as he'd been when their conversation had been interrupted. He may have been even more so.

"I don't want to hear anything about Gold River Highway except that it's dead."

"You know it's not up to just me, and when we do vote . . ."

There was still plenty of noise, but Everett didn't need to be screaming. "I'll tell you how to vote and—"

"No you won't."

It was a new voice, and they were both a bit startled at it. Randy blinked just to focus, and there beside them was Wade Harris.

"He can vote however he wants," Wade was saying, "and you're acting like an idiot."

Everett couldn't even speak, and for a moment Randy was pretty sure that the man was going to explode, or at least some vital organ was going to blow out like a tire. Randy decided to take advantage of the silence.

"Good evening to you, Wade. Sue Ann, let's go on."

He scooted. He took Sue Ann's hand in his and got caught up with the main part of the crowd, and a minute later they were out into the dark night.

They waited there at the curb, and even though it was good and cold, it actually felt nice after the hot gymnasium. Car engines were starting and head lamps coming on, and it was all as much a part of the game as everything else. Randy breathed in the cold air and helped Sue Ann straighten out her coat.

"Well, Randy!" she said.

"I think we got away."

She was looking back. "I don't see him coming."

"I really am afraid Everett's going to have a stroke one of these days."

"I think he will! The poor man."

"And this road thing's going to go on for months."

Then Kelly came running out to them with a big coat over her cheerleader outfit and they talked just a minute about the game and she told them she'd have a ride home with her friends, and of course she could really even walk if she had to, they were that close. Then she ran back in, and the parking lot was clearing out, and Randy and Sue Ann walked out to their car.

Halfway there, Randy stopped beside a big black sport vehicle that was just starting up and tapped on the window. The window glided down and Wade's face looked up out of it.

"Wanted to make sure you were all right and hadn't suffered too much back there," Randy said.

"Oh yeah, no problem. I'm fine. He started up yelling when he caught his breath, but I just left him there."

"Well, thank you. I did appreciate it."

"Hey, Randy. Don't let the guy bully you."

"He has been for a long time, and I try not to let it get to me. But now, Wade, don't get a wrong idea about him. I'll vote the way I see best and not just for whoever's the loudest."

"Whatever. See you later."

"Good night, Wade." The window glided back up and the big car glided away as Randy and Sue Ann clumped over to their own little car.

Sue Ann was in and Randy had closed her door and was walking around to his own side when Kyle came running up to them. He hadn't even changed out of his uniform yet, but he didn't seem cold.

"Dad," he said.

"Good game!" Randy said. He was ready to point out some of Kyle's finer moments, but the boy had something to say.

"Sheriff Hite wants you. He sent me out to try and catch you."

"All right, I'll be right there. Let me get the car started and warming up for your mother, and you go tell him I'll be right in."

Trotting back to the gym, he was trying to think what he could have forgotten in the bleachers, as they had their coats, and that was all they'd taken in. Or maybe Gordon was still fretting over the furniture factory.

Sheriff Hite was back away from the twenty or so people still talking. Randy sidled up beside him. "Kyle told me you needed me?"

The sheriff lowered his head and his voice.

"Randy, did I see you and Everett Colony having words up there in the stands?"

"Sure, Gordon, but it wasn't anything. You know Everett."

"I do. And he looked even more worked up than usual."

Gordon Hite was round and jowly, his face set up high on a big long heavy frame. Even with him leaning down, Randy still was looking up.

"It's this road," Randy said. "That's the problem. He can't abide the thought of it."

Gordon was nodding slow and deliberate and sort of undecided, about the same as the way he did everything, including think. "Well, it's not a secret, since it's public record, even if people don't always know it. Randy, Everett's got a concealed-weapon permit."

Randy was thinking. "What would he want with a gun? I don't think he hunts, does he?"

"Not that I know of," Gordon said. "What I mean is, I think you should just keep an eye open. Especially when he's throwing a fit like tonight."

It was finally getting clear, at least maybe. "What are you saying?"

"I'm just saying you should keep an eye open."

"Well, how long has he had the permit?"

"Just got it last week."

"There's nothing to that, Gordon. I'm sure there isn't."

February 24, Friday

"Joe Esterhouse!"

Joe knew the voice. He had the spark plugs he needed and he was ready to be getting back to the tractor.

"Morning, Luke."

"Good morning, Joe. Called the farm and Rose said I might catch you here."

"Just these," Joe said to the cashier. She took his money and he took his bag and walked out to the parking lot with the reporter beside him.

"I want to ask you a question," Luke said.

"Go ahead." They stopped beside Joe's truck.

"It's about the county's long-range plans. Is there anything that's been on the books longer than Gold River Highway?"

"You might just check with Patsy about that."

"That'd be work, looking through papers. I figured you'd know."

Luke should do his own work and let Joe get to his. But it wasn't easy to be rid of him.

"Nothing longer than Gold River. You have Patsy get you a copy of the plan from 1974. That was the first one we took serious. Look through it and see for yourself what's been done and what hasn't."

"1974. Okay. I'll check."

That would be some work. He didn't feel like listing all the projects they'd put in that year, but he could have. That had been Mort's first year on the board. The two of them had worked long and hard together, dreaming up parks and improvements and new things. Back then it seemed like putting them in the plan meant they might happen, sometime or other. He knew what Luke would find, that hardly a one had ever come to pass.

"Anything particular from then you wish had been done?" Luke asked. "You personally?"

There were a few. "I'll just be glad we've got done what we have."

"How about Mort Walker? Wasn't Gold River Highway one of his pet projects?"

"I think you should get that plan from Patsy. Good morning, Luke."

"Thanks, Joe."

Then Joe was out of the hardware store parking lot and away from the questions. Precious little had come of those plans, with money always tight and a board that was never intent on spending it anyway.

And now that there was a chance for something real to happen, Mort wasn't here to see it.

The herbs, faint but still pungent; the smell of wood everywhere; coffee; soap, almost like fresh flowers; and woodsmoke. And no wind inside!

"Good morning, Eliza."

"Good morning, Annie Kay, good morning."

"How are you?"

Another deep inhalation and she was a part of the room. "Very well. And how warm it is in here!"

"Sit by the fire, dear. Warm up."

Eliza passed the bins of oats and rices and grains, and the apothecary of extracts, and sat in the rocking chair by the woodstove, between the breads on one side and the stacked firewood on the other, beneath the shelf of books.

"Do you need anything, dear, or are you just stopping in?" Annie Kay leaned over from behind the counter. "I don't think we'll ever see spring. There's just no end to this winter."

"There's an end, in time," Eliza said. "I'll find a few things in a moment. Is Jeanie in today?"

"She's off today. She's with Zach at the outfitters."

"Tell her I was in, when you see her."

"I will."

Presently she rose from her place and began her collecting. Oil for the lamps, a spool of thread, a few other things.

"I'll put those on the account." Annie Kay looked under her counter. "No mail for you this week. And take a loaf of bread with you."

"I have enough at home."

"Go ahead. It's so good."

"Thank you, then."

And then, back into the wind, a difficult acquaintance for the day.

Louise peeked in the window. It was always so dark in there. She went in anyway.

"Well, Louise Brown, howdy!"

It took her a minute to find him, but there he was. "Why don't you put on a light, Luke? I can't see a thing."

"Guess I forgot. It's always bright in the morning, and then the sun goes up over the building and leaves me in the dark."

He had his feet up on the desk and his hands behind his head and he might have been sleeping in his chair, just like he did at the board meetings. The computer screen was the brightest light in the room.

Louise flipped the switch on the wall and one little bulb on the ceiling turned on. It hardly made a difference, except to show what a mess the room was. File cabinets and magazines and old newspapers in stacks. "For goodness' sakes," she said. "You couldn't find anything in here."

"Why would I want to?"

"Because I want to. I want to find a newspaper from fifty years ago."

"Fifty? Well, let me see." He got up and she followed him back a hallway and down some stairs, and it got darker and mustier every step. "You want 1956? That would have been Woodrow. No, Ezra. Ezra Dawkins."

"You know, I think I remember him. With the long white beard?"

"That was Woodrow. Ezra was before him. Here's a box."

It said *1956* on the side, and it smelled terrible.

"That's the whole year in one box?"

"It was only once a week then, twenty-four pages."

She opened the lid and touched the top paper inside. "It's all stuck together."

"Probably got wet in the flood."

"That was thirty years ago," she said.

"Then it should be dried out by now."

It was dry, more or less. "I guess I can just look through them."

"What are you looking for?" he asked.

"If I told you, you'd go and print it and everyone would know. And I want it to be a surprise."

"I can keep a secret."

"Well, I can, too," she said. "You go back to your nap."

"Hey, Corny." Wade had the phone tucked in between his ear and his shoulder. "I got a house sold."

"I didn't know you had anyone coming in."

"They were here a couple weeks ago. Just got the call."

"Good for you, Wade!"

"Yeah, and it'll get Charlie off my back for a couple days, too. Hey, I was thinking. When Meredith's here. Let's take her rafting."

"She'd love it."

"I'll call the outfitter and make the reservations." The front door opened. "Talk to you later, somebody's coming in."

"Dinner?"

"Yeah, I'll be there."

A man was gawking around the room.

"Hi, there," Wade said. He didn't get up. Now that he saw him, the guy didn't look real likely—more like a salesman than a buyer.

"Hi." The man stopped at the big map board and blinked. He was maybe forty-five, slacks and a sweater, but the sweater was thick wool, dark gray. Not standard country club bright polyester/cotton mix. The shoes could pass for work boots.

"Just look that over," Wade said. "Let me know if you have a question."

"Sure. Thanks." He squinted at the board and scratched his head. Diamond ring on his right hand. Wade stood up. The guy wasn't city, but there was money somewhere.

"So, where you from?" Wade asked.

"Wardsville. More or less."

Well, this was a first. "I don't think we've met. Wade Harris."

"Jeremy Coates."

That rang a bell, but he couldn't quite place it. "Do you get up to Gold Valley much?"

"Uh, no." He looked around the big room at the stone, heavy beams, wood floor. "I'm not buying. Just curious."

"Sure, sure. Can I show you around?"

"Can I drive around myself?"

"Help yourself. Take a map. The black roads are the ones that are done and paved. The red ones are going in this year."

"What color's Gold River Highway?"

Wade caught himself and made sure he thought before he opened his mouth. "Let's just call it real light pink."

"I think that road's going to wipe out Wardsville."

"I think it might be a big help to the town."

"Then you're wrong. You wouldn't know anyway."

"Maybe none of us know what's going to happen. You can't let that stop you."

Jeremy Coates didn't like that. "Something has to stop you." There wasn't anything to say, but the man was already leaving anyway.

Wade just smiled. "Stop back in if you have any questions. Be glad to help."

The door closed and Wade opened the phone book. Just think about Meredith. And rafting. The outfitter they usually used . . . Zach . . . something. Water should be up real high.

And he'd have to ask somebody who Jeremy Coates was.

"Jeremy! Jeremy Coates!" Good gravy. Randy pulled over to the curb, right there on Hemlock, where Jeremy was just walking down the sidewalk like he always had.

"Randy?"

"Of course it is! How are you doing? It's been forever!"

"It's been a year since I was back." Jeremy leaned down to look in the car window. "You've heard what he's doing?"

"Roland? Well, yes, I have heard, and most people in town have, and it's been a shock, too, I'd have to say."

"The old fool."

That answered most everything that Randy might have asked. "Did you come to talk to him?"

"We talked. Over at the factory. We talked and talked. All morning. If you could call it talking. It wasn't worth the gas driving up."

"I'm sorry about that, but we all know how your father gets an idea in his head and just won't let go."

"You think I don't know that? The old fool."

"But tell me what you're doing with yourself, Jeremy." It seemed wise to change the topic of conversation.

"Waiting. I've been in Asheville, waiting for the old fool to retire. Waiting a year! And now what?"

"You have a place down there?"

"Just an apartment. And managing a furniture store."

"Well, that's not bad!"

"It's more than bad," Jeremy said. "But at least it wasn't going to be forever."

"And now you're just thirty miles away in Asheville, and this is the first you've been back home?" It seemed wise to change the topic of conversation again.

"What would have been the point? But I did drive around this afternoon. And now I'm looking around at the neighborhood."

"It hasn't changed much, and your father's house is just where it's always been."

"Nothing changes around here."

"Hello, this is Randy McCoy. Louise? Is that you?"

All she could do was giggle. "It is. I can't help it."

"What has come over you?"

It was so fun!

"Randy," she said, "did you know the board used to start terms in March instead of January?"

"March? What are you talking about?"

"Because I've got a little idea, and nobody's going to stop me."

Randy sounded so worried. "Louise. I hope you're not going to cause trouble."

"Randy, I'm going to cause all kinds of trouble!"

March

March 6, Monday

And there it was, time to start. Randy leaned back to watch.

Joe knocked his gavel and the room got quiet. It was going to be a show, one way or the other.

It was pretty obvious from the big crowd that something was happening, and of course Joe was going to have heard about it, but he wasn't giving one bit of a hint that he had.

And people were still coming in. Gordon Hite was there, and Lyle with the whole staff from the county offices, and Billy Flockhart, who'd been on the board back in the eighties, and even Tim Grant, who'd been on it in the seventies or so, back when Randy'd been in high school. Not any other board members from before that.

But lots of other people, especially from around Marker, and Randy knew a fair number. The Methodist pastor, and Eileen Bunn, who owned the Imperial Diner, and all Joe's neighbors.

And of course, Luke Goddard was back in his corner. Someday that plywood patch in the ceiling was going to fall down and hit him right on the head. For now he was writing and writing.

"Come to order," Joe said, and still not a word that anything might be happening. "Go ahead, Patsy."

"Mrs. Brown?"

"Here." She was grinning like a Cheshire cat.

"Mr. Esterhouse?"

"Here."

"Eliza?"

"I am here." Could Louise have even gotten Eliza in on the party?

"Mr. Harris?"

"Here."

"Mr. McCoy?"

"Right here," he said.

"Everyone's present, Joe."

The door opened and Everett Colony took about two steps in and stopped. There was not a single chair open. He found a place to stand, scowling himself blue in the face.

"Thank you, Patsy," Joe said. "Jefferson County North Carolina Board of Supervisors is now in session."

Randy was still putting names to faces while they accepted the minutes. Louise must have used half the phone book inviting people.

Then Joe leaned back in his chair, acting like he was first noticing the packed room, and every eye was on him. "Next is receiving public comment," he said. "And it looks to me like someone's been stirring up trouble." He still seemed to be in an even temper, at least. "And we've got agenda items left over from last month. So I've half a mind to dispense with comments and move on to business."

He was probably serious enough to mean it, but not serious enough to stop Louise.

"Oh, no you don't, Joe," she said, and she wiggled her finger at him. "I'd like to know what everyone has to say."

"Suit yourself." He put his hands together behind his head and leaned back even more. "I'll be using my prerogative as board chairman to cut off comment if it gets too long or repetitive." He looked like he meant that, too. "Please state your name and where you live."

Everybody seemed to be waiting. Everett Colony started to move, but Gordon Hite put his hand on the doctor's shoulder.

Then the back door opened. A boy walked right in, about eight years old, marching down the aisle like he was the governor, looking straight ahead and not at the seventy or eighty people all staring at him. Randy hadn't ever seen the child before.

But it was pretty obvious Joe had. In fact he leaned forward and started paying real close attention.

The boy came up to the podium, just barely looking over the top.

"My name is Joseph Clay Anderson Junior and I live at 4218 East Cypress Circle in Tampa, Florida. I have an important matter to bring to the attention of the board this evening." The child was reciting by memory, a speech written for him, most likely, and his voice was as high pitched as a flute, carrying through the whole room. "Most people probably do not realize the time and effort required to serve as an elected official on a county Board of Supervisors or the importance of having wise and experienced citizens volunteer their time to do so."

Joe was frozen like a statue, like there was no one else in the room but just him and the speaker.

The boy kept going. "Jefferson County is very fortunate to have a chairman of its Board of Supervisors who has served longer than any other elected official in the state of North Carolina and as of tonight has been on this board for fifty years and has been chairman for forty-two years. He has never asked for or expected anything in return for his service.

"There are many citizens of Jefferson County here tonight who would be able to describe how this community is a much better place because of the leadership and vision of this man, and who admire him for his character and integrity, his hard work and his dedication, and his godliness.

"However, even the members of this board, who know better than anyone else how many outstanding qualities he has, may not realize the most important of all, that their chairman is the best great-grandfather in the world and I love you, Granddaddy Joe."

And then the boy walked right up in front of Joe and *climbed onto the table and put his arms around Joe's neck.*

There was not a dry eye in the place. So after that, with Rose coming in with a whole crowd of family and someone else with a cake, there didn't seem much chance of business happening. Randy stood back from his chair as everyone came up toward the front. Joe put his great-grandson in his own chair and stood behind it and let people shake his hand, and he didn't have any real choice but to let it happen. And people were taking pictures and Louise was cutting the cake, and Everett had disappeared. It was truly a night to celebrate.

Then the telephone rang on Patsy's desk, which Randy could not remember ever happening during a meeting. Nobody knew who was supposed to answer until finally Patsy did.

Her eyes got big and she grabbed Randy's elbow because he was close by.

"It's the governor!"

"Say that again?" Randy said.

"It's Governor Johnson. On the phone. He wants to talk to Joe."

"Good gravy, get Joe, then. Tell him we're getting him." Randy pushed his way over. "Joe, you have a call."

Joe got to where he could reach the telephone. "Joe Esterhouse," he said, and everybody got quiet to listen to him. "Well, thank you, Mr. Governor. . . . Yes, sir, to tell the truth it does seem like fifty years. . . . Now, that would be up to the voters, but I don't think another fifty is too likely. . . . Thank you, I appreciate it." Then there was a longer pause. Luke Goddard's camera flashed a picture of Joe on the telephone.

"Now, that's something I might use," Joe said. "Let me write that down." Patsy handed him a pink telephone message slip, and he wrote whatever the governor was telling him. "Thank you again, sir. Thank you for calling."

Joe put the pink paper in his wallet. Then he looked up at everyone looking at him and frowned a bit. "Well, I don't think we're getting much done tonight," he said, while the room was still quiet, "so I'll consider the meeting adjourned." And everyone laughed, and of course it all kept going on.

Sue Ann was bringing him a piece of cake. "Best meeting I can remember," he said to her. "Nothing done means nothing done wrong."

March 8, Wednesday

Rose sat down at the table.

"Cold morning to work in the barn," she said.

It wasn't particular cold. "I'll be out to it anyway," Joe said. "I was going to make a call on the telephone first."

"I have laundry." She put coffee in his cup and went out to the hall.

He took the book of telephone numbers and found the one he wanted. Bunch of numbers. Then he took the telephone itself and pushed the buttons, checking the book on each one. Then he waited.

Right away a girl answered. "Thank you for calling the office of Marty Brannin, representing the forty-fifth district in the North Carolina House of Representatives."

"I'd like to talk to him," Joe said.

"He's not available at the moment, sir. I'd be glad to take a message."

Fool telephone. "Tell him Joe Esterhouse is calling."

"What number should we call you back at, Mr. Esterhouse?"

"Just go in and tell him. I'll wait."

"Well . . . I don't know if he's . . . I'll see if he's in."

"Thank you."

It didn't take a minute but Marty was talking to him. "Joe. Hi there."

"Morning."

"It's been a while. What can I do for you?"

"I want to ask you about a road."

"Well, sure. What do you want to know?"

"We applied for a grant back in January. I'd like to know how that's coming along."

"January? Now Joe, you know those things take forever. Do you have a project number or anything?"

"I'll tell Patsy at the courthouse to call your office with that this morning."

Marty waited a minute to answer. "Joe. When Daddy was vice mayor in Asheville and I was running for state assembly the first time, he gave me a few pieces of advice."

"I knew your daddy real well, Marty. I expect his advice was worth hearing."

"It was and it's sure come in handy. And one thing he told me was to keep an eye on you."

"Oh, he did, did he?" Joe allowed himself a smile.

"He did. He said if I ever heard from you, I should pay close attention and do as I was told."

"That's been twenty years ago."

"Yes, it was, and you and I have talked fairly often over these twenty years. But I think this is one time that Daddy's advice might especially apply, at least that I should pay close attention. Because I don't think you'd call me about a simple road grant unless something wasn't so simple."

Marty was a smart boy, just like his father. "I'd be glad to hear that there's nothing to it, but I'm doubting that's what you'll find. I do appreciate your time, Marty. Just when you get around to it."

"I'll call you back, Joe."

Rose was watching him in the doorway, holding her laundry basket. "Decided you can still make a difference," she said.

"I suppose."

"Little Joey called you a godly man, in front of all those people."

"People can think what they want."

"I think he's right."

"Meredith can't come rafting?" Wade said. First hint of warm weather, and there'd been five walk-ins. Nice to have a busy day, finally, and nice to get home after it.

"She will be working on a class project." Cornelia looked real comfortable in the recliner. "And Lauren is going to a concert in Charlotte."

Take off the coat. "So who cares about good old Dad anymore. Just as long as he pays the bills."

"They are both very sorry. Lauren offered to stay home."

Hang up the coat. "No." Toss the briefcase into the computer room. "It's okay." Drop into the chair. "I don't mind."

"They would love to spend time with you. They are both feeling guilty and despicable. Meredith wanted to talk to you herself, and Lauren was almost crying."

"Okay, okay!" Women. He was outnumbered three to one in his own family. "If I give them each a new car, would that make them feel better?"

Corny smiled. "Maybe. I'd need one, too."

"Hey, and what am I supposed to do with this rafting trip? I already paid for it."

"Can't you cancel?"

"I'd lose my deposit." Nothing was ever easy. "For Pete's sake. You know anybody to go rafting with? Or should I just give the trip to somebody?"

"Well—there must be somebody. Do you have any clients?"

"Not that I'd want to spend a day with." And then, a strange idea. "Hey, wait. You want to try something different? Randy McCoy. From the board. And his wife, what's-her-name. Sue. Sue Ellen. Sue Ann."

"Us? And them? Together? Do you want to?"

"Not hardly. But maybe I could shmooze him into voting for the road. Hey, I'll think about it. There must be someone we know."

March 13, Monday

The secretary walked the two steps over to the office door where Roland Coates was sitting plain as day, as short and round and bald and shiny as to make a person think of a bowling ball, and as visible to Randy as Randy was to him.

"Mr. McCoy is here," she said.

"Come in, Randy," the man himself said, and Randy did.

It was true that Randy saw Roland Coates once a week at church, where they would say hello and mention the weather, and they lived just two blocks apart. They only had an actual conversation once a year, though, when they negotiated Roland's insurance contract.

It was not Randy's favorite annual event. He always worked out the very best offer he could make and then added just a whisker onto it so he'd have something to give up.

Randy felt confident enough to ask him a question as they got started.

"Now, Mr. Coates, what's this we all hear about you selling the factory?"

Well, that struck a nerve, and he'd known it would as it really was about Jeremy. But the gentleman took the comment in stride.

"I got a good offer. Not as much as it's worth, but as much as I could expect."

"When might that happen? I'm only asking so I'd know the term of this year's insurance contract."

"Not for a while. There are still a few details to iron out. If there's time left on the contract, I'll have you give me a refund."

With that they settled down to their routine. The furniture factory was really a larger business than those Randy mainly dealt with, although that did not mean any particularly larger profit on the deal, what with the way Mr. Coates didn't see why he should be putting money into other people's pockets.

"I'll just remind you," Randy said, with the papers arranged on the desk, "that it's a basic policy, like you tell me you want, and doesn't have any bells or whistles. It's a high deductible and it'll get you back in business if you have a major disaster, but not too much else. And the liability coverage is just what you're required to have and no more. That's to get you the lowest premium."

"The factory never has had use for the policy, not in eighty years. Money down a rat hole, mostly. And the premium is high enough."

"Mr. Coates, I hope you never have to use the policy. But if you do, you'll be glad you have it."

Roland humphed and snorted, but he signed on the dotted line, and Randy was wondering if he'd get enough other business that month to cover what this one would be costing him.

"But tell me about this road."

That took just a moment for Randy to catch up with. "You're meaning Gold River Highway?"

"If that's what they're calling it. I'm talking about the one that's coming over the mountain and into Hemlock."

"Yes, sir, that's Gold River Highway." He hadn't heard Coates' opinion on the possible effects to the neighborhood.

"When is it being started?"

"Started? You mean, when would they start on the construction?"

"What else would I mean?"

"Now, you don't need to be concerned as it's not even certain that they ever will. We don't have funding for it yet, and even if we did, the Board of Supervisors would still be voting whether to accept it, and there are already a few of the neighbors expressing their opinions against it. And I'd guess the board is leaning just a little bit toward a no vote. So I'm recommending that everyone stay calm and we'll see what happens."

Mr. Coates was just staring at him. "They might not build the road?"

"I'd call it far from certain."

Roland did not look calm. "You'll be voting on the road?"

"Well, sure. And I'll be protecting the interests of Mountain View and Wardsville."

"What are you going to vote?"

"That's what I was saying. I want to keep that road from barreling right down Hemlock as much as anyone."

"McCoy, what are you going to vote? Yes or no?"

"Well, no. That's what I'm trying to say."

"No? Against the road?"

"Yes. Or I mean, yes, I'll vote no."

"Then you're a bigger fool than I thought. Rip up that paper. I'm not insuring my business with a fool."

This was going to take a bit of working out. Randy stared for a moment, sort of frozen, and then he got himself breathing again, and then thinking. "Now, Mr. Coates, sir, you're telling me you want the road built?"

"Of course I am. I'm speaking plain English, and you could learn to do the same."

"Well, sir, now, so far I've only heard opinions to the contrary. But if that's the case, that you're favoring the road, and it really only does make sense that you are, that's an important piece of information. Very important. On the weight of that, I'll retract my statement and just say that when and if the funding comes through, I'll make sure I've heard from everyone on both sides."

"Now you're saying you'll vote for it?"

Randy took another breath and tried to pick just a few words out of the crowd that came to mind. "I haven't decided yet."

"Haven't decided. When will you decide?"

"When it's time to vote."

"And when will that be?"

"If we get the funding, which is hardly likely to my mind, then we'll have the last vote in December."

Mr. Coates didn't like that, either, but it didn't look like he'd be yelling at Randy over it. "I won't know about the road till December?"

"That's the schedule, and there isn't anything that would change it."

"December. Very well. Go ahead and take that contract before I change my mind again. But you'll be hearing from me."

"Yes, sir, that's why I'm here."

"Bunch of political foolishness. Give me stroke before it's over."

About the last thing Randy was going to suggest was that Roland have a doctor check his blood pressure, as that would be Everett. But on the other hand, that might just be taking care of two birds with one stone, with the two of them each giving the other a stroke.

With that unworthy thought, he left for his walk back home. It was a perfect blustery March day and the wind was tugging on his coat, just like a lot of different thoughts were tugging at his brain.

Well, sure Roland would want the road. It would be a help for his trucks in getting out to the interstate. And his house wasn't right on Hemlock, either, but at the back of the neighborhood, against the mountainside.

"Randy!"

If he hadn't been quite as distracted, he might have noticed Everett and possibly even turned off Hemlock a block earlier. But there the man was, home for lunch, standing beside his car.

"Howdy there, Everett. Nice breath of spring we're having."

"Did I see you coming out of the factory?"

"Well, yes, I was. Just talking insurance with Mr. Coates."

"What's he saying about the road?"

Either the doctor was reading minds or the road was the only thing on his own mind. "To tell the truth, I got the impression he'd actually prefer to have it built."

Everett didn't seem as surprised as Randy had been. He just calculated a few seconds. "That man is set to ruin this neighborhood. First his trucks, and now this."

"Now, it might be that the second would fix the first, if you understand what I mean."

"Has he got you in his pocket, Randy? Is that why you've been voting for it all along?"

"No, Everett." He was finally feeling a little put out by it all. "And I haven't been voting for it. There's one vote in December that counts, and when that comes, I'll do what I think is best."

Everett was calculating all the more. "Then I'll have to take care of it myself, and I've got until December to do it." He turned away and marched up his steps and into his front door.

Randy sighed and took up his own stroll home. Maybe he should try to get the two of them together, Everett and Roland, and just see if there was a single thing they might possibly agree on. Well, probably that they both were highly dissatisfied with Randy and his representation of their interests on the board. Now, if they were complete opposites in their views, how could he be making them both mad? It almost defied common sense.

Two birds and one stone still seemed like a good idea. And why in the world had Everett gone and bought himself a gun?

Louise couldn't help herself. She pulled her car into the spot right next to Byron's, between the warehouse and the factory, and checked her watch. Just right. Byron would be starting his lunch break.

She trotted around the side of the factory to the door the workers used and peeked in there.

That's where he was, just sitting down on the bench in front of her. She practically ran with the envelope in her hand.

He looked up. "What are you doing here?"

"Just wait till you see," she said, and sat beside him, a couple other men moving aside to give her a place. There were big saws and wire benders running out on the floor, and the lathes turning, and piles of wood, and the overhead crane swinging along. She held the envelope under his nose.

He looked a minute at it and then he saw the return address. "Matt?"

"All the way from Baghdad."

"What's it say?"

She pulled out the piece of paper. It wasn't very long but it was written by hand. "'Grandma and Grandpa.' See? He hasn't forgotten about us. 'I'm in the mess hall. We just got back from patrol and we're taking it easy for a while. I want to tell you I just got my orders that we'll be coming home around September. I want to come see you as soon as I can. You be looking forward to it, all right? Because I sure am. Matt.'"

"September," Byron said. Then he frowned a little at her. "Now don't you go crying here in the middle of the factory."

"I'll cry wherever I want. He told us to be looking forward to him coming."

"Still a long time till September. Don't wear yourself out."

"You're just as excited as I am."

"Sure, but I don't go caterwauling about it."

But then the man next to him gave him a nudge and pointed his chin toward the front of the big room. Byron followed his look and frowned again. "Looks like they're at it again."

Mr. Coates' office had a big window out onto the floor and people could see in as well as he could see out. And right there in front of everyone, Mr. Coates and Jeremy were standing, facing each other, and both talking at the same time, with Luke Goddard right beside Jeremy, memorizing every word, by the look of him. No one could hear them through the window or the noise, but a person wouldn't need to, to see that they were shouting at each other and both as furious as they could be.

While they watched, Luke said something, and the two Coates' turned on him and started laying into him as hard as they had been at each other, and quick as lightning he escaped, and that left Mr. Coates and Jeremy with just each other to be yelling at.

Louise turned around to where she couldn't see the window, and Byron turned with her. She held his hand to get rid of the thought of yelling and anger. Just being next to him it made her feel like everything would be all right with Matt, and with the Coates and with anything else that she might think of.

They sat there together while he ate his lunch, even if she should have been getting back to the salon, and Byron took a few minutes extra. Then a couple of men were standing up. There was a loud whine and a saw was starting. The crane thudded and whacked and started lifting a big pallet of lumber.

"Time to go," Byron said.

"Me too," Louise said, and gave Byron a little peck on the cheek. The front office was empty.

Randy would have just gone on down to the office, but when he stopped in at the house, Sue Ann was taking a nice big ham out of the oven, and he just couldn't let that get past without a little taste, and that led to a sandwich, and that led to sitting down at the table and enjoying Sue Ann's company.

Of course the telephone rang, which a person could count on if they were having a quiet moment, even though it was only Patsy at the courthouse.

"Randy, Luke Goddard is here and he's looking for you. He says he was at your office and it was locked."

"Patsy, tell him I locked it because I saw him coming. But I'll be there in a little while."

"He says he's in a hurry."

"Then tell him I'm not."

And just to be sure he wasn't, he gave Sue Ann a hug and a kiss, and walked slowly out to his car and started for downtown.

When he got to Hemlock, he paid the price for not being in a hurry. A line of trucks was headed out from the factory—six big, lumbering elephants—and the first one was just passing in front of him. So he waited for them to get by, one by one, and then he'd be behind them all the way to the office. At least it wasn't far, as nothing in Wardsville really was.

And when the last truck roared past, going too fast, really, for that street, it must have kicked up a bit of gravel or something on the road. Instead of two birds getting hit by one stone, it was Randy's windshield.

It was just an instant of time but lots of different impressions. There was a fairly loud crack, a sharp sound like a hammer on a nail, but the first thing he really realized was the glass in front of him suddenly turning white. And it wasn't white but filled with cracks, and all splitting and popping and splintering and not clear to look through. He saw how the whole right side of the window looked like circles on a pond coming out from a center spot where the rock must have hit, and even for a moment the nice round hole, and then the whole sheet of a thousand pieces collapsed into his lap and onto the seat beside him and onto the floorboards. And even with all that going on, he still had enough of his senses left to barely feel the seat next to him shudder a little.

"Oh, for goodness' sake!" he said. "Look at that!"

He was in shock at how sudden it was. One second everything was normal and the next a mess of shattered glass and shattered nerves. "Of all things! Oh, for goodness' sake!"

The earth was breathing, deeply, ending winter, receiving spring. No leaves had budded, but the thought of them was alive and stirring the trees. Already the ground was awakening, and patient seeds and slow beating hearts were feeling the quickening warmth.

It was time to prepare for her own planting. Eliza had thought of what that would be, how her garden should be. She had her list.

"Here you go, Eliza. And a couple letters."

"Thank you, Annie Kay."

A few small bags, mostly seed. The laden shelves here were always a temptation to her. But she had what she needed and she always chose to never take more. And the letters were the kind she didn't understand, the kind that Zach called junk and had told her she could always throw away.

"And I'll put it on the account," Annie Kay said.

"What has that come to?" she asked. The whole winter had passed without a request for payment.

"Just today's. That's all there is on it."

"But surely there would be more."

"Jeanie's paid it off. It wasn't much, anyway."

"Jeanie?" Oh, that Jeanie!

"A few days ago, what was left. But Eliza, it wasn't much at all. I almost hate to keep track of it."

"Did someone ask her to?"

"No, of course not. She worked here all winter—she could look at the accounts anytime."

"Will she be in soon?"

"No, she's working with Zach at the outfitters all the time, now that it's warm enough. But she's still in once or twice a week."

"I'll see her soon. She comes to check on me. But please thank her for me! As soon as you see her again."

"I will."

Eliza took her bags and left the store. The sun and the wind both tugged at her coat, but she chose to keep it on, and she began her walk home.

"Somebody shooting at you, Randy?"

"No, Gabe, nothing like that." He'd driven straight over to Gabe's garage. "Just some gravel from one of the furniture trucks."

"Well, I never seen gravel knock out a whole windshield like that. You sure it wasn't somebody shooting?"

"Why would anybody shoot my windshield? It was just a rock. Now give me the bad news. What's it going to cost to get a new window in there?"

"I'll look it up. You got insurance, Randy?"

Gabe thought that was pretty funny, and he was still laughing and looking in his parts books while Randy called Patsy at the courthouse and asked her to run across the street and tell Humphrey King that he'd be a little late for his appointment, and maybe they should just try again later.

"Randy, Luke is still here waiting for you."

"Good gravy, I forgot. I'm down here at Gabe's if he wants me."

And when he did get the bad news, which was worse than it really should have been, Luke Goddard was standing next to the car with his camera.

"Hey, Randy. What happened to you?"

"A big truck and a little pebble, and my windshield was in the wrong place at the wrong time. "

Luke was still staring at the car. "There might be a picture for the front page here. 'Insurance Salesman in Car Accident.' "

"Not much of an accident, although it still costs plenty."

"Not much of a picture, either," Luke said. "Say, Randy, I'll tell you what I was talking to Patsy about, and why I was looking for you. I'm doing a story about Roland Coates selling the furniture factory. I was up there talking to him, and I was wondering: If someone bought the place and wanted to do anything to it—what would they be able to do? With the zoning and all, I mean."

"Did he tell you what they'd want to do?"

"Tell me? Roland Coates wouldn't tell me the time of day. I don't know why. But I did get to watch a first-rate head-butting between him and Jeremy."

"I was just up there."

"I might even have heard your name mentioned," Luke said, grinning like a jackal. "Although I wasn't able to witness the entire conversation."

"Why did you even get to witness any of it?"

"Guess I was just in the right place at the right time. I was there to ask Roland about selling the factory and Jeremy interrupted us. Very interesting."

With Luke, *interesting* meant *troublesome*, and for Randy, *troublesome* meant *not interesting*. "But did he tell you anything specific about doing something to the factory?"

"Maybe not exactly. Just Jeremy saying Roland would never get his plan approved, and Roland saying he'd have you approve anything he wanted approved."

"Me?"

"And then I was suddenly unable to continue listening."

"Which of them kicked you out?" Randy said.

"There are at least a few things on which the two of them are still able to cooperate. But that was fine, as I was more interested in locating you than remaining with them. So now, that's my question. If they wanted to do anything to that place, what would they be able to do?"

"It depends on what kind of anything you mean."

"Well, I don't know," Luke said. "Say Roland wanted to tear it down and build a grocery store."

"Tear it down? You don't mean they really are closing the factory?"

Luke was shaking his head. "No, no, I'm just making up examples. What could someone do with that land the way it's zoned?"

"Well." That thought had been so unexpected that Randy had to get over his sudden panic, and he wasn't going to all the way, with that new idea in his head. "About anything would need some special use permit. The furniture factory was there a long time before the county got around to zoning, so they just gave it a special use permit for light industrial, and I don't think much of anything can be changed."

"What's 'light'?"

"I don't know. Light. Not that it's very likely we'd get any heavy industry around here. There might be a list back at the courthouse. Where are you getting these ideas, anyway? Are you sure you're just making that up?"

"I'm just stirring you up, Randy. Wouldn't Humphrey King have a fit if someone wanted to build some new grocery right up from King Food?"

"Well, he would. Don't you go give him a stroke."

"There'd be lots of strokes. It'd be good business for Everett Colony. But not for you and your insurance. Anyway, I'm just asking. And don't you give it a second thought."

March 14, Tuesday

"Well, Lyle!" Louise was stopping in at the courthouse. "How are you doing?"

The poor man spun around and almost tipped his chair right over. "Oh. Hello, Louise."

"I was just going to say hello to Patsy."

"Patsy isn't here." Lyle started hunting through Patsy's desk, and he looked more likely to knock anything off of it as to find anything on it.

"That's all right. I can come by tomorrow."

"She has the papers for next month's meeting. I saw her copying them." The hunt continued, and Patsy's telephone hit the floor, and Lyle almost hit the ceiling.

"That's really just all right," Louise said, but Lyle looked up with a big smile.

"Here they are!" Five folded sets of paper. He grabbed the top one and held it out.

She almost had her fingers on it when it got yanked back.

"There's envelopes they're supposed to be in," Lyle said, and knocked those on the floor next to the telephone. He picked them up and found the envelope with Louise's name, and put the papers in it.

Louise carefully took it out of his hand before anything else happened.

"Thank you, Lyle. That's a big help."

Lyle was putting the other papers into the other envelopes. "We try to do our best."

Louise got herself out of the courthouse and then she had to take a breath. Lyle's flustering was contagious! Then she took her papers out of the envelope, and there on the first page was written in big letters, *For Joe Esterhouse*. It was just Lyle doing his best.

The papers were all the same, so it wouldn't matter that everyone got each other's. And she wasn't about to go back in there and try to straighten it out.

March 16, Thursday

"You have a letter," Annie Kay said. Eliza took it carefully from her. It was weighty, both in her hand and in her mind.

"This is from the council," she said. "It's for our next meeting."

She opened the envelope with reluctance. She didn't like these papers and their hardness, but it was the council's tradition to send them. The first paper had written on it, *For Randy McCoy*.

"I don't know what that means," she said. There was always something new and strange. Then another paper fell out from among the others.

"Very strange."

In large printed letters it said,

The windshield was your warning
No road
OR ELSE

"What does that mean?" Annie Kay asked.

"There is so much that I don't understand," Eliza said.

Nice clear night. Lot of stars for once, and that was good. There'd be no rain for a few days. The fields needed to dry some and not wash out. Roads were already worse than usual.

"Joe? It's the telephone for you." Rose was in the kitchen door. "It's Marty Brannin."

No moon. The stars alone were bright enough to see Mount Ayawisgi up northeast.

"I'll be right there."

Just barely see the one gap where Gold River Highway would go through. The mountain had been there a long time without being bothered. Now that was likely over.

"This is Joe," he said.

"Marty Brannin."

"Evening, Marty."

"You, too. I hope it's not too late to call."

"It's not."

"It's about your road, of course, and I'll keep it short. I'm not to the bottom of it yet, Joe. But I can tell you what I know. The appropriation was down in the fine print of the Clean Air Act we passed last summer. I voted for it, and I sure didn't notice this one paragraph."

"Is that an usual place to put a road?"

"It is not usual."

"I suppose you can find out how it got there?"

"I'm going to. It can be tricky, but I know how this game is played. I've played it myself."

"Then I'll be curious to know what you find."

"I'll let you know. It might be a while. The legislature's in session and everyone's busy."

"Don't put yourself out. Just when you get to it."

"Well, I'm curious now, too. There's definitely something going on here. And besides, somebody's pulled a trick that I've never seen before, and that's saying a lot. It would be worth figuring out how it was done."

Marty laughed. "I might be able to use the same stunt if I ever want a road built myself. Talk to you later, Joe."

Then back out again under the stars. Cold, black night. Same as what was inside some men.

Every word said about this road made his own insides feel black and cold. Of all the words said, not a one gave him rest from thinking about Mort dying when he did.

"Was he a help?" Rose asked, beside him in the cold.

"Just making it worse."

"What would have happened if Mort Walker had died earlier?"

"Just a few days earlier and someone else would have had time to put their name out for write-in votes. A few days later and the election would have been over and the board would have filled the empty seat. But just that day, and with Eliza Gulotsky running, was the one sure time to swing a vote to be against the road."

What was it about a road? They were plain things, for getting from one place to another. It came down to where people were, and where they wanted to go, and how bad they wanted to get there. And what they'd do if something was in their way.

"Would anyone want that bad to stop it?"

Was there evil in the world, and wickedness? "I'd say it could be." A road wasn't evil itself, but it pulled evil in. Greed on the one side, in the men who wanted it. Hatred and fear on the other.

"I can't think of anyone else besides Randy," Wade said.

"Then call him." Somehow Cornelia had gotten to liking the idea.

"Yeah." He still didn't want to. But there was no one else. "Okay." Or they could just go by themselves and not use the other two tickets.

He picked up the phone and pushed buttons.

"This is Randy McCoy."

Oh well. "Randy, Wade Harris."

"Wade, how are you doing? This is an unexpected pleasure."

Right. Unexpected, at least.

"Yeah. Hey, Randy, wonder if you could help me out."

"Help you? Well, sure, if I can. What can I do for you?"

"Have you ever been rafting?"

Long pause. Wade could almost hear the gears trying to shift. "Rafting? I'm not sure I quite follow you."

"Whitewater rafting. You ever noticed those outfitters on every road in the county? They've got big signs that say *Whitewater Rafting* on them."

"Well, of course I've seen them. I just wasn't sure what you meant."

Okay, don't be mean. Take a breath. "I was wondering if you'd ever taken one of their trips."

"I can't say I have. Those establishments are usually more for tourists, aren't they?"

Got to love the way his brain worked. "I think once in a while they make an exception. Anyway. I've got four tickets for a week from Monday, and I need two people to use them with Corny and me."

"Well, now, I can think on that, Wade, but to tell the truth nobody comes to mind right away. I could ask a few people."

"I meant you, Randy. And your wife. Do you want to go rafting?" This was getting priceless. He should write a book and make Randy the main character, except no one would ever believe a man could be this dense.

"Sue Ann and I? Well, Wade, I don't know what to say. I'd never thought of such a thing, actually, and I don't know what to say, and that's for certain. I don't believe it had ever even occurred to me. We've never done any of those tourist type things."

"I won't tell them you're from around here. If you're with me, maybe they won't notice."

"Goodness sakes. Let me talk this over with Sue Ann. Wade, thank you for thinking of me here. I sure do appreciate it. It'll take some thought."

Wade took another deep breath. This is how it would feel to get stuck in quicksand. "You think about it and let me know."

March 17, Friday

Fool business, complete fool business. Here he was at the police building and he still wasn't turning around. But he couldn't. He got out of the truck and went in the front door.

"Go on back," the girl said. Gordon's door was open.

"Well, Joe," he said. "Morning! What're you doing in town?"

"Passing through." No reason to waste time. "I've got Mort Walker on my mind."

"Mort Walker? What's brought him up?"

"It was Minnie that found him, and you went when she called."

Hite was flustered. Joe waited for him to get his thoughts caught up. "Well, sure, that's how it was. You're talking about when he died?"

"And then the doctor came."

"Everett Colony. He got there a couple minutes after I did. Now I remember. I was in the house with Minnie when he came, and she was carrying on, before I'd even been out to the barn to see for myself, and Everett took a quick look at Mort and then he came and sat with Minnie while I called Roger Gallaudet at the funeral home."

"You saw him, though?"

"Mort? Sure, I went out. But nothing for me to do."

"And Dr. Colony said it was a heart attack?"

"Well, he was Mort's doctor. So I guess he already knew what it was going to be. Joe, what's on your mind?"

"A bunch of fool things. He was a friend. I want to know what happened to him that day."

"Well, sure. There wasn't much to it, to be honest. He was pitching hay down from the loft to his cows and his heart just gave out. Banged his head when he fell. Might have been that as much as his heart."

Nothing had been said about that. "Hit his head?"

"Up there in the loft and falling into the stalls, sure he'd hit something. He'd have to."

Or something hit him.

"I suppose he would."

"Louise, I hope you aren't busy." Louise wasn't. And if she had been, she'd still have fit Grace Gallaudet in somehow.

"What is it, Grace?"

"I'm having my picture taken," Grace said. "They're doing a newspaper article on me."

"Now, what's that about?" She had Grace sit down, and she was already looking at what had to be done.

"For Founders' Day."

"Now, that will be interesting to read about. Is Luke writing it?"

"I'm letting him use my Grandfather Ward's letters."

"I can't wait to read it," Louise said. "Will it be the whole story?"

"That's what I told him he should do, from Haggai Ward on through the whole family. At least to my great-grandfather."

"It'll be nice to have it all written out. Nobody's family has more history than yours, Grace. Of course, the Fiddlers have been here a long time, too, and others. The Fowlers, for instance, and even the Goddards."

"Well, the Fiddlers, yes," Grace said, and not gracefully. "But those others didn't leave anything to show. The Wards and the Fiddlers built this town."

March 27, Monday

Well, here they were. He and Sue Ann standing beside the Gold River, looking at that water pouring by, looking at the little rubber boats, feeling like Noah must have.

It was a crowd, with Wade and Cornelia, and the two of them, and a dozen tourists from Greensboro and Charlotte and other distant points. Randy was feeling real out of place, and it didn't help a bit that they were all of them jammed into rubber suits and looking like astronauts.

Maybe some of the tourists were a bit heavy and didn't cut much better figures than he did, but Wade looked trim and fit, and his wife Cornelia had a movie star kind of figure. He and Sue Ann didn't hold too well in comparison.

"You're sure you've never done this before?" Wade asked.

"I'd remember if I had," Randy said.

"Then come on in."

There were three rubber boats for the group of them. The guides divided them up, and Randy found himself and Sue Ann in the back seats out on a little practice pond with Wade and Cornelia in front of them, and then a tourist couple from Greensboro in front, and up in the point of the boat a cute little button of a girl bellowing at them like a drill sergeant.

"Right!"

Now, that meant Randy pulled forward on his paddle, as he was on the right, and Sue Ann pushed back on hers, as she was on the left.

"Whoa, stop! Okay, back there, let me explain it again!"

She did, making it all completely clear, and they tried again. "Right!"

Now, that meant Randy pushed back on his paddle, as he was on the right, and Sue Ann pulled forward on hers, as she was on the left. The boat turned right much better than it had the last time.

"Forward!"

The girl's name was Jeanie and she really was very nice, just a slight bit forceful. She might possibly remind a person of Everett Colony. And of course she had to be that way as captain of the ship, so to speak. She didn't try to remember the names of the crew, as she was mainly used to calling them out by their positions.

"Back right, pull it!"

He pulled it, just as hard as he could.

Randy could have used even a bit more practice, but Jeanie seemed satisfied after a while and she started going over a few more fine points.

"The water's high, so a lot of the rocks are submerged. I know most of them anyway. You'll need to act fast when I call a direction and pull hard. The water's fast. We just have to be faster.

"If we hit a rock, it can swing the boat around facing backward. If we can turn back around, I'll call a hard right, but we might just need to stay backward till we get somewhere calm." Randy listened while she described situations that were each worse than the one before, and what to do if they got into them. "If the boat gets turned over in some rapids, the first thing is to get out from under it."

Randy expected that would be some fairly vigorous rapids they'd be wallowing around in, while trying to get a boat off their heads. "If you're in the water, get a good breath every time your head's in the air," Jeanie said, and Randy added breathing to his list of things to remember.

Now she was talking about hydraulics, which Randy had usually associated with the brakes of his car, but this wasn't the same.

"You can't fight them. If you get in one, don't try. It'll suck you down, but eventually you'll be out of it. Just wait till you're out of the grip and then get to the surface. And the most important thing to remember is to not panic."

If that was the most important rule, then Randy was already on the verge of breaking it. Even with all the instructions and knowing what to do, he was not feeling completely reassured.

"I'm just wondering," he said, "how likely that is, that a person might fall out of the boat?"

"It doesn't happen often," Jeanie said. "As long as everybody does exactly what they're supposed to when I call a direction."

Randy was guessing that he looked about as white as Sue Ann.

The lead guide was a wiry young man named Zach, and it must have been his company, as it was called Zach Attack Whitewater.

"Let's get going," he said to the whole company, and going they got, carrying the boat like Lewis and Clark right over to the Gold River and then getting in it, leaving the nice solid ground behind.

"Forward!"

They paddled about two strokes and then the river had hold of them, and it was moving them a good deal more vigorously than they could have themselves, or was really even necessary. And if Randy was hoping for a nice easing in, he didn't quite get that, because right away there was a sort of a drop and a push sideways at the same time and Jeanie hollering, "Right! Forward! Right! Left, hard! PULL IT LEFT!"

About that time Randy finally worked out that he should just do whatever Cornelia was doing in front of him, and that made him feel confident enough that he even leaned over to Sue Ann and said, "I think I'm getting it." And she nodded, but she had her eyes glued onto Wade's paddle ahead of her.

After that first place the water settled down, and they both could catch their breath.

"Good job! Good start! Two more short falls after the next turn, then we'll have a smooth section before we start the real stuff!"

That had seemed very real, but when Randy looked back, it was a shock how little the one fall they'd already done actually looked.

Wade leaned back. "What do you think?"

"I haven't had a chance to yet," Randy answered.

"Forward!"

Wade gave him a nice encouraging smile, and then they were off paddling right at a drop that really looked to be better off avoided.

Good day, so far, with the water high and fast. Wade leaned back against a rock and chewed his ham sandwich. He'd been afraid the whole thing would be a bust.

Randy's face in the last rapids had been worth the price of four tickets all by itself.

"Tell me about this furniture plant," Wade said. Randy looked like he needed something to take his mind off moving water.

"Oh, well, the factory." That looked about as upsetting to him. "I don't even know what to make of that."

"So this is a big deal, right? Getting bought out?"

"I'd say so, and most everyone would agree. A hundred fifty people working there, and that makes it the biggest employer in the county, except for the schools."

"But it's not closing," Wade said.

"Maybe it isn't, and I wouldn't have thought so, but now I've heard that they might even just tear it down and build a grocery store."

Suddenly this was real interesting. "A grocery store?"

"That's just a rumor, and I've only heard it one place so far."

"Could someone build a grocery back there?"

"Not by the zoning. But we could always change that."

"It's not a good place." Wade was figuring. "It wouldn't make any sense to put it back there. Uh—not unless the road went through. I was hoping that the Trinkle farm would get developed sometime, but it sounds like that won't be for years."

"If it depends on the Trinkles, it won't be for years."

"They're as bad as I've heard?"

"You should see the stack of lawsuit letters the county has gotten. It might be the only way the title will ever get clear is if the county condemns it to auction for back taxes."

"The taxes aren't paid?"

"Not in years. But lawyers cost so much, there's hardly anything left for the county if we do take legal action, and it just seems so harsh, so we don't usually get around to it."

"Is it that they just can't agree on selling it?"

"More than that. Hermann Trinkle didn't leave a will, so that makes it muddier. And even before that—the Trinkles came over with the other Austrian families after the Civil War, and some of them got their land legal and some didn't, what with courthouses burned and landowners missing and occupation troops and carpetbagger judges. So there's not much record of who owned that land before, and if the current Trinkles are any indication, the early Trinkles wouldn't have cared anyway."

Wade laughed. "Then it's a mess. If there won't be any stores in Gold Valley, we need the road, and a new store right there in Mountain View."

"Everett and them would tar and feather me," Randy sent a mournful glance down at himself. "Not that I'd look much worse than I do now."

The guy had a streak of humor. "You're doing fine, Randy. Whatever anyone says."

"I'll keep that in mind next time one of my constituents suggests otherwise, which they often do."

"That's what constituents do. It's their job."

"So what's our job, Wade?"

"Ignore them. Hey, so why's Coates selling the factory, anyway?"

"Now, for one thing, it hasn't happened yet, so there might still be some negotiating to do. But for why, most people could tell you. It's about Jeremy."

Jeremy Coates. Of course. The walk-in last month. "That's the son?"

"That's Roland's son. All in line to take over, just like Roland did from his father. But Jeremy wanted to go ahead and make his own changes without waiting, and Roland just didn't see it, and they quarreled. Roland's dad died young, so Roland didn't have that chance to get impatient waiting to take over, and I suppose he just doesn't understand the situation from Jeremy's side. So I think Roland's sort of decided that Jeremy doesn't want the business anymore, and now Roland himself's just wanting to be done with it."

"Right. I've met him."

"Roland? Or Jeremy?"

"Jeremy. He was up at the sales office a few weeks ago."

"Looking to buy something, you mean?" Randy asked.

"I don't think so. He said he was curious about Gold Valley, and then he told me how much he hated Gold River Highway."

The sun was shining and it was warm and pleasant beside the river. Sound of rapids in the distance. He could make himself take a nap.

"Let me ask you a question," Wade said. "No politics. Do you really think Gold River Highway will mess up Wardsville that much?"

"It'd change a lot of things, and that's not usually good, from all that I've ever seen. Now take Mountain View, for example. You've been through it, haven't you? You'd have to admit there's going to be more traffic. So either they widen Hemlock and tear up everything on it, or else they don't and it stays a little two-lane road with that many more cars. You see my point, don't you?"

"Yeah. Yeah, I know. But do you see what it'd do for Gold Valley? And from where I come from, change and growth are good. And Wardsville would get a lot of new development, too."

"I can see that, Wade, from your point of view. But now, I'm looking down this river right now, and at all its trouble and confusion you've talked me into going through. And it's maybe like this road. You're looking forward to it, and I'm not particularly, maybe like the way we each live our lives, where I like to stay away from problems and you seem to run right at them. Well, maybe one of us is right and one isn't about this road, or about how we live our lives, or maybe there isn't a right, anyway, and all we can do is just each of us try to take care of ourselves. I guess you'd say we were each on our own road."

"Roads are supposed to go somewhere."

"I wonder if many people know where they're going," Randy said.

If there was an answer to that, it wasn't obvious. At least Wade didn't feel like looking for it, except that it was the first conversation with Randy that had ever made sense.

"Are you ready for dinner?" Rose asked.

"Still some patching on the toolshed." Winter was hard on the older buildings. "Take maybe an hour."

"It's the roast from Sunday. It'll keep till you're ready for it."

It was a long day and Joe was about ready to be done. "Might just leave the rest for tomorrow." Then the telephone rang.

"It's Marty Brannin," Rose said. "He says he calling from Raleigh."

It wasn't a welcome call, not at the end of the day and before he'd eaten his supper. And as much as he could hope for it, he doubted it would in any way set his mind at rest.

"This is Joe Esterhouse."

"Hi there, Joe. I'm finally getting back to you again."

"Good of you to do that."

"It's been a busy few weeks. But I just heard from my spy in the Department of Transportation. Joe, looks like you've got yourself a new road."

That was that. "Is that so."

"Yes. Sixty-seven counties applied and you got it. The whole thing. Twenty-five million dollars for a beautiful new highway right over the mountain."

"That's real interesting."

"And you don't sound surprised."

"I guess I'm not," Joe said.

"You know, I'm not, either. Listen to this: Every other application was disqualified. Your project was the only one that met all the requirements."

"I'd have been surprised if there was another project in the state that did."

"Right. Exactly. Clever way to get a specific road funded without anyone knowing it. Anyway, don't you tell anybody, since it's not announced. You'll get your letter, and then you have to wait till your official board meeting."

"I'm not in a hurry."

"Good. And there won't be an announcement in Raleigh. That's another quirk. The counties that win will make the announcements, and that's it."

"Not too many big city reporters at the Jefferson County board meetings."

"Oh really?" Marty laughed. "I'd never have guessed that. Well, I think I'll have a chance to get back to my detective work next week and find out where this road comes from. Talk to you later, Joe."

"Thanks for your call, Marty."

Rose had the table set for the two of them. She sat down beside him.

"That's proof," he said. Jefferson County had got the road over every other county in the state.

"I'm sorry, Joe."

"So am I." He was. It was just as black evil as it could be, and now there was no use hoping it wasn't.

"What are you going to do?"

"I don't know." There was no good thing to do. "Marty'll find out who's behind the road, and that's where there's evil. Then I need to find who's against them, and there's evil there, too. Then I'll know what happened to Mort."

"There are a lot of people on both sides."

"Just fighting on either side's not evil by itself. Or the road. It might or might not make sense, but it isn't evil in itself. But there is evil."

"There always will be, Joe. But there's good, too."

"Seems harder to find. I'll wait for Marty to call again."

April

April 3, Monday

The moment had come; the gavel fell.

"Come to order," the heavy voice said, and the air itself became still and silent, waiting. "Go ahead, Patsy."

The ancients had held their councils, in sacred groves, beneath holy mountains, gathered under each moon for each moon's ritual. Still, in this different world, the rites were maintained.

In the past, powers were invoked. Today there were still spirits that presided and moved, unknown and unrealized but also undiminished, intervening as they always had in the decisions made. The words spoken were more than those speaking them knew.

"Mrs. Brown?"

There was a circle. Each one of them would be taken into it. Any tribal elder would have understood this prelude to the exercising of ritual power.

"Here."

"Mr. Esterhouse?"

"Here."

"Eliza?"

And now she herself was called.

"I am here." Just the statement of presence, of existence, was as profound in itself as the ceremonial declarations used in other ages.

"Mr. Harris?"

"Here."

111

"Mr. McCoy?"

"Right here."

"Everyone's present, Joe." The acknowledgment was the closing of the circle.

"Thank you, Patsy. Jefferson County North Carolina Board of Supervisors is now in session."

It was an act of creation. In this place, in this moment, a living thing was brought into existence. It was the merging of their will, their purposes, into a fire, alive in itself and beyond themselves. They were only the coals that were its fuel. The flame had power and authority, joined with the unseen powers that were gathered.

"Motion to accept last month's minutes?"

"I'll move that we accept last month's minutes."

"I'll second that."

"Motion and second," Joe Esterhouse said. "Go ahead, Patsy."

Eliza listened.

"Mrs. Brown?"

"Yes."

"Mr. Esterhouse?"

"Yes."

"Eliza?"

No guidance. She still did not understand many of this councils' rituals, but that would come. "I vote no."

"Mr. Harris?"

"I vote yes."

"Mr. McCoy?"

"Yes."

"Four in favor, one opposed," Patsy said.

"Motion carries," Joe said. "Minutes are accepted."

In times to come, she would be given words to speak.

"Next is receiving public comment," Joe said. Eliza turned her thoughts outside the circle.

The doctor, the man of anger. No one else understood, not even him, but he was a spokesman. Eliza saw deep, that there was a fire in him, that he was speaking words given to him.

"Everett Colony, 712 Hemlock in Wardsville. I'm here, and all of us are here, because we thought there was supposed to be an announcement about the road. We were told the state funding decision would be made by April first. I've called the office here in Wardsville and I've called the Department of Transportation in Raleigh, and nobody can tell me anything. I think someone is trying to hide something—as they have been through this entire process. I would like to know two things. Why won't anyone tell me anything, and has this road been funded or not?"

Joe Esterhouse, the leader, raised his hand. The single motion of authority silenced all others.

"I'll discuss that," Joe said.

He held in his hand a paper like fire itself. Eliza shrank from it.

"Received this today by special delivery, dated March thirty-first. Addressed to me as chairman.

" 'Mr. Esterhouse. The North Carolina Department of Transportation hereby informs the Jefferson County Board of Supervisors concerning project—' bunch of project numbers and code sections and application numbers—'that the funding for completion of Gold River Highway as described in application number—' bunch more words, you can look at—'has been approved.' "

"Approved?" The man facing them spoke and his fire lit the room. "What does that mean? I was told this board would vote before the road was approved. This is an outrage. Esterhouse, you've crossed the line here, and you're not getting away with it."

Again, Joe Esterhouse spoke. "I'm reading this letter and I'll return to public comment when I'm finished. I'll require quiet until then."

Joe waited for the quiet to be complete. Next to her, Wade Harris wrote words on his papers, underlining them fiercely. Then Joe read again.

" 'The information in this letter is confidential and may be announced only at the next regularly scheduled meeting of the Board of Supervisors.' Going on—'Preliminary engineering plans will be provided for July meeting . . .' Going on—'Final acceptance will be contingent on vote of approval by your board by December 31.' That's the main points. Patsy, could you take this back to the office and make a dozen copies?"

"The copier takes a while to warm up, Joe."

"Get it started then. And, Lyle, why don't you wait on it back there so Patsy can be out here writing down the comments. We'll resume the comments now, and anyone wants to see this letter complete before they speak, we'll wait on them."

The man facing them spoke again. "I don't believe this." The fire had subsided, down to hot coals. "This is incredible. I've never heard of any government department acting like this."

Joe Esterhouse looked directly at the man. "Dr. Colony, I have to say I am in complete agreement with you on that."

Those strange words were the beginning. The papers were brought from the offices; Eliza would not touch them.

But though there were many speakers, there was only one voice. And Eliza knew the voice.

There was also fear. They spoke of destruction and disturbance, though Eliza knew the one speaking through them had no fear.

Some spoke of justice, and injustice, and the burden they would carry unfairly. Some described the loss they would suffer. Always, with each word, Eliza was hearing more clearly a single voice, and one she knew well.

Do not desecrate, do not defile, do not violate.

It was the Warrior.

The Ancient One, far older than this people, even older than her own people, was speaking to her.

Do not desecrate, do not defile, do not violate.

She listened closely to the words of one man.

"I don't even know who wants this road. Not Wardsville—it doesn't go anywhere we want to go. And everyone says Gold Valley wants it, but I don't know why. They don't want to come here. It's just going to be a road to nowhere."

But deeper, beneath the man's words, she heard the deeper voice, *Do not desecrate, do not defile, do not violate.*

Another voice spoke, but the deeper words were still the same.

"I live just two blocks from Hemlock Street, and if you build this big road, how am I supposed to sleep at night with trucks at all hours and kids drag racing and all that highway noise? Who'll be using this road, anyway? It won't be the residents of Mountain View. But who'll have the traffic and noise right in their front yards? The residents of Mountain View. We'll be the ones picking up the trash that those cars leave behind, and we'll be the ones hiding in our homes for fear of crime, and we'll be the ones who can't use our own front yards because of cars flying through."

But the Warrior was saying, *Do not desecrate, do not defile, do not violate.*

"Wait a minute."

A different voice. From beside her, Wade Harris was speaking.

"Who do you think is going to be on this road, anyway? For Pete's sake, half the people in Gold Valley are retired. We're talking grandparents here, driving into Wardsville to buy groceries. What do you mean they'll be throwing trash in your yards?

"And maybe the reason no one ever goes from Wardsville to Gold Valley or the other way is that they can't. You say it won't go anywhere? Well, that's what it does now." Suddenly his words had their own great strength behind them. "I'm tired of living on a road to nowhere."

Those words . . .

She felt power against them but also power behind them. Two strong powers, two mountains moving slowly against each other.

From his words, there was more anger, and discord.

To Wade, the truth was simple, and he didn't understand why the anger against him was so strong. He didn't know that he was opposing a much greater strength than he could see, or that he even knew of. But Eliza knew that the anger was great because it was against more than one man.

Just as the other speakers were giving voice to the Warrior, Eliza had heard a different voice speaking through Wade Harris. In his few words, Eliza had heard a faint whisper of that voice, a voice she didn't know.

The words went on, and Eliza felt her attention move from them.

The room was strange—old as any building, carved and ornamented, but neglected. The ceiling had images, unfamiliar to her, but broken in places, and patched and covered. One large corner was covered entirely. Even the room was in conflict with itself.

Then Joe Esterhouse spoke, and the discord ended. The anger remained. The conflict was between forces too great, and it was plain that the time for peace was still far off.

"We'll get on with our business. You all have your agendas, and they include the items left from the last two months."

"Joe?" Wade was speaking. "I've got a question."

"Go ahead."

"Is there any official estimate of what the traffic on Gold River Highway would be?"

"There is," Joe answered. "Estimates were made in 1987."

"Anything recent?"

"That would be the most recent."

Wade spoke again. "I want to make a motion that we get some kind of new estimate. How does that work?"

"We can request it from the state or pay for it ourselves," Joe said.

"Mr. Esterhouse?" It was a voice from the audience.

"I'll recognize Mr. Stephen Carter of the Planning Commission."

It was the young man from the other meetings.

"I know a person in the Department of Transportation district office in Asheville. I could get him to work up some quick estimates."

"I object to this." This was the man who always spoke first, Everett Colony. "He's from Gold Valley. He'll manipulate those numbers."

"We are not accepting public comment at this time," Joe said. "If you can do that, Mr. Carter, we'd certainly appreciate it. Lyle."

What a strange man this Lyle was. So nervous. "Yes, Joe?"

"Work with Mr. Carter on that."

"Yes, sir."

"And I don't think we'll even need a motion for that. Now, let's get on with the agenda."

Joe Esterhouse led them on. Eliza listened for direction, but she only heard the echoes from before, *Do not desecrate, do not defile, do not violate.* The words rang in her ears!

She had nothing to say, nothing of her own and nothing given to her. The time for her to speak would come, but not yet.

And she watched the man next to her, Wade Harris. There was danger; the powers now in conflict were very strong.

"What a crackpot!" Wade stuffed his coat into the closet and made for the kitchen. "What do I want to eat?"

"Heat up an enchilada." Cornelia was at the kitchen table reading a magazine.

"I figured I'd about seen it all," Wade said, squinting at the shapes in the freezer. "But good old Eliza takes the cake." He found the enchiladas. "She takes the fruitcake. She *is* the fruitcake. The whole meeting she doesn't say a word but, 'I vote no,' in this solemn wheeze." He closed his eyes and held his nose up in the air. "I vote: noooooo."

"Does it make a difference?"

"What difference does any of it make? Change a zoning, appoint some bozo to the Recreation Commission. None of it makes a difference. So it's all four to one, four to one. 'I vote no.' "

Cornelia giggled. "I want to meet her."

"Sure, do it. I don't think she's contagious. The one thing . . ." He punched the button on the microwave and sat at the table to wait. "The one thing is Gold River Highway. That makes a difference, and she might make *the* difference."

"What about Louise Brown?"

"Yeah, exactly. She's wavering." He finally got himself slowed down to where he could look his wife right in the eye. "Corny, I want that road. I don't think I've cared about anything since we moved here, but I want that road."

"So Charlie Ryder can sell more houses?"

"Not for him, and not for what I'd make out of it, either. I don't know." The food was hot and he dumped it on a plate. "Maybe I just need to care about something once in a while. It's almost . . . like I've found something that's . . . that's right."

"Right, like in right and wrong?"

"That's it, Corny. The road is right. All those Mountain View nazis are wrong. I want right to win. We've lived here for four years on this dead-end Gold River Highway road to nowhere, hating every minute. Now it might go somewhere."

"Wardsville."

"Right. Wardsville. But if that's where it's going, you know, I don't mind. That's where we'll go with it."

She smiled. "Then I'm with you, Wade. On to Wardsville."

He raised a forkful of enchiladas as a salute. "On to Wardsville."

April 10, Monday

Time to start.

The soil was dark, like he'd always remembered it. Always brought back a lot of memories.

He remembered plowing with a horse, walking beside his granddaddy. Would have been seventy-five years back. Pretty soon after that they'd got the first tractor.

That'd been the hard times, not that he'd known it. Chickens, the milk cows, the horse for riding. Big kitchen garden. They hadn't known they were poor. They had all they needed.

Joe started the tractor. The blade bit the ground.

Turn over the soil, turn it over like everything got turned over. It was good soil, now, with years of fertilizer. Back then it'd been worn out with a century of tobacco taken from it. If his granddaddy or his daddy could see how much grew out of it now.

But those times were turned over and buried and the memory of them withering. It was only roots that dug down and back. No one saw roots, but they were there, pulling out from what was buried.

He was half done before he knew it. He knew this field, and the others, to where he could be doing this in the dark, hardly thinking. He could have plowed just by the smell of the soil.

Once it had been forest. Cherokee had lived on it. There were still arrowheads to be found, even in the fields. No telling how long they'd hunted up and down the creek before the settlers came.

They had a deed, signed by Thomas Jefferson himself, dated 1806. That family had been the Hardisons, and they cleared the fields and built a cabin by the creek, and then a house. Then the North had burned it and no one of that family had come back from the war. Jacob Esterhausy had bought the land when he came from Austria in 1868. It took all the money he had.

Into the next field, cutting into it.

That had been a big family. Dozen children and a big house that Jacob built for them, real big for the times. Joe's own granddaddy had been one of the dozen.

Big empty house now for two old people. And no one after them.

Fields that would grow grass and scrub if no one plowed them. Then saplings and then the fields would be back to forest and the house gone and the memory of it withered. His own children left with the only living memory of the land as a farm and after them nothing.

Into the last field, tearing at the ground and leaving it scarred behind him. But the scars would be gone by fall, forgotten after that. Who would have known, twenty years ago, forty years, seventy years ago, he'd be here at this far end of time still plowing.

Leaves fallen in the creek from some lost autumn, and now one left, miles downstream, still riding the water, in unknown times so far from where it had grown.

He was on a long road with not much left ahead, and no going back, and it had been hard and a man might wonder what the use of it had been. What was the use of a road, when a man didn't know where it was going? Or even if he thought he did. Was it any good to be godly, to try to be? A church sermon had good words, but at the end of life, it wasn't words. It was what was true, and had the life been lived by what was true.

He let himself think about seventy years of plowing, as there wouldn't be many more, or any.

The earth had so much life. It was the source of so much, of all life.

Pull the hoe through the dark dirt, open it to light, plant the seed. The life of one year reborn in the next.

Eliza worked the hoe, one slow row and then another, pulling and working, then planting and covering.

Give to the earth and it gives back so much, each turn of the circle.

Every beginning came from an end before it. There was no beginning or end. Every road returned to where it began because there was no beginning or end, only the appearance.

She understood this in part. She saw it each spring, when the seed became a plant, and each fall, when the plant became a seed. There was coming forth and returning, there was opening and closing, but they were only appearances of beginning and end.

Birth appeared to be a beginning, and death to be an end, but there was no beginning or end.

The Warrior had no beginning or end. If a man or woman did, it was only the appearance of it.

But thinking of her own husband, long dead, made her often wonder.

"That about does it, Gabe." Randy tapped the papers on his desk to even them all up. "And I hope I see you again next year."

It was funny with Gabe, how easy and friendly he was in his garage, and how uneasy he was with business details such as insurance.

"You're sure it's okay, Randy?"

"Just right. You don't have a thing to worry about."

"Thank you so much. It's all above my head, you know."

"Well, that's my job, Gabe." He was glad to be doing it, too, and now just a little light conversation to erase the nervous feelings. "And now tell me, have you had many more broken windshields to replace?"

"Broken windshields? Oh—hah! Yours is okay, isn't it?"

"Not a single problem with it."

"Good. You know, I did have another one just like it a few days ago. Roland Coates, in fact."

"Mr. Coates? His window got broken, too? Well, I wonder if it was one of his own trucks that did it."

"Might have been," Gabe said. "It was just like yours, the exact same way. Except I still don't think it was a truck. Never saw a pebble do that."

"We'll call it a freak accident. And it's business for you either way."

"Sure thing, Randy. Well, thanks again. Appreciate it."

Gabe left and Randy set to filing and doing his own forms to send in the renewal, but he hadn't got two minutes into it when he looked up.

"Randy?"

"Well, Jeremy, come right in. Sit down." Randy wasn't sure if he should be leaning forward or back for this exchange, as Jeremy wasn't much of one to shout and scream, but he likely wasn't here just to buy some insurance. Jeremy didn't sit, though. He just stood in the door.

"Just up from Asheville for the afternoon," he said. "I heard what happened at the meeting." Then he kind of tilted his head, like they both knew something together. "You're against the road, aren't you?"

The desk felt solid enough. "Well, I'm just waiting awhile longer before I make up my mind. I've been hearing quite a few people's opinions."

Jeremy did not seem pleased by the answer.

"I was thinking people were pretty much against it."

"Some are and some aren't, and maybe more are against it, but it isn't unanimous, including a certain mutual acquaintance, if you know who I mean."

"The old fool? You aren't listening to him, are you?"

"I'm listening to everybody, and there's still months to go."

That made Jeremy stop to think. "Aren't you, um . . ." He seemed to be looking for just the right word. "Um, *worried* about what might happen if you do vote for the road?"

"I know what it'll do to the neighborhood, and all the other concerns, as I've heard them all very clearly."

"I mean, to you. Aren't you worried about what might happen to you? Because of what's already happened?"

Randy wasn't too sure what Jeremy seemed to mean, especially as his tone didn't sound natural.

"Well—when the next election comes around, I'm sure people will remember how I voted, one way or the other. Is that what you mean?"

"That's not what I mean." Jeremy stood looking at him, frustrated about something, and Randy didn't know what to say. "Well, see you later, Randy." And then he was gone.

April was the month. May, June, September, October, they were all good, but April was the big one. Wade had appointments stacked up for three weeks and the phone ringing off the hook. Corny working mornings to keep up with paper work.

Call the boss.

"Charlie, it's Wade."

"What do you want?" Charlie said.

"More money."

"Forget it, I'm busy."

That took care of the pleasantries.

"I heard something a couple weeks ago," Wade said. "There's a furniture plant in Wardsville, right where Gold River Highway would come into town. Somebody's buying the place. And what I hear is that it might be so they can put in a grocery store."

"Say that again. I didn't get it. What about a grocery store?"

"Somebody might build a store in Wardsville where Gold River Highway would come into the town." There. It always took at least a couple of times for him to get it.

"What? A grocery store?" Make that three times.

"It's a rumor," Wade said. "I think you should find out for sure."

"What's the name of this place?"

Did it have a name? "I don't know. There's no sign. I don't know who's buying it, either."

"Wait a minute. You say it's in Wardsville?"

"Yes."

"That's not in Gold Valley?"

"No." One-syllable answers. He should be able to handle those.

"Then something's wrong. I thought it was going to be in Gold Valley. Is this a done deal about the factory getting sold or just talk?"

"I think it's a deal. And I need to go, I got a customer."

"Why is it in Wardsville?"

"Talk to you later." He hit the button. The man was going crazy.

The front door opened. Maybe he really did have a customer. He put on his happy face.

Then he put on his for-real happy face. "Man, I'm glad you're here."

"What a morning," Corny said. "The bus never came. I had to take Lauren all the way to school."

"I figured it was something. Hey, I had a couple in first thing from Charlotte. They came because they heard about Gold River Highway."

"How did they know?"

"Some cousin in Asheville called them. The word is getting out. Look at this." He tossed her the newspaper, the *Wardsville Guardian*. "Believe it or don't, we have an ally in Luke Goddard."

" 'Gold River Highway Funded,' " she read. " 'In another secretive Board of Supervisors meeting, Joe Esterhouse announced that the state has funded the unpopular and wasteful Gold River Highway extension.' I think Luke is not happy."

"I think he is not. But there's no such thing as bad publicity. That was the only report anywhere about the road, but now the Asheville paper has picked it up and the word's getting out. So I say, thank you, Luke. Anyway, there's a pile of offers and contracts to go through."

"It's nice to be needed," she said. "And Meredith says she will definitely be home next weekend for Easter."

"Easter?" Wade checked his calendar. Easter was always huge.

"She would love to go rafting."

"The outfitter's going to be booked solid and I'll be in the office the whole weekend, and I'll need you here, too. I'll get some tickets for later in the week."

"We could have Meredith and Lauren show models."

What a concept. "Do you think they would?"

"I could ask."

"You're pure gold, Corny. And genius, too."

April 12, Wednesday

Louise was just beside herself. She couldn't even remember the last time she'd so looked forward to a morning.

Becky was cheery and Stephanie had been laughing, and even Serena was in. And they only had one appointment for all of them for the next hour.

"Is she coming?" Becky asked and everybody jerked around to look at the clock. It was still five minutes till.

"Of course she is." Louise looked back at her books of styles. Well, she still was not one hundred percent sure about this. The more she looked, the more she wasn't sure at all.

But that was part of the excitement! Her fingers were just itching to get started.

"There she is!"

They all saw her at once, stepping down the sidewalk as grand as the queen of England. Becky was at the door and swept it open, and Eliza swept in.

Oh, what hair!

"Eliza! What a treat it is to see you!"

"Thank you, Louise. So much." Eliza was just glowing. "How I appreciate you doing this."

"Thank you for coming!"

And Eliza smiled her smile that seemed like it had worlds in it. "Thank you for making me welcome."

"You are welcome. You're always welcome." Louise put on her stern face for business. "And I said this is on the house. It's my gift for you." Then she giggled. "I just hope we can come up with something you'll like!"

"I can hardly imagine what you think we should do. And thank you for your gift. I wouldn't have money for a luxury like this."

"Then all the more I'm glad to be doing it. Now, this is Serena, and Becky, and Stephie. Serena, you start her at the sink to wash and shampoo. Use the . . ." Louise put her hand up to run it through the lightning bolts of black and white and gray. This would be the first important decision. "Use the moisturizing one, the Glisten. And the cream rinse." She'd never felt anything like it.

They settled her down in the chair and she leaned back, and Serena turned on the water. And while the girls washed and rinsed, Louise went through it all one more time.

No perm, of course. That wouldn't be right at all, not for Eliza. And no coloring. There was nothing that could improve on those streaks of black and white. Just cutting and shaping. And if she couldn't make something marvelous with what she had to work with, she didn't deserve to ever touch a pair of scissors again.

She made her final decisions. She was ready.

Doctors, lawyers, funeral directors. Businesses might have hard times and close up, but those three couldn't be got rid of.

Joe looked in the front door of the funeral home. The Chapel room was empty. Roger Gallaudet was in the back office.

"Joe?" Roger didn't look particularly busy. "Well, what are you doing up this way?"

"Had a question." He didn't much want an answer to it.

"Go ahead."

"About Mort Walker."

"Oh, sure. What's on your mind?"

"Gordon Hite says the doctor called it a heart attack."

"I think that was the cause of death on the forms."

"I suppose you didn't think any different."

Roger sat up and scratched his head. "What is it on your mind, Joe?"

"He was a friend. I'm just wondering if he was taken care of right. Some doctors might not look real close if they think they already know what they'd find."

Roger was still scratching where his hair used to be. "Is there some reason you're asking?"

"There might be."

"That's not a good thing, Joe. Are you thinking Everett Colony missed something? Or that he was covering something up?"

"I wonder if Mort might have died of something else than a heart attack."

"Well, he had a big wound on his forehead, if that's what you mean. I cleaned it up myself. But that was from his fall. He was up in the loft throwing down hay. And it might have been that the heart attack didn't kill him but the fall did. That gash would have done it."

"And the gash would have come after the heart attack."

"Must have, Joe. Wouldn't make sense the other way."

"I suppose."

"Well . . . now, he might have fallen, just from losing his balance. Then hit his head, and that caused the attack."

"You could tell he had a heart attack?"

"No, of course not. Just from Everett filling in the form." Roger was drumming his fingers on his desk. "Wait a minute. What are you talking about?"

"What I said. Did Dr. Colony make sure about that heart attack or just take it for granted?"

"I don't question Everett Colony."

"He knows his business."

"He does, but that's not what I mean. I mean I don't tangle with him. He doesn't like questions."

It was enough. "Thank you, Roger. I'll leave it at that. And Gordon Hite didn't think it was anything but a heart attack, either?"

"Gordon doesn't like trouble any more that Everett likes questions."

"I suppose."

They stepped back to look. The girls hardly knew what to say, but they all started talking at once, chattering and excited. But Louise knew exactly what to say.

"It's perfect, Eliza."

Eliza turned to see the mirror for the first time since she'd come in. Her hand flew up to her mouth and then she froze and stared.

Louise waited. Some people might not have known what Eliza was thinking, but Louise had seen that expression before. And she was so excited she could pop.

Black, white, and every gray and silver in between. But now each vein had its place. And it was all still long, but not wild. But it was wild. That hair always would be! Now it swept around her face instead of shooting out from it.

"It's marvelous." Eliza touched it, very carefully, feeling what had been done. "It's splendid—Louise. I could never have imagined." She laughed. "Is it really me?"

"More than ever," Louise said. "Let me show you. It's easy as anything to do. You'll brush it back around this way, and just put about four hairpins under here, and two more here. See? That's all it needs. And when you braid it up at night, it's shorter on the sides."

Eliza was still staring and staring. "How did you know?"

"It's just what I do, dear."

Eliza stood out of the chair and took Louise's hands and held them, and looked right into her eyes. "You don't even know what you have done."

April 14, Friday

"Now, you let me know if you have any questions," Wade said. "I'll be right here all morning. And . . . let me check . . ." He looked at the map in his hand one more time before he handed it to them. "Yeah, looks good. The red stars are the models and they're all unlocked. Just help yourself."

And off they went. A newly promoted corporate vice-president from Asheville and his sales account manager wife. If Wade could have gone with them, it would have been a sale, guaranteed. On their own . . . seventy percent chance. But they were just the first ones in, noon on Friday, and the long weekend was only starting. He barely made it to his desk before the door opened again. Real fast glance back across the big room.

Young lady. Rugby shirt, new blue jeans. Real young, too young to be buying a house. Checking out the main room. College kid. Then a younger girl, her little sister.

Attractive girls. Knock-down ravishing gorgeous, actually, and then their mother came in, every bit as gorgeous and more. Wade was there.

"Hi, sweetie, you made it," he said, and gave Meredith a big hug.

What days these had been. Planting, warmth, growth, and now the transformation of the whole forest. In the full year, of all the climaxes and riches, this moment had power that no other did. In just days the sky disappeared, the trees were absorbed, everything changed. Everything. The leaves became everything.

And of all times, dear Louise—dearest Louise—had chosen this moment to work her own unfurling. Eliza would never have imagined, but just as the trees, she herself had been transformed! She still wasn't sure of what it meant, but there was significance.

Now it was time to be out and be seen. She wasn't ashamed, but she felt strange, displaced, that there would be attention. Did the trees feel this way?

"Well, Eliza! Is that you? What did you do?" Annie Kay even came from behind the counter to draw close.

But Eliza could only laugh. "I don't know."

"Well, who did that?"

"My friend. Louise, my dear friend. Look at me, Annie Kay. Would you ever have imagined?"

"No. Absolutely not."

"It's spring. Everything is changing—and so am I!"

"Then I have a little surprise, too. Eliza, just stand there. I'll be right back."

Annie Kay hustled off, through the shelves and into the back rooms. Eliza stood. The smells of the place surrounded her, new and springlike. Flowers. Herbs. So many things. Then someone was coming back through the aisles, shorter than the tall shelves and unseen among them, but not unheard, and then bursting out right in front of her.

It was Jeanie. Jeanie, always so full of life and energy. Her hair was in a long braided tail and her eyes open and all-seeing.

"Jeanie!"

Jeanie put her hands on her hips, as she always did, and her voice was like the sharp silhouette of the mountains against the sky.

"Mother!"

"Yes, child?"

"What have you done to your hair?"

"Nothing." She always felt like laughing with Jeanie. "Louise did it."

"Who is Louise?"

"My friend."

"I never know what you're going to do next."

Eliza had to laugh. "Neither do I!"

"What a day. What a beautiful day." Randy was on the porch swing looking down over the front yard, which Kyle had just mowed yesterday, and Sue Ann's tulips were as bright as light bulbs, and all freshly tended from where she'd been working all morning. "Sue Ann, why don't you come out here and just help me enjoy it?"

"I will," she said from inside the screen door. "I'll be right there."

Good Friday. Some years Easter was too early to really be spring, but this year the timing could not have been more perfect.

"There you are," he said as she came out. "And look at that." She had a tray of iced tea and a few little snacks. "I was thinking it had all been perfect before, but I hadn't realized what I was missing."

"It is beautiful out here, isn't it," Sue Ann said.

She'd worked so hard to get the tray ready that she hadn't even gotten cleaned up from weeding and planting. She even still had her gardening sandals on.

"Now, don't you move," Randy said. He jumped up and ran into the house himself, right into the kitchen, and right back out in just a moment with a wet washcloth.

"What are you doing?" Sue Ann smiled as bright as the tulips.

"Making you a little more comfortable." He slipped off her sandals, one at a time, and wiped off the bits of grass and dirt. "You're always working so hard." Then he got back to his chair and leaned back and there they were, the two of them, with a beautiful yard, and a comfortable house with a relaxing front porch, and a dear family, and each other.

"It is a beautiful day." He handed her a cracker. "And a beautiful place to be enjoying it." He filled up her iced tea glass. "And you're the most beautiful of all."

There was the Yukon pulling in. Smiling people getting out, strolling toward the office.

"Welcome back," Wade said, opening the door. "Everything okay?" He couldn't remember the wife's name.

"Just wonderful," she said.

"You saw everything you wanted?"

"So far," the husband said. "I think we'll just drive around some on our own." Whatever their names were. Smith, whatever.

"Just help yourself. Did I give you that map? Yeah, that's it. I'll give you some more information, too, before you go." Turn to Corny as the couple left. "Did they fill in that information sheet?" Another couple was coming up to the office.

"Lauren's putting it into the spreadsheet right now."

"Great." Anyone who took the time to write down their address was already twenty percent sold. "You know, they don't call it Good Friday for nothing."

Turn to the windows. No, back to Corny. She was even better than the view.

"You know, I love this."

"Selling houses, Wade?"

"I don't know. There's something about it all." So then he had to think. "Forget Charlie. This is about building a place. People move in and they connect and live." Right. "Their roads are here. The roads they're on come through here, just like a real road."

"Some people don't want new roads."

"Forget them, too. I don't care if they show up with pitchforks and torches and arrest me. I've sold almost three hundred houses in here in four years. This fire's lit, and they can't blow it out now."

Fool newspaper man, he'd done it again. Standing right there beside Joe's truck. Waiting for him.

He pushed open the door from the hardware store.

"Joe! Well, what a coincidence, you just happening to be here. And I was wanting to ask you a few questions! Didn't that work just right?"

"What do you want, Luke?"

"I've been trying to get ahold of you. It's been almost two weeks since the board meeting and I never have got to ask you about the road."

Joe just waited.

"Well, anyway, everybody knows you tried to hide everything, and how you wouldn't announce it until they made you. Not a peep out of the state, and not a peep out of Patsy or anyone, and when Everett Colony finally was there demanding that you say whether we'd got the road or not, you finally admitted we had."

There was nothing to say.

"So, Joe, everyone's pretty upset with you, and they're all throwing around those accusations. Aren't you going to say something? I'm only worried that nobody's hearing your side of it."

"You're not telling the truth, Luke."

He laughed at that. "The only thing that's true is what people think is true."

Eliza walked slowly, each careful step an effort on the dusty road. But she kept on. There were tired days like this on occasion, when she felt the effort of every step.

She shifted the heavy bag from one hand to the other. Annie Kay was so generous, saving out for her wheat and rice and beans, and any other useful thing. And she'd offered to even drive them up to the cabin.

But these were Eliza's burdens to bear.

So she walked, slowly, step by step, along the dusty road.

It had been a nice day, with both of them home, and Louise had a nice supper of chicken and rice and carrots. They hadn't been in a hurry at all. The kitchen was clean before seven o'clock.

Now they each had a bowl of ice cream, watching the news and just as comfortable as they could be.

So, of course, there had to be pictures and talking about the war. Byron didn't even wait for her to say anything.

"He's all right."

"I hope so," she said.

"He is. Matt can take care of himself. And they're all looking after each other anyway."

She watched tanks and ruined buildings. "When he left, it was like he'd died. That's how it seemed to me."

"He's coming back, Louise. Just be patient."

"That'll be a day to celebrate, when he does."

April 16, Sunday

Easter! Finally. Louise had on her bright yellow dress, and she'd been for months waiting to wear it. And right in front of the church was a whole long row of tulips exactly the same color, and another row exactly the same red as Byron's tie.

All the other ladies were as bright as the flowers. They were a whole garden! The children were in their little dresses and white shirts, and their hair combed and brushed. Now, this was spring.

Maybe it was warmer now and the flowers were blooming, but Easter was what really made it spring.

They'd sing Easter hymns and hear a good Baptist Easter sermon, and everyone would be there.

Oh, what fun!

Up the steps, Rose beside him like always. Old granite church walls, big wood doors. Marker United Methodist hadn't changed since they'd got married there.

Third pew on the right. Leonard Darlington and Maggie in front of them. They'd been married there, too. Forty years ago.

Other farmers and their wives filling in. Not many young folks.

Pastor was an old man, too. He'd come two years ago. Most pastors who came were just biding time till they'd retire.

Everybody was looking nice and tidy, all made up, Kyle such a treat in his new suit and Kelly with her hair all done up. Sue Ann just as pretty as a picture. They parked on Main Street and walked to the Episcopal church right beside the courthouse and made to look like it. Easter Sunday already—how time flew by. It was this time of year that morning sunlight came through the stained-glass windows right onto the altar. Those windows were worth every penny.

The little children were all lined up in front like a row of dolls, just like the top shelf in the kitchen where she had all the little porcelains. They were singing all the songs they learned in Sunday school, fidgeting and sitting down and standing up and being little children. They hardly knew anyone was watching, they just concentrated on singing, or on nothing. Louise was remembering when Angie was little like that, and when Matt was. And thinking of Matt made her squeeze Byron's hand.

"Corny. I can't eat another thing." The table stretched a mile in front of him, covered. Waffles. Sausage. Eggs.

"You've eaten enough anyway," she said.

They were all in the same stupor. The girls were done and gone to the kitchen. Wade looked across the wreckage at his wife.

"I could sleep till noon."

"That's one hour."

"Noon tomorrow."

"We're rafting tomorrow, remember?"

Randy stood up and shared his hymnbook with Sue Ann. The choir had their purple shawls on, and they had a trumpet for "Christ the Lord Is Risen Today." Wonderful addition to the service, just wonderful. Very touching. Very fitting.

A strenuous walk, through the forest, up the side of the mountain. Eliza did not hurry but accepted the difficulty of the climb, and the value it gave to the height.

Finally she sat, on a fallen tree, with the immensity of the valley before her. The trees were cast in fresh green, and the torrent of unfurling was clothing the mountain.

"And what happened in that cave on that morning?" The farmers and wives were all straight and still, as was proper for church, while the pastor read his sermon to them.

"He arose, he arose," Louise singing as loud as anybody.

"And what does it mean to us?" the rector asked.

Randy noticed that Everett Colony and his wife were sitting a few rows forward from where they usually did, as far as he could from Roland Coates, and Roland and Miranda were returning the favor.

"Could something that happened two thousand years ago have any importance in our lives today?"

In fact, now that he looked around, Randy was noticing that there were a few families there in that back corner with the Coates, and a space between them and the rest of the congregation. Roger and Grace Gallaudet were back there, and Ed Fiddler and Emma.

"What relevance does this event, this story, this resurrection, if you will, have for us? I believe we each need to answer that question for ourselves."

It was surely just a coincidence, but those in the back corner were the families who'd said they were in favor of Gold River Highway, sort of cut off from everyone else who was against it.

"Why do we, today, need that resurrection of long ago?"

"To think, He would die for us!" The pastor waved his Bible and Louise glued her eyes onto it. "And you can't ignore it. Every man, woman, and child will have to decide what they're going to do about that. What side will you be on today?"

The sharp edges of the mountain ridges, across the valley from her, and far off, also, drew hard lines against the sky. As if they were saying,

Here is mountain, and, *Here is no mountain*, and the line between mountain and empty sky is hard and unmoving.

Often there were shades and depths in the Warrior. Now there was a boundary, dark and light separated.

Wade opened his eyes to see what his ears were hearing.

The television was on, right in front of him. "Brothers and sisters, He did die for each of us, for me and for you." Shiny hair, shiny teeth, shiny voice.

"What's that for?" Wade asked, everything still blurry.

"It's Easter."

"Oh."

"Once a year we should watch a church service. It's good for you."

"Like broccoli." He'd got his focus working and he stared at the bright, shiny screen. He made himself pay attention. Corny was right, it was Easter.

"Do you love anyone enough to die for them?" the teeth asked.

April 20, Thursday

Potatoes. Celery looked nice. The carrots didn't, but what was a roast without them? Louise pushed her cart down the vegetable aisle, looking for anything that might spice up dinner. King Food just wasn't the place to look for surprises.

It was always crowded this time of the afternoon, and they would run out of things soon. She kept looking. Back to the produce line.

A pile of turnips, of all things. She smiled at the thought of Byron finding a great big turnip on his plate beside his roast.

She stopped beside Humphrey King loading up the soup shelf.

"Now, where did these turnips come from?"

"Howdy, Louise. Those are from Duane Fowler's greenhouse."

"They're the best I've ever seen," she said. "But the carrots could use some improvement."

"There'll be more in a couple days."

"Then I'll be back." She started moving, but Humphrey called her back.

"Louise? I just want you to know that not everyone in Mountain View is against the highway. I'd be glad to get some new customers."

"I'm glad to know that, Humphrey."

"Charlie. You wanted me to call?"

"Yeah, where've you been? I haven't heard from you."

Wade took a few seconds to put his feet up on the desk. "I've got better things to do."

"Like what?"

"Sell houses."

"Since when have you been selling houses?"

Same old lovable Charlie. "Since when haven't I? It's April. People buy houses in April. Seven so far this month, done deals. Twenty more prospects to follow up."

"You could give me a report once in a while."

"You get all the paper work."

"I don't read papers. You know how much paper people send me?"

"That sounds like a personal problem, Charlie. Hey, did you ever find out about that grocery store?"

"Oh yeah, I know that story, down to how many spaces in the parking lot. You don't need to worry. Nobody's stopping that thing."

"So, they're tearing down the factory?"

"What factory?"

"The factory in Wardsville, where they're building the store."

"What store?"

"The grocery store."

"They're building a grocery store in Wardsville?"

"That's what you just said."

"I didn't say that. Factory, huh? I'll find out. Didn't you say something about a factory before?"

Wade could only stare at the phone. Charlie's voice kept coming.

"Forget that. I want to talk about Gold River Highway."

"We got the funding, we wait for July to see the plans."

"No waiting. I'm putting it in the ads. Big new road, buy your house before prices go up."

"It's not a road yet."

"I think it is. You said you'd get it through the county board."

"No I didn't."

"You said it was three to two."

"No I didn't. I said I didn't know how Louise Brown would vote. It's two to two, with her on the fence, and the vote isn't till December. So don't put any road in the ads."

"December's too long to wait. We'll lose the whole year, and we'll lose the shopping center, too."

No. Don't try to figure it out. "I'd be right with you, Charlie, but it really could go either way."

"Then get to that lady and make a deal. How much will it take?"

"Charlie, what is your problem? What happens if I offer Louise money and she blows the whistle? Because the first thing she'll do is tell me to stuff it, and then she'll tell the other board members, and it'll be in the newspaper the next day. I'm the only guy on this whole board who even knows how to take a bribe."

That shut the guy up. For six seconds. "Give me her number."

"Forget it. You can look it up yourself," Wade said.

"She's a politician," Charlie said. "There's never been a county supervisor that couldn't be bought. What's the point of even getting elected?"

"Charlie. You call her, I quit. I mean it. I will flat out quit."

"What's your problem, Wade? Since when do you care?"

"I'm saying that that's not how it works out here. I don't want the whole Gold Valley project to end up on the trash heap, and I personally don't want to end up in jail, and if you talk to Louise Brown, you will do both of those."

That bought twelve seconds, and when Charlie finally got his mouth moving again, he was finally just a little humiliated.

"So what am I supposed to do?" he asked.

"Just wait."

His humility was all used up. "That's not good enough! Wade, I want that road and I want it now! I said there was no stopping it, and there better not be!"

Bang!

Charlie had slammed his phone down real hard, and Wade was back to staring at his.

He walked out into the main room of the lodge with the big fireplace and beams and windows. Beautiful place. Take a deep breath, look out at the mountains. Ayawisgi. What did *Ayawisgi* mean, anyway?

Then he made his own call.

"This is Joe Esterhouse."

Joe and Charlie within two minutes of each other. He might get vertigo.

"Joe, this is Wade Harris. Hey, I'm sorry to call—I know you don't like people interrupting you with calls. I'll be real quick. Did you ever find out anything about Gold River Highway? You didn't sound like you'd be able to, but I thought I'd ask."

Short pause. "I did find out some," Joe said. "Not much yet. It's someone in Raleigh behind it, but I don't know who. Somebody devious." Another pause. "I think we need to talk, Wade."

"Yeah, I think so, too. Uh . . . man, it's busy these next couple weeks. Maybe before the board meeting in May?"

"I could do that."

"Okay. If something else opens up before then, I'll call. Hey, Joe, thanks. I'll see you."

"Sue Ann, now I think that's about the last thing I ever expected you to fix for dinner."

"Is it all right?" She looked almost fearful. "I saw them at the store and I remembered my mother's recipe."

"Well, of course it's all right, sweetie, just a little of a surprise. I can't even think when was the last time I had turnips."

"There's ham I could fix real quick."

"No, I wouldn't hear of it. Now, I'll get Kyle and Kelly, and you finish whatever you need to, and we'll all just sit down and enjoy those."

"I think I will warm up some ham," Sue Ann said. Poor thing, she must have been fretting all afternoon. "Just to make sure everyone has enough to fill up on."

"You do whatever you want, dear, because I don't think I can remember a dinner you've made that wasn't just delicious, and now I'm sure looking forward to tonight's."

"You should have heard him," Wade said. Man, he was looking forward to supper. It smelled good, too. "Blew about every gasket he had."

"More than usual, you mean?" Corny said.

"Way more. I've never heard Charlie that out of control." Supper and then bed. He could sleep twelve hours. "He wanted me to bribe Louise for her vote on the road."

"Louise?"

"Yeah. Louise. As if she'd even know what a bribe is. Hey, what's that cooking?"

"Stroganoff."

"So when I say I won't talk to her, Charlie wants her number."

"No. Really?"

"Really. Try to picture Charlie Ryder sweet-talking Louise." He did have to try. "Can you even imagine that?"

"I don't know her as well as you do."

"It doesn't take long. Unless you're Charlie. He'd never figure her out." He was hungry, he was tired, his brain was spinning too fast from the whole long day. "People really are different here, Corny."

"You've said that a lot."

"Yeah, I guess. But this afternoon, talking to Charlie, and then I called Joe Esterhouse. Night and day. Or compared to Louise, either. Or even to Randy. Charlie and I go way back, but I'm getting real fed up with him. He's such a slimeball."

"Then wash your hands, Wade, because dinner is served."

Byron was just staring at his dinner plate, and then up at her.

"What's come over you?" he said.

"Nothing's come over me. They're turnips."

"I can see they're turnips."

"People have turnips for dinner all the time. Why shouldn't we?"

He was back staring at them. "I had my fill of turnips when I was a boy and we couldn't afford better."

"You can eat your roast plain, or you can eat it with turnips. It doesn't matter a bit to me what you do."

"I don't know what's come over you. Everybody's acting senseless."

"What? Did somebody try to feed you turnips at lunch today?"

"Of course not. It was Mr. Coates."

"Mr. Coates being senseless?" She was feeling a little sorry for him. He *had* been worrying so much over the furniture factory. "Has something else happened?"

"No, it's not that, and he's not being senseless, not Mr. Coates. But he came up to me today, right out on the floor, and it wasn't even break or lunch time, and he said, 'Byron, what do you hear about this road over the mountain, out to the interstate?' "

"Gold River Highway? Why was he talking about that?"

"That's what I mean, people are acting strange. I said, 'Well, I hadn't thought about it much, to tell the truth,' and he said, 'Then let me tell you, Byron, that road's important. You be thinking about it.' And then he turned right around and was back in his office. Now, what do you make of that?"

Louise just shook her head. "I couldn't guess. Did he talk to anybody else about it?"

"Not that I saw, and I would have. No, it was just me."

"Well, Byron, you've been there as long as anybody. Maybe he really wants to know what you think, just like he said."

"Then that would be the first time," Byron said. And he'd gone and eaten half the mess of turnips without even noticing.

April 21, Friday

Knock on the door.

"That'll be him," Joe said. He took himself out to the front door. Sun pouring through it. "Afternoon, Marty. You come on in."

"Hi, Joe. Thanks." Marty Brannin followed him back to the kitchen. "Well, hello, Miss Rose."

"Good afternoon, Marty," she said. "That's been a long drive for you today from Raleigh. And you aren't even home yet."

"At least I'm back in the mountains. I just thought I'd stop in here to talk a little before I got back to the house."

"I appreciate that," Joe said. They sat at the table and Rose was at the stove with a pot of stew.

"I can't even think of the last time I was sitting at this table," Marty said. "Must be ten years."

"Not much has changed," Rose said, and Marty laughed.

"And that's a good thing," he said. "Oh, look at that!"

He'd caught sight of the cherry pie Rose had cooling by the window.

"We'll be expecting you to have a piece," Rose said.

"I won't even be polite and pretend to say no," Marty said. "I'd love it. I've been smelling it since I came in. It just took me a minute to find it."

They sat there a few minutes more. Rose served them each a piece of the pie and Marty gobbled his down.

"I skipped lunch," he said partway through, and, "Best pie in the state," when he was finished.

Rose thanked him for the compliment, and Joe allowed himself a smile. Rose wouldn't put much store in a politician's flattery.

Then it was time for business. Marty shook his head.

"Well, Joe, it's a mess there in the statehouse. I'm afraid I still can't give you much of an answer about your road, and I've got a lot more questions myself now. But I've dug out a few things and I'll give you the short version of it all."

"That's all I'd want."

"Even the short version's not real short. I started by asking how that grant got stuck in the Clean Air Act. There's supposed to be a revision trail so you can answer questions like this. Well, I've been through the Commerce Committee to the Technology and Communications

Committee to the Energy Committee to the Transportation Committee, and right back from there to where I started.

"Anyway, there's this section on research on improving roads to reduce emissions and travel time and congestion. And that's where the funding for this grant was."

"Not much congestion around here."

"That's what I would have said. Of course this bill doesn't mention Gold Valley or Wardsville, just the list of qualifications for the project— which is what got you wondering. I've never seen anything like it on any transportation funding.

"So I found where the committee reviewed one version of the bill without this specific project, and then later when they voted on it, the section had just sort of magically been added. It was finally the Transportation Committee chairman who remembered anything, and he said he thought it was a request from the Appropriations Committee. And there are eighteen people on the Appropriations Committee, and that's the biggest snake pit of the whole House."

A fool mess, and just what anyone could expect from that bunch in Raleigh. "This kind of thing happen very often there?" Joe asked.

"I don't think so. But I guess I don't know. I've been there twenty years and I haven't ever seen it done this particular way. But now that I have, I can see how someone could get away with it. It wouldn't work with an interstate or U.S. route, because the federal government would have to get involved. Even state roads would be more complicated. But county roads are under all those radars. The only catch is you—your Board of Supervisors has to approve it if it's a county road."

"I suppose they expected that wouldn't be a problem."

"I bet they'd already investigated you and Wade and Mort and decided they'd have a majority. It looks to me like someone's been through all the angles on this deal."

"So who would that be, Marty?"

"Right. Someone with some clout in Appropriations. That's the short answer. That narrows it down to five or six of the eighteen."

"I'd still be interested to know who it was."

"The next step is getting to the clerk of the Appropriations Committee and digging around a little."

"That'll be up to you."

"Well, Joe, that's why I thought I'd stop in for a visit. Part of me wants to follow this through, sort of on general principles. I'm long past trying to clean up the muck at the statehouse, but I still think people shouldn't get away with tricks like this. There should be a bit of a fuss, at least.

"But, it's going to take time, and I'll probably have to assign somebody specifically to do the digging, and I don't know if it's really worth the effort when there's so much else that needs to get done."

Marty stopped and squinted his eyes and gave Joe a look. "So I thought I'd ask you."

And Joe took his time to think about that. "I think I'd rather you did, Marty."

"Now, that's interesting. We both know that this road is somebody's underhanded little project, but of course most roads are. And I hear there's a fight brewing in Wardsville over the final vote. But even knowing all that, I'd still expect you to just shrug and let it work itself out. Sure, you might call me about it, like you did. But at this point you'd say, *Never mind*. Is there something else? Besides all the usual Raleigh antics?"

Joe took his time to answer that, too. "That might be."

"With you, that means yes, but you don't want to tell me yes."

Joe smiled a little. "That might be."

"Then I'll just be quiet and do as I'm told. But are there any clues that would make it easier for me?"

"There's a man on the board, name of Wade Harris, and he works for a developer who's building all the houses up in Gold Valley. Charlie Ryder, he says, in Raleigh. Now, you know developers. Wade says this Charlie Ryder is sure wanting the road built. Enough that Wade got suspicious and asked me to make some calls."

"Charlie Ryder. I'll look him up. But even if he is, is that what you're looking for?"

"I have a thought, and it's bothering me." He had to stop, to decide what to say. "I don't care much to know who's behind the road or how they pulled their tricks or what they even want from it.

"Marty, if you can find who's behind this road, I just want to know one thing." Rose had turned around from the stove to listen. "I want to know if they're evil."

April 25, Tuesday

"I did it."

Cornelia looked up from the sofa. "What?"

"I quit." Wade dropped his briefcase by the front door and then himself onto the sofa next to her. Corny waited for him to stop moving.

"Tell me what happened," she said.

"I don't know. I mean, I don't know why. Charlie called and we screamed at each other like usual. But this time . . . I don't get it."

"I'll just sit here and listen," Cornelia said. "And I'll let you know if I figure out what you're saying."

"Okay. This is what he said. He wants to know who's buying the furniture place. I said I didn't know, I'd call this Coates guy and ask. No. We can't let him know it's Charlie trying to find out. He asked if I could break in."

"You're kidding."

"No. That's what he said. So when I told him to forget it, he said he'll make his own offer for the building."

"Now you're kidding."

"No."

"Why would he do that?"

"I don't know. Maybe he wants to develop it into a shopping center. It's the wrong location and it's too small. I don't know. But it sounded like someone is pushing him."

"Pressuring him?"

"Yeah. The way he was talking. So I asked him why he wanted to know, and he wouldn't tell me. So I told him I'd quit if he didn't tell me what was going on, and he still didn't. So I quit."

"This is for real?" Corny said.

"Yes. It is. I'm not putting up with this anymore. Charlie doesn't believe me, but I don't care. I told him end of May. June first, I'm out of that office."

"What will you do, Wade?"

"I don't know. I don't know anything! But it sure feels great." Maybe *great* wasn't the right word. "Let me just sit. I think I've blown a fuse."

"Everything will be okay."

He could even close his eyes. "Sure, it's okay. Now I need a job." He did close his eyes. "So what do I want to do when I grow up?"

"When would you ever grow up?"

April 28, Friday

"I think we're half done, at least." Randy had to stand and stretch, with his back sore from hunching over the table all afternoon and his eyes seeing spots from looking at page after page of the tax ledger book.

"We'll finish Monday," Patsy said. She looked a bit bleary herself.

"I suppose most counties do it all with their computers, but it's not really that much work for just twice a year. And someday we'll foreclose on some of these. When did the county ever do that last?"

"Eight years ago, we had a lawyer do all the work. Most of them paid and the county only closed on fifteen or so, and it hardly covered what the lawyer cost."

"That doesn't surprise me a bit.

He was still standing and thinking it would be so much nicer if Patsy at least had a window down here in the middle of the courthouse basement, when a cloud covered her door.

"Look at you, Randy!"

"We're just finishing for the afternoon, Luke."

"Everybody pay their taxes this year?"

145

"Almost," he said. "Just a few, like always."

Luke settled himself onto the desk, right in the middle of all their work. "Here it is, sort of ironic. You make up this list every six months of all the unpaid property taxes in the county and publish it in my newspaper. So the more that haven't paid, the bigger the advertisement you have to buy, and the more I get out of it. And here I am, hoping nobody pays their taxes, because that gives me the biggest ad."

"Then we wouldn't have any money to buy the ad," Randy said.

"But you have to. It's state law. Maybe I'd give you a hardship discount."

"Well, it's not likely, anyway, as most people do pay." Randy sat back into his chair, and Patsy stood up.

"What about the Trinkles?" Luke asked. "They paid up this time?"

"They're not on the list so far, so I guess we haven't got to them yet. It'll be a lot, though."

"What do you mean?"

"You know, Luke. It's been years since they paid. Isn't that what you were asking?"

But Luke didn't seem to quite catch what Randy meant. "Nothing," he finally said. "Just wondering."

"And what I'm wondering is," Randy said, "are you here for any good reason, or just being nosy?"

"Part of each. I wanted to see if you were about done with that."

"Monday."

"That'll be fine. It helps to have some time, since it takes me a while to set it. And as long as I'm being nosy," Luke said, "I'm counting a few noses. What's the latest with all of you on Gold River Highway?"

"Now, Luke! That's the last thing I want to talk about."

"It's not the last you will hear about it. I'm just keeping the public informed."

"Keeping the public inflamed."

"When it comes to Gold River Highway, those two are the same. Now, I'm saying Joe Esterhouse and Wade Harris are for it, you're against it, Eliza Gulotsky always votes no, and Louise is trying to decide."

"I don't know," Randy said.

"But you don't say I'm wrong on any of those?"

"I don't say anything."

"Then I'll quote an unnamed board member, and everyone will know it's you."

"Why don't you just ask each of us?"

"That's work, and I already know what they'll say."

"Then why are you asking me?"

"So I can quote you."

"Then talk to Wade Harris, so you can quote him."

"I am, actually. When he's in town next Monday. And he gives me better quotes than you. Now I've thought of another question."

"Good gravy, Luke. Why don't you just make up your answer to it?"

"I can't for this one. Who owns the land on the mountain where they'd build the road? Over on the other side, it's all Gold Valley Development land, but what about on the Wardsville side?"

"I don't know. Do you know?"

"If I did, why would I ask you?"

"So you can misquote my answer," Randy said. "I'm trying to think. Whoever does is going to make some money selling it to the state."

"That's what I was thinking. Who'd have thought that old mountainside would be worth anything?"

"That's the thing about owning land."

"I wish I owned some," Luke said. "Just what family you're born into, I guess."

But just then there was a clatter in the hall. Patsy had her things to leave, but she backed into a corner to make room for whoever, or whatever, was coming, and Luke finally stood up from the desk.

Kyle came bouncing in as eager as a puppy.

"Dad?"

"Right here, son." Sue Ann must have told him that he'd be here in the courthouse.

"Mrs. Clark, Mr. Goddard." The boy nodded to the other adults, polite as his mother had taught him to be. "Dad!"

"What's after you?"

"Coach put up the list for varsity football." The boy dropped onto Patsy's chair, but he was leaning so far forward he was hardly touching it. "I'm quarterback."

"Well, sure you are." Randy felt a big smile spreading across his own face to match Kyle's. "Starting?"

"Yes, sir. Starting quarterback."

"Congratulations, Kyle." Randy took hold of Kyle's hand and shook it. "What I would have given to say that to my dad. But you deserve it."

"Practice starts in May. And Coach wants seniors for weight training all summer."

"You've got some hard work ahead of you. Kyle. I am so proud of you."

And at that point, a handshake just wasn't the right thing, and he stood up, and Kyle did, too, four inches taller than his daddy, and Randy gave him the biggest hug he could.

There was a bright flash, and they both looked around to see Luke and his camera both smiling at them.

April 30, Sunday

Sweet sunset. Wade finally had a minute's pause, just in time to appreciate it. He'd take a picture, but how many sunset pictures could one person use?

Corny was coming out from the back office. "I took a call," she said. "Somebody from last month, wanting a second look."

"It's a busy week."

"He wanted Monday evening, tomorrow. It's the night of your board meeting, but I think it'll be early enough that you can fit it in."

"Uh—okay. Whatever. I'm going in to Wardsville for the afternoon, and I was going to meet Joe before the meeting. I'll figure it out. I'll just catch Joe afterwards."

"And I'm out of here," she said. "I'm thinking stir-fry."

"Whatever's easy. I'll be about an hour."

"See you at home."

Off she drove, into the sunset, and Wade settled into his chair. Paper, paper. No job was finished until the paper work was done.

The front door opened.

It was kind of late on a Sunday for a customer, but anything could happen in April. Wade started out to the main room.

Oh boy. This was going to be a disaster.

"Dr. Colony," he said. "Welcome to Gold Valley."

"Thank you."

Calm words, the first Wade had heard from that mouth. Maybe they were going to be adults for the evening.

"I guess you're not here to look at houses," Wade said. "But I'd be glad to talk." He waited. "I'd be glad to try to find some common ground."

"I don't think there is any." Colony had a big bulging thick manila envelope in his hand. "Not here. I want to make you an offer."

"Okay. Come on back to my office."

They abandoned the big room. Wade offered a chair to his guest and then sat himself. Then they were facing each other, and Wade waited.

"You moved here to sell these houses," Colony said. "You aren't from here. I don't think you even like it here."

"It hasn't been real welcoming."

"Why don't you move back to Raleigh?"

That was a question that could mean a lot of different things. From the way he said it, Wade couldn't tell which.

"My job is here," he said.

"There must be other jobs back there." Colony set the envelope on Wade's desk. "This place doesn't mean anything to you. You don't care what happens except to make money. Well, here's money."

Wade stared at the envelope. "What are you saying, Dr. Colony?"

"Look at it."

Wade picked up the envelope and looked inside. Lots of hundred-dollars bills, bound neatly in bank wrappers.

"It's fifty thousand," Colony said. "If you'll leave, or resign, or anything, but just kill that road, then you can have it."

"It's worth that much to you?"

"It's worth that much."

"I think I'll have to say no."

Everett Colony started to blow his top. But he held back.

"Why? Isn't it enough?"

"It's a lot." Wade had to give him points for generosity. "It's better than the going rate. But I'd make more than that selling houses if the road gets built."

"Then how much?"

Wade shook his head. "That's not it. I'd have to trust you, and you'd have to trust me. Not just now, but for a long time. That's how these deals work."

"It's cash. There's no record."

"It might be marked. You might have the serial numbers recorded. There'll be a record of you withdrawing it from your bank. See, Dr. Colony, you're an amateur at this stuff. That's enough of a reason to turn you down."

"Then how should I do it?"

"Don't." Now he was feeling sorry for the guy. It had taken a lot of guts for him to get this far. "I'd get fired anyway."

Except that he'd already quit. That was where it got complicated. Why not take the money? He could use it, and Colony was taking the bigger risk.

"Besides," he said, "that still might not kill the road."

"I think it would."

Wade pushed the envelope back. "Thanks anyway. But keep it."

The envelope was snatched and the chair shoved back and then the front door was slammed. And Wade was alone with his thoughts.

May

May 1, Monday

Time to start—already! Poor Byron, left there at the dinner table alone with just a heated up noodle casserole, of all things. That was *not* going to be enough of a supper.

Joe knocked his little wood hammer on the counter.

And she hadn't even left him any green beans or . . . or even a glass of milk! They were still in the refrigerator.

"Come to order."

Well, Louise was trying to come to order. But she couldn't get that picture of Byron out of her head.

"Go ahead, Patsy."

"Mrs. Brown?"

The man was just going to have to survive on his own. "Here," she said, and tried to pay attention.

"Mr. Esterhouse?"

"Here."

"Eliza?"

"I am here."

"Mr. Harris?"

It took a moment before Louise realized something wasn't right. Well, Wade hadn't answered! What with worrying about Byron, she hadn't even had a chance to look around the room. His chair between Joe and Eliza was empty.

"Mr. McCoy?"

"I'm here."

"Four present, Joe," Patsy said. "Mr. Harris is absent."

"Thank you, Patsy. That's a quorum. Jefferson County North Carolina Board of Supervisors is now in session."

"Do we know where he is?" Louise asked.

"I was expecting him," Joe said. "Did he talk to you, Patsy?"

"No, Joe."

"He's probably running late," Louise said.

And now she'd had a chance to notice the crowd in the first rows of chairs. "Or maybe you all have scared him off," she said. It must have been half of Mountain View sitting out there. That meant it was looking like a long meeting tonight, and Luke Goddard was even awake. Well, at least Everett Colony wasn't in the room.

Someday she'd put a mirror up on that sheet of plywood over Luke's chair so she could read in it what he was writing.

Steve Carter was there, and maybe one or two others who looked like they were from Gold Valley.

"Motion to accept last month's minutes?" Joe was all business.

"I'll move that we accept last month's minutes," Louise said. It was going to have to be her and Randy, with Wade gone and Eliza never voting for anything and Joe was chairman and couldn't move or second.

"I'll second that," Randy said.

"Motion and second," he said. "Any discussion? Point of order, with only four members voting, it still takes three votes to be a majority to pass a motion. Go ahead, Patsy."

Louise still couldn't think where Wade might be.

"Three in favor, one opposed," Patsy said.

"Motion carries," Joe said. "Minutes are accepted. Next is receiving public comment. Looks like we'll have some this evening. Please state your name and address."

Well, Joe was right about that. She'd been on this board eight years and there'd been hot tempers before, but there'd never been anything like this road. Why, most of these people had never set a foot into a Board of Supervisors meeting, and now look—more than half the room full.

There was a little looking around while people were deciding if they'd be first. Then Fred Clairmont got to his feet. Louise only knew him through his wife, Lynn, but she did know they lived in Mountain View.

"Fred Clairmont. 715 Washington Street, in Wardsville. I know there's been a lot of comments on Gold River Highway and Hemlock Street. I just want to make sure all of you know just how much all of us are against that road. There might be reasons for building it, but I don't think any of them are worth the damage that thing will do to the Mountain View neighborhood."

And just at that second, the door slammed open and Everett Colony barged right in.

"I guess I've said all I wanted." Fred said to Everett.

"Well, I've got quite a lot more to say," Everett said and pushed past and set himself right at the podium. Most of Louise's thoughts of Byron had gotten pushed away, too. It was time to be listening now.

"You know what we've got to say," Dr. Colony said, and not in a good humor. "First I want to say that I don't understand why this road is still being considered—"

"Excuse me," Joe said. "You'll need to state your name and address."

"You know who I am!"

"Required by law," Joe said. "Otherwise you'll need to step down."

"This is ridiculous! Oh, all right. Everett Colony, 712 Hemlock, Wardsville. We're all here tonight to show you that we're not putting up with you or anyone forcing this road through our neighborhood."

He kept on from there, and Joe let him go past five minutes. Watching him reminded Louise for all the world of one of the five-year-olds in church throwing a temper tantrum. He didn't say a single thing he hadn't said before, and he didn't leave out a single thing he had said before.

But he finally sat down. While all his neighbors were just starting to see who would come up next, a man in the back row got right up and beat everyone else to the podium.

The whole front row of Mountain View folks saw him coming, and they started whispering and frowning.

"Good evening. My name is James Ross and I live at 4500 Eagle's Rest Drive in Gold Valley. I want to comment on Gold River Highway."

He looked like a Gold Valley person, too, with his bright sweater and tan pants and loafers. There probably wasn't a sweater that color of green in all of Wardsville. "Frankly, I'm surprised at what I've heard here tonight. When I heard that the highway had been funded, I was thinking it would be automatic that the board here would vote to approve it. It's been on the plans forever. I bought my house in Gold Valley partly because I understood that the highway would be built when the funding came through. It had never occurred to me there'd be any reason for it not to be."

Mr. Ross leaned forward, toward the board, leaning on the podium a little and smiling a little.

"I looked through the plans. There's some interesting wording there. Those plans aren't just a daydream. They're published so developers and planners know what to expect."

There was something about the way he was talking. Louise couldn't take her eyes off of him.

"And of course, this board has approved all the Gold Valley subdivisions. Gold River Highway is a big part of those plans."

In fact, she was hardly breathing.

"I would consider the plans a type of legal commitment, in fact."

Mr. Ross had paused. Nobody was breathing.

"And if the board didn't carry out its responsibility in that commitment, legal action might be appropriate."

He was staring right into her eyes. She couldn't even move.

"He's a lawyer!"

She was startled. Everett Colony had jumped up and was pointing at the podium.

"He's a lawyer and he's trying to threaten you! Don't listen to him."

Joe Esterhouse hadn't moved, but now he tapped his hammer. "Mr. Ross is entitled to his comments."

"What was that first name again?" It was Luke.

"Let me be clear that there are to be no further interruptions from the audience," Joe said.

"Joe?" Louise said, once everyone had settled down. "Is that right?" A lawsuit sounded serious. "Can people sue us if we don't go by the plan?"

Joe shook his head. "Transportation planning and implementation is government policy, and policy is set by due process of government action. That's the law in North Carolina, and government action would be this board voting."

"With all respect." Mr. Ross was still at the podium. Louise knew what he was reminding her of: those courtroom shows on television with the lawyers talking to the jury. "A judge might have a different opinion about whether this constitutes breach of contract."

"He might," Joe said. "I'll just say I doubt it."

"The law notwithstanding," Mr. Ross said, "I hope you would abide by the spirit of the planning documents you've published for years."

He left the podium, but there was an air he left behind, kind of like smoke, that lingered. Everyone seemed a little afraid of walking up to where Mr. Ross had just been.

But then Richard Colony broke the spell. He wasn't as loud as his brother, but he still had the family boldness. After the lawyer, he was almost a relief—just straightforward bullying.

Louise listened to him lecture. Simply because they were all really just being selfish didn't mean that they weren't right. Now a lady was speaking, and Louise had seen her in the salon once or twice but couldn't remember her name. It was hard to think of telling all these people they had to have a road they didn't want. It did seem like it would ruin their homes, and Louise wouldn't want crime and trash and traffic all around her house.

The door opened in the back of the audience and a sheriff's deputy eased in. He was a young man in uniform, and he looked a little like Matt.

The people were still talking and it had been almost an hour. Joe wasn't going to take much more. And what was she supposed to make of it all? She had no idea what she thought.

"I'm just worried about the children," the woman was saying. "We've always had such a nice, quiet neighborhood for them to play in. They could walk over to the park. They could even play out on the streets. Not Hemlock, but the side streets—Washington, Henry, Maple. Now we'll have . . . well, a highway. Right through the middle. Would any of you want that? I don't think—"

Bang! Louise jumped—everyone did. It was Joe's wood hammer.

"This meeting is adjourned."

Joe sounded as hard as Louise had ever heard him. But he looked terrible, all pale and so old. The deputy was standing behind him.

"Well, Joe . . ." she said, but Everett Colony interrupted.

"You can't just adjourn this meeting—"

"I said the meeting is adjourned. Board members, could you come with me."

Even Dr. Colony took a breath. "What's happening?"

But Joe was up and walking toward the side door. Randy stood up and followed him, and Louise did, too. She went through the door and down the stairs, and Joe and Randy were just going into Patsy's little office. Louise squeezed in with them and the deputy, and then even Eliza was there with them standing in the doorway.

"Close the door," Joe said.

Eliza closed it and there they were, the five of them all packed like sardines. Joe looked terrible.

"What is it?" Randy asked.

The deputy coughed a little to clear his throat. "Gordon called me. He asked me to come in here and inform you all. There's been some kind of accident up on the mountain, and Wade Harris was in it."

"Does that thing work?" Joe was pointing at the two-way radio set up on a shelf.

"I think it does."

"Get Gordon on it."

"Well, he said–"

"Now."

The deputy was sure not going to argue with a voice like that. He had to push himself over to the shelf between Randy and Joe, and then diddled and poked and talked police talk into it.

The door opened and Luke Goddard was trying to get in, too.

Joe only looked at him, but then they heard Gordon Hite himself on the radio thing.

"Sheriff Hite, over."

"Um, Gordon, this is Russell. I'm with Joe Esterhouse at the court-house and he wants to talk to you."

"Put him on."

"You push here to talk," the deputy said and showed Joe how to work the thing.

"This is Joe," he said. "What happened up there?"

"Well, I'm still working at it."

"It's Wade Harris?"

"Sure is."

"Where are you?"

Gordon's voice came loud and scratched out of the speaker. "Up on the dirt road, Ayawisgi road. Looks like he was coming over the mountain, coming to the board meeting, I guess. And he went over the side."

"How bad is he?"

"Well, he's dead, Joe."

Joe's face didn't change. It was like stone. Somebody started breath-ing real fast, as loud as talking.

"Oh my," Randy said.

"Are you sure?" Joe asked.

"Of course I am," Gordon said. "Is Everett Colony there? I was trying to reach him but he's not home."

"He's up in the main room."

"Have Russell bring him up here."

"I'll take him," Luke said, but nothing people were saying seemed to mean anything. They were just sounds.

"Oh my," Randy said again, but it didn't look like he even knew he was saying anything. Louise realized she was the one breathing so loud. And Eliza had her eyes closed, all hunched over.

"Just a plain accident?" Joe asked.

"That's what it looks like," Gordon said. "He must have been hurrying. It looks like he missed a turn somehow and went rolling. It's a real mess here, Joe. I need to get back to it."

"Go ahead, Gordon."

Louise was shaking. She wasn't even sure what she'd just heard.

It couldn't be real.

May 5, Friday

People filing in.

It was a wicked, evil shame.

They waited in line to sign the book. Then they went in. There were Louise and Byron, and they sat next to them.

Goodness sakes. What an awful thing to happen. He still couldn't get over it. He wrote his name and Sue Ann's and Kyle's and Kelly's in the book on the podium with the silver pen.

Gallaudets' was all done up and the flowers were real nice, and the organ playing. He just couldn't get over it. It was a tragedy, that's what it was.

The poor family! She just couldn't stand it. How could such a thing happen? She was sobbing and she couldn't help it. Joe sat down next to her and Rose with him, and Randy and Sue Ann were back behind, all dressed sad and dark. Joe's suit was so black he looked like death itself in it.

She had to hold Byron's hand. It was the only thing to hold on to.

What solemnity there was.

She crossed the threshold and was taken by it, and she was humbled.

She knew the powers of the land, that had been here for the ages before any man had been.

She had heard the voices of other powers and she knew of their conflicts.

Here in this place was a power she had never known.

She felt shaken, and she took a place far from the altar.

There was Cornelia. To think they'd been rafting just a few weeks ago, the four of them, and she'd looked so modern and happy and stylish, with her movie star gold hair, and the way she was just so relaxed and casual. And there were his girls, too, that they'd talked about, and he'd seen the younger one at basketball games, who looked just like her mother, and the older daughter had more of Wade in her. He could imagine what they looked like usually—fashion models just like their mother. Now they looked just like their mother, torn to pieces like she was.

And it was more than a shame. Eighty years of seeing what men would do. He knew how terrible they could be. But this made him sick. It made him ready to die himself.

That poor Cornelia. What in the world was she going to do? Surely she'd move back to Raleigh. She must have family there. That would be her mother in the seat beside her.

Louise had to let go of Byron's hand to find another tissue, and then she grabbed on again.

She couldn't imagine what it must be like to lose her husband like that. To have that police car come up to the house and the officer knock on her door.

She held on as tight as if she were drowning.

He might have stopped this.

Two men dead, Mort and now Wade.

Gordon Hite on the other side by the windows. Not likely he'd be a match for such wickedness.

Rose was looking over at the sheriff. She'd be thinking the same.

What was the meaning? What had happened? The man who they had seen and heard speak was now unseen and unheard. But he was still with them! He was unbound. He was merged with all of them.

She knew it. She knew he had to be still among them. Not thinking and walking as he had been, but now part of all life.

As they all would be.

It had to be.

They were singing "Holy, Holy, Holy." It was her favorite hymn.

" 'Early in the morning our song shall rise to thee.' " She sang it almost as loud as she could because it was the only thing that seemed to make any sense of it all, and also because otherwise she'd be bawling just as loud.

It was tearing at him inside. A waste of a life, destruction of these other lives. It made him so sick. The one who'd done this was still among them, and hiding what he'd done. " 'Though the eyes of sinful man thy glory may not see.' "

He hardly wanted to look around himself at the people there singing.

" 'All thy works shall praise thy name in earth and sky and sea.' "

No, it was wrong! *Thy works?* Whose? What did the words mean? She knew the earth, and the sky, and ancient mountains. These words had no meaning.

He'd come to appreciate Wade these last couple months, despite their differences on quite a few things, particularly Gold River Highway. That rafting trip had been such a nice gesture, even if it had been somewhat of a new experience for Sue Ann and himself. These last two years that Wade had been on the board, he wouldn't have said they'd really gotten along, but he'd just recently started thinking that maybe he could get to know the man, that there was more than just everyone fighting for their personal desires. In fact, that there was anything at all besides just everyone's personal desires.

" 'Only thou art holy; there is none beside Thee, perfect in power, in love and purity.' "

The reverend was ready to say his piece. The program said he was from a big Baptist church in Raleigh. Looked like he'd done his share of funerals.

"Friends. Cornelia, Meredith, and Lauren, and all of the family, want to thank you all for coming.

"We are together today because of Wade McMillan Harris. We knew him and we shared in his life. Now we have been touched again, together, in this grief."

Joe had been to his own share of funerals.

There were a fair number of people there, and that was good, not that he recognized many of them, and not a single other person from Mountain

View. Well, that was at least somewhat because they wouldn't have known him, with there being so little coming and going between town and Gold Valley. But it would also be about the road. It wasn't worthy to think it, but there'd be a few who might be glad that Wade wasn't on the board anymore. But nobody would have wanted it for this reason.

And Luke Goddard was even in the back pew with his pad out, writing, but at least dressed half decent.

"I knew Wade from years ago," the pastor was saying. "His parents were close friends at Jackson Street Baptist in Raleigh."

There'd be a memorial gathering in Raleigh, the program said, and some of these people here today would be from Raleigh, which was quite a drive, but of course most of the folks who had known him back there would just go to the service there.

An interesting point was that Wade was being buried in Gold Valley, in a little church cemetery. It was an old church, built by the Austrians when they came after the Civil War.

The thought of being buried had always been uncomfortable.

There was hardness in the words.

"Yes, we know this has been a tragedy. We all feel this shock and this loss. And we ask why."

But there was no answer to *why*.

"And we ask how it could be."

But there is no answer! Only the ancient powers knew such answers!

"And we stand face-to-face with the pain of this world—and we know we need a Savior.

"And as we each travel our road, we see how much we need a reason and a destination."

The man speaking the words was in bondage to vain hope. Eliza felt anger and was surprised at the force of her hostility.

"Some people will see this tragedy and say God is cruel or uncaring or just nonexistent. I say that He is deeply loving, because despite our evil and hate, he still offers us salvation and forgiveness. I don't know why he allowed this to happen. But I know we can run to His open arms at this time when we need Him so much."

Oh, that was so good to hear.

"Now life will go on. It will not be easy for Meredith and for Lauren, who have lost their father, and for Cornelia, who has lost her friend, her companion, her husband. We don't have Wade anymore."

Louise was about to break down again.

"We do have hope," the pastor said.

Yes, that was it. She sniffed and held it in. There had to be hope.

Fitting words. Difficult to have fitting words for a funeral like this. But the man knew his business.

"And I want to ask you who knew Wade and who know Cornelia to stay with her through the days to come and do your part to help her."

His part. Somehow he would.

The last prayer was over and people were starting to get up, and Randy took a quick look around. Everett Colony was standing by the back door. There were plenty of empty seats and he could have been sitting, but it might just have been that he'd only just gotten there.

It was an honorable thing that the man had come. But the sight of him there, late coming and at the back door, pricked a little thought, of the last board meeting, when Everett had come in late.

"Joe. Rose. Thanks for coming." Roger Gallaudet was at the door, shaking hands with ones he knew.

"A sad day," Joe said.

"Joe?" Roger leaned close to talk quiet. "Could you come in soon and talk? Maybe the sooner the better."

Randy was in his armchair, which was usually one place where he could get his mind off troubles and have a little peace. Now, after that funeral service, he was finding that troublesome thoughts weren't respecting his armchair at all.

"Sue Ann, I just don't know." And he didn't. He just couldn't stop thinking about it. "One day Wade is right there and going along and doing his business. The next day he's gone. And there is nothing to do about it. No matter how much any person might want him back, there's not money or anything that could do it."

"Cornelia must be wanting him back so bad," Sue Ann said. That started her sniffing again.

"I know she is." Randy gave her a tissue and then held her hand. "Everybody's wanting him back."

And he was sure they were. It wasn't imaginable to think that they weren't. But he was still imagining it.

He picked up the newspaper, although most often it did not help his peace of mind, and in fact the front page article was no help at all. *Is Gold River Highway Dead?* the headline asked, and the paragraphs underneath pointed out much too soon after Wade's accident, in Randy's opinion, how that accident might affect the highway. He turned the page, and that wasn't much better, just the whole long list of unpaid taxes he and Patsy had spent those hours putting together.

Then the front door opened and Kyle and Kelly both were getting home from their after-school football and cheerleading practices, and were passing by toward their rooms.

"Hi, Dad."

"Let me ask you two a question," Randy said, and they stopped in the living room. "Do either of you ever see anything of Lauren Harris there at school?"

"Not really," Kyle said.

"She's a senior, I think," Kelly said, being just a sophomore herself.

"Well, if you do," Randy said, "you might be extra kind."

May 8, Monday

"Joe? Sorry you had to come all the way into town."

"Doesn't take long to get in." It was more that he hadn't wanted to.

He knew Roger Gallaudet wouldn't have anything good to say. But he had to hear what it was.

"Well." Roger was looking like he had worse to say than Joe was even expecting. "I won't mince words. I think you're making a mistake, and I shouldn't be saying this to you, since you'll take it wrong. And I don't see it's your business anyway."

"I've got enough to tend to that is and I don't much want more. But I'm thinking it might be my business."

"Then I'll say it. And if you know something I don't, don't tell me what it is."

"I won't."

That made Roger look even more gloomy. "You asked about Mort Walker, and since then I've kept thinking about him. I was thinking about him while I was taking care of Wade Harris."

"I see."

"When they brought him to me, he'd been cleaned up, but I still had all the usual work to do. That included making him presentable for viewing."

It was sickening, the thought of it.

"What did you find, Roger?"

It was plain he was feeling the same that Joe was.

"A lot of trauma to the body. It was a real bad wreck. I suggested a closed casket, but the family wanted a final viewing. His face wasn't as injured, so I could oblige them." It took a sympathetic man to be a funeral director, but also a hard man. "Joe. I'd say he might have had a bullet. Right through here." Roger tapped his chest, right over his heart. "That's just *might have had*. I can't say for certain at all. I haven't seen many bullet wounds, but I have seen a few. That was where the steering wheel impact was, so I wouldn't have had anything to see at all, but there was an exit from his back. That's harder to notice than the entry. But when I saw it, I looked until I found where it might have entered." He pointed his finger. "And I'm not sure at all that's what it was. It might have been anything else, too, from how bad that wreck was. Do you understand?"

"I understand. And that's two board members dead in six months."

"I can count that high myself," Roger said.

"Did you talk to Gordon Hite about it?"

"I made that mistake."

"What did he say?"

"He got plenty angry. He told me they had a cause of death as accidental, automobile accident, and he wasn't going to have anybody raising questions about that."

"Gordon said that."

"We've had these run-ins, Gordon and I, where I just ask. I'm not accusing him, I just ask, and he tells me not to stir up trouble. So if you're going to start pushing Gordon, tell me now so I'll know."

Joe shook his head. "I won't talk to Gordon yet."

Roger had to think about that. "Now, I'm not saying anything about Gordon except that he doesn't like trouble, and that's all that was on his mind when he said that. It's not that he's trying to hide anything."

"That's likely."

"It wouldn't be him hiding anything. Joe, here's what I'm really worried about. Everett Colony is so dead set against that Gold River Highway. Now, I'm saying it again, I'm not accusing anybody, and I don't know anything for certain anyway. But it wouldn't do him any good for people to think that someone killed Wade Harris."

"Would he hide it?"

"I don't know."

Joe was still sick from it all. Easy to kill a man in this county. The sheriff didn't want to see anything, the doctor would just as soon have the man dead anymore. "I'll thank you for your time, Roger, but not for what you've told me."

"I wouldn't want thanks for it." Roger stood up. "It's a hard world we're in."

"It is that."

Randy put his hand on the door. He couldn't believe he was doing this, and he didn't even know what he was doing anyway. But he made himself push the door open.

"Good morning," he said.

"Good morning." Everett Colony's receptionist looked up at him from her window. He didn't know her, which was probably a good thing. "Can I help you? Dr. Colony isn't in this morning. He's in Asheville at the hospital."

"That's fine." He still didn't know what he was doing, but the fact that Everett was out was a great relief.

"What can I do for you?"

He wasn't sure. "I wasn't here to see him. I just had a little question." What would he say? "I was remembering this morning I had an appointment scheduled with him last Monday afternoon and I missed it."

"Monday?"

"That's what I was thinking."

"He takes Monday afternoons off after he gets back from the hospital. I can look up your appointment if you'd like."

"No, that's fine. My arm hasn't been hurting at all, and that's why I didn't even think to come." He had his hand on the door and now he was real anxious to be out of that room. "Whenever the appointment was, I'm sure it's past by now. Thank you, good-bye."

"That's been a day," Byron said. He dropped into his television chair like he'd never get back out.

"Is something else wrong now?" Louise said. She had the table set and the chicken and cheese casserole warm in the oven. Whatever Byron wanted, to eat or wait, she'd be ready.

"Wrong? Something must be. And I wouldn't know what it was, but Mr. Coates was about fit to be tied."

"How could you tell?"

"How could you not tell?" Byron shook his head. "Storming and yelling and throwing fits. We all know the man has a temper, but I've never seen him like today."

"I wonder what he was mad about. Anyone there in the factory?"

"Anyone crossed his path was like to get an earful. Poor Grady, he got the worst of it. He was having trouble with the crane, and he said to Doris that he might need her to order some parts, and she said, 'Which parts?' and Grady said, 'That same hydraulic pump that Jeremy ordered a couple years ago.' And he hadn't noticed, but Mr. Coates was right behind him, and when he mentioned Jeremy, Mr. Coates hit the roof. 'Don't you ever say that name in here again!' he said. 'You understand? I don't want to hear it again!' Everybody in the factory heard him."

"Has he been that angry at Jeremy before?"

"Not like that. Not ever like that. He was just wild."

"Jeremy must have done something new."

"I'll tell you, that boy must have done something criminal for Mr. Coates to be as angry as he was today."

"I've just been to Everett Colony's office," Randy said to Sue Ann. She was concerned. "Aren't you feeling well?"

"I know it's complete foolishness on my part, but I can't get the thought out of my head."

Sue Ann looked at him as if it were his head that wasn't right. "What are you saying, dear? Aren't you feeling well?"

"Well, it's just that I keep thinking how much Everett is worked up about this whole road business."

"He's just being himself."

"I know that. And it's not a worthy thought, I know that, but I can't get it out of my head how he was late to the board meeting that night that Wade had his accident. Even *while* Wade was having his accident."

"He probably had a patient."

"That's what I thought. That's what I was hoping, in fact."

"I still don't know what you mean, Randy."

"Then just don't think about it. Never you mind." He didn't want to mind, either, and he looked for something to take his mind somewhere else. The last few newspapers were still in the rack and he pulled one out. It was still open to the list of people who hadn't paid their taxes, and he just stared at it with his mind still stuck on Everett.

"Well, look at that," he said out loud.

"What, dear?"

"I didn't even notice when we were making this up, Patsy and I. Trinkle farm isn't on it."

"It isn't?" Sue Ann sounded even more confused.

"They must have paid their taxes. I would have just gone past that page when I saw the zero balance on it and never noticed."

"Joe?" Rose was at the barn door. "Marty Brannin called."
"What'd he say?"
"He said he'd just read about Wade Harris, and he was offering his sympathy. He asked that you call him back."
Anything else Marty had to say, it would be about the road. And Joe didn't want to hear anything about it. He didn't want to hear anything.
"I don't think I'll call."
"When you decide to, the telephone number's written down," Rose said.

May 11, Thursday

"Howdy, Louise."
"Hi, Gordon." Louise was up to her elbows in a perm, and this was not the moment to be distracted.
"The wife said I should drop these off and say thank you."
Louise looked around to see, even though she knew what it was. Gordon had the two big baking pans that Artis had borrowed for the last church potluck.
"Thank you, Gordon. You could just set them on my desk back there if you don't mind."
She squeezed the tube of Lifelike onto the next curler and clipped it into place. Gordon clumped past behind her, the pans clank-clank-clanking against each other.
"Russell to Gordon. Hey, Gordon, are you there?"
Louise almost dropped her curler from the popping and snapping sounds and the loud voice.
"Russell, this is Gordon. Go ahead."
"There's a call from the furniture factory," the voice said.
"What is it?"

Louise could hear her desk creaking with Gordon sitting down on it. Here she was trying to concentrate, and he was yakking into that radio of his.

"Mr. Coates just said he wants a policeman over there right away."

"Well, did he say why?"

"No."

"Now, Russell, you're supposed to find out what people want when they call. How am I supposed to know what to do?"

"But it was Mr. Coates, Gordon. He just said to send someone over right away."

"He's not your boss, Russell, I am. Oh, for heaven's sake, I'll go over there."

"Okay."

Gordon went grumbling by, talking to himself. "Okay. Okay. Mr. Coates says so, and so that's what we do."

"Gordon, tell Artis she can have them again any time," Louise said.

"What? Oh, sure, Louise. See you later."

"Patsy, would you do something for me?"

"Sure, Randy." She looked buried behind her desk.

"Find the page in the tax ledger for Trinkle farm."

"Do you know the parcel number?"

He smiled at her. "No, I don't."

She gave him a smile right back. "Then you know how long it's going to take me."

"Nothing urgent. Just when you have time. I noticed that they weren't in the ad last week."

"They weren't?" Now she was curious, too. "I don't remember them paying. Maybe Lyle deposited the checks that day."

"Does he do that often?" The thought of Lyle writing in the tax ledger made Randy kind of nervous.

"Sometimes. But I don't think he's ever made a mistake. And we have to deposit the checks right away, so if I'm not here, he has to do it."

"Well, see if you can find them in the book. It's somewhere near the front, I seem to recall. In fact, why don't I just start myself."

"Letter for you, Joe."

He washed his hands. Handling pesticides all morning.

Handwritten, no return address. "What's that mean?" he said.

"I don't recognize it."

Asheville postmark. He opened it.

"What are those?" Rose asked.

Two pages printed. "It's state laws." A paragraph was highlighted yellow. "Code of North Carolina." He read the paragraph.

And he threw the papers down on the table. Blazing angry.

"Joe?"

"Wicked evil thing," he said.

"Look at that." Randy just stared at the big zero at the bottom of the column.

"They really did pay," Patsy said.

"Sure looks like it. You don't think Lyle put someone else's payment on the wrong page, do you?"

"It's for the exact amount. And see how it's fifteen different payments all on the same day? It must have been an envelope full of checks."

"That sounds like the Trinkles, to pay that way. But it doesn't sound like them at all to agree on such a thing. And that was a good-sized deposit. And see the date? September last year."

"I was gone that week of Labor Day," Patsy said. "So Lyle would have been depositing checks."

He smiled. "Well, good. It's nice to know that's taken care of. I really should find out what all those lawyer letters are about. There's five of them on my desk. I tried reading them a few weeks ago, and I've seen enough contracts and legal papers, but those I just could not figure out."

"Maybe that lawyer in Gold Valley could help you."

Randy groaned. "I don't think we'd get on real friendly together, as much as I'd try. We'll have to call down to Asheville like we usually do." He was looking at the tax book, just sort of absentmindedly flipping through pages, and then he stopped. "Is that what I think it is?"

Patsy looked over his shoulder. "What do you think it is?"

"Two hundred and forty-five acres, and I think that's on Ayawisgi Mountain over Wardsville. Now, I should check the maps, but I think that's the land where the new road would go."

"That's it," Patsy said.

"Owner is Warrior Land Trust. I wonder who that is, because they might make quite a bit of money selling that land for the road if it gets built."

There was Byron. Louise heard the front door open and close, and she ran out to meet him in the hall.

"You won't believe it," he said, before he even got to his chair.

"I will," she said. She followed him into the television room.

"No you won't. I wouldn't have believed it myself."

"I will believe you, and I've been waiting all day to hear."

"What do you mean you've been waiting?"

She sat beside him. "I know that Mr. Coates called for Gordon Hite."

"Now, how in the world . . . !"

She couldn't help it, even if it did annoy him purple when she already knew something he was about to tell her.

"Mr. Coates called the sheriff's office this morning while he was in the salon dropping off my baking pans."

He just stared at her with the biggest scowl. "What in the world was Mr. Coates doing with your baking pans?"

What was the man talking about? "Well, nothing." The day *had* been too hard on him.

"Then what was he doing in the salon with them? And what was he doing in the salon anyway?"

"He wasn't in the salon."

"Louise!"

But she had finally worked it out. "It was Gordon in the salon. And don't you yell at me." Then she started giggling.

"I wasn't yelling!"

"What I said was that Mr. Coates called the sheriff's office while Gordon was in the salon."

"That's not what you said, you said Mr. Coates was." He was red in the face from being mad, and being worn out from working a hard day. So she poked him in the side and he started laughing, too.

"Mr. Coates in the salon!" she said when she could catch her breath.

"With your baking pans," Byron said.

"He doesn't have any more hair than you do!" Louise said, and that slowed Byron's laughing but not hers.

"It's no wonder I've lost my hair, worrying over the factory," he said, "and paying the bills, and making sure we have food on the table, and all your foolishness."

"Well, there is food on the table right now." And they were both already up and on their way to the dining room. It was only after they'd settled in and both made a good start into the green bean and tuna casserole that she finally got Byron talking again.

"It was right at lunch," he said, "and some of us had gone outside to eat, and right there in the front parking lot were Mr. Coates and Jeremy yelling at each other, and Gordon Hite watching."

"What were they arguing about?"

"I couldn't hear most of it, until Mr. Coates started just plain screaming at Gordon. 'What are you waiting for? Arrest him now!' "

"*Arrest him?* Jeremy? I don't believe it!"

"Now, didn't I say you wouldn't? Didn't I?"

"Well, I don't."

"But he did."

"Right in the parking lot?" Louise asked.

"Right in front of everyone."

"His own son! Gordon didn't, did he?"

"Of course not. I didn't hear what Gordon said, but nobody got arrested. And Jeremy just stormed off, anyway, and Gordon stayed and calmed down Mr. Coates. Then they went into the office. And when we were back in after lunch, they were gone."

"Even Mr. Coates?"

"Him, too."

"Well," she said. "Well, goodness sakes. Even before, they never were acting like that."

"I wouldn't have believed it if I hadn't seen it," Byron said.

May 15, Monday

Randy had a million things on his mind. Three client appointments this morning. Sue Ann feeling a little under the weather with a cold, poor thing. The yard needed mowing, and ever since Ed Fiddler next door had got his promotion at the bank, he'd been making comments about appearances being important in the neighborhood.

And now, Roland Coates wanted to see him soon as possible, which meant that afternoon at the latest, no matter what else he might have planned for the rest of the day.

He slid himself into his car and felt something under his shoe on the floorboard. Another piece of broken glass.

That was a dozen or so he'd found since the windshield had been broken. He might even mention to Roland, while he was out there this afternoon, that his trucks should maybe drive a little more gently on Hemlock.

Probably Everett had already pointed that out.

Randy looked at the little pebble of glass. He'd been thinking about broken car windows lately—now, what had that been about?

Well, Wade, of course.

He hadn't seen Wade's car, but from what Gordon Hite had said, it must have been a terrible mess.

Sort of a strange thought, two windshields broken between the two of them, him and Wade, like one more little connection they had together.

The whole thing was playing on his mind in a funny way, and uncomfortable. But he couldn't stop thinking about it—all that glass shattered.

Gabe should have vacuumed out the car better when he replaced the glass. Randy ran his hand down the passenger seat, underneath, around, in the cracks, to find any other pieces he could. He didn't want to keep having them show up every time he sat down in his car.

His finger caught something on the seat. Just a hole, over on the far side. What was that? The car had been through a lot, but he hadn't noticed that hole before.

And there was something down in it. He slid over to sit in that seat so he could get his finger down better. Something . . . he got it fished out and looked to see what in the world it was.

For goodness' sakes, it looked like a bullet. Of all things. How would that have gotten in there?

"What does that mean?" Of course, no one answered. No one else was in the house. But Louise didn't mind talking to herself if she didn't have anybody else. She was trying to work out what the pages said.

Goodness, it was hot! The first hot day of the year.

But time was getting on. She had laundry to finish and sweeping and vacuuming and no time for all those big words in little tiny print. Some of the words were marked with yellow.

She'd have to work them out, though. A letter with no return address, mailed to Louisa Brown, and two pages of some kind of state laws. They'd wait until she and Byron could look at them together. And she'd have him put the air-conditioner in the window for the summer.

She only took one afternoon a week off for housework, and time was wasting.

"Good afternoon, Mr. Coates, and here I am. What can I do for you?"

Randy was trying to be real friendly and helpful, because Roland Coates looked about ready to spontaneously combust. His face was red and his neck was bulging out over his white collar and his eyebrows were squeezed down toward his nose like two white wolves going after a rabbit hole.

"I'll tell you what you'll do for me."

Randy started working out just what might come of losing Roland's account, as that seemed to be the worst that Roland could do, and he was looking like he wanted to do the worst he could. And even if there wasn't really much profit in the account, there was still a tidy sum of cash involved, and also the honor of handling the furniture factory.

"Tear up the contract from March," Roland said. "That thing's worthless."

"Well, I'll do that, Mr. Coates. I'm sorry that—"

"And make a new one."

Randy had taken in a breath, but now he wasn't remembering exactly how to breathe it out again. "Now, I don't think I quite—"

"I want the best. You said that last one didn't have any bells or whistles. Well, put them all in. And double everything."

"I'm not quite sure I understand . . ."

"*Not quite sure?* How can I make it any plainer?"

"What I mean is, there are some questions I'll need to ask, and there are laws about over-insuring. I don't know if I can double everything in the policy, as that's likely to exceed the 150 percent of replacement value . . ."

But Roland had used up all his forcefulness, like a balloon out of air.

"Then just do what you can. Especially fire. What if there's a fire? What will that policy do for me?"

"It'll pay back the cost to replace whatever's been destroyed. Up to the whole factory."

"Make the fire damage as much as you can. Triple it. I'll pay whatever it takes. If there's a fire I want it to pay every cent it can."

"I'll see what I can do," Randy said.

And now Roland was even more done in, limp and slack and weighted down like a wool blanket out of the washing machine. Randy started getting up. It didn't seem like Roland even knew he was there.

Then his inside fire suddenly burst out again and Roland jumped up and reached right over the desk and took hold of Randy's necktie and pulled his head to just two inches from Roland's own.

"McCoy. Make sure they build that road. Do you understand?"

It was a little hard to talk. "I understand, Mr. Coates."

Roland let go and sank back into his chair, but his eyes still had the fire in them.

"Don't let anybody stop you. Just make sure they build it."

Supper was over and the dishes were done. Here it was, her favorite part of the day, when she could sit down next to Byron and watch a

175

little television and not have to think about anything. And while she'd been in the kitchen, Byron had brought the air-conditioner up from the basement and set it in the window. It wasn't as hot as in the afternoon, but they had it on anyway. Just because.

"Oh, I forgot. I got something in the mail today."

"What was it?" He hadn't really heard her. It was more just a reflex.

"I don't know. Let me get it."

She found the envelope and plopped back into her chair, and plopped the papers onto his lap.

"What's that?"

"What I got in the mail today. Now does it make any sense to you?"

He had to get his reading glasses on, and then he squinted, just like she had.

"Where'd these come from?"

"It didn't say. See the envelope? They even have my name wrong. Louisa."

"I can't hardly make sense," he said. "But I think I don't like it."

"I could hardly make sense of it, either."

He put his finger on the yellow paragraph. "Well, it's about county boards, and it's about voting on roads."

"State-funded road projects."

"And board members 'serving by appointment.' "

"Good," she said. "That's what I thought it was talking about. Now what does that mean about six months?"

"They have to wait six months to vote."

"*Serving by appointment*—I think that means when they're appointed instead of being elected."

"Like you'll be doing to fill Wade Harris's place," Byron said.

Suddenly it made more sense. "Well, yes, we will."

"How do you do that, anyway?"

"I should ask Joe. I think we just pick someone and vote. But when we vote on a road, they can't vote till six months later?"

"That's not what it says."

"It says six months right there." She pointed at the words.

"That's not what that means. It means they have to wait till they've been on the board six months before they can vote on these road projects."

Now it made complete make sense. "But if we appoint someone to take Wade's place, they won't be able to vote on Gold River Highway."

"No." Byron was adding up months. "You'll vote on it in December. So you'd have to appoint someone by June."

"But that's our next meeting. Well, I had no idea there was such a law. They can vote on anything else, but not on state road projects."

Byron was scowling at the papers. "And here . . . here's somebody wanted to make sure you knew about that."

May 16, Tuesday

"Gordon?" No one at the front window, so Randy was just poking his nose down the hall toward the office in back.

"Randy?" The sheriff himself came lumbering out. "Is that you?"

"Not anyone else. I'm just stopping in for a second, and I hope I'm not disturbing you." He was feeling sort of nervous.

"No, just sitting back there."

"Good, good, I'd hate to be an obstacle in your line of fire, and . . . no, I'm sorry. I meant to say in your line of duty." Of all things to slip up on, to say such a thing. "Well, either of them, to tell the truth." Now he was feeling all the way nervous.

"What are you talking about?"

"Nothing. Don't mind me one bit."

"Well, why'd you stop in then?"

"Oh. I had a question, and I don't know if you can answer it but I thought I'd stop in and try." Randy took a moment and got himself calmed down, and he tried to sound natural and not use too many words. "You mentioned back in February, I believe it was, at the basketball game, that Everett Colony had got himself a gun."

"I guess I did. Way he was acting, I thought you should know. Foolish thing for me to say."

"Now, I'm wondering, would you know what kind of gun it was?"

"What kind? Why would you want to know that?"

This was the point Randy had been wondering about himself, whether he could really believe such a thing at all, let alone say it to someone else. "You see, I found a bullet. And—" he was thinking as fast as he could—"it wasn't far from my house, and I thought that was sort of strange, of course, in a neighborhood like Mountain View, until it just occurred to me it might be from Everett target practicing or such, and I didn't want to ask him, thinking that he might ask how I knew he had a gun, and when you'd told me he had that permit maybe you hadn't meant for him to know you—"

He'd been talking faster and faster up to as fast as he'd been think-ing,. But Gordon had cut right in.

"Everett Colony target shooting? In his own backyard? Randy, that's the looniest thing I ever heard."

Randy took a good slow swallow. "I'd have thought so, too, but it's just one of those things, finding a bullet there, and I was curious."

"Do you have it?"

"What?"

"The bullet."

"What bu . . . oh, of course. Yes, of course I do. Right here."

He held it out to Gordon, and the man took it and frowned. "Not Everett's. This is a rifle bullet, and he only has a little handgun." He kept looking at it. "At least, that's what he has the permit for. He might have a whole arsenal of rifles in his living room, for all I know, just not any permits to carry them concealed."

"I doubt that. I expect you were right the first time, it isn't Everett's. And that means I don't know whose it is, but I'm not really so concerned about it anyway."

"Did it hit anything?"

"It . . . it might have, I don't really know—"

But Gordon was still staring at the bullet.

"Mind if I keep it?"

Randy was wishing he hadn't stopped in. "Now, why would I mind? I don't have any reason to hold on to something like that, and it hardly counts as mine, anyway, as I was just the one who happened to find it."

"Thank you, Randy."

Gordon Hite swung around in the narrow hallway and clumped back the way he'd come.

And that was a relief, not that it had been but just the wildest of thoughts, anyway, to know that it hadn't been Everett shooting a gun at his car. Well, not that the bullet maybe even had anything to do with the broken windshield anyway. It might have been in that seat for years. Maybe a stray from someone hunting.

"We actually met this guy," Jeanie said, her words like the spicy scents hanging about them. Eliza was rocking beside the woodstove. There was not wood piled in it but a mass of field flowers instead, a daisy blaze.

"The one who got killed?" Zach asked.

"See?" She held up the newspaper. "He was in my raft, back a couple months ago."

"I don't remember. You knew him, right, Eliza?"

"Yes. I knew him." So much was in the air, the scent of every herb and fruit and grain in the store. And Eliza's own thoughts.

"He was a real estate salesman," Zach said, "and he worked for the developer that's cutting all the roads on the mountain. Sounds pretty slimy."

"He crashed in his SUV," Jeanie said.

"Live by the sword, die by the sword. So do you get to kick all those guys out of the county?"

"I don't know," Eliza said. "I don't know what I can do. I don't know what I've done so far."

"Have you ever stayed for one of her meetings?" Jeanie asked.

"No way," Zach said. "I can't think of anything worse."

"Mother, what do you do at those things, anyway?"

Eliza shrugged. "They all talk so much. I listen."

"That's what I thought."

"I still think it's crazy," Zach said. "Eliza getting elected. I mean, it was kind of cool, filling in the forms and getting the signatures. I never thought she'd win."

"If I'd known you were going to win, Mother," Jeanie said, "I would have stopped Zach right at the beginning."

"What was meant to be, is." Eliza had put her own doubts aside.

Zach smiled. "Oh, right. The Powers and the Ancestors. Who was the chief, again?"

"Her great-grandfather," Jeanie said. "Follower-of-the-Wind."

"Right. Grandpa Follow-the-Wind."

"It is my place to be on the council," Eliza said. "It was my ancestors' place."

"To be on the Jefferson County Board of Supervisors?" Zach said.

"To be an elder." Zach was a joy to her, but he was of his own world, and he didn't understand hers. "And it has come to me. It is all for a purpose."

Randy leaned back in his desk chair. There was no danger of desk pounding or loudly spoken viewpoints. There was just Louise.

"Now, this is a treat," he said. "Whatever do I owe this honor to?"

"Oh, Randy." She smiled, but of course for Louise that was hardly unusual. "That's nice of you to say." But then the smile lost a bit of its brightness. "I wonder if you got one of these?"

She handed him two papers folded like they'd been in an envelope, and he took them a little carefully, considering the way she was handling them. Then he started reading them, and then he started making sense of them.

"They came in the mail?" he asked.

"But there was no name on the envelope. And marked in yellow just like that."

"For goodness' sake."

At least no one was pounding on the desk. But it might as well have been.

"Let me get this straight," he said when he thought that was how he had it. "There's a state law from—let's see—" he checked the paragraph reference—"from 1970 that says that a person serving on a county Board of Supervisors by appointment, which I suppose means he was appointed and not elected, that that person can't vote on state-funded road projects unless he's been on the board for at least six months."

"That's what Byron and I decided it meant. But I don't know why they even have a law like that."

Randy was thinking about that. "Well, I might guess. I'd think it was to prevent shenanigans. Now think . . . say an important vote was coming up and it was going to be close. If somehow a person could be forced off the board, the members who were left could maybe appoint that person's successor based on how they thought the new person might vote on the issue coming up. So this law would keep that person from voting for six months."

"But just on roads."

"Well, I can think of two reasons for that. One is, roads are the main thing the state has a say over, and so that's why the state government could make a law about county supervisors voting. And the other reason is, about nothing makes as much trouble as roads."

"That's the truth, Randy." Louise was looking genuinely sad. "Now, why would someone send us those papers?"

"They didn't send them to me."

"I don't understand that, either."

"I think I'll guess about that, too. I'd say whoever it was that sent you that is for Gold River Highway, because it's really about Gold Valley having a vote, which would be a yes. And since people probably think I'm leaning toward a no, it wouldn't do any good to send that letter to me."

"For goodness' sakes. I'd have never thought."

"That's what so special about you, Louise." Which was the truth. "But what do you think we should do?"

"About the papers?"

"About a new board member."

"Oh—my! Well, that's right. We do need to do something."

"Or else we don't," Randy said. It was an interesting point, that if they didn't appoint someone right away, that would be the last word on the highway. There'd only be four voters, and two of them would be Eliza and himself. "If you don't mind, I'll make a copy of those pages."

"Hi, Joe, it's Louise."

"Good afternoon." There was wood to be split and that would take till dinnertime. No time for talking on the telephone.

"Sorry to call on the phone, but we need to talk."

"Go ahead, then."

"Whether we need to appoint someone to the board at the next meeting."

So they'd mailed her one, too. Made him sick.

"Don't like being hurried."

"Well, I don't, either. But I found out there's a state law that I hadn't known about before."

"I got the letter."

"Oh." That took her a minute to work out. "Oh, well then you know about it."

"I do."

"Now, Joe, I know what you're thinking. And I think you're right, that it's an awful thing to send out those letters without saying who they're from, and they even sent mine to Louisa Brown instead of Louise. But that doesn't mean we should just ignore them."

He'd prefer to. "I understand."

"And I think it's about being fair. I think Gold Valley deserves a vote on the highway, and they won't get it unless we appoint someone in June. Now, I did talk to Randy about it."

Randy McCoy wouldn't be thinking about fairness. "Imagine he wasn't in a hurry, either."

"Well, you know Randy. It's hard to ever get him to decide on a thing. But what do you think, Joe? Do you think it's important?"

"I suppose."

"Well, I think it is. And I think we shouldn't let it go by. We should decide to either appoint someone or not."

"Who do you think that might be?"

"For goodness' sake. Joe, I don't know. It would have to be someone in Gold Valley, wouldn't it? Of course it would. Who do we know over there?"

There was work to be done outside.

"I'd have to think it over," he said finally.

"Oh—well, I think we all should think about it. And if I think of anybody, I'll call you back."

They hung up their telephones, and he frowned at his. He'd rather he didn't even have one. Never anything good came from it.

Then he took himself outside in the sun. It helped his disposition to do that. Rose was in the garden.

He looked into the tool shed and took down his axe. Two old trees from down by the creek that had fallen in the April winds. They were easier to split green, but there hadn't been time with planting. They'd been half dead anyway. They'd be dry enough to burn by December.

Leonard Darlington from the next farm over had cut them down to length. Joe didn't use chainsaws anymore. But he could still split wood.

It was his daddy's heavy old axe he used, and he kept it sharp. Most logs snapped right apart with one strike.

That was a big pile of wood. Could be discouraging to look at, but he just took one piece at a time. Then another. And another.

The goal wasn't to finish, it was to just not stop. Finishing would take care of itself. That was from his daddy, too.

Rose had gone in to start dinner.

The pile of split wood was getting bigger. Might not get it all this afternoon, but at least there'd be an afternoon's worth done.

Just lift the axe. It could do it's own falling, and the logs cracked, one and then another.

If they put another man on the board, then that just might be another accident, and another funeral. Particularly if the man was voting for the road.

"I heard you're picking someone to replace Wade Harris."

Randy stared at the telephone plain confused, partly for what the person was saying, but mostly for not even knowing who the person was.

"Now, you'll have to give me just a second," he said, not wanting to offend someone who might be a client or a constituent. "And just to be fair, as I said who I was when I picked up the telephone, I think I should have the honor of knowing who it is I'm talking to."

"What do you mean?"

"Oh." That had been just enough more of the voice to recognize it. "Now, you need to say, *This is Luke Goddard,* when you call someone. Like I said, it's only fair, especially if I've already told you who I am."

"But I know who you are. I called your number. Who else is going to answer? And who are you picking? That's why I called."

"Well, no one that I know of, not yet anyway."

"But what about Gold Valley having a vote on the road?"

Randy was still feeling reasonably confused, but he could think fast enough to realize what that meant.

"Now, Luke, how do you know about that law?"

"State law is public information. But I asked Louise when you'd pick somebody, and she said you had to do it this month, and she said she'd told you, too. So what are you going to do? You have to pick somebody at the next board meeting or else Gold Valley doesn't get a vote."

"I hardly want to say a thing for fear of what you're going to put in that newspaper of yours."

"*No comment.* Got it. Is that with an exclamation point, or a comma followed by some excuse?"

"Luke! That's not what I said."

"Or maybe you won't appoint anybody. That would about kill the road, wouldn't it?"

"I don't know, Luke."

"In my article, I'll be sure to mention that you made that point."

"Then have Eliza say it. Nobody will call her to complain. Anybody besides me. And that's made me think of a question for you."

"I don't answer questions, I only ask them."

"Well, answer this one. When you were in the courthouse there a couple weeks ago and I was asking you to quote somebody else, you said you were going to be talking to Wade Harris. Did you ever catch up with him?"

"No. It was going to be that day of the board meeting. He called and said he had to show a house. So he never came into town."

"Joe?" Rose looked into the front room, where he was reading. "It's Louise on the telephone."

"Take a message, if you don't mind."

He didn't know what to do. He couldn't just hope he was wrong about it all.

Couldn't call Gordon Hite. Might as well not have a sheriff.

Mort Walker and Wade Harris. Two men dead. Two board members dead who'd have voted for the road.

The fool road.

"Joe. Louise said to give you this name. Stephen Carter. She said if that sounded good to you, she'd leave it to you to talk to him."

"Carter. I suppose."

"Is that for the board?"

"It is."

"You'd put someone new on?"

"Louise wants to."

"He'd be voting for the road."

"Likely he would be."

"Can you stop it?"

"Might be that Randy and Eliza will." What else was there to do? It was like a room filled with smoke. Trying to see what was good and evil, and what was true, and it was all hidden.

"I wonder who owns that land, anyway," he said.

May 17, Wednesday

A beautiful spring day for a walk. But Randy hadn't enjoyed it, mostly because the walk had been just over a couple blocks to Everett Colony's house. All things considered, it seemed best to break the news himself, before Everett read it in the newspaper.

"This does it then!" Everett waved the papers under Randy's nose. "Gold Valley won't have a vote."

"Louise Brown is thinking we'd appoint someone this next meeting." Randy said.

A cloud passed over the sun. A thundercloud.

"She's trying to stack the board," Everett growled. "She's decided to vote for the road, and she knows Joe Esterhouse will. She has to get one more yes vote, so she's going to appoint one."

"I don't think that's it, Everett. I don't think she's even decided herself yet."

"It's the only reason she'd try to make an appointment."

"I really think it's what she said, that she's trying to be fair."

"Well, stop her."

"I can't stop her bringing the subject up, but I don't know how likely we might be to vote a new person in. It would take three votes out of four. And I don't even know if she's come up with a name."

Everett didn't answer and Randy waited. The doctor was thinking.

"I have an idea. Don't wait for Louise. You nominate someone. Someone who'd be a sure vote against the road."

"I . . . I don't know right off who that would be."

"Anybody. Anybody here in Mountain View."

"They'd have to be from Gold Valley."

"Gold Valley! What right do they have to be on the board, anyway?"

"It is part of the county."

Everett was getting louder. "And why do you keep taking their side? Don't you know who you're representing?"

"I do, Everett. I do. I'm just pointing out what anyone could point out, that those are the rules. It's Gold Valley district that has the vacancy, and that's where the replacement has to come from."

"Then find someone from over there who's against the road. There must be someone with sense."

"I expect most of them would rather the road did get built."

Everett looked like he might start yelling, but then he must have decided it wasn't worth the effort. "All the more reason they shouldn't be allowed to have anything to do with it. And they won't, as long as there's no new board member appointed next month."

Randy had a lot to think through walking back home. Everett seemed even more upset than he generally was, to not even be caring about straightforward county rules. It must be that he was that upset about poor Wade.

May 19, Friday

"The men won't do it," Louise said. And they wouldn't.

"So you'll be traipsing all the way out to that crazy woman's house?"

"Byron, she's as sensible as anyone."

"Anyone sensible would have a telephone," he said.

"Then there's different kinds of sensible. She's on the board and we can't just ignore her."

"And you yourself said she votes no on everything."

"That's her choice and she can vote the way she wants." Honestly, the men could get so tiresome at times! Well, Byron was never very cheerful at breakfast. "But I'm going to talk to her about Steve Carter, and that's that."

"Then go do it. Mark my words, though, that I say you won't get any sense out of her."

"I've marked them," Louise said, "and you might just be eating them tonight for dinner."

"If you take the whole day driving out there and back, you won't have time to fix anything else."

"Oh, you!"

She finally got him out the door for work, and then herself, too. Stephanie would take care of the salon.

And Louise would have herself a little adventure!

Joe checked the signpost. *Lofty Ridge Road.* Fool place to build a road, up and down the side of a mountain.

Gold Valley. Fool place to live at all, middle of nowhere.

Still, seemed to be a fair number of people living on the road, or houses at least. No telling what they were all doing here.

Strange road for a man to choose to live on.

Louise pulled into the gravel parking lot. When was the last time she'd been out this way? This building—it had been something once. Well, of course. It was an old schoolhouse.

And now it was some kind of store. She was really going to have to get out more. All she ever did was drive up Coble Highway to Wardsville, and back home again. And there was a whole big world out there in the rest of the county.

They might know which of these roads was Cherokee Hollow.

Louise looked in the front door. Well! It looked like her adventure had already started. The room looked just like her own pantry, as neat as it could be for being just too packed—even if most of what she saw might not have been exactly what Louise would have had in her pantry. Bins of all kinds of beautiful beans and rices and, well, everything. Bags and boxes and bottles on the shelves. And smells. She was remembering her grandmother's kitchen on the farm.

It even all seemed a little mysterious. And wonderful!

"Hello." A lady was standing behind the counter in the middle of it all. She was short and stout and had long white hair in a ponytail.

"Hello!" Louise said. "Good morning! What a lovely store!"

"Thank you." The lady was looking at Louise with a big smile, and she must have known she wasn't the regular kind of customer. "Can I help you with anything?"

"Oh! Yes! I'm looking for a road, and I haven't been out this way in forever. Cherokee Hollow."

"That's it right out of the parking lot, up the mountain."

"It is? Now, tell me, do you know Eliza Gulotsky?"

"Eliza! Of course I do."

Of course she would. This was just the kind of place Eliza would like. "I'm Louise Brown. I live down in Coble."

The lady's eyes had gotten big. "You're Louise?" The lady leaned forward over the counter, and her hands flew up to her ponytail just by themselves. "You did Eliza's hair?" And before Louise could even answer, "What would you think about a French braid?"

That would be the house. Joe parked on the side of the driveway. He rang the doorbell.

"Hello?" A young lady. "Mr. Esterhouse?"

"Joe Esterhouse."

"Please come in. I'll get Steve."

He stood in the front hall. Walls and floor were clean and bare. Children's toys in the living room.

"Mr. Esterhouse. Hello." Stephen Carter was holding out his hand. He shook it. "It's Joe."

"Sure. Joe. Come on in. This is Natalie."

Joe nodded to her.

"We'll just duck in here. The older kids are outside, and Andy's down for his nap. I think we'll be okay."

"Appreciate your time," Joe said.

"Sure, no problem."

They went into a side room, more bare wood floors and light-colored walls. The room had a desk and a wide table, and shelves, and computer screens. Rolls of blueprints on the table.

"Sit down."

Joe sat on a chair that was all rubber cushions and steel tubes. Steve sat in his desk chair on wheels, to look like a bank president.

"So, what's up? I guess it's about the Planning Commission?"

"Not that." This man was so young. He'd probably learned more in college than people had even known fifty years ago. "I'm wondering what you might think of taking Wade Harris's place on the Board of Supervisors."

"Oh . . . wow."

Oh . . . dear.

The road should have warned her. It had hardly been a road at all. Bending and twisting and doubling back. Louise had no idea which direction she was even pointed in. Everything here was confusing, and if it made sense to anyone, it didn't to her. What a strange road to be living on!

But now she'd come to the end, and what a sight it was! A bit of open space tucked between two steep sides of the mountain and a creek running as fast as it could through, and right against one steep side was the most adorable little cabin she could imagine. She had a mountain cabin on her kitchen shelves that she bought at a tourist gift store once, but that wasn't the sight this one was.

And there was even a front porch with two rocking chairs. And Eliza was sitting on one.

Louise bounded out of her car, and Eliza came sweeping down the stairs from the porch, and they met with the biggest hug right beside the stream. It was just the natural thing to do, and Eliza hadn't even known she was coming.

"Louise! You've come to visit!"

"I have, dear, and I'm so glad I did." She sat herself in the chair next to Eliza. "It's so beautiful." She had to breathe deep enough to get it all in. "But it doesn't look easy."

That was the next thing she was thinking now that she'd gotten over her first impression. The whole of the small clearing was tilled and planted in one big, neat garden, and green things were already sprouting out of it. There was a woodpile off the end of the porch and smoke coming from the pipe chimney.

"No, it isn't easy," Eliza laughed. "But I don't want it to be!"

Louise knew Eliza wouldn't mind her asking. "Do you have plumbing?"

Joe just sat and let him consider.

"You mean—you're asking me to be on the board?" Steve said. "Is that how it's done, you just choose a replacement?"

"More or less. There'd be a vote by board members at the meeting."

"Uh—well—I could think about it. When would you want to know?"

"Before the June meeting."

"That fast?"

"There's reasons. I expect you'll hear them all soon enough."

"Okay. I'll talk to Natalie. But I guess I could. It's for how long?"

"About a year and a half until the next election."

"I guess I could. It doesn't look like it's as much work here as in some counties. I mean, I know it is work. But you're not approving new subdivisions all the time or doing lots of rezoning. I guess the main thing that's up right now is the new road. Gold River Highway."

"That's the main thing."

"I do," Eliza said. "My friend, Zach put it in. As long as the creek is running, there's water. But I haven't let him put in electricity."

"It doesn't look easy at all," Louise said. She settled back in the rocking chair. "Eliza, I have to admit. I didn't just come to visit. I have some business to talk about."

"Very well." Eliza had such a solemn way of talking about some things.

"We need to appoint someone to replace Wade."

The minute she said it, she felt bad that she'd had to. It didn't seem right at all to be talking about poor Wade so soon.

"How is that to be done?"

"We pick someone and vote. And the reason I wanted to talk to you was, there are only four of us and it'll take three votes. If you're going to vote no, then we other three have to all agree. But I want to know what you think."

Eliza set her eyes right into Louise's.

"What I think?"

"I'll think about it," Steve said at the door. "I'll let you know."

Joe nodded and walked to his truck. Two children were down back of the house and the wife, Natalie, watching them. They didn't look to be even school age.

Two men dead. Two board members dead.

"I would not think," Eliza said.

"Not . . . what do you mean?"

"I would listen."

Listen. It was happening again. Sometimes Eliza made her feel so turned around.

"Listen to what, dear?"

"Just listen. And wait for something to be said."

191

"But . . . by who?"

Eliza had turned away and was just staring out into the valley.

"By the one who speaks."

Louise leaned her chair back and couldn't think of what to say.

"And I would hear," Eliza said. And then, like she was telling a secret, "And I know who would be speaking."

Oh well. Maybe Byron was at least part right. "What do you think of Stephen Carter?"

"Stephen Carter. The young man of exactitude."

"Of what? Exactitude. Well, yes, that sounds like a good word. I think we should appoint him."

"Then I will begin listening."

"You do that, Eliza. Does that mean you might vote yes?"

"That could be."

"Did you come up with somebody?"

Randy stared at the telephone the same as last time, but at least he knew who he was talking to.

"I told you that you need to say who you are."

"You know who I am. Who is it?"

"It's you, Luke."

For about the only time Randy could remember, Luke didn't jump back with an answer. When he did, it didn't mean anything.

"But I don't live in Gold Valley."

"Of course you don't."

"Come on, who is it?"

Randy had to stop a minute. "Why, you're talking about the board. Don't confuse me."

"I'm not. Are you telling me or not?"

"It's Steve Carter, from the Planning Commission. It's Louise's idea."

"Steve Carter. So are you voting for him, Randy?"

"Luke, I don't even know for sure that he wants to be on the board."

"I'll find out. If he does, how are you going to vote? If Louise and Joe vote for him and Eliza Gulotsky votes no, then it'll be up to you."

"I'll have to think about it."

"I'll give you a day or two," Luke said. "Then I'll call you back."

"You don't need to bother. I won't tell you."

"No problem, Randy. I'll just make something up. You know, *Sources close to McCoy say he'll be voting for the new board member.* Something like that."

"What sources?"

"Me."

"You'll cause me all kinds of trouble if you do that," Randy said. "But that won't be anything out of the ordinary."

What a glorious day it was. Not a cloud in the sky and all the gardens blooming. Just exploding! Every color a flower could be.

Byron had been wrong. It hadn't taken more than half the day to see Eliza. And it surely had been an adventure!

Louise parked her car on Main Street just down from the salon to leave the spaces right in front for the customers. The ladies wouldn't want to walk down the block to their car in the breeze right after they'd had their hair done.

And there was the courthouse sticking up over everything. That building would always remind her of Wade.

She peeked into the salon, just to see what went on when she wasn't there, and then she pushed the door open. The girls jumped up from where they were sitting in their chairs talking.

"You won't believe where I've been," she said.

She was just getting ready to tell them when the door opened right behind her, and she had a sight she wouldn't have believed.

"Joe! Well, look at you here."

There he was, tall in the doorway, as out of place as a first gray hair.

"Afternoon," he said. He didn't seem to even notice the hair dryers and the pink floor, and the pictures on the walls of hairstyle models.

"Sit down right over here," she said and she took him back to her desk. She just couldn't imagine what he was doing there. She just barely kept from giggling. "Now, are you here to get your hair done?" He'd had that same short cut for at least thirty years.

"Just need to talk," he said, dour as ever.

"Then go right ahead."

"I talked to Steve Carter."

"What did he think?"

"I expect he'll decide he's willing."

"Then we need three votes."

"I don't see that happening."

"Did you talk to Randy?"

"I haven't. But this would be a way to put an end to the road."

"Joe, you always think the worst of people. I think he'd want everything to be fair."

"That might be."

"Well, it might not matter anyway." This would be her surprise. "Because I talked to Eliza this morning."

If Joe could have looked more sour after she said that, she'd never seen it. "Oh, you did?"

"I did. And she said she might vote yes."

She waited for Joe to answer, but she might as well not have. She could have waited forever by the way he was scowling.

"Anyway," she said, finally, "I'll move we appoint him."

She waited again, and this time she decided he'd have to say something. And she waited more, and Joe might as well have been just an old dusty block of granite. But she kept waiting and smiling, and he finally said what was on his mind.

"I wonder if you should."

"Well, Joe. Of course. Why shouldn't I?"

But that was it. He stood up and said a good-bye. Nobody would accuse Joe Esterhouse of not having any sense, but he was about as hard to understand as Eliza was.

June

June 5, Monday

Empty chairs, just sitting there.

Time to start. It was all that Randy could do to not stare at them.

Joe knocked his gavel, as if it were just the same as always. "Come to order." Of course, Joe would be seeing the two empty chairs like everyone else. "Go ahead, Patsy," he said.

It was like last December, when Mort's chair had been empty and they'd all known why, or like last month, with the other empty chair. But now two empty chairs!

"Mrs. Brown?"

"Here."

"Mr. Esterhouse?"

"Here."

"Eliza?" Everybody looked around, even though they knew she wasn't there. "Eliza Gulotsky?"

They waited a moment, but of course she wasn't there.

Then Joe said, "And Wade's not here, either." Just like he had in December. That way Patsy didn't have to call out the name, which would have been just terrible. "Mark that seat vacant."

"All right, Joe," she said. "Mr. McCoy?"

"Right here," he said. Good gravy, where was Eliza? He was suddenly having real terrible feelings.

"Three members present, Eliza Gulotsky is absent, and one seat vacant, Joe."

195

"Thank you, Patsy. Jefferson County North Carolina Board of Supervisors is now in session."

"Joe?" Louise looked pretty upset. "Do we know where Eliza is?"

"Anybody know that?" Joe asked and waited.

"I thought she'd be here," Louise said.

"We'll just go on," Joe said. "Motion to accept last month's minutes?"

Randy looked at Louise. It was just the two of them to do it, and they did, like they always had. But then a voice interrupted them from the audience.

"Do you have a quorum?" It was Luke Goddard.

"Well, we don't," Randy said, "do we?"

"What is quorum?" Louise asked.

"Four of us," Randy said.

"Two-thirds," Joe said, thinking.

"Then we're short," Randy said, doing his math. Three out of five was less than two-thirds. "We'd need four members."

Louise was doing math, too. "But is it two-thirds of five or two thirds of four?"

Joe had finished thinking. "Quorum is based on members, not seats. Three present is more than two-thirds of the members. We have a quorum."

"Wait a minute," Everett said. "This won't stand. You're short of quorum. You can't vote."

"No, he's right." That was the lawyer from Gold Valley, Jim Ross. "They do have a quorum."

Bang! Joe was back in action.

"This board has four members, and more than two-thirds are present."

"Have we declared the position vacant?" Randy said. "Officially? Because if it isn't vacant yet, don't we need a quorum to say that it is?"

"Of course it's vacant." Louise was looking at him like she might do some violence. "We don't need to vote on that."

"But that's only because you said so." Luke Goddard had jumped up again. "Is that all it takes to make it official that the seat is vacant? I'm just asking, Joe. Are you sure that's all it takes?"

For the moment there was quiet, and everyone was watching Joe. And Joe stared back at them all.

"The man is dead," he said. "His seat is vacant."

The silence after that was like running into a wall. Randy leaned back in his chair, being real careful so it wouldn't creak, just getting out of the way of the silence because otherwise he didn't know what might happen.

The back door of the room opened.

Every eye turned to see who it was. Randy felt a sweat break out, just picturing the sheriff's deputy coming in like last month.

It was Eliza Gulotsky. "I apologize," she said. "I was delayed."

"Mark that Eliza is present," Joe said while everybody watched her glide up the aisle to her seat. "Point of order for the evening, as the board has an empty seat, vote of a tie on a motion is considered that the motion does not pass. Three votes majority is required for a motion to pass. "We have a motion and a second to accept last month's minutes," Joe said. "Go ahead, Patsy."

"Mrs. Brown?"

"Yes."

"Mr. Esterhouse?"

"Yes."

"Ms. Gulotsky?"

"I vote no." Well, that hadn't changed.

"Mr. McCoy?"

"Yes."

"Three in favor, one opposed," Patsy said.

"Motion carries," Joe said. "Minutes are accepted."

Just that little struggle had worn Randy out, and he was going to need all his energy for the meeting. He looked out at the room and tried to smile. Somebody needed to.

There weren't many other empty chairs in the room, and Joe was glaring out at all the filled chairs in the audience. "Next is receiving public comment," he said, "and I'll make a few comments of my own first. Most of you are aware we're likely to vote on appointing Mr. Stephen Carter to the board this evening. I'd prefer it as much as anyone that we had more time to consider the decision. However, state law requires that if the new member is going to vote on Gold River Highway in December, he has to be appointed at this meeting. It is also completely legal for us to appoint him, or anyone, by a simple motion tonight without any prior notification or waiting period.

"Now, we've heard from a number of you already on the subject and we're real open to hearing your comments tonight. However, we would appreciate you keeping your comments short, and I will not allow personal attacks. And please state your name and address."

"Everett Colony, 712 Hemlock Street in Wardsville." And here it came. Randy felt his shoulder hunching up a bit, automatic.

"Everyone here knows I had my differences with Wade Harris," Everett said. "However. I want to state here this evening that despite that, I always had the greatest respect for his work and dedication. I, for one, will miss him greatly, and I regret his loss as deeply as anyone here."

Randy clamped his jaw. It was good to hear Everett's real feelings about Wade, as Randy had somehow missed realizing them up to this point.

"To honor him properly, the decision to name his replacement should not be made in a reckless manner." Everett's manner changed a bit, from being reasonable to more of his normal tone. Randy found himself leaning forward to get a good hold on the table. "Frankly, I find this unseemly haste appalling. Are we taking his years of service on this board and discarding them in just a few short weeks?

"If you proceed with this vote, it will lack legitimacy. You will be tainting the whole Gold River Highway project even further.

"Therefore, I demand, out of respect for Wade Harris, that this vote be delayed for at least another month. It is the only proper and honorable thing to do."

There was something of a murmur of agreement in the audience. The highway might be a consideration, that was for sure, but the more important issue was respect for Wade. It was a nice point, except for Everett Colony being the one making it.

There was the usual rustling and coughing as people were deciding if they'd go next.

"I'm Fred Clairmont. 715 Washington Street in Wardsville. I'd like to say that I'm sure Mr. Carter is a wonderful man, probably just what this board needs, and what Gold Valley needs representing them. But I have to agree with Everett that this is just too fast. That's my only concern, just that it's only been a week that we even heard the name."

"Richard Colony, 713 Hemlock in Wardsville. I agree with most of what has been said here so far, except I'm not as sure Mr. Carter is as qualified as has been suggested. He's been a resident of the county for just five years and he's quite a bit younger than most people who serve on this board. More importantly, he has his own business, I understand, and that could bring up some conflicts of interest if he were to be voting for the benefit of his own business over the interests of the county. In fact, it seems kind of callous of him to be pushing himself onto the board, and I'd have to wonder what his real motives were.

"I also want to point out that Steve Carter is on the Planning Commission. We're supposed to have one person on the commission who's on the Board of Supervisors, and that's Randy. We're not allowed to have two. So I don't know if you even can appoint him."

Louise had been looking pretty annoyed, and finally she just couldn't hold it in.

"Poppycock," Louise said. "If he's appointed, he can resign from the Planning Commission. Or Randy can. That's no reason. And Richard, I've got my own business, and so does Randy, and Joe runs his own farm. Do any of you have anyone better to suggest?"

"No, of course not," Richard said. "But if there were more time, someone else might come up."

"Does anybody have someone else better?"

In her own way, Louise could be almost as intimidating as Joe, especially as she wasn't nearly as often. Richard sat down, and it was going to take a brave person to be the first to comment after that.

Then someone stood up, and the Mountain View people eased back in their chairs, away from the podium, as if they were afraid of catching the plague.

"My name is Jim Ross and I live at 4500 Eagle's Rest Drive in Gold Valley." The lawyer.

"I think we need to be very clear," Mr. Ross said. "These objections aren't about Mr. Carter, or even about honoring Mr. Harris's memory. These objections are all about Gold River Highway, and trying to prevent a representative of Gold Valley from having a vote on that highway.

"I believe we need to consider Mr. Carter strictly on his merits. If he is qualified, then appoint him. There's no need to delay. If he isn't qualified, then wait to find someone who is. That's the commonsense issue.

"Furthermore, I believe the record shows that Mr. Carter is qualified. Five years residency is far more than the six months required by state law, and is manifestly adequate to qualify him to represent Gold Valley. To be successful as a consulting civil engineer demonstrates the highest level of proficiency in the very fields of expertise necessary for service on this board. Finally, Mr. Carter has always demonstrated the highest integrity and character. Speaking personally, as a resident of Gold Valley, and as a friend of Mr. Carter who knows him well, I would be sincerely honored to have him representing me and my district on this board."

It must have been an effort to not finish with, *I rest my case.* But before Mr. Ross would have even had a chance to, Everett was on his feet.

"He doesn't mean a word of that. He doesn't care who's representing him, as long as they'll vote for Gold River Highway."

Crack, and everyone jumped. Joe was waving his gavel.

"That'll be enough," Joe said. "Dr. Colony, I believe you've already had your turn for this evening. I also won't allow personal accusations. I'll close the comment period if this continues, and require that people leave if they can't maintain order."

But Everett had made his point. And Mr. Ross had been right, too, of course. Nobody was saying anything they really meant. It was the highway over everything.

Steve Carter had moved up a row, to behind James Ross's seat, and once Mr. Ross sat down, Steve leaned forward to speak to him, quietly. Mr. Ross didn't seem to care at that point, though.

Another minute passed after that, and between Louise frowning and Joe staring and Everett scowling and Mr. Ross glaring, nobody else could make themselves stand up.

It might also have been because most of the people there were from Mountain View, and they'd been counting noses, which Randy could do just as well. Louise would vote yes, and Joe, too, and then Eliza would vote no, and it would come down to him, and all his neighbors in Mountain View probably were assuming they knew how he'd vote. That assumption would be that he'd vote no, and of course, that was the assumption he'd been making himself. Then that would most likely be the end of Gold River Highway.

"Then we'll close public comment," Joe said. "Now we have a number of other items on the agenda and we'll cover those fast as we can, and then we'll be open to new business, which this would be."

Joe read the items one by one, and Randy hardly paid attention, which was what they deserved. It was the responsibility of the Board of Supervisors to treat each item with due consideration. About thirty seconds' consideration for each item was plenty.

"Is it time now?" Louise asked.

They'd gotten to the end of the agenda items, where they could propose whatever motions they wanted.

"Go ahead," Joe said.

"I'll move that we appoint Stephen Carter to fill the empty seat."

"There is a motion," Joe said, "that Stephen Carter be appointed to the vacant seat on this board, representing the Gold Valley district. Is there a second?"

Silence. Now, that would be a problem right there. The rule was that the chairman could not make motions or second them. And as it was that no pigs had sprouted wings lately, Eliza did not appear to speak.

Louise was looking at him.

Now, a regular vote yes or no was one thing, but just letting the motion die was something else. And Louise was still looking at him.

"Well, I'll second that," he said.

Everett was on his feet, but Joe's stare was enough.

"Just so there'll at least be a vote," Randy said.

"That's a motion and a second. Any discussion?"

"Yes!" Everett said, about to walk up to the podium.

"I'm referring to board members," Joe said. "We are not receiving public comment at this time."

"I'll discuss it," Louise said, and she locked her eyes right onto Everett Colony. "I'm surprised at all of you." She went right down the front row, one by one, giving each a good stiff look, for all the world lecturing them like they were misbehaving children and she was their own mother. "The things you all will say! Now, I don't know what we're going to do about that road, but Gold Valley should have a vote on it. This is a matter of plain right and wrong, and all of you know it.

"And here's Mr. Carter, who's willing to give up his time to be on this board, which I doubt any of you would do. And the things that were said about him this evening." She gave Richard Colony a specially withering look. "That's terrible."

Then she turned to the other board members, and particularly Randy. "Now. I'm expecting this board to be responsible and do what they know is right."

And that about did it for discussion. Randy wasn't about to say anything after Louise's sermon, and Eliza didn't look like she was ready to break her vow of silence, and Joe wasn't much for discussing . . . well, he wasn't looking real well, either. He'd been glum as usual through the evening, and maybe more so, but for the last few minutes he'd just had his own eyes on Stephen Carter there in the audience, and when Louise had said that about doing what they knew was right . . .

That was when Joe had just seemed to cave in.

He hadn't moved except maybe his expression, and that only a tiny bit, and maybe Randy, being next to him, was the only one close enough to see it. But those words had meant something to him.

"Go ahead, Patsy," Joe said.

"Mrs. Brown?"

"Yes."

"Mr. Esterhouse?"

"No."

"Eli—sorry, Joe, what did you say?"

But he'd said it plain and clear. Randy felt his mouth hanging open. Then his brain caught up, at least enough to close his mouth, but not enough to even start trying to work out why in the world . . .

Of all things. What in the world was going through the man's head? Louise was looking at Joe like he'd turned into a giant turnip.

Joe was looking down at Patsy. "You heard me."

"Sure, Joe."

Then Randy realized what it meant, at least as far as he himself was concerned. After Eliza's no, his own vote wouldn't matter. The motion was as good as defeated already, and so was Gold River Highway.

He let out a sigh.

"Eliza?" Patsy said.

"I vote yes."

Randy rubbed his eyes, and looked again, close. He hadn't got the two of them mixed up. That one was Joe, and that one was Eliza. And now it was Joe's turn to stare at Eliza.

And Louise was looking at the two of them like she was about to burst out laughing. And then she did.

Randy could only imagine what he was looking like. What in the world? Of all things. It didn't make a bit of sense. What in the world was going on?

And everyone was back to looking at him!

"Mr. McCoy?"

He was a little too stunned to remember what he was going to do.

"Just a second, there, Patsy," he said. "I'm trying to work out what's just happened here."

The two of them, Joe and Eliza, were both as stock-still as they could be, which for both of them was close to being frozen. Eliza was peaceful and smiling a little, like she was seeing something the rest of them couldn't.

Joe was haggard and hard and staring at something terrible the rest of them couldn't see, either.

And then Randy finally looked back around toward the audience and saw Stephen Carter there with his head cocked over a little and looking somewhere between being amused and bewildered. A couple seats over was Everett, but Randy kept from looking there.

What in the world . . . Randy had found his thoughts again and got them back in some sort of order.

Gold River Highway. And that was the most important thing. He could stop it all right here and now.

Do the right thing. What was the right thing? Was there even right and wrong?

"I'll vote yes," he said, before he could stop himself.

"No!" That was Everett.

"Three in favor, one opposed," Patsy said.

"Motion carries," Joe said. He looked like someone had just died. "Mr. Carter, congratulations on being appointed to this board. Patsy'll get you up on things you'll need to know. Is there anything else? Then this meeting is adjourned."

And why had he done it? Now Everett and Fred and Richard and everyone were going to be on him. But he couldn't help himself. It had just been too right a thing to do.

Everett was headed right for him, and several of the other neighbors, as well, and Randy knew what that meant. Real quick he turned to Louise, to try to be in a conversation before they reached him. But Louise was already running over to Eliza. Randy turned to Joe.

Joe still looked fully grieved and unlikely to talk. Randy was just getting ready for the onslaught, though, when Joe suddenly spoke up himself.

"Who owns the land where the road would be built?"

Randy had to think hard a minute, and he let it show. Everett did actually pause, not that Randy let on that he realized the crowd had gathered, just keeping his eyes on Joe.

"I noticed that, Joe, as a matter of fact, just a few weeks ago. It's a trust, and it's called—now, let me see—Warrior Land Trust. That's it."

Joe didn't say another word.

"Let me even look that up, downstairs," Randy said, standing. Joe wasn't paying attention but Randy pretended he was and left through the side door as busy and official-looking as he could.

"What a night!" Louise didn't usually keep Byron up after she got home, but this meeting was worth talking about. "That dear Eliza came through, though. I was so proud of her."

"But Joe voted against the man?"

"He did, and Randy almost fell out of his chair from it."

"Must have had a reason. You know this man Carter at all?"

"Just a little, but I'm sure he's fine. I don't think that was it."

Byron shook his finger at her. "But he must have had a reason."

"Well, maybe he did, but if he's not going to tell anyone, then I'll just ignore it. He came over to the salon that one day, but you know Joe. He wouldn't say a thing."

"If Joe Esterhouse votes against a man, I'd sit up and pay attention."

"I didn't even know he was going to. And I'd already voted. And Joe was the one who went out and asked him face-to-face."

"Must have seen something out there."

"But he didn't tell me. Or anyone. I'll talk to him." But asking Joe Esterhouse a question like that on the telephone wasn't going to get much of an answer at all. He'd be a hard enough nut to crack in person. And she was really more feeling excited than worried. "But Eliza came through. What a dear she is. And I'm glad for Steve, too. I'm looking forward to him being on the board."

"Joe against the man, and that crazy woman for him. Some recommendation, if you ask me."

"Fool business."

"Joe." Rose looked worried as he was. "Call the newspaper reporter and tell him you'll vote against the new road. He can put it in the newspaper, and then people will know the road won't get voted for."

"It wouldn't be true."

"It could be. You could vote no."

"It wouldn't be right to."

"Then how will you feel if Stephen Carter is killed?"

"You know how I'll feel."

"Is there a right thing to do?" she asked.

"There always is."

She knew that as well as he did. "Will you talk to Gordon Hite?"

"I don't think he's up to this," Joe said.

That was another problem, something about Gordon and all of this.

"Who, then?" Rose asked.

"State Police. That's who to call outside of county jurisdiction. State law."

"Then call them."

That would be a terrible thing, letting loose a world of commotion, and no stopping it. No telling what would happen.

"I'll call Marty Brannin in the morning."

Randy was feeling just worn out. "I was as flabbergasted as I've been, and that's for sure," he said to Sue Ann over the kitchen table.

"Well, you did the right thing," she said.

"I hope I did, if there even was a right thing. It seemed mostly like it was two wrong things to choose. Either be outright hateful to that poor Stephen Carter, and unfair to Gold Valley to boot, or else give up the best chance I might have to stop that road. And I dearly want to stop it, Sue Ann."

"We all do."

"I know Everett and all the rest are being just hateful themselves, and I think it's wrong for them to be, but the facts are the facts. Bringing Gold River Highway down into Hemlock is going to ruin this neighborhood, and maybe the whole town."

"I know it will, Randy."

Or maybe not. That was part of the problem, really knowing anything for certain. "And I couldn't vote no. It just wasn't fair to him, or to Gold Valley. Oh, thank you, dear."

Sue Ann handed him a nice tall glass of iced tea. She was always so considerate, and the children had learned that from her.

"You've got grown men and women," he said, "standing there talking to the board and saying things they don't believe for a minute, and we on the board don't believe them, and everybody knows that nobody believes them."

Randy leaned his head down and propped it on his hand. It was all so confusing, knowing what to think.

"Sue Ann, sometimes I wonder if anything is really true. Just by itself, not depending on what a person wants. Two plus two is four, and no one argues with that, but when you're building a road, is there anything that's true by itself? And is there anything that right or wrong?"

"That's why they elected you, Randy. Because they trust you to make the right decision."

"I wonder if I'm very good at that." He hardly felt strong enough to hold his head back up. "And if I thought I knew anything about anything, I'd have thought Joe would vote for Stephen, and Eliza would vote no like she always does. Now, what do you make of that?"

"You could ask them."

"I might. And besides Gold River Highway and whether he's been here long enough and everything, there's one objection I have against Steve Carter."

"What, Randy?"

"I just wish his name was something that came after McCoy. Because I'm still in the hot seat casting the last vote on all these things."

Beneath the stars. Eliza stood listening. Gentle rustling of the wind, furtive movements within the forest.

Deep silence from the mountain.

There was no anger from what had passed that evening. This new man had been brought into the council. The Warrior had allowed him to be; the Warrior would have a purpose.

And it had been strange, as well, that the sheriff had stopped them as they drove into town. Zach had spoken to him for a long time. She knew nothing about how to deal with such people.

"So three to one, and I'm in," Steve said. "Meet Mr. Supervisor." What a long, strange trip it had been. But kind of fun to watch.

"I wish I'd been there," Natalie said.

"You could have brought the kids. That's all we needed for it to be a complete circus. You could have enjoyed the slandering and maligning of your dear husband. Especially being as callous as I am to snatch Wade Harris's seat just a month after he died."

"You didn't ask to be appointed. Joe Esterhouse asked you."

"He did." Steve shook his head. "He was right here, in this house, and he said, 'I'm wondering if you'd be on the Board of Supervisors.' Didn't he? I don't think I'm making it up."

"That's what you told me."

"And then he votes no, which is bizarre. The one guy I figured was a sure vote, and he says no. Then Eliza Gulotsky, who won't even vote for the minutes, she votes yes, which is highly bizarre. Then Randy McCoy, who treats me like some kind of trespassing space alien for even being there, he has the last vote, and he votes yes."

Natalie pushed the cookie jar toward him. It was a very important member of the family, and it lived on the kitchen table, where it could participate fully in household affairs.

He looked inside. "Someday I hope we can get back to oatmeal cookies."

"Raisins," she said, "and therefore inedible."

"But the kids like raisins." Josie would eat a whole pound if they let her.

"A plain raisin and a raisin in a cookie are entirely different species."

"It doesn't make sense."

"If you want logic," Natalie said, "read a math book. Don't ask a four-year-old about cookies."

Life with preschoolers. "Way more logical than the vote tonight."

"Are you sure you want to be on this board?" Natalie asked.

"Oh, I guess." Politics was a whole different world. Life with preschoolers was good training for it. "Probably good experience." He munched his iced chocolate chip cookie. "I think I want to meet this Jim Ross guy."

"Have we ever met him?"

"No. But I'd say he knows me pretty well. Impressive experience and education. 'Highest level of proficiency in the very fields of expertise necessary for service on this board. Highest integrity and character, too.'"

Natalie smiled, her little mousy look. "I guess you're going to believe everything anyone says at these meetings?"

"Sure. Why not? I'm sure that truthfulness and objectivity will be uppermost in every person's mind."

"And the common good."

"Oh, right, I left that out. Truth, objectivity, and the common good. Yeah." He rubbed his forehead. "What do you think Joe Esterhouse was thinking?"

"I don't know. I only saw him ten seconds when he was here."

"I'm just talking to myself. He didn't say anything to me about why he'd vote no. So that's going to bother me."

"Ask him."

"I will, I guess. Maybe when I get to know him a little better. He's kind of intimidating at those meetings."

June 6, Tuesday

"I'm trying to think. Did I forget to call you?" Marty sounded worried.

"You did call," Joe said. "Afraid I didn't call back."

"I'm finding my notes. Okay . . . I should have called agin. The man behind your road is Jack Royce."

"I might have heard the name," Joe said.

"Let's just say I'm not surprised. He represents High Point and he's kind of known around here for monkey business like that."

"Do you have any thought why he'd be interested in Jefferson County?"

"I doubt he'd tell me anything. But let me run this by you. Different representatives here get in kind of cozy with different special interests, and Jack's got a couple specialties. First, he's the man for the furniture industry, since he represents all those plants around High Point."

"Furniture."

"Is that important?"

"Might be."

"And also he's big friends with developers. That made me think of the man you told me about back in April. Charlie Ryder. So I looked him up, which wasn't hard, and he and Jack are a perfect match. It looks like Ryder works more with representatives from the mountains, where his projects are, and I didn't find a specific connection with him and Jack. I wouldn't be a bit surprised if they were in cahoots, though.

"But that's as far as I'll get without putting Jack in a headlock."

"I appreciate your help," Joe said.

"And what we talked about last time, there in your kitchen. I don't know, Joe. Jack's an oily snake—but I wouldn't call him evil. There's somebody pulling his strings, but Jack's not the man you're looking for. Oh—and now that I'm looking at my notes, sorry to hear about Wade Harris."

"Appreciate that."

"I never met him. Isn't that the second board member you've lost out there?"

"It is."

"Now wait—that was the member you said was working for Ryder."

It was time. "Marty, when are you out this way again?"

"Every weekend."

"If you would stop by, I'd appreciate it. Something to talk about in person."

"Okay. This weekend's busy. Friday night next week?"

"That would be fine."

June 9, Friday

"And here's the mail," Kelly said. She always checked.

"Thank you, thank you," Randy said. "Well, look." It was a formal little invitation envelope.

"That's a graduation announcement," Kyle said.

"But they would have gone out a month ago," Kelly said. "Who's it from?"

210

"Let's see," Randy said, and opened the little envelope. "Well, well. Sue Ann?" She was in the kitchen, and she came out to see. "Look at that. It's for Lauren Harris."

June 12, Monday

This was a large sheriff.

"Hi. I'm Steve Carter."

The eyes were pretty far back behind the puffy cheeks, but they narrowed even more.

"What can I do for you, Mr. Carter?"

A southern large sheriff. The Rod Steiger kind, not the Andy Griffith kind. Blue uniform, open collar, pink jowly face, topping out at maybe six foot four under thin gray and reddish hair. Not overweight—more of an overhang

"I'm on the Board of Supervisors," Steve said. "I took Wade Harris's place."

It had seemed like a good idea, meeting the sheriff, cultivating a professional working relationship.

"Now I remember you," Mr. Hite said, but it didn't make any difference in the way Steve was being inspected.

Stupid idea. Really stupid.

"I'm sorry to bother you. I was just stopping in to introduce myself. I guess I should have called."

"No, that's fine. Pleased to meet you." Right in the middle between annoyance and outright hostility.

Now what? Uh . . . professional relationship. Right. "I don't know if the Sheriff's Department ever works with the Board. I was . . ."

"Not much. I'd probably call Joe if I needed anything."

"Oh. Well, whatever." He should probably just turn and run before he got arrested. What could he say? "Did you know Wade at all?"

"Never talked to him."

Wade must have been too smart to tangle with Frankenstein. "I guess you handled his accident." Steve was just blurting now. Just cut and run! Don't chatter!

"Of course I did." Something had hit a button. Pure hostility, and a whole lot more muscle behind the answer. "And I don't prefer to be questioned about it."

"Oh—I didn't mean . . ."

"And if it's Roger that's been putting you up to it, tell him I've had enough."

"No, um, really, I was just . . ."

The telephone was ringing. Oh, please, let it be for this gorilla.

"Sheriff's Department," the receptionist said. "Gordon? It's for you."

Hite was still breathing fire, but his attention was diverted.

"Who is it?" He took the phone.

Steve backed across the hall to the front door. Whoever it was would be reaping what they had not sown.

Out the door into the afternoon sunlight, with a little wave that nobody noticed. Fortunately.

Roger? Who was Roger?

June 16, Friday

Black night.

"There he is," Rose said. Joe had seen the headlights himself.

"I'll let him in," he said. Almost eleven o'clock.

He had the door open when Marty got to it.

"Hi, Joe," Marty said. "Finally made it."

"Sorry you're out late," Joe said, and let him in to the hall.

"Things come up. Good evening, Miss Rose!"

"Good evening, Marty." She had coffee and a plate of pie on the table for each of them.

"Thank you."

They sat and Joe let him talk awhile, about Raleigh politics and people Joe didn't know anymore. But then the pie was finished and it really was getting late.

"Marty. I appreciate that you've taken time to look into our road. It's been a help."

"Glad to, Joe. It's part of the job. Especially for you."

"Then tonight I'd like you to just listen. I'll keep it short."

"Go ahead."

"Last November, Mort Walker died. He'd been on the Board of Supervisors for near thirty-two years. In May, Wade Harris died. He'd been on the board for two and a half years. They were both fairly strong in wanting Gold River Highway built."

Marty was watching, nodding slow. "Okay."

"The one was a heart attack, the other a car accident. The undertaker here in town thinks each of those might not be accurate."

"What does the sheriff say . . . Hite, isn't it?"

"Gordon Hite isn't open to discussing it. Plain truth is, he doesn't want trouble."

"Okay. And that's why you want to know who's behind the road."

"I do want to know."

"Whew." Marty was a smart boy, and he wouldn't need any more said. Joe gave him a minute to think.

"I'd just as soon be wrong," Joe said.

"Sure. Good grief, Joe. Do you think that's all the sheriff is worried about? Just not wanting trouble?"

"I'll hope so."

"Yeah, I will, too. Is anybody else thinking along these lines?"

"Roger Gallaudet, the funeral director, for one."

"Who around here's against the road?"

"Fair number of people. One is the doctor who assigned the cause of death."

"Oh." It was more a groan than a word. "Joe. I hate roads."

"There's nothing that's more trouble."

"That's the thing!" Marty was getting mad, now he'd had a chance to think. "Because this could be for real. I'll tell you, there are people who would kill over a road. Either way. If they want it and they're greedy enough, or they don't want it and they hate enough. Okay. Let's talk about the State Police."

"That's what I was thinking about," Joe said.

"There are two ways we can get them involved: either lack of local resources and expertise, or else suspicion of complicity."

"Don't have many resources here."

"But then it can't be kept secret. You or Hite would have to request help, and it would be public. You could make the request over the sheriff's objection, but then there'd be a hearing with a judge."

"I'd hate to do that."

"How sure are you, Joe?"

"Plenty sure. But not sure enough to turn the county upside down."

"Right. Exactly. So what are you supposed to do? Have you even discussed it with him at all?"

"I haven't."

"Because the other way is for you to make a confidential request for help against the sheriff, where you'd testify to a grand jury, and then a judge would authorize a secret investigation."

"I'd hate to do that, either."

"You'd be accusing your sheriff of murder, Joe. But here you are, telling me all this, and you haven't talked to him. Would you?"

"I haven't wanted to, but it's time. But I don't know what I want to happen, and so I don't know what I want to do."

"I can only help if you ask me to do something. I can't make up your mind for you. How sure are you that Mort Walker would have been for the road?"

"Anyone could tell you he'd have been for it. He was for roads. He knew what changes they made and he was for it all. When they built the interstate, he fought to have it come through the county and have the exits it did."

"Did he know about the funding? He got that letter from Raleigh?"

"The envelope was already opened when his wife brought it to me."

"And I guess he would have smelled the same rats you did."

"He would have."

"Would he have maybe even owned a few of them? I mean, could he have been behind the deal somehow?"

"No."

"How do you feel, Joe? Do you even want a road that's this corrupt?"

"Wouldn't be any roads at all otherwise."

"Okay. Too bad that you're exactly right."

"It's late and you need to get yourself home," Joe said. "I'll give you a call in a few days."

"Okay. And if I think of anything else, or I find out anything else about the road, I'll let you know."

"Thank you. The best help would be to know what's happened in Raleigh."

June 19, Monday

Eliza watched as the car came slowly through the trees, some moments visible, mostly a slight clouding of dust. But on it came and she sat on her porch to wait.

The car could also be heard, and she soon knew, from its sound and from the glimpses she had of it, that it was not a car that she knew.

It reached the edge of the trees and entered the open space, and the stream. There it stopped. Its door opened and out of it came a man.

All around him the life of the mountainside shuddered. The birds became quiet, the smaller creatures fled. She could hear them escaping. Even the trees, even the grasses held back from him.

He stomped toward her. He was plump and short and carried much. His light was dark red, the color of harshness and ignorance. And pain.

He looked quickly around at her quiet place and she saw him condemn it in his mind. Then he stood at the porch steps and spoke.

"Are you Eliza Gulotsky?"

"I am." She felt peace. She was protected here. It would take a strong power indeed to bring her harm in this shelter.

"Glad to meet you. Roland Coates." He looked around again. "This is where you live?"

"This is where I live," she answered. "Come, join me."

He did not. His choices were full of hardness. "What a heap. Anyway. You're on the Board of Supervisors?"

"Yes, I am." She was watching the pain in him. The coarse stone of his hardness caused it. "Please, join me."

"Might as well." He crossed the steps and came beside her and sat on the other rocking chair, and a softening had taken place. "I came to find out what you're voting on the road. Gold River Highway. I want that road."

"The road." Hard stone hammering against hard powers. Pain, indeed. "It is important to you?"

"Of course it is. Why shouldn't it be? I've got a lot depending on that road."

"There is great anger about this road."

He laughed, abruptly, and it was filled with the anger. "Oh, you've picked that up, have you? Those boneheads on Hemlock. Sure, they're squealing at every meeting, but most people would be glad for the road. Jobs, development, all that. The county needs that road."

Eliza had heard these words before. She knew of the Warrior's scorn for them. But Roland Coates spoke them weakly, without force.

"But what is your desire?" she said.

"My—my what?"

"What is important to you, Mr. Coates?"

"Well, getting the road built. I don't know what you're talking about." Anyone would see the cloud all about him. But piercing it only needed a light breeze. "What are you talking about?"

"There is sorrow in you."

He didn't speak. He stared at her, pulling away in his chair. Then he looked again at the porch and cabin, and his eyes narrowed from their wide openness. "They're right. You are crazy."

She laughed, and she saw another softening in him. "I suppose I am, if so many people think it."

"You don't look dangerous, though."

"Oh my!" She had to laugh again, longer. "No, not at all!"

"Most people are crazy, now I think about it."

"Then I hope you won't mind it in me."

At this, he laughed. "I guess it doesn't matter anyway. Except for this road. How're you going to vote on it?"

"Vote," she said.

"What's it going to be, yes or no?" He had already gained some peace, just being in this place, but not any wisdom.

"Yes or no." She rocked slowly, summoning peace herself. Yes or no. A hard line between yes and no, as if it were just one or just the other. "There are many more than two colors."

"Colors . . . what's that? I'm talking about the road."

Anger and hardness, like rocks beneath the surface of the water. But sorrow, too. "You fight many battles, Mr. Coates."

"Of course I do, that's business." He wasn't angry as he had been before, but confusion swirled around him like leaves in a whirlwind. "But I'm talking about the road."

"Yes, the road." She held up her finger to keep him from answering. "It is more than your business, or the road." Something deeper. "Tell me about your family, Mr. Coates."

"What's that got to do with this?"

"I don't know! That's why I'm asking."

She waited.

"My family?"

"Yes."

"I've got a wife."

"What is her name?"

"Miranda."

"And do you have a son?" Eliza asked.

All of the softening was gone. The anger and the hardness had returned.

"What is his name?"

"Jeremy." He put all of the anger and hardness into the name, but he was suddenly emptied, rocking slowly in the chair on her porch, with the stream speaking comfort, and the breezes peace.

Eliza waited.

"His name is Jeremy," Mr. Coates said again, but there was no anger left. Just pain.

"Joe, I have been wanting to see you." Louise smiled her biggest smile.

"Then I guess you are."

She ignored his silly old scowl. "I guess I am." And when he turned to look at Patsy, she didn't let him get away with it. "And don't you fuss at her. I told her that she had to call me the next time you set foot in the courthouse, so it's not her fault."

"Then what's on your mind?"

"Just this mop of old white hair." She couldn't help saying it. And he just stared, annoyed with her as ever. "Let's find a room," she said, when she thought they'd both had enough. "I want to ask you something."

"Tell me about him," Eliza said.

"Well, what's there to tell? The boy's a hotheaded fool."

"What has he done?"

"I don't know why I'm saying all this."

"But I want to know." Eliza made her voice as peaceful as the calming water. "Please tell me."

"He's always been impatient. Never would listen, never would be satisfied. Finally just walked out."

"Walked out . . . of where?"

"The business. Hasn't hardly been back since. Even left town."

"He moved away?"

"Far as I hear, anyway. Asheville."

"Now, Joe." They were in the county records room at the end of the hall. She wasn't about to sit in one of the chairs around that old wood table, covered with a lot more dust than Patsy should have let accumulate, so they were standing by the door among the filing cabinets and boxes of copying machine paper, and a bucket and mop, and an old typewriter, and a shelf of staples and paper clips and such.

"I know you make your own decisions and let the rest of us make ours." She folded her arms and looked him right straight on. "But you have some explaining to do."

"Jeremy . . . you wanted him to be with you at your business."

"It's natural, isn't it? Thought we'd work together, and he'd take over after me. But he was too impatient. Always wanting to have his own way. Thinks he knows everything.

"So now he's on his own, and I'd say good riddance. But he's not letting go! He's threatened me, and worse, acting the fool. I had to call the sheriff. Gordon Hite says he didn't have anything to do with Wade Harris, but I still wouldn't put it past him, not after what he did to Randy's car, and to mine. So then he said he'd burn my factory down. My own son."

Eliza waited.

"But that's not the concern here," Roland Coates said. He had closed the door. "And you don't know what I'm talking about anyway. It's the road." He leaned toward her, and the peace between them was forced back. "Now, I guess you've heard, too, about selling the factory. Everybody's heard. Well, I'm going to. Not for what it's worth, but it's enough."

"Yes. I've heard this said."

"And I need that road."

Joe just waited. Louise was thinking she'd need pliers. "I want to know why you voted against Steve Carter."

Nothing.

"When you came to the salon that day," she said, "I should have known you had something you were chewing on. So now we've got him voted on, thanks to dear Eliza, and Randy, too, which proves he's not as bad as you think. But I cannot make sense of you."

Not a peep out of him.

"And I have all day." She was right between him and the door. "And you're too much of a gentleman to push me out of the way."

Roads and factories and "development." They didn't matter to her, or even have meaning. She only knew that those who spoke of them spoke with the voice of her enemy.

Her enemy. This power from outside that was contending with the Warrior. Even now the Warrior was speaking.

"The road," she said to Mr. Coates, "and your factory. They are together."

"Together?" He pulled back away from her. "Together? Now, who told you that?"

"You speak of them in the same way, as if they are the same."

He was watching her as a dog would watch an unfamiliar animal—suspicious, alert, but not fearful. "Well, maybe I was."

Then he made his decision, and came back close. "All right. Tell you what. I'll level with you, but I don't want this getting out. You probably don't talk with anybody anyway. Sure the road's important." His voice got quieter but still was noisy and harsh. "It's part of the deal."

"Fool business."

He still had a voice. Louise waited. She had him over a barrel.

"No, I'm not talking to you about it," he said.

"That just makes me all the more determined. There is something going on here."

"There is," he said. "And you should just let it be."

"Well, I'm not going to, Joe."

"Fool business." He was spitting the words out. Then he finally decided to let out another few words. "This fool road."

"The deal?"

"Yeah. You see, the people that want to buy the factory. They say they'll only do it if they can add on another set of saws and lathes. Too small as it is now. That'll mean building another room—it'll about double the place. But they won't do any of that if there isn't a road out to the interstate. Big plans, big changes, lots of hiring and jobs, lots of good for Jefferson County. More than anyone has a right to expect. We just need the road. You understand?"

Eliza didn't understand.

"The road and the zoning," he said. "That's the other rub. Can't do it the way the place is zoned now, so I'll need that changed. Once we get the road. That's why it's important."

But it was strange. She saw this man's pain and disappointment, and she wanted to bring him healing and peace.

Yet she felt anger against him, not her own. The Warrior was against him and his road. She was saddened for him, but the great forces could not be turned back.

"Gold River Highway?" Louise said.

"I'd just as soon he didn't get tangled in it."

"Now, Joe, we talked about all of that. It was just the fair thing to do. Without Steve on the board, Gold Valley doesn't have any say about the road."

Joe fixed his stare on her like he would have melted her. "It would have been for the better."

And that was that. Louise knew she'd pushed him as far as she could. And that last thing he'd said, somehow it made her . . . well, scared. Just from the way he'd said it.

"I don't understand," she said. But then she just turned and marched out the door into the hallway. She didn't want to be there with him anymore.

She didn't even say good-bye to Patsy. She just walked out into the sun and the hot day. And she didn't understand.

All the families filing into the auditorium, and the band on stage playing, and everyone dressed up so nicely, and still seats left but filling up quick.

"Dad," Kyle said, "over there."

"Let's sit by them," Randy said.

The four of them edged down the row to the empty seats near the end, and there wasn't anyone else sitting close.

"Good evening, Cornelia," he said.

"Good evening!" She smiled at him, a real smile, but also forced. "I'm so glad to see you. Sue Ann. And these are . . . Kelly and Kyle?"

"Well, yes, they are." So now he had to remember. "You've got Lauren graduating, and this is Meredith, isn't it?" They looked so much better than at the funeral.

"Mr. McCoy was on the Board of Supervisors with your dad," Cornelia said to the beautiful young lady next to her.

They went on a little, as was proper, and Randy did his best to make them all feel welcome, because even though the Harrises had lived in the county for four years, it was mostly Wardsville and Coble and Marker families in the auditorium that Cornelia might not know well. And then they stood with the band playing "Pomp and Circumstance" while the seniors wearing their blue gowns marched in, and listened to Stephanie Balt give her valedictory speech, and to other appropriate comments from the school officials, and then listened to names of each of the hundred forty-three seniors as they walked across the stage. There was even a special extra applause for Lauren Harris, and she waved at her mother and sister.

Then afterward out in the foyer with the lemonade there were quite a few parents who came up to Cornelia to wish her and Lauren well, and Randy stepped out of the way and talked with his own neighbors and friends.

"Randy—you know most of the people in Wardsville. Do you know Jeremy Coates?"

"Well, yes, I sure do, and I've known him for years, since he and I graduated together right up on that same stage, and I know his family real well, too."

"It's his family that owns the factory?"

"Yes, it is, although he and his father are not on good terms right at the moment. In fact, I understand he's down in Asheville these days, last I talked to him. Now, where have you come across Jeremy?"

"I talked with him the night before Wade's accident. He made an appointment for the next evening, before the board meeting. I believe he would have been the last one to see Wade."

"Jeremy? Of all people. You've never talked to him?"

"No. I will sometime, but I'm not ready yet."

"Does anyone else know?"

"The sheriff asked. He was filling in his forms, that was all. And—you must know Everett Colony, also."

"Oh yes. And Wade was getting to know him, too."

"We've talked about him. He came out to Wade's office that Sunday night."

"Everett Colony?" He didn't say it, but that must have been some fireworks.

"Wade didn't get to tell me what they talked about. He wasn't talkative at all when he came home that night, and then we didn't have a chance the next day."

June 20, Tuesday

Steve was staring at the green binder. Charlton Heston on Mount Sinai staring at the stone tablets.

"I haven't looked through it," Mrs. Harris said.

He touched the thing. It felt like any other big heavy notebook.

"Well—thanks. I'm sure this'll help." Short pause. He'd have to force himself to pick it up.

"Do you have children, Mr. Carter?"

"Three little peanuts. Max was six last week, he's the oldest."

"He was in kindergarten?" She was being friendly. It made him feel a lot better.

"Natalie kept him home. It's such a long way to the school, and we didn't want to throw him on a bus. She's been teaching him."

"It was hard for Meredith and Lauren to adjust. We moved here in the middle of the school year. Meredith was in eleventh grade."

"Will you go back to Raleigh?"

"Sometime. It's too hard to think about."

She looked like a faded Hollywood starlet, old and tired, a washed-out Lauren Bacall.

"If there's ever anything we can do, we'll be glad to," Steve said.

He said good-bye, and then thanks, again, then another *whatever we can do,* and then he finally got himself to shut up and leave the poor woman alone.

Not fun. He backed out of the Harrises' driveway.

What would Natalie do if he died? Time to check the life insurance.

The binder was beside him on the car seat. Now he was kind of looking forward to going through it.

No, really, he was. Somebody had to be a geek.

He came to Gold River Highway and turned south, up the mountain. Just for fun.

Half a mile to the end of the road. The barricade was getting kind of rusty after whatever it was, seven or eight years, since the road had been built this far. And just before the *Road Closed* sign, the old dirt road branched off. He'd driven that thing maybe twice. When did they ever go into Wardsville, anyway, besides him for the meetings?

But he felt like trying it. *Trust your feelings.* Off road, here we go!

Stupid feelings. After the first quarter mile, he was ready to go back to being rational. This road was wretched. The vertical distance to the top was maybe a six-hundred feet, but bouncing up and down out of ruts and holes probably doubled that. And the winding—the horizontal distance was at least tripled.

He'd have turned around if there'd been a place to.

But somehow he got to the top, and stopped.

Wow.

It was a whole new definition for *vast.* Two huge valleys, Gold River on one side and Fort Ashe River on the other. Still more of Ayawisgi towering above the gap. Fiddler Mountain etched by streams and shrouded in green. The bridge in Wardsville a little Tinkertoy, and the town itself a pile of building blocks. A couple of mottled flat spaces, way off. And mountains everywhere. *Everywhere.*

Who'd have ever thought the world was flat?

And it seemed like a good place to look through Wade Harris' papers.

Two and a half years of agendas and minutes and . . . stuff. What a tiny, mundane little world it described. Enough to drive most people off a cliff.

Scratch that. Bad thought.

But Steve himself actually found it all sort of interesting. There was the civil engineering involved. But something else. He'd seen plenty of counties where the board of supervisors was trench warfare. Every vote would be three to two, two to three. Here, it was as close to unanimous as any board with an Eliza Gulotsky on it could be.

It must be Joe. Actual leadership. How rare.

Wait, here was Wade voting no. Parking meters? Oh, right, he remembered that meeting. Everett Colony's first appearance. Wade had lost his temper.

And here was April, Wade's last meeting. The night the funding had been announced.

An actual handwritten note. The first one in the whole notebook. Right beside the agenda item about the road. And all it said was, "Charlie. That crook." *Crook* underlined three times.

Suddenly Dave Brubeck was playing "Brother, Can You Spare a Dime" in his pocket. Cell phone, here? Actually . . . there was line of sight in every direction.

"This is Steve Carter."

Clicks and crackles. Then a voice. "Hello? Hello? I want Steve Carter."

"Yes. This is Steve Carter."

"Steve. Great. My name's Charlie Ryder."

Bizarre. Yes, Wade's note really did say *Charlie.* "Yes, Mr. Ryder?"

"I called your house. Your wife gave me the number. I guess it was your wife. Anyway, you won't know me, but I was a friend of Wade Harris. In fact, he worked for me. So I hear you've taken his place on the Board of Supervisors."

"Yes, sir, I have."

"Well, congratulations." No mention of Wade's death. "Now, I wanted to get you caught up on a few things Wade was working on for me, mainly the new road. Gold River Highway. You live there in Gold Valley, I hear?"

"Yes, sir, I do."

"Good. So you know how important that road is. Wade was working hard to get it built, and I wanted to make sure I could expect the same from you."

"Do you live here in Jefferson County, Mr. Ryder?"

"What? Live there? Are you kidding? No. I'm in Raleigh."

"Um . . . maybe you could tell me why you're interested in Gold River Highway?"

"Why, I'm . . . well, why not? It's obvious the county needs that road. We'll never get Gold Valley developed the way it is now."

"Oh. You're a developer?" Steve asked.

"What do you think I am?"

So this was a game, and Steve was supposed to guess. Except that didn't sound like what Mr. Ryder meant. "Go ahead and tell me, if you don't mind."

"Look, I want to get that road built." So Mr. Ryder did mind telling him. "What do you do, anyway?"

Several witty retorts came to Steve's mind, but they would have just prolonged this agony. "I'm an engineer. A civil engineer."

"Well, how about that." Suddenly the voice turned as sweet as a frosted chocolate chip cookie. "I've got civil engineers working for me. What are you making?"

"I'm fine. Really."

"Think about it. Roads and subdivisions, right? I've got seven projects up and down the mountains. But that Gold Valley, that's the one. You could do real well just working on Gold Valley. How would you feel about sales? I've got an opening up there."

Sales. That would have been Wade's old job. . . . "Excuse me, Mr. Ryder. I'm not interested."

"And you get that road built, I think I can make a real nice offer."

"Mr. Ryder, I don't work that way."

"Look, Steve, this is too big a deal to get your feelings hurt. I own half that valley and you're going to have to listen to what I say. And it's better all around if we're working together. You understand that?"

"I understand exactly."

"And there's something else, too. That grocery store they're building in Wardsville where the factory is."

"I don't know about any grocery store."

"Block it, okay? That's important."

"I don't know what you're talking about."

"Wade did. You will soon enough. And I'm going to be in touch."

"I guess that's your right."

"You bet it's my right. And you'll pay attention if you know what's good for you."

"Mr. Ryder, that sure sounds like a threat."

"Mr. Carter, I don't care what it sounds like."

What calm! What peace! Jeanie and Eliza in the rocking chairs and Zach sitting on the steps. Only the gentlest breeze flowed over them, and the creek whispered.

"Eliza," he said. "I won't be able to take you to your next meeting. I've got a group that's camping overnight."

"I'll take her," Jeanie said. "Maybe I'll stay and watch."

"Okay—but be careful. The cops are on to us."

"What are you talking about?"

"They stopped me last time."

"Going to the meeting?"

Eliza smiled to herself. It had been an adventure, and she listened to Zach tell Jeanie the story of it.

"Two weeks ago. We're just driving along, everything normal. Then here comes the cop car. Lights *and* music. So I pulled over to get out of the way, but he's actually after me. 'Out of the car. Driver's license, registration.' "

"You're kidding."

"No, really. Then he was on his radio calling in my license plate, and I'm waiting for him to start a strip search. It took him five minutes. And then, finally he starts writing a ticket."

"Zach! What for?"

"My brake light is out."

"The police stopped you for that!" Jeanie's anger was so sharp!

"The ultimate crime. So I figured I'd try playing with the guy's mind. It couldn't be too hard, right? I said, 'Excuse me, Officer. I'd be glad to stop in at the station later to finish this, but I'm actually on county business right now, and it's kind of urgent. I've got a member of the Board of Supervisors with me and we're trying to get to the meeting in Wardsville.' So he stares at me, and his mouth drops open, and he squints. Like this."

Eliza had to laugh—it had been just like he was saying.

"So he says, 'Who do you have in there?' Just like that. 'Eliza Gulotsky,' I said. He looks in. 'Just a minute.' And he's back on the radio!"

"Was he calling the sheriff?" Jeanie asked.

"This guy *is* the sheriff! And then he finally comes back, and he says, 'You can go on, Mr. Minor. But please get that light fixed.' "

"I was late to the meeting," Eliza said, and she was still laughing. "So many strange things happen."

Two weeks on the board and not even at a meeting yet. What was the record for fastest resignation?

Joe had been dealing with this for fifty years. No wonder he'd tried to keep Steve off the board.

He looked at the page again. *Charlie. That crook.* Maybe he should add his own underlines.

And this was the road Wade had been driving that night. So now, he was on Wade's road. As if he wasn't already being dangerously erratic in coming this far, he decided to keep going.

The road on this side was worse than the Gold Valley side. He found himself going very slow. It was almost hypnotizing, this dense green world and the road disappearing into it. And then he stopped again.

How long had it been—seven weeks? Almost two months. But this must have been the place. There were torn bushes and broken branches and a big gouge out of the side of the road. And one tree thirty feet from the road missing a lot of bark.

But this couldn't have been the place. The road was curving to his left, going down toward Wardsville. The gouge and the tearing went off to his right, at a straight line tangent to the road coming up. Either he was coming down the hill and turned real hard, or he was coming up from Wardsville and just went straight over. Not that either of them really made sense.

June 23, Friday

Gordon was sitting at his desk. Joe sat himself across in the one other chair.

"What can I do for you, Joe?" Gordon said. He paid attention that Joe had closed the door.

"We have a problem."

"Sorry to hear that."

"I think Mort Walker and Wade Harris were both murdered."

Gordon Hite squinted his eyes and dropped open his mouth some. The rest of his face just went slack.

"Now, what's given you that idea?" Annoyance was about the main part of his voice.

"I'd say it was a reasonable thought."

"That Roger." Now he was just sounding mad. "That does it. How many people is he out talking to behind my back?"

"I went to him." Joe let his anger show. "Because two supervisors are dead in six months, both set on voting for Gold River Highway."

"Gold . . . Gold River Highway? What does that have to do with anything?" Gordon didn't look to have any idea.

"You don't know what a road will make people do."

Gordon just shook his head. "Now you're being crazy. Joe, you've got to stop listening to people like Roger Gallaudet. He's out there telling everyone he sees that Wade Harris was killed, but for the life of me I don't know how anybody could have while Wade was driving down that road."

"Who else has Roger told that to?"

"Roland Coates, for one. He had me out at the furniture factory to arrest his son, Jeremy, for being the killer. And Randy McCoy, asking about bullets in that sneaky way of his."

"Bullets?"

"Well . . ." Gordon scowled. "There's business there between Randy and Jeremy that's best not discussed. But Roger's got it mixed up to think it's with Wade. And then that new man on the board, Steve Carter, he was in here himself asking about Wade's accident, and where else would he have heard it?"

"Then why haven't you done anything?" How could the man be ignoring it after all that?

"I just said I was going to. I'm going down and have it out with Roger. What else would I do?"

No sense answering that. "I think we need the State Police in," Joe said.

It was like a mule had kicked the man. "You *are* crazy! Nobody's killed anybody. What would the State Police do here?"

"Gordon. I'm bringing in the State Police. Now, either we do it together, the sheriff and the Board of Supervisors, or I'll do it myself over your head."

"You can't do that! Now, look. Let me get back with Everett. Give me a chance here to look into it myself."

That was all he really wanted for now. "All right, then."

"And it'll take a few days. He's out of town for the week."

Joe left him stewing and went out to the street. Plenty to think about. Roger Gallaudet talking to Roland Coates or Randy or Steve Carter. Must be a reason for that.

If Roger really had. And that look in Gordon's eyes, right at first, in that squint. Something in there.

July

July 3, Monday

Okay. Just walk right in. Pretend like it's nothing. Steve checked his watch. Ten minutes to go.

It was going to be a big night. Supposedly they'd see the plans for the highway. There was going to be a huge crowd, and comments till midnight, and everyone blowing his top.

Take a deep breath. There was the door. Just open it and walk right in.

He put his hand on the knob. And turned it. And walked in.

No one else was in the room.

Empty room. Okay, no problem. Should he be sitting at the table when the others came in? That would look stupid, like he'd been waiting for an hour. Just kind of standing there? More stupid. Or . . . he could go back outside a minute, and then come back, after other people had come in. But what if he met Louise or Randy in the hall? They'd wonder why he was leaving. Real stupid.

Just stand over by the table. Hand on the chair. No, back off. A couple feet away.

"It won't bite you."

Steve Carter, rushed to the hospital from his first board meeting due to heart attack. "Oh. I didn't see you."

A man back in the dark corner. The newspaper guy.

"I guess not. First meeting, right?" the guy said. "They'll all be here in a minute. Just take it easy."

Steve wandered toward the voice. He could be talking to someone while everyone else came in. That would look okay. Luke Goddard was the guy's name.

"Real show there last month," Luke said. "Shameless bunch, aren't they? And pulling those tricks to get you voted in. Are you worried about whether you're even on the board legal or not?"

"I think it's legal."

"When that Gold River Highway vote comes up, there'll be people wondering if you should really be there. You think it'll pass?"

"I don't know."

But then the door by the table opened and Patsy, the clerk lady, stomped in. The lights came on. The main door flew open and a row of citizens swarmed the front row of chairs, with Randy McCoy nodding and laughing in the middle of them. Patsy left. More citizens. Eliza Gulotsky swept down the aisle and enthroned herself. Patsy returned, Louise Brown beside her, and then Louise sat down beside Eliza and those two mouths started flapping. Jim Ross, the lawyer, rode in, and a whole new posse of supporters with him. Randy extricated himself from his admirers and sat in his chair, leaning forward, still holding three conversations. Chairs scraped, and Wardsville and Gold Valley citizens split to separate sides like the Red Sea parting. Louise scooted over to her own chair.

And Luke's attention had drifted away.

Steve took a deep breath. Check the watch. One minute fifteen seconds to go.

Now the place was noisy and full, and he was getting squeezed tighter back into the corner. He was a spectator, almost as if he didn't even exist. His attention drifted away.

The whole ceiling was painted, but he'd never really looked at it. Sort of the Sistine Chapel of Jefferson County—signing the Declaration of Independence—the pilgrims landing at Plymouth Rock—a Civil War battle—what was maybe some pioneers founding Wardsville?—and a big portrait of Thomas Jefferson. Of course. But the corner up above him was covered with ancient plywood painted the same color as the walls.

"Aren't you going up there?"

Steve jumped. "Oh, right," he said to the reporter. They were deep in the Wardsville side, but no one had noticed them.

He scooted up to his own chair.

"Welcome to the board," Randy said, standing to shake his hand. Louise was right behind him and he got a hug. He turned and nodded to Eliza.

"Good evening."

"Good evening," she said. Sepulchral. But a friendly sepulchral.

The room was getting quiet. Something was supposed to happen, and people were waiting.

"For goodness' sakes," Louise said. "Where's Joe?"

Check the watch. Twenty seconds late.

"I haven't seen him," Randy said, "or Lyle either." He looked worried. "I guess we'll just give him a couple minutes. I can't hardly remember him ever being late before."

"Well, he's so absentminded," Louise said. "He probably just forgot."

Everyone knew that was a joke, and they laughed and started talking again. Randy leaned over toward Patsy.

"Why don't you go check if his truck is out back." Patsy left. "And I was sort of expecting someone from the Department of Transportation this evening," he said to Louise.

"Were they coming from Raleigh?" Louise said.

"They'd come from Asheville," Steve said.

He hadn't said it loud. It was just a reflex—he hadn't even meant to say anything at all. But suddenly everyone was looking at him.

"It's the local office. The local regional office." It was still quiet and they were all still looking at him. "They have an engineering staff there."

The side door opened and Patsy looked out. All eyes turned to her, to Steve's relief.

"It's his truck, but I don't see him, or Lyle."

Now Randy was the center. "Well . . . I hope nothing's wrong."

But something was wrong. And somehow, it would all be Steve's fault. He knew it.

The sheriff had been wanting to arrest him since that first meeting. Someone else was coming in the side door. It was. . . .

"Lyle!" Louise said. "Where is Joe?"

The little county manager looked at the room, one side to the other, his mouth wide open, and he started shaking. Physically shaking.

County manager, rushed to hospital from his last board meeting due to heart attack.

"Joe . . . he's . . . he's . . ."

"He's what?" Randy said.

"He's . . . he's down in the basement. In the . . . the records room. With those roads people from Asheville. We've been down there all afternoon talking."

Louise had stood up, like she would have gone racing down there. "Well, go tell him the meeting has started!" She plopped into her chair, quivering a little herself. But not from being nervous.

Lyle ran. Fast. They all heard his footsteps in the hall, and then on the steps, disappearing.

Finally, the slow, heavy tread of a group, and then Joe Esterhouse marched in and two men and a woman, and Lyle scampering last.

Joe took his chair, boiling mad, right beside Steve; and Lyle melted into his seat; and the DOT three sat in a little front row that Patsy had set for them. Their briefcase was now the center of all attention.

Bang!

Everyone in the room was glad he was not Joe Esterhouse's gavel.

"Come to order. My apologies for the delay. Go ahead, Patsy."

Steve was petrified.

"Mrs. Brown?"

"Here."

Pause.

"Mr. Carter?"

Another pause. But this one wasn't ending.

Joe turned and looked right at him.

"Are you waiting for something?"

What . . . ?

"No! Here. I'm here. Sorry."

"Mr. Esterhouse?"

"Here." Then, that aged, cragged face leaned close to him. "I need to talk to you."

". . . any time."

"Eliza?" Patsy said.

"I am here."

"Mr. McCoy?"

"Here."

"Everyone's present, Joe," Patsy said.

"Thank you, Patsy," Joe said. "Jefferson County North Carolina Board of Supervisors is now in session." Joe was still angry, and he wasn't trying to hide it. "Motion to accept last month's minutes?"

"I'll move that we accept last month's minutes."

"I'll second that."

Was it some kind of seniority thing? Always Louise then Randy.

"Motion and second," Joe said. "Any discussion? Go ahead, Patsy."

"Mrs. Brown?"

"Yes."

He was next.

"Mr. C—"

"Yes."

"—arter? Mr. Esterhouse?"

"Yes."

"Eliza?"

"I vote no."

"Mr. McCoy?"

"Yes."

"Four in favor," Patsy said. "One opposed."

"Motion carries," Joe said. "Minutes are accepted."

The last chairs had filled up and there were a few people standing. Wardsville still had a big majority in the room, but most of the people who'd come in late were Gold Valley residents.

And front and center was the star attraction. The trio was wearing Department of Transportation polo shirts to seem friendly. In the middle lap was the closely guarded briefcase.

"Receiving public comment would be next," Joe said. "I expect most of you are here to see these road plans. I'll open the floor for comments after we've seen them."

So they wouldn't get to start with Everett Colony's primal scream. Steve was remembering that he was supposed to get sworn in, or something, but he wasn't about to interrupt Joe.

All right. Into the agenda. For these, he was ready.

First up: request for a special use permit for roadside lights.

He'd been through each item and checked the topographic maps and plat outlines and utility easements, and reviewed the zoning ordinance to make sure he had it all right. The roadside lights looked good.

"Mr. Carter?"

"Yes."

Firm, authoritative. This was what he was here for.

"Four in favor, one opposed," Patsy said.

"Motion carries. Next item."

He knew what he was doing. If there were any questions, he was ready. Not that he really expected any questions. There probably had never been any questions, ever. But he was ready.

"Mr. Carter?"

"Yes."

And then the next item, and the next, and the next. It was easy. This was how it was supposed to be. This was engineering.

"Next item, Fourth of July picnic," Joe said. "The public is invited to Memorial Park in Wardsville tomorrow at noon for the annual county picnic sponsored by King Food."

Finally, it was time for the fireworks.

"We will now have a presentation by Mr. Robert Jarvis of the North Carolina Department of Transportation."

"Thank you, Joe." Mr. Jarvis had a deep voice

Joe pointed his gavel at the audience. "And I will not accept any interruption during the presentation. There will be adequate time afterward for comments."

Jarvis had opened his briefcase.

"We can ask questions, can't we, Joe?" Louise said.

"Board members may ask questions or make comments."

"You can just jump in any time, Louisa," Jarvis said. First names apparently went with the polo shirt friendliness policy. Although he should have tried to get the first names right.

But Steve was checking out the projector. Cool! He leaned closer to see. The thing popped right out of the briefcase.

And the lady was handing them each a notebook. Louise and Randy and Joe each set theirs on the table without opening them.

Steve got his. Just like Christmas! He started paging through.

The projector was on, pointed at the wall to their left. "Gold River Highway Extension," in big letters. Patsy was closing blinds.

And Steve was cranking through the pages. Cross sections . . . elevations . . . proposed right-of-way acquisitions.

What a massive project.

He found the design criteria section. Only one page—this was a minimal summary. Real minimal. There was hardly any information. A few design assumptions . . . traffic projections . . . very strange.

"I think we're ready," said Mr. Jarvis. "I'm here this evening to present NCDOT's plan for the completion of Gold River Highway in Jefferson County."

And present he did.

Maps, pictures, lots of long sentences filled with long words. It did not take Steve long to realize something very strange was happening.

Was Mr. Jarvis really just caught up in the engineering of the whole thing? Somehow he wasn't saying anything understandable. Randy and Louise looked completely confused. Joe had no expression. Eliza was staring at the notebook in front of her like it was a dirty diaper. Well, like he would stare at a dirty diaper. Like he usually did at two o'clock in the morning.

"Vertical change of altitude standards for limited access roadbeds will require an excavation as shown in this diagram." The diagram projected on the wall showed a black line and a red line dropping down in a V shape under it. The scale was in meters, with nothing for comparison.

Steve felt words building up inside. He couldn't let this get past. "Mr. Jarvis?"

"Yes, sir." Deep voice. Patronizing. Steve hated to be patronized.

"The North Carolina grade standard for vertical change in a limited access highway is only applicable when the limited access requirement is based on anticipated vehicle speed and traffic count, and I don't see that either of those is pertinent here. In fact, there's no assumption basis for a limited access design at all. Or am I missing something?"

Mr. Jarvis didn't answer right away.

"You don't have much in the way of design assumptions at all."

Mr. Jarvis found his voice. "Those would be too technical for a presentation like this."

"I think not." Steve was feeling like his cookies were being stolen. "I sure want to see them. How are we supposed to evaluate these plans?"

"The engineering department has done a complete technical evaluation."

"Then I want to see it. For instance, the cross-section on page thirty-two. A twenty-foot median? What's up with that? Two-lane roadbeds on each side, median, shoulders—this thing is eighty feet across. The existing section in Gold Valley is thirty-five feet, and Hemlock is what, twenty-four feet? Who did the design work on this project? NASA? It looks more like a runway for the space shuttle."

"You need to remember that this is a significant opportunity for Jefferson County," Mr. Jarvis said. "I realize it may seem large . . ."

"Seem? It is! It is large. Look at this cut." The diagram was still shining on the wall. "Is that really a thirty-five-meter notch? A hundred and ten feet?"

"Compared to the mountain itself, that's actually fairly small."

"Fairly small? You name one other cut in North Carolina that's that big. It'll be visible for twenty miles, at least, and it'll change the whole ridgeline. Where are you even going to get enough dynamite to blast it? Or put all the rock you blow out?"

"I'll be glad to have the engineering staff answer your questions."

"Good, I'll expect them to. I want design assumptions, in detail, a geologic core sample analysis to see if that cut is even possible, the whole environmental impact statement, which only has a two-sentence summary in this binder, a much better set of images showing the scale and visual impact of that cut, and I mean with the cut superimposed on them."

"We'll certainly work on that. . . ."

"And next, do you have a slide of page forty-one? I think you need to put it up on the wall."

"I don't believe that was part of our presentation."

"You're kidding."

"This is meant to be a general overview, we won't get into details."

"I think most of the people here came to see that one map."

"We can make it available after the meeting tonight."

"No, let's see it now." Steve held up his notebook. "You have this document on that computer, don't you? You can get page forty-one displayed on the projector."

"I don't know. . . ."

Steve was out of his chair. "Here. I'll do it."

He leaned over the briefcase projector and got his hand on the mouse. A little searching—the hard drive was a mess. Dozens of presentations mixed together. Didn't they ever put them in subfolders? Finally he had to search—he typed in some text off one of the pages. The document was buried in an e-mail. Open it, find the page, project it.

"There."

He stood up from the computer to see the map on the wall better. He looked around to see what everyone would think.

They were all looking at him.

Randy had his elbows on the table and his chin in his hands and his eyes narrow and his brow wrinkled—Louise was slumped in her chair with her eyes wide open—Eliza's mouth was tightly closed, like she would start crying—Lyle was about to start screaming—Patsy was just blank—Mr. Jarvis was still startled and bent sideways from where he'd gotten out of Steve's way at the computer—the rest of the audience members were in every other shade of confusion and bewilderment.

They were all frozen and staring right at him.

And Joe Esterhouse was smiling.

"I'm sorry," Steve said. "I didn't mean to hijack the meeting."

"You just go right ahead," Joe said. Smirking.

"Well—look at the detail map." Steve pointed up at the wall.

"Maybe you could tell us what it is," Joe said.

But it was obvious. "It's Hemlock. This shows the project taking fifteen feet out of every yard on the street."

"Sue Ann, you have never seen such a ruckus." It was well after midnight. Randy sipped his iced tea, and he was mercifully glad for the peaceful and quiet living room and that comfortable chair. "I truly thought that Everett was having an attack. He couldn't say a thing for at least five minutes, and you know how unusual that is for him."

"It must have been such a shock," Sue Ann said.

"It was that, let me tell you. Most of the people from Mountain View were having conniptions."

"Now I don't know what to think!" Louise said. "There was more shouting and name-calling than I've seen in eight years on that board."

"Glad that road isn't coming this way," Byron said.

"I'm not sure it's going to come any way, after tonight."

"Mr. Coates is wanting it, I know that."

"I don't know why he would," Louise said. "It couldn't make as big a difference to him as it would to everyone in Mountain View."

"But he does want it."

"I spent the whole afternoon with those state people," Joe said, "and I couldn't get a single answer. Just, 'We know what we're doing and don't you worry.' In five minutes Steve Carter took them apart."

"Wouldn't he be on their side?" Rose asked.

"I'd have thought. But I'd say he might have about stopped that road. Those people are going to have a real job of it now."

"You don't seem worried about that."

"I'd say anyone who was against that road would call Steve Carter their biggest friend."

"Oh, Natalie." Steve was drowning his sorrow in No Sugar Added SuperKids Apple Juice Made From Concentrate. "I made such a fool of myself."

"You always say that. Everyone else says what a professional job you did."

"Everyone on that board must hate me. Or at least think I'm an idiot."

"Steve—they don't. They're glad you understand all those engineering plans. None of them do."

He had to snicker, a little bit at least. "You should have seen the place blow up when they saw that map of Hemlock. Man. I'm glad no one had any weapons or those DOT guys would never have gotten out alive."

"They would really have to tear up Hemlock?"

"The road comes over the mountains and hits that one narrow stretch of six blocks in Mountain View, then it widens out again down the hill to downtown Wardsville. Engineering-wise, it's obvious. The point is, though, why does the whole thing have to be so big scale? It doesn't make sense."

"They must think there will be that many cars."

"I don't get that, either. The projections in the report look way too high."

"They think there will be lots more houses?"

"Maybe. But a couple months ago, I got some projections from the office in Asheville. The board asked me to, the month before Wade Harris died. They're completely different than the ones in the report tonight. If they'd used the projections I had, the road would be a nice wide two-lane with a couple switchbacks and no cut at the top."

Tonight was a bright moon. There was no need for candles. Eliza sat by the window in the pure, thin light.

How terrible the meeting had been. Those people with their haughty smiles and deceiving words and papers. She had never touched the book offered to her. Patsy would have found it on the table after the meeting.

The Warrior would take retribution on those bringing this assault.

July 4, Tuesday

"I have no idea what to expect," Steve said. They were turning onto Hemlock from Main Street.

"You've said that five times," Natalie said.

"That means I'm nervous."

"I know."

"I figure, I'm new on the board, I should go to the picnic. I didn't even know the county had a picnic until they invited us last night. What are we supposed to do at a county picnic?"

"Eat?"

"Yeah, I mean what else? Shake hands and kiss babies?"

"You aren't running for president, Steve."

"I really have no idea what to expect."

The Fourth of July picnic was usually one of Randy's favorite events, with lots of Wardsville neighbors and Humphrey King grilling hamburgers and hot-dogs by the dozen, and congenial conversation and watching the children play at the park, but this year the thought of lots of Wardsville neighbors didn't quite go with congenial conversation, especially with the board meeting just the night before still fresh in everyone's mind. So he settled himself at a table near the grill and sent Sue Ann to get him a plate, and waited for the neighbors to find him.

Well, there were enough people, even if Byron had stayed home. Even Mr. Coates was there.

But Louise wasn't worried about Mr. Coates. She put her cooler by the drinks. There was food to take care of.

"Randy!" It was Everett. Randy put on a big smile and leaned against the table. And Everett's brother Richard was with him, and both wives, and they all sat right around Randy's table. But they didn't look like they were really enjoying the holiday.

"Look at him," Steve said, pointing at Randy. Max and Josie were on the swings and Andy was asleep and he and Natalie were actually just sitting. In peace.

"He's sure popular," she said. Randy was surrounded by a dozen citizens.

"I'm not sure that's the right word."

"Do you know any of these people?"

"Uh—oh, come here. It is time for you to meet Louise."

The baby was adorable! Louise couldn't stand it. "Look at him!" And Steve and Natalie, what a nice couple they were. Andy was just sleeping away, dressed so cute, and their other two were precious, and playing so nice on the swings.

Louise was so glad to meet them all! She made sure they got plenty to eat.

"Let me get my breath," Natalie said when they were sitting again. "How could anybody be so friendly? It would wear me out."

"She's like that continually. Except when somebody isn't playing nice, and then it transforms into righteous fury."

"I need to come to one of these board meetings. So, are there any fireworks tonight?"

"People go to Asheville. If you want fireworks, look at Randy." The guy was engulfed. There were now twenty irate people around him.

"At least there are no Gold Valley people here," Natalie said. "Nobody even knows you."

But his phone was ringing. "Hi, Steve Carter." Then he looked at her, and smiled, and listened. "Jim Ross," he said after the first pause. "He'd like to discuss Gold River Highway with me. He doesn't think I represented the district's interests very well last night."

July 6, Thursday

Gordon Hite looked up from his desk. "I'm kind of busy, Joe."

"Have you talked with Everett Colony yet?"

Gordon shook his head, like he was tired. "Yes, I did, a couple days ago. We had a long talk. I think you need to just drop this whole idea you've got about Mort and Wade Harris."

"What did Dr. Colony say?"

"He wrote *Automobile accident* on the death report and that's what it was, and a person can read the report for himself if he has any questions."

"And Mort Walker?"

"Heart attack, plain and simple."

"Is that all he said?"

"We had a long talk, but that's the main part of it."

Fool business. Fool sheriff, fool doctor, the whole lot of them.

"What else did you talk about, Gordon?"

"Well—we weren't just talking about this. Some other things, too, but they're not part of this at all."

"Because Everett Colony says so? That's not good enough."

"I'm making my own decisions, not what he tells me."

It was time to make his own decision. "I want to know if you're going to do your job or not."

"What am I supposed to do?" Gordon looked as frustrated as Joe felt.

"Go to Asheville and get the State Police."

"I can't do that."

"Why?"

"Because they'll come up here and nose around and make all kinds of trouble and leave me looking a fool. And people'll be asking why I need help to do my job, and I'm up for election again fall next year."

And people would have a right to an answer. "There might be people from out of state involved in this," Joe said. "You'd need the State Police to help with that."

"Out of state? Of all things, Joe. What do you even think is happening here, anyway? Killings? Out of state people involved?"

"Because it's a road."

"I don't believe it," Gordon said. "There is nothing happening! Nothing! And you'll be the one who's left looking a fool if you bring in outsiders and there's nothing to find."

"I'll go talk to Everett Colony."

"Well, go right ahead, Joe, and don't blame me for getting your head bit off."

That's what Gordon had got, and that's all it would take for him.

"Did you search Wade Harris's car for any bullets?"

"Of course not. In that wreck, there's no chance you'd ever find something that small. And it's never crossed my mind at all to look for a bullet, not until you came in a couple weeks ago."

"Where's the car now?"

"They towed it off from Gabe's a month ago. Wasn't even good for parts. Are you really going to see Everett?"

"I am."

"Luke?" Louise frowned at the front of the salon. "What are you doing in here? And close the door."

"I was just wondering."

"Wondering what?"

He looked back and forth. There was no one else in the shop. "Do you give haircuts?"

"I think I can," Louise said. "You need one anyway."

"The last girl I had for a secretary at the newspaper used to cut it for me," Luke said, "but she's gone."

"Just sit there."

She put him in the far back chair so he wouldn't frighten off any real customers.

"Now, that meeting Monday night was a real whopper," he said.

Louise was giving the mop a critical look. "Everybody should just calm down."

"Careful about those ears!"

"Well, you never use them."

"Of course I do," Luke said.

"From what you write, I don't think you do."

Luke was moving his head too much, and Louise finally put her hand down on the top and pushed, to hold it still.

"Speaking of listening," he said. "What do you think about this road?"

"That I don't want to ever hear about it again."

"I think you will. I don't think it's very popular."

"In some neighborhoods it isn't. In some it is."

"Gold Valley, sure, but they've got along forever without it. Have you thought about what it would do to your shop here?"

"What would it do?" Louise said. "New customers, if anything."

"Roads go both ways, you know."

"What do you mean?"

"Some old customers might go the other way."

"There's nothing in Gold Valley."

"Not now, but there's no road to it, either."

"McCoy? This is where you work?"

Randy jerked his head up, part because he recognized the voice and part because he didn't believe his ears.

"Mr. Coates? Well, come on in. Come right in! Have a seat."

Roland Coates stared around first, as if he still didn't believe he had the correct place, and then as if he didn't trust the chair Randy was offering him.

"You can't afford any better than this?"

Randy thought about Roland's own threadbare office. "I don't like to waste money, to tell the truth, and this old desk has stood the test of time."

That was an answer Roland would appreciate, even if it wasn't exactly accurate, as Randy wouldn't mind at all a fancy new office set.

"For all the money I send you, I'd have expected something frivolous. Anyway, I'm not here for that. I want my zoning changed."

"Your zoning . . . you mean, for the furniture factory?"

"Of course that's what I mean."

"Now, that land's zoned special for the factory just the way it is."

"I don't want it for the way the factory is. I want it so I can do anything I want."

A vision of a shopping center appeared before Randy's eyes. "What do you have in mind?"

But Roland's mouth clapped shut and then only opened enough to say, "Just anything."

"You'd have to give us some idea."

"I won't. Now, what do I have to do to fix the zoning?"

"Well, you'd fill out the forms for the Planning Commission, and they'd look it all over and vote on a recommendation to the supervisors, and then we'd vote."

"You're on the Planning Commission, aren't you?"

"I am. But we'll need to know what you want to do."

"Just give me the forms."

"Patsy has them down at the courthouse."

Roland remained planted in the doorway. "What about the road? Would it make a difference if it gets built?"

"The road? Well, it might, and I'm almost afraid to say anything for fear of it coming back around at me. But my guess is that if the road does get built, and the factory has a big highway out to the interstate, then the zoning would be a completely different kettle of fish. And without the road, the chances of a zoning change would be a kettle with no fish."

"Mr. Esterhouse? Dr. Colony can see you, back in his office."

Thirty-minute wait. "Thank you."

Joe followed the woman down the hall, and Everett Colony was sitting at his desk.

"Sit down," Everett said. "You have a question?"

"I do." Joe sat in a padded chair. "About Wade Harris."

"That's what I thought." At least the man wasn't having a fit yet. "He died of massive trauma due to an automobile accident."

"Could he have been shot first?"

247

Colony set his jaw, like he'd bite through a fence post. "Sure he could have. He might have been poisoned, too, and clubbed on the head and stabbed. I'm not going to look for all those things when he's in a car that's wrapped around a tree."

"What if you'd known someone had been wanting him dead?"

"I'd have expected Gordon Hite to tell me."

"I'll tell you a few things, then."

"What Roger Gallaudet's told you? That's the real problem. It's what he's telling everyone. It amounts to slander."

"I went to Roger first, and not the other way."

"I know what he's been saying. He's wrong."

"I don't think he's been talking to people like you claim he has anyway."

"When people start asking questions about Wade Harris being shot, I'll have to assume Roger's been pushing them. Not that Harris didn't half have it coming, the way he made enemies around here.

"Last February, Roger Gallaudet came to my house to talk about the new road. He wants it and tried his hardest to convince me to side with him."

"He was arguing for it?"

"More than arguing. Roger threatened me."

"How?"

"It wasn't outright." Dr. Colony pointed his finger. "But I could tell. He said if I fought that road, there'd be people fighting me. And after he left, I realized it was a threat."

"What was he threatening?"

"I didn't know then, but I took measures to protect myself. And now I've found out what he meant. He's slandering me and trying to ruin my reputation. He's telling people I covered up a murder."

"It might be a murder anyway."

Colony frowned. Then he was real angry. "What are you saying, Esterhouse? You're accusing me of killing those two, and over this road?"

"It had crossed my mind."

"That will be worth a lawsuit."

248

"Don't waste your time, Dr. Colony. I'd tell you straight out if I really thought it. But if they had been killed, it was your job to realize it when you looked at them. Now, did you give either of them the time you should have?"

"It's just a road! No one's going to kill a man over a road."

"You've been making threats yourself."

"Not to kill anyone! I'll get a lawyer! This is going too far."

"Do what you have to," Joe said, "but I want an answer."

Colony took his time. "All right. I understand. But you still haven't given me any reason why someone would want to kill either Wade Harris or Mort Walker. Besides Gold River Highway."

"That's enough of a reason."

"It isn't."

"It is. With this road, it is. There's people behind it and money enough involved. I'll ask you again. Could Mort Walker have been killed by the blow to his head? Could Wade Harris have been killed by a gun?"

He was still thinking his answers through.

"If I say yes, what are you going to do?"

"Bring in the State Police."

"Then I'll say no." He said it right away. "They couldn't either have been killed any other way than I said in the first place. That's final."

"Then I'll bring in the State Police anyway, and their own doctors."

That made the man think even more than he had before.

"Don't," he said.

"Why not?" Joe asked.

"There's more to it than you know," Colony said. "And I won't say what. I'll tell you this: nothing happened to Wade Harris and nothing happened to Mort Walker. But if you bring in the State Police, they'll think they have to find something, and they'll look until they do."

"You're saying there's something they'd find?"

"Yes. It's nothing to do with Wade Harris, but they'll think it is."

Fool business. "I'm not much satisfied with that, Dr. Colony. You're hiding something."

"I don't care whether you're satisfied or not. You'd do better to just stay out of it. If you don't, you'll wish you had. I'm warning you."

Wicked, evil business. "I'll consider that," Joe said.

"Consider it, Esterhouse. Then don't make the wrong decision. And don't listen to Roger Gallaudet."

Time for a little telephone call to Asheville.

"Department of Transportation, Mike Fletcher."

"Mikey! It's Steve Carter."

"No one else calls me Mikey."

"Somebody needs to. I got a question."

"Shoot."

"Remember back in April? You gave me some traffic estimates for the proposed Gold River Highway."

"I remember."

"Good. So, I finally saw the plans, and they're out of whack. NCDOT wants to build an interstate over our mountain."

"That doesn't sound right. It was only a couple thousand cars a day."

"Right. But the twenty-year estimates they used were fifteen thousand."

"There aren't that many cars in Jefferson County."

"So—what kind of funny business is somebody up to?" Steve asked.

"Well, the usual kind, I guess. I'll try to find out."

"Sit down, Joe. You look beat."

"Thank you, Roger." The funeral home had nice soft chairs, and anymore Joe was appreciating an occasional rest.

"How's Rose?"

"Well as I am."

"That doesn't tell me a thing."

"I suppose." He was tired, now that he'd sat. "I'm here to have a talk, and after Gordon Hite and Everett Colony, it's a relief to not be contending and adverse."

Roger laughed at that. "I can't promise I won't be."

"Don't think you'll match those two. And I suppose you know what we've been talking about."

"I suppose!" Roger looked as tired as Joe felt. "It's enough to make me retire. Maybe I'd open a restaurant. Tell me what they said, Joe, if you want, but you know I don't really want to hear it."

"You don't need to, except a couple things. Gordon says you've talked about Wade Harris to Roland Coates and Randy McCoy and Steve Carter."

"He said what? I know Roland and Randy, but who's the other one?"

"Steve took Wade's place on the Board of Supervisors."

"I've never met him, much less talked to any of them about anything."

"That's what I thought. But they've all been asking Gordon questions about Wade, so he's blaming you for stirring them up."

"I've only talked to you, Joe, and to Gordon himself. What questions were they asking?"

"I don't know. I'll have to find out." Too much to think about. "Roger. You've said that you and Everett Colony have tangled before. Now Gordon's told him you're spreading rumors about him."

"Sounds like they're the ones spreading rumors about me."

"Any other reason Everett Colony would be set against you?"

"I don't know, Joe. Can't think of anything else."

"Any other reason you'd be set against him?"

Roger thought about that question. "What do you mean?"

"He's against Gold River Highway. You tried to change his mind."

"That was months ago." Roger was showing his own temper. "I talked with him as a neighbor just to be cooperative, but it turned out we didn't see eye to eye. Grace said I should."

"How do you feel about the road?"

"I don't know." The man was frustrated, too. "I suppose I'm for it, but it's more a nuisance than anything else." Then he shook his head. "And it's not any reason for me to say that I'm worried about what happened to Wade Harris. I'm saying that on my own, and I'm saying again I don't know anything for certain anyway. Talking to Everett Colony was my mistake, and I should have known not to bother."

July 10, Monday

"Stevie. It's Mike Fletcher."

"No one else calls me Stevie."

"Somebody needs to. You asked about traffic estimates?"

"I did."

"When I did those for you, I just used standard linear assumptions. We guess what the development will be based on the population, and then we guess what the population will be based on the development. Basic circular reasoning. You know."

"Right."

"Well, your highway has something bigger planned."

"What?"

"I don't know. This is one of those special jobs where we use confidential plans from a developer. Only the team engineering that highway has access to the information, and I'm not on that team. You'd have to talk to Bob Jarvis."

"I don't want to. I've met him. So there is something, you just can't tell me what."

"That's it. If I told you, I'd have to kill you."

"Don't worry, there are people here that might do that anyway."

"But here's a clue. When I was talking to Jarvis, I just said a friend of mine had called to ask. Apparently, someone's been bugging him, and he wondered if it was the same person. He asked me if it was some lady with the Warrior Land Trust."

"Never heard of it. Was there a name?"

"Yeah. It was the owner of the trust. Um—some weird last name. Started with Gul- or Gel-something."

"I have no idea who that might be," Steve said. "Uh—well, the one lady I can think of doesn't even own a telephone."

"Then that's all I know."

"Well, then thanks, I guess."

"You're welcome, I guess," Mike said.

"Randy McCoy, can I help you?"

"This is Joe Esterhouse."

Randy had to swallow down his surprise at that, because he hadn't got more than two telephone calls from Joe in his whole life, and maybe not that many, and surely it wasn't just his imagination right now.

"What can I do for you, Joe?"

"I heard you talked to Gordon Hite. About bullets."

It must be his imagination, because it was impossible that Joe could have heard about that.

"Well, I did, I guess, but it wasn't anything particular or serious."

"What did you ask him?"

"I'd found a bullet and I just happened to be going by the sheriff's office, and I stopped in to ask if he knew where it might have come from." And if that wasn't about the silliest answer he'd ever given, he didn't know what was.

"You found a bullet and you asked him where it came from."

"Now, Joe, there's more to it, but that's all I said to Gordon."

"Where'd you find the bullet?"

He didn't have much chance of putting off Joe when Joe wasn't wanting to be put off, and Joe Esterhouse usually had a reason for asking a question, and there wasn't really any reason not to tell him anything anyway. And Joe calling Randy on the telephone was almost as much a show of respect as Randy driving down to Marker for breakfast to meet Joe.

"Well, I found it in my car. Now, this has been months ago."

"Just laying there?"

"No, down in the seat. Inside the seat, where I dug it out."

"Did somebody shoot at your car?"

"I can't believe they would, Joe, and that's the truth. It wouldn't make sense. And I'd be all the more sure they hadn't except that the windshield got broken to pieces around the same time, and I thought it was just a rock because it happened just as one of Roland Coates' furniture trucks went by, and I'm still sure that's what it must have been, but I decided to just see what Gordon might say, even though it ended up not being much."

"Did you tell him it was in your car?"

"No, I didn't, just that I'd found it, as I didn't really want him to be jumping to any conclusions."

That got a pause out of the telephone.

"What conclusion did you think he might jump to, Randy?"

"I don't know." Why did Joe always have to cut through everything to the bone? "I don't know. Oh, Joe, it was right there, at the same time as Wade's accident, and I just wasn't thinking straight. Because if someone shot at my car, they could have done the same to Wade, and I know that's just too ridiculous and terrible to be the least bit true, but I just wasn't thinking straight to even have the thought in my head."

"So it was all just your own ideas?"

"Well, sure, and not for more then a few days at that. Why are you asking all this, Joe?"

"Because there's no trouble like there is with a road."

"You say that a lot, Joe, and I wonder what you mean by it."

Joe's voice out of the telephone was dry as an August creek bed. "Roads mean change, like nothing else. Building the interstate, building the first part of Gold River Highway, even the new bridge in Wardsville. They were all fights."

"Before my time, I suppose," Randy said. "But it's true that I've never seen trouble like with this road."

July 19, Wednesday

"You know, it's nice out here. Peaceful." Roland Coates rocked back and forth like a machine, and Eliza just listened. "Good to get away once in a while. Not that the business doesn't need constant watching. But I'm getting old."

"Not old at all," Eliza said. "But sometimes in need of rest."

"I am that. I could use a lot more than I get, but somebody has to keep things running. Anyway, that's why I'm out here. I need the board to fix my zoning."

Another of those words! Zoning! What things people worried about.

"What is broken?"

"Broken? Oh . . . well, the zoning. If anybody's going to build on to the factory, the county needs to change the zoning. I don't know what it all means."

Perhaps no one did! "I don't either!"

"At least we agree on that. You see, I'm worrying that the road might not happen. So I'm going to try for the zoning anyway. Maybe that'll do it, and I can get that factory sold without the road."

"You wouldn't need the road?" This thought seemed to step out from the forest of his words.

"I don't know how likely I am to get it. Everett Colony and his crew are squeaking louder than all the other wheels put together."

"Squeaking?"

"But there's more. Eliza, I can talk to you. Now, this is just between you and me, you know. You wouldn't go telling anybody else any of this."

"I don't think I could!"

"Good. It's Jeremy. I don't know what he's up to, but it's no good. He's going to break this deal one way or the other, if he can. Shooting out car windows! As if that would change a person's mind. More like to get the boy sent to jail. I had him tell that fool of a sheriff what he'd done, and he said he'd let it by. But he'll do more, I know it."

"What will he do?"

"We'll find out. I've got my suspicions. But it all comes down to the board. When you vote on the zoning, there's nothing he can do about it. And more than anything, when you vote on that road. That's the only thing that counts anyway."

July 20, Thursday

"Over here."

Now, where was that voice coming from? Steve was around some-where. Randy could hear him. There was Grace Gallaudet across the street by the funeral home . . . Ed Fiddler just coming out of the bank . . .

"Randy! Over here!"

There he was. Way out on the middle of the bridge. Randy waved and jogged across Main Street and over onto the bridge, where Steve was waiting for him.

"There you are," Randy said. "I was starting to wonder where you'd gotten to."

"I'm sorry," Steve said. "I was looking at the flood plain."

"I guess we can see it all from here."

Randy looked at it. Along here, with the far side of the river being that sharp bank, the flood plain was basically downtown Wardsville. The first row of buildings backed against the river, then Main Street, and then the second row of buildings across from the first, with the courthouse right facing the bridge and the Episcopal Church next to it, and the drugstore on its other side, and more stretching out either way from there. King Food down at the end, and the stoplight for Hemlock, and Gabe's garage down at the other end. Then Ashe Street parallel to Main Street and its buildings, with Randy's own office in there. Then all the houses of River View scratched into the hillside where the land started rising up, and Mountain View up and out of sight.

"What was the flood like, back in '77?" Steve asked.

"It was a mess, let me tell you. We lost the bridge, and I guess to kind of make it up to us, the river left a foot or two of mud everywhere."

"What did people do without the bridge?"

"We went down to the bridge at Coble. It seemed like forever getting this new bridge built, but I think it was just about eight months."

"That was fast."

"Even for back then, it was fast. Looking back, I think Joe Esterhouse must have had something to do with it. But Steve, this bridge doesn't look like it's going anywhere. That old one was a pretty rickety affair and it was no surprise it washed out. I don't think we need be worrying about it now."

"Okay." Steve was looking down at the Fort Ashe River. "I've been through the engineering drawings. I agree with you, it would be one massive flood to take this bridge out. But it's still the only way into town, except Coble Highway and Ayawisgi Road. Doesn't that worry you?"

"It would," Randy said. "It would, maybe, but I've lived here my whole life, and except for that one time, it just hasn't been a problem, and it might be years and years before anything like that happens again. And if there was a big road up to Gold Valley, now, what is that going to do? It won't go anywhere. It'd be twenty miles out of the way for anyone to get into or out of Wardsville."

"I know," Steve said. "I'm getting real familiar with that twenty miles."

"So I'd just say we won't worry about the bridge washing out. Then we wouldn't have to bring up Gold River Highway at all."

"Come on, Randy," Steve said. "If it wasn't for all the business about Mountain View and Hemlock, wouldn't you say the road was important for the county?"

"You can't break it apart like that. That's why the Board of Supervisors has the last word, so they can look at everything, not just maps and plans. And that brings up a point about the Planning Commission."

"What?"

"Well, the rule is that there's supposed to be one member of the Board of Supervisors who's also on the Planning Commission, to help them work together. But the other four planning commissioners are supposed to be independent."

"Right," Steve said. "I remember how that was commented on. So one of us has to quit one of our boards."

"And I'd like to suggest that you stay on the commission, and I'd step down."

"Uh—sure. Is that what you want? I remember you weren't real keen on me being on the commission."

"Well . . . I think we've all seen that you know the business a lot better than the rest of us."

"Whatever. That's fine."

"And while we're talking about that, let me tell you about one zoning request that's just come up, and that's from Roland Coates."

"I've heard of him . . ."

"He wants to get his zoning changed on his factory."

"That's a special-use permit for light industrial."

"I think that's what it is. But he's filling in forms now to hand in for the next commission meeting."

"What zoning does he want?"

"I don't know, and I don't expect that he does, either."

"Uh . . . so what are we supposed to do?"

"That'll be up to you."

"Okay. I guess I'll look at his forms."

"They might not tell you much."

"I'll go see him. Um—I might have a guess. I heard about a grocery store."

"Oh no!" That was completely unexpected, as Steve wasn't likely to be hearing rumors from the likes of Luke Goddard. "Where has that idea come from? Because I've heard it, too."

"A developer called me. But he wanted to kill it. Don't ask me, Randy. I don't have a clue what he was talking about. But I have another question. When I was reading about the 1977 flood, it mentioned the mayor a lot. What happened to Wardsville's mayor?"

"You might say the whole town was canceled due to lack of interest. It was, let's see, about 1983 when the people in town decided there wasn't any point in paying taxes for two governments, town and county, so they just sent their charter back to Raleigh and dissolved the municipal council and mayor."

"And the county just took over."

"That's right. And that was about the time the town started fading, you might say, and there were the first empty windows on Main Street, and they stopped putting up any new houses in Mountain View, and since then we've been holding on at best, or maybe slipping a little."

Good leaves. Heavy, thick, good smell to them. Joe got down on his hands and knees to look under them, to look for worms, for beetles, anything. Not a one.

He stood up. Not as easy to stand up as it was even last year.

He got back down so he could stand up again.

Walk back to the house. Rose was in the garden weeding, on her own knees.

"I'll do some of that," he said, and he knelt next to her, over a row, in the beans and tomatoes. She'd planted those two together since he'd known her, a stake of one, then of the other, back and forth. They'd always been beside each other.

"Thank you, Joe," she said. Then they were quiet. They worked down the row together, side by side. Pulling the weeds, pinching off the weak branches, straightening the stakes.

They came to the end of the row. Once again Joe stood up. He took Rose's hand and lifted, to bring her up beside him.

"Thank you," she said again. "I think that's enough for today."

"We could do a walk," he said.

"We could."

He took her hand again. Her step was stiff at first and he went slow, but when they'd passed the chicken coop and come to the lane, she had her usual stride, and he did, too.

He kept her hand and walked the dirt of the road together, past the field and down. Past the line of trees at the creek and up beyond it, past the pasture. The neighbors had their cows in it. Joe had sold his own cattle when it had got to where he wasn't strong enough to handle them. That had been four years ago.

Then they were to where the creek bent around again and the pond was, where they'd skate in the winter if there was enough ice. He'd done it as a boy, and the children had, and the grandchildren.

Woods on the other side of the lane. They stopped and he let go of Rose's hand, and she pulled a few of the weeds from around an old thorny bush, one of a line along the roadside. There'd been her grandmother's house where the trees were now, and a yard and garden along the roses. It was where he'd known her as a girl. Just the bushes now and they didn't bloom.

There was that telephone ringing. Louise had just that moment put the last plates back up in the cupboard, and she hadn't even had a chance to breathe and there was the telephone.

"Byron? Could you get that?" It was right beside his elbow.

"It'll be for you."

It always was. She got her apron off and ran across the hall.

"Hello?"

There wasn't anybody there, just some scratchy sounds. "Hello?" she said again.

"Hello?" It was man, talking loud. "Anybody there?"

"This is Louise. Who are you?"

"Louise Brown?"

"Yes. This is Louise."

"Good." There was a loud clank and then the voice sounded a little bit better. "Getting off that speaker phone. The Louise Brown on the Board of Supervisors?"

"Yes!" It was starting to get just too silly.

"Good. Finally. That last one wasn't. Can't tell a thing from those addresses. I'm Charlie Ryder. I want to talk to you."

Louise had finally settled down in her chair. It was silly, but it was a little bit fun, too. "Well, then talk, Mr. Ryder." Who in the world was Charlie Ryder?

"It's about this road. Gold River Highway. Now, look, I want to know what it's going to take to get you to vote for it."

Charlie Ryder. She just couldn't remember knowing a single Charlie. "Do I know you?"

"I don't know you. You are supposed to vote on the road, right?"

"Of course I am."

"Good. That's why I'm calling. I want to get that road built, so I'm calling to see what it's going to take."

"Well, it's going to take us voting for it," she said. She couldn't help but giggle.

"Great. Great. That's what I wanted to hear. We're communicating. Now, we're two against two, and you're in the middle. You get my point?"

"I think so."

"So that's why I'm calling, to see what it'll take."

"What it will take?" What in the world was he talking about? "I don't understand."

"What it would be worth to you. There's a lot involved here, and I can be generous."

"That's very nice, Mr. Ryder, but I still don't really understand."

260

"Okay, I see. You don't know me, and you're being cautious. That's good. You're smarter than some people I deal with. Just think about it and I'll get back to you. Now, here's another thing. About some new grocery store. Do you all have to approve that, too?"

"What?" Louise was enjoying herself, but she was starting to get dizzy. It was like talking to Eliza. "What new grocery store?"

"A guy told me they were going to tear down some factory. Somebody was buying an old factory in Wardsville and they were going to use the land for a shopping center."

"Who told you that?"

Pause. "A guy who used to work for me."

"Mr. Ryder, that couldn't be right. In Wardsville?"

"Yeah. Where the road was coming in."

"I think you're mixed up," she said. "There's only one factory in town, and that's the furniture factory."

Byron looked up from his television program.

"Right, that's it," Charlie Ryder said.

"No! I don't believe it."

"You don't want it, believe me. You've got to make sure that thing doesn't get approved."

"That won't ever happen."

"Good, good, we're communicating on that, too. That can be part of the deal, and like I said, I can afford to be generous."

Louise was not enjoying the conversation anymore. At all.

"Mr. Ryder, I'm starting to wish you had never called."

"Then I never did. I like working with you, Louise. And that's just right, I never called. And I'll be in touch."

The telephone went dead, and Louise wasn't feeling much better herself.

"What's all that about the furniture factory?"

"I don't know, Byron," she said. "I have to think. That man must have thought he was talking to someone else."

And then the telephone rang again.

"Hello? This is Louise."

"Hi—this is Steve Carter."

"Oh good! That's so much better! How are you, dear?"

"Oh, um, fine. Do you have a minute for a question?"

"Go right ahead, Steve. I'm just sitting here answering the phone."

"Okay. Um, it's about the factory in town? The furniture factory?"

For goodness' sakes. "Not you, too?" she said.

"Me, too?"

"Go ahead."

"Okay. This isn't really official, but maybe you can help me figure this out. I've got these forms that Mr. Coates has just submitted to the Planning Commission. He wants to rezone his land."

Louise put her hand up to her cheek. Goodness, goodness, goodness! It was true! Byron was back to watching the television.

"It's Steve Carter," she said to him, "and he's asking about the factory." She talked into the telephone. "Does it say what he wants to do?"

"That's the thing. He hardly filled anything in. It just says to zone it for general use."

"What does that mean?"

"It doesn't mean anything. There isn't any general use category. I'll go talk to him. But do you have any clue, Louise?"

"Oh, Steve. I think I do, and I hate the thought!" She was watching Byron, and he had his eyes right on her. "I just talked to a man who said they want to tear down the factory and build a shopping center."

"A shopping center!" Steve said. "I still can't believe it."

"You've heard that, too? Mr. Coates said he was selling the factory, but we all thought that meant someone else would be running it."

Byron was just staring at her.

"Maybe the new owners just want the land," Steve said.

"It's terrible, Steve! We can't let that happen."

"Well, I really don't know anything. Let's just wait, Louise, and I'll talk to Roland Coates."

"You won't be the only one!"

Oh dear. Oh dear, oh dear, oh dear! Goodness, goodness! Oh dear!

"What's this?" Byron said as soon as she had the telephone put down.

"I don't know!" She was almost crying. "Would they do that?"

"Do what?"

"Just tear it down?"

"Tear down the factory?" Byron's mouth was hanging open. "What? Why?"

"To build a shopping center with a grocery store!"

"That's crazy!"

"Oh, Byron! Would Mr. Coates do such a thing?"

"Maybe it's the people buying the factory."

"But he's the one who wants the zoning changed."

"Let me talk to the man," Byron said. "Don't go and have a fit, Louise."

"I will if I want to."

"Then do it in the kitchen so I can think."

And then the silly telephone rang again!

"This is Louise." She was almost crying.

There was a little pause and a click or two.

"Hello?" said a voice, and it sounded far away.

"Hello. This is Louise!" Now she might get mad. Everyone calling her was saying terrible things.

"Grandma? It's Matt." She could hardly think what that meant. "Are you okay?"

"Matt? Matt!" Matt! It was Matt! "It's Matt, Byron. Go get on the other telephone, quick. It's Matt!"

"Grandma?"

"Yes, dear. Oh, where are you? Are you all right?"

"I'm okay," he said, but he sounded worried. "Everything's okay. Are you okay, Grandma?"

"Oh, Matt, I'm just fine. It's so wonderful to hear you! Where are you?"

"At the base. In Baghdad. Mom said I should call you to say hi. I'll be home the last week of August, and I'll be right up to see you."

It was dark when they ate. That didn't happen often in the summer. He and Rose both were early to bed most nights. But their walk had brought them back late.

The phone rang, loud and harsh.

"Joe Esterhouse."

"Joe. Marty Brannin here. Just checking on you."

"That's thoughtful of you, Marty."

"It's been a few weeks since we talked. I was sort of expecting to see something happen pretty quick. Have you talked to the State Police?"

"Not yet."

"But what about the road?"

"It's not looking real likely that the board will vote it in."

"What do you mean? Does that make a difference?"

"If somebody's trying to stop the road, they might have done it. So there might not be a reason for them to do anything else."

Long pause. "So you aren't pushing it because you don't think anyone's in danger?"

"Something like that."

"Joe! What about two murders?"

"I know, Marty."

"We have to do something."

"I know."

Another pause. "I can call the State Police."

"I can, too. But I'm not sure that's the best thing just now."

"There might be a murderer on the loose. Now. In Jefferson County. And whatever you think, he could kill someone else any day."

"He might. I don't know as much as I thought I did, Marty. Bringing the police in from outside might even be worse."

"Okay. Who on the board is the next most likely to vote for the road?"

"Hard to tell. I'm not sure there are many votes for the road."

"The new person, from Gold Valley?"

"He's doing more to shoot it down than anyone."

"Louise Brown?"

"She didn't seem too pleased by it, either. I think what I need is to know more."

"I'll keep trying. The police could do a lot better job."

"I understand."

"I don't think I should just let you run your own show on this."

"You do what you think is best, Marty."

"Did you drive my daddy crazy like this?"

"Maybe once in a while."

Pause. "Then keep in touch."

"I will. Thank you for calling."

Joe put the phone down and looked up at Rose.

"Thank you for our walk this evening," she said.

"We should do that more often," he said.

July 21, Friday

So this was the infamous furniture factory. Steve sat in his car for a minute in the lot, checking it out. An actual brick factory. Hadn't they heard of corrugated steel?

Twelve acres, according to the plat maps. But only seven flat acres, and the rest was going up the mountainside. Not real promising for retail development, but it would be okay for a small strip center.

He looked back at Hemlock through Mountain View. It was too easy for him to picture what the road would look like through those houses and yards, or what would be left of them. Ouch.

Then the other way, up the mountain. Four lanes, divided, slicing though that mountain like a Barbie through warm Play-Doh—a picture fresh in his mind from breakfast that very morning.

It was crazy.

So could a retail development right here generate fifteen thousand cars a day? No way. Not big enough, and not enough customers anyway.

Oh well. Time to meet Mr. Roland Coates. Into the building.

And into the nineteenth century. The industrial revolution, phase one, brought to life!

"May I help you?"

"Steve Carter. I'm here to see Roland Coates."

"Just a minute."

At least she looked modern. Wood floors. Plaster walls. The building itself was museum quality.

"Come in!"

Thick, squat nasal voice, and person to match.

"Hello, Mr. Coates. It's good to meet you."

"Where's Randy McCoy?"

Huh? "Um, I don't know . . ."

"Why isn't Randy McCoy here? They told me someone from the Planning Commission would be here."

"I'm on the Planning Commission."

"I thought Randy McCoy was."

"Actually, he isn't, now . . ."

"He said he was."

"He just stepped down a couple days ago."

"Oh, he did, did he?" Coates' eyes narrowed—Edward G. Robinson. *You dirty rat . . .*

"He had to. There were two of us on the board and the commission . . . it's complicated."

"Complicated? Sounds pretty simple to me. That man will do anything to squeeze out of making a decision."

Roland might just have a point there. "Anyway," Steve said, "maybe you could tell me about what you're trying to do here?"

"I want this zoning changed."

"Right. You want it general use, but there isn't a category with that name. Maybe if you could tell me what you want to do."

"I won't tell you."

Steve thought about that. They hadn't covered this kind of thing in any of his engineering classes.

"Um, that makes it kind of hard. Can you tell me just generally whether it's commercial or industrial or residential?"

"Doesn't industrial mean the same as commercial?"

"Commercial is, um, stores and stuff. Retail, like a grocery store or shopping center, or maybe offices."

Mr. Coates growled. "Who says it's going to be a grocery store?"

"I meant that as an example. You see, Mr. Coates, the road and the neighboring areas aren't really compatible with lots of traffic."

"What if the new road gets built?"

"Gold River Highway. That would change a lot."

"But we won't know till December. Well, I don't want to wait. And I don't want to count on it."

"You'll probably have to."

Mr. Coates did not choose to hear that. "This is what I want. You fill those forms in however they need to be for me to do whatever I want here. It's the supervisors that vote on it, isn't it?"

"The more specific it is, the more chance they'd vote yes."

"Well, I'll get them to vote for it anyway. It's not about roads and traffic and being compatible and all that talk. I know how it works now. It's about getting three votes out of five."

"Mr. Coates, let me ask you one thing. I had a call from somebody a month ago, from Raleigh, about a shopping center where the factory is now. Is that what this is about?"

"I don't know what you're talking about."

"Okay. Okay, Mr. Coates, I'll see what I can do."

"Did you talk to him?" Louise felt like a moth fluttering around a candle.

"I talked to him. Let me get in the door." Byron wasn't much of a flame. She let him get to his chair, and she was right behind him.

"Did you go up to the office?"

"That's where he was, so that's where I went. He'd been with some young man all morning, so it was almost lunch before I got up there. And he said, 'Come on in, Byron.' So I came in, and I said, 'I have a question, Mr. Coates, if you don't mind.' And he said, 'Go ahead.' And I said, 'I've been hearing a rumor, and I hope it's not true.' "

"That's right," Louise said. "It is only a rumor."

"So he said, 'What is it, Byron?' So I told him."

"You told him about tearing down the factory?"

"More or less. I said, 'We all know you're selling the factory here, and I guess you'll let us know when it happens. But there've been a couple people calling Louise because she's on the Board of Supervisors, and they're asking about some kind of shopping stores to get built here.' "

"What did he say?"

"He looked at me like he might have blown his top. But then he said, 'Sit down, Byron. Let's talk.' "

"Oh my! Is it really going to happen?"

"Now, let me tell you just the way he said it. Because he started out saying, 'I'll tell you but I can't let people be knowing this. Not anybody. Understand?' And I said, 'What about Louise?' And he thought, and then he said, 'Byron, I want you to tell Louise. But nobody else.' So I said, 'We won't say a word, either of us.' Then this is what he said. 'The people buying the factory want to expand it. The only way they'll buy it is if they can add on another row of saws. And they want a road out to the interstate. A real road. They wouldn't even talk to me until last February when I told them we'd be getting one.' "

Byron started talking quieter. "Then he got real serious. 'But this is important,' he said. 'They say if the word gets out, the deal is off. They don't want it getting out! So don't tell anybody.' Then he looked at me, and he said, real firm, 'But you make sure your Louise knows all that.' So I'm telling you everything he said."

"And not anything about grocery stores?"

"No."

"Byron, do you see what this means? More people working at the factory."

"I see it plain. Lots of changes, but maybe for the good. Just don't let it get out. I'm telling you because Mr. Coates said to."

"I won't tell a soul."

"Women never could keep a secret."

"Well, I will." Finally, some good news. After all these years, she was sure they could trust Roland Coates. As long as he wasn't being lied to by whoever was buying his factory.

Oh dear. That was a terrible thought, but anymore she was starting to not trust people like she should.

July 24, Monday

Oh, weeds! They didn't mean to offend, but they did! And in her garden, Eliza would not allow them.

She was on her knees, uprooting each bold, shameless stem. Anywhere else on the mountain they would be welcome to any spot or soil they could find, but not here!

Being intent, she was startled when a car tumbled out of the forest into her clearing. And she was not in a peaceful mind.

The man who stepped into the tall grass was familiar from the council meetings. She stood to see him.

"Good afternoon," she said.

"Afternoon. Luke Goddard, Wardsville Guardian."

"Welcome, Mr. Goddard." He didn't seem like a guardian.

"I was hoping to ask you a few questions, Ms. Gulotsky."

"Please. Just call me Eliza."

"Sure, glad to. Can we sit down?"

The first question was simple! "Please."

They sat on the porch. "Eliza, I'm here to ask you about Gold River Highway," he said. "My readers are plenty interested in your opinions."

Why would his readers be interested in her? "What do they read?"

"Everything I write, especially about the new road."

"What do you write?"

"The truth. Now, I think most people in the county expect you'll be voting against the road. I'd like to hear what you think, though."

"I don't know what they're expecting."

"Oh . . . well, what I meant was how you'll be voting on the road."

Eliza was still thinking of weeds. She might have been friendlier if he had interrupted something else. "I don't know."

"So that's undecided?" He was writing what she said! "Waiting for more information? Or just not committing yourself?"

"I'm waiting," she said. She felt herself bewildered, listening to him. Was it the way he spoke? Or his eyes? His gaze was like mist.

"What might push you one way or the other?"

"I'll know at the right time."

"So why do you vote no for everything?" he asked. "Even the minutes?"

"I haven't any reason to vote yes."

"So will you have any reason in December?"

"I don't know." This was too confusing! He was harrying her, like a raccoon after a bird nest. "Please. You're asking about things to come, and we don't have answers. We have to wait."

"Now, that's a new one. You know, Eliza, that's a good quote. I think I'll use it."

"Come along back here," Joe Esterhouse said.

Steve nodded and came. *Walk this way . . .*

He'd never been in this part of the courthouse. What a labyrinth, and it didn't look this big outside. Maybe they were sliding into a different dimension.

Or maybe there was a white rabbit in front of them, that only Joe could see, looking at its pocket watch.

Get the imagination under control, here.

"Appreciate your coming," Joe said, opening a door.

"No problem. It's fun to drive into Wardsville all the time."

No reaction.

It was a big room, dusty, old file cabinets and . . . wow. A typewriter. A *real Woodstock!* Five hundred bucks on eBay. Did it work?

Joe closed the door. There was an old wood table with chairs, and Joe sat in one of them. Joe's work pants might not care about dust, but Steve's nice tan pants were screaming, *No! No!* Their voice sounded oddly like Natalie's.

But he couldn't stay standing. Oh well.

"Some things you need to know," Joe said. "And some questions I have."

"Sure."

This guy was eighty years old and he still worked his own farm. Good grief.

"Fool business."

Steve was not sure exactly what that meant. Just hoped real hard that he was not in trouble somehow.

"Fool business. It's this road."

"Gold River Highway."

"You know much about roads?"

"There are some things I know real well about roads," Steve said. "I'm finding out there are some things I don't know about at all."

"I'll tell you a couple." There were pauses every couple sentences. "There's no trouble like a road. Bad trouble, I mean. And I'm afraid you're part of it now."

He was in trouble. Bad trouble.

"Did I do something?"

"Not you, except to let us put you on this board."

"Okay. I guess you've been through this before?"

"The interstate. The first part of Gold River Highway. The new bridge in Wardsville. Those were the big ones. Do you know how this new road money got to us in the first place?"

"Sort of. I read the papers from Raleigh. I know there's something screwy about it."

"What do you know?"

"I called my friend in Asheville about the traffic estimates, because the ones that Bob Jarvis used were real different than the ones I got back in April, and he couldn't tell me much except that there's some big development planned."

"Do you know what that is?"

"It might be something in town, where the furniture factory is."

"You know that for sure?"

"There is a development. I don't know if that's where it'll be."

"Did your friend mention Jack Royce?"

"I don't think so."

"In the state assembly. He's the one who snuck it all through. Likely he's the one giving Jarvis his orders."

"So, this is all his idea?"

"Likely there's someone behind him."

"Joe—have you heard of Warrior Land Trust?"

Steve waited. Was the guy still alive?

"What about it?"

"I just wondered if you knew anything about it. Because I think they, or it, or whoever, is involved, but I don't know why. There's a person who owns it, a woman named Gul-something. I was wondering if it was Eliza."

Rose was at the stove when he came in, but she sat with him at the table. "Did you talk to Steve Carter?"

"Some. Not much," Joe said.

"Did something happen?"

"I don't know what it means."

She waited for him.

"I don't know if there's any truth."

"There's always truth."

"I don't know if there's any I can find."

"There is something going on," Steve said. "Something strange."

"Like what?" Natalie asked. The kids were in bed wide awake, and she was half asleep.

"Joe was about to tell me. We were in the secret chamber, we'd checked for listening devices, I was about to hear the plans for the new nuclear power ray he'd just invented, and then I opened my big mouth."

"What did you say?"

"I told him about this land trust that Mike told me about on the phone. And Joe just froze. Then he said, 'I think that's all we need to say now,' and we were done."

"He left you there?"

"I followed him out. I'd never have found the way myself."

"Do you have any idea what it was about?"

"Gold River Highway, and I think Eliza Gulotsky. That's all I know. And there's trouble. *Bad* trouble."

July 27, Thursday

"Now look what Luke's gone and done," Randy said to Sue Ann, the newspaper spread out on his knee, and Gold River Highway spread out all over the page. " 'In an abrupt change of direction,' " he read, " 'Eliza Gulotsky held out the possibility of voting for the road if certain conditions were met. She would not, however, elaborate on what those conditions might be. That information, she said, would come at the right time. "The answers to these questions will have to wait," she said in an interview exclusive to the *Wardsville Guardian*.' Well, now, who else would interview her, anyway? Sue Ann, all our neighbors are counting on her to vote no, and now they'll be all the more agitated, and we both know full well that she probably didn't say anything like any of this."

July 31, Monday

"Joe Esterhouse."

Woman's voice on the other end. "Mr. Esterhouse? Good afternoon! How are you?"

"I'm fine, thank you."

"Good! Mr. Esterhouse, my name is Sandy Lockwood, and I'm with Regency Atlantic Associates in Atlanta. The nice lady in the office at the county government gave me your number."

"What can I do for you, Miss Lockwood?"

"Sandy. And can I call you Joe? I'd like to come up to Wardsville next week for your Board of Supervisors meeting and present some exciting new plans to you and your board."

"What would those be?"

"I can't say very much yet, Joe. Just that Regency Atlantic is so excited about Jefferson County! And we're looking forward so much to working with you!"

"Who is Regency Atlantic?"

"We'll tell you all about us when we come."

"Why don't you tell me now."

"Sure, Joe. Regency Atlantic is the premier developer of new retail centers in underserved and growing small communities in the Southeast and Mid-Atlantic. We operate more than sixty grocery store–anchored strip shopping centers in seven states. We'll be working very closely with your board, so that's why I want all of you to be the first to hear our news!"

August

Time to start. Louise just felt nervous, and out of sorts.

Bang! She jumped. Why did Joe have to hit that thing so hard?

"Come to order. Go ahead, Patsy," Joe said.

"Mrs. Brown?"

"Here." She took a deep breath to calm her nerves. She was just so fidgety! And for once, it should be just a normal meeting, or at least as normal as it could be with the room full of angry people.

"I'll move that we accept last month's minutes." She said it without even thinking! Joe must have asked for a motion.

"I'll second that," Randy said.

"Motion and second," Joe said, "any discussion? Go ahead, Patsy."

"Mrs. Brown?"

"Yes." They did all look so angry—and there were still months to go before they finally got this road business done.

"Four in favor, one opposed," Patsy said.

"Motion carries," he said. "Minutes are accepted. Next is receiving public comment. Please state your name and address."

There were just a few empty seats. In the back row were a man and a lady, dressed real nice, that she'd never seen before.

But here came the comments. Of course Everett Colony was first. Louise was not feeling very sympathetic to him these days.

"I have these figures from the North Carolina Department of Transportation," he was saying, " showing that intersections of two-lane

275

residential streets with large four-lane roads have the highest accident rates of any type of intersection." He slapped the podium, whap! Louise jumped again. "What is it going to take to convince this board just how dangerous this road will be? Here it is, in black and white!"

"I'm Annette van Marten," the next person said. "That's M-A-R-T-E-N. Van Marten. I live at 2970 Lofty Ridge Road in Gold Valley." She looked like it, too. She had a nice purple polo shirt with the name of a golf course up in the corner, and bright silver hair. "I've lived in Gold Valley two years, and I'd like to say I'm in favor of the new road. When I bought my house over there, I did some research. I looked at the county planning maps. Now, you all might not realize it, but Gold River Highway is actually on those maps. They show it going straight into Wardsville. From what I could tell, it was added in 1967. Now, I don't expect anyone here would remember something from that long ago. But you check those maps—it's right there."

She smiled and went back to her seat.

Louise had so much else to think about, and everyone was just going on and on and on.

"Humphrey King, 605 Jackson Street in Wardsville. I know that it isn't popular in Mountain View, but I'm kind of warming to the idea myself. I could maybe use a few extra customers coming in to King Food, and that road would make it a lot easier."

"Roland Coates. 801 Henry Drive, Wardsville. So this is what these meetings are like? Bunch of foolishness. Listen, all of you, especially you, Randy McCoy. This county needs jobs and it's high time some improvements got made around here. And some bunch of boneheads who don't like anything to change are going to wreck the whole thing."

"Richard Colony, 713 Hemlock in Wardsville. I just have to say that's the first time I've ever heard Roland Coates say he wanted something to change. Why, if his grandfather walked into that factory of his right now, he'd recognize every stain on the carpet. That's pretty fine to say you want changes when it's not in your front yard. We could ask Jeremy Coates whether Roland likes changes or not."

Roland exploded like a tube of toothpaste being stepped on by an elephant. "Leave that boy out of this!"

"Thank you, everyone," Joe said. "I think we'll go on now."

"You're cutting us off again, Esterhouse," Richard Colony said.

"You all have a copy of the agenda," Joe said, just ignoring him. And he deserved it. "First item is subdividing a parcel on Crooked Hollow Road past Marker."

And on they went, just like always, everything passing. She was feeling better now because they were doing good things and helping people, like they usually did. Everyone had common sense and they were getting along. If only it weren't for this road.

"That completes the main agenda," Joe said. "We have one new item that's been added."

"I wish to make a motion."

Louise couldn't believe her ears, or hardly her eyes.

It was Eliza!

Joe turned in his chair to look.

"You?" he said.

Eliza looked right back at him. "Yes."

"Of all the . . . Then go ahead."

"I wish to move that the obstruction be removed from the ceiling."

"The . . . what?" Joe said. Every head in the room was looking up, and then they were all zeroing in on the plywood up in the corner over Luke.

"Does anyone know what it's for?" Randy said. "It's been there forever, that I can remember."

"Why do you want to take it down?" Louise asked.

"It should not be there," Eliza said.

Then there was one of those long silences that happened when anyone was talking to Eliza.

"Is there a second?" Joe said.

"Well, I'll second it," Louise said. "If it doesn't have to be there, I think it would be fine to take it down."

"Can it come down?" Randy said. "It might be there for a reason."

"It doesn't look structural." Steve had stood up and was staring at it. "It's been there a long time but it doesn't have any discoloration. So it must not be because the roof was leaking."

"I'd worry about taking it down if we don't know why it's up," Randy said.

"I could check," Steve said. "I'd have to look at it close."

"Any other discussion?" Joe said. "It sounds like we're voting on having Steve and Eliza look into removing the plywood on the corner of the ceiling here in the council room. Go ahead, Patsy."

"Mrs. Brown?"

"Yes."

"Mr. Carter?"

"Uh, yes."

"Mr. Esterhouse?"

"No."

Louise could only shake her head. What was getting into the man? It must be just spitefulness, to vote against Eliza.

"Eliza?"

"I vote yes."

"Mr. McCoy?"

Randy was looking back and forth between Joe and Eliza.

"Well, it's already passed. Yes. Might as well."

"Four in favor, one opposed," Patsy said.

"Motion carries," Joe said, but he didn't seem too bothered. "I'll leave it to the two of you to work that out." He even seemed—amused a little? But with Joe, who could ever tell. "We are now going to receive a presentation by Sandy Lockwood of Regency Atlantic Associates."

It was the nicely dressed man and lady. The lady was smiling and Louise just suddenly liked her so much! She seemed so friendly.

"Thank you, Joe," she said, and turned around part way toward the audience. "I'm Sandy Lockwood of Regency Atlantic, and this is Roy Donaldson.

"And good evening to all of you! My, what a crowd tonight! And I'm so glad you're all here, because we have some very exciting news!"

The man, Mr. Donaldson, was setting up a stand and unrolling a poster to clip onto it.

"Regency Atlantic Associates is the premier developer of new retail centers in underserved and growing small communities in the Southeast and Mid-Atlantic. We operate more than sixty grocery store–anchored strip shopping centers . . ."

Louise lost track for a moment. It was like the lady was talking in a foreign language.

". . . completed eight new centers in just the last two years. Five of those are already ninety percent occupied . . ."

It was so hard to concentrate, to understand what she was saying.

". . . full cycle development with design, construction, marketing, and operation of the center . . ."

Mr. Donaldson had his poster up. It had drawings of parking lots and trees and long lines of big stores all glassy and shiny. Louise was feeling glassy.

It was all true! The furniture factory would be torn down and there would be big stores instead, and Mr. Coates had been deceiving them!

". . . and so, Regency Atlantic is now pleased to announce our latest development."

Oh my. Oh, my, goodness. What would Byron do?

Sandy Lockwood smiled and held her hand up to the poster just like they did on game shows when they were pointing at the big prize.

"Regency Center at Trinkle Farm."

Why would they call it that? The Trinkle farm was way over in Gold Valley. It wasn't even going to have a Wardsville name!

"Wait a minute!" Luke Goddard was practically jumping up and down, and now he came running over to the poster. Sandy turned to see who he was.

"I'm Luke Goddard," he said, "with the *Wardsville Guardian* newspaper. How did you get ahold of Trinkle farm?"

Randy answered. "Did you know, they did actually pay their taxes? I only noticed it recently. I should have known something was happening." And Joe just stared.

Sandy's smile had stayed just as bright. "I don't know those details, but I believe the property owners approached us first."

"Where are you building this?" Louise said. She was starting to figure it all out.

"At the Gold River Highway Exit off the interstate, in Gold Valley! I was up there this afternoon, and it is beautiful!" She turned back to Luke. "Mr. Goddard? I'm so glad to meet you, too. We'll want your newspaper to know all about our new Regency Center at Trinkle Farm."

"But why are you building it up there?" Randy asked. "How is anyone going get to it?"

"Once the new Gold River Highway extension is completed into Wardsville, we feel we'll have just the right population and growth potential to make this a very successful center."

"That's what it's all been about!" Everett Colony shouted.

That finally got Joe to move. He slapped his hammer on the table. "Let's get back to order, please. Sit down." He waited until everyone had. Sandy just kept smiling.

"What if we don't build the road?" Randy said.

"Oh, I hope you do!" Her smile had cracked just a little.

"But what if we don't?"

"I'm just sure you'll have that road open before we even know it! It's such a wonderful opportunity. And Regency Center at Trinkle Farm is going to be such a beautiful shopping center."

"What will you have in it?" Louise was still reeling, but she was starting to get back upright.

"We are already in talks with several regional food store chains, and the other spaces will fill right in once we start construction."

And then, Louise had the worst thought she'd ever had in her life. "Would there be a beauty salon in there?"

The biggest smile yet. "It's Mrs. Brown, isn't it? Louise? Louise, more than half of our centers have a national chain hairdresser in them. Just think—in just a couple years, or less, you can get pampered and taken care of and your hair done at a bright new modern salon just a couple miles from Wardsville. And all your friends, too! Won't that be wonderful?"

"I should have known," Randy said to Sue Ann. "When those Trinkles paid their taxes, I should have known something was happening."

"And right when they decided to build Gold River Highway," Sue Ann said. "There are all kinds of things happening."

"Now that you mention it, Sue Ann, it's kind of interesting that they're happening at the same time. And what would you think of a new shopping center just over the mountain, and a big road right to it?"

"I don't know what I'm supposed to think."

"I don't know what I'm supposed to think, either," Randy said. "But Everett and the rest will be sure to tell me."

"It's terrible. I still can't believe it!"

"Calm down, Louise." Byron actually had the television off to listen to her. "Not the end of the world."

"It might as well be," she said. She was sitting in her chair, but she could hardly feel it. "I never dreamed anyone would ever want to go and build some big, huge shopping center right in Jefferson County."

"High time, I'd say," Byron said.

"No! It's terrible!" The man must be blind. "What is that going to do to us? What will happen to Wardsville?"

"It'll still be there."

"It won't! Don't you see, Byron? All those big fancy stores will open up out there in Gold Valley, and Wardsville will just dry up like a . . . a—" she couldn't think of what—"like an old loaf of bread."

"Already pretty stale if you ask me."

"I'm not asking you."

"You should. And besides, remember what Mr. Coates said. He especially does want that road."

"Mr. Coates! He just might not get what he wants!" She pushed back a sob and tried to get calm. "But at least that means they aren't tearing down the factory."

Then that terrible phone rang, even though it was late, and she picked it up before she had a chance to think maybe she wouldn't.

"This is Louise."

"Louise Brown?" Oh, it was that man! "Charlie Ryder. I figured you'd maybe be there. You have your meeting tonight?"

"What do you want?" She didn't even mind sounding rude.

"Were they there? Did you see the plans? They were supposed to show them off tonight."

"I saw those plans!"

"Good. Nice place, isn't it? Okay, so you're probably voting for it anyway, aren't you, the road I mean. But I want to make sure. You've had a chance to think. What can I offer? Like I said, I can be generous."

"You!" Now she knew! "Mr. Ryder, don't ever call me again!"

"What? What's wrong?"

"It's your shopping center! You sent those people here!"

"Me? My shopping center? No! I wish it were! It's not mine. But I'm doing everything I can to help out. So what's the problem?"

For the first time in her life, Louise hung the telephone up without even saying good-bye.

"I think that did it," Steve said to Natalie. "You should have seen Louise at the meeting. I don't think you could even pay her to vote for that road now."

"When would they build this thing?"

"They could have it open in two years. It just depends on the road getting approved."

A deep, intense look came into Natalie's eyes. "I will dig the road myself. I want that store, Steve."

"I will take that into consideration," he said. "As a constituent, your views are very important to me."

"As your wife, they had better be. Maybe you would like peanut butter sandwiches the rest of your life? Or haven't I described what it is like to make one shopping trip per week? One? Per week?"

"You have described that, yes. I will arrange for you to meet with Randy and Louise. Even Eliza."

"It's the Trinkles," Joe said to Rose. "It's them behind the road. It's to make their land worth this Regency company buying it."

"What does that mean, Joe?"

"I need to make sure. I'll see if Marty can find out anything with that name."

"After all these years. It's like that family won't ever let go."

"Hermann Trinkle and my daddy tangled more than once. I remember it."

"Would you hold a grudge, Joe?"

"No. Hermann's long gone anyway, and Jacob and Willhelm and Franz. It's their children now, Hermann's grandchildren, and I've never seen any of them."

August 10, Thursday

"May I speak with Mr. Robert Jarvis, please?"

Steve waited. There were happy lunchtime sounds coming from the kitchen, and the sun was shining and he was looking out at his grand Gold Valley view. How nice. And he was now going to jump into a swamp.

"Bob Jarvis."

"Hi, Mr. Jarvis. My name is Steve Carter and I'm on the Jefferson County Board of Supervisors. We met when you were up last month to show us the DOT plans for Gold River Highway."

"Oh. Yes, sure, I remember you."

"Great. Maybe you remember I had some questions at the meeting?"

"I do remember."

"I was waiting for a call. You said you'd have someone in engineering call me."

"I'm sorry, Mr. Carter! I do remember that some questions came up, but I didn't realize that was an official request."

"Then let's make it official. And I'll even make the call myself if you give me a name." He knew half the people there, but it would be interesting to see who Jarvis directed him to.

"Well, now, why don't you remind me exactly what the questions were? So I'll know who you'd need to talk to."

"I had questions about the actual construction, just for my own professional interest. I listed some of them at the meeting, remember? But what I want to know now is about the design assumptions. Specifically, where you came up with the traffic projections."

"That's a fairly involved process, Mr. Carter. But let me assure you we've taken everything into consideration, current and future, in determining those."

"I'd like to see the process."

"We don't always provide that level of detail to the public."

"Why not?"

"I know it may sound strange, but we actually work with confidential information at times."

"Right. Well, we just had a big announcement for a retail development in Gold Valley, right off the interstate. If that's the information you were working with, it's not confidential anymore."

"I'm sorry, but it's a matter of policy—not just in this specific case."

Be a tough guy. Robert Mitchum in *Cape Fear*. "Okay. Mr. Jarvis, let's start over. I'm not the public. That road has to get through the Board of Supervisors, which includes me. This isn't an interstate, as much as it looks like one, or a U.S. route. That means there's nothing you or Raleigh or Washington, D.C. can do to force us to take it. The Board of Supervisors of Jefferson County has absolute authority over county road improvements. And right now, you'll be lucky to get two votes out of five. Even one vote—I'm leaning against it myself."

"I understand, Mr. Carter. And of course, no one here is trying to influence you in your decisions. I will mention, of course, that Raleigh would be paying for this road, and they do provide Jefferson County with quite a bit of transportation funding, some of which is discretionary, depending on how well they feel the money would be used."

Okay. Humphrey Bogart mode. "So, you'll get us on the blacklist. Let's start over again. The whole appropriation and award of this road is more crooked than a snake. I think you've been assigned the job of hiding it all from anybody who might ask questions. So, what happens if you don't deliver? Does Jack Royce in Raleigh come after you, or is he on the firing line, too? Is it Regency Atlantic or the Trinkle family that's making a deal you can't refuse? But wait. Don't answer those.

Just this to start. Is the Regency project contingent on Gold River Highway?"

Long wait. Seconds going past.

"Um."

More seconds.

"Mr. Carter—I do happen to know that, just by chance. I believe it is."

Bingo. The bluff pays off big time. Now, go for broke.

"Do you have a copy of their agreement?"

"There might be a binder in the files that Regency provided us."

"I want a copy."

"Mr. Carter, I can't do that, of course."

Switch to Jimmy Stewart. We can be friends! "Here's why I want it, Mr. Jarvis. If that road has any chance, it needs a strong advocate on the board. It's mainly in my district. I really do want it built, but I need to know what's going on with the road and the shopping center. Everything. Or else it's nothing. Can we work together on this?"

"I'll see what I can do."

"Thanks."

"Joe! How are you doing?"

"Just fine, Marty. There's just a few things I want to say."

"Okay. Just a second, that's the governor calling back."

Joe waited. Sitting in the kitchen, out of the heat. It was cool when Rose wasn't cooking.

"I'm back," Marty said. "And I'm getting my notes. One thing right off. Charlie Ryder. He's West Carolina Development. I slid up to Jack Royce last week and asked if he knew the name. I don't think they're connected."

"He told you that?"

"It's all in how you ask. When I said I was interested in working with West Carolina and Charlie Ryder on some deals, Jack smiled and said I could have him, no problem. Jack's actually a very generous guy."

"I see," Joe said. "Here's two new names. Regency Atlantic Associates in Atlanta, and the other name is Trinkle."

"Trinkle. I knew a Trinkle. Thad Trinkle. His father was in Asheville, and his grandfather farmed up there somewhere. I knew him in high school. Haven't seen him since."

"That's like to be one of them. It's them and Regency that just announced a new shopping center in Gold Valley. That's the farm."

"The shopping center and the road. Sounds like they were made for each other."

"I'd say."

"But which came first, the chicken or the egg? Okay, I'll send them up the flagpole and see who salutes. What does this do to the vote?"

"It lost them Louise Brown. I don't see much chance for that road now."

"I was thinking, Joe. What about you? Are you voting for it?"

"That's been my plan. But there's been a lot to persuade otherwise."

"It sounds like you might be in the crosshairs yourself. Why don't you just tell people you're inclined against?"

"It's crossed my mind. Right now it doesn't seem necessary."

"And it could make everyone on the board safer."

"I understand. But I don't think I will, at least yet. Marty, there's been a few more things come up, and I'm not as sure as I was."

"Sounds like nothing is sure. I just know that anybody on the board who's for the road had better be real careful."

August 12, Saturday

"Eliza, dear, here's a letter," Annie Kay said.

Eliza sat in the chair beside the stove, now filled with apples.

"It's from Cornelia Harris," she said.

"I don't know her. Do you want anything today?"

"I do. Potatoes and rice, and cornmeal. And molasses."

The letter was brief and quiet, but rooted in grief.

"Cornelia wants to come visit. She saw what was written in the newspaper and was reminded she had wanted to see me. I'll write a letter back to her."

Randy was on the porch swing enjoying the afternoon breezes, which were almost enough to make a person think it wasn't as hot as it was. The sky he could see was blue, but it had a feel of thunderstorms in it.

"I believe I'll go for a walk," he said, leaning around to see in the screen door. "Now Sue Ann, don't you think you should, too?"

"That would be so nice," she said from inside. "I'll be right there."

She was, too, and in not even two minutes they were strolling down the front walk to the street, and then along the sidewalk, holding hands just like they were in high school.

They ambled the length of Washington Street and said hello to Ed Fiddler trimming his hedge and Emma weeding in the flower garden, and stopped a minute with the Clairmonts playing in their front yard with their little one-year-old just walking, and waved at the Wards on their front porch.

Then they turned the corner and ended up on Hemlock, under the big hemlocks and oaks pushing up the concrete walk, and the high school down the road, where Randy could even see the white jerseys of the football team out practicing.

Back behind the school, and in about every direction, was Ayawisgi. Even with the trees in full leaf along the road and in all the yards, the mountain was visible everywhere. It made a person feel like Mountain View was just a little dot in the middle of something so much bigger. And the big clouds coming over the ridge only added to the drama.

"I think that's the prettiest view a person could have," he said.

"I wouldn't want anything else," Sue Ann said.

From the immensity of the mountain right down to the snapdragons and hollyhocks just inches long, it was all as perfect as it could be.

"Randy!"

"Well, good evening, Everett."

The doctor was out in his own yard, just standing, like he'd been on guard duty. He didn't do his own yard work, of course, especially with Ed Fiddler's boy Ken just two blocks away, and a fair number of other teenage boys in the neighborhood, and a whole high school of them down the street, and a fair number of those having taken note of Everett's daughter. And one thing no one would dispute about Everett Colony was that he didn't scrimp on paying for yard work, as long as the job was done right.

"What do you think about this shopping center?"

As fast as he could, Randy tried to decide what Everett wanted him to think. "Well, it's a surprise, that's for sure."

"It's a disaster. All that talk about how there won't be more than a few cars on Hemlock. Now we see the real game going on here."

"Well, hello, Ed." Randy had just caught sight of Ed Fiddler coming down the block behind his old beagle, with enough huffing between them to hear a house away.

"Evening, Randy. Everett."

Waiting for Ed gave them a moment of silence, and Randy even thought about him and Sue Ann slipping away. But Ed and Fortunatus had picked up their pace.

"While I've got you here," Ed said to the two of them, "I think we need to talk about this Trinkle Center."

"That's just what we were doing," Randy said. "Everett was giving me his thoughts on that right as we saw you."

"Good. Everett, we'll need a united front on this."

"The whole town's against it," Everett said.

At that moment, Randy had a sudden strange feeling, deep down past his thoughts and even into the pit of his stomach, because of the look on Ed Fiddler's face.

"I mean the new shopping center," Ed said.

"That's what I'm talking about," Everett said.

"I'm not against it."

"Ed, that's why they're trying to build this road."

"Of course it is. That's why it finally makes sense."

"It doesn't make sense!"

For Randy, observing the conversation was interesting, being for once that *he* was the observer and not the recipient.

"It makes perfect sense. I'd like to pick up more loan business at the bank from Gold Valley. We might put a branch out there in the new shopping center. And it's about time we're finally getting someplace modern to go shopping."

"And they'll put a big modern road right through here."

"I don't think it'll be that bad."

"It's going to be terrible!"

"Not back where I live," Ed said.

At that point, Randy decided that intervention might be necessary, as painful as it might be, in the interest of saving Gordon Hite a trip up to Mountain View. "Now, of course, it's still a few months away from the vote on that."

"The board's going to vote it down anyway," Everett said.

"I don't know about that," Ed said. "The last I saw in the newspaper, Esterhouse and Carter are leaning yes and Brown and Gulotsky are leaning no. So it might be up to Randy here."

The feeling down in Randy's stomach twisted like a knife. "I wouldn't count on those," he said. "Luke is only guessing anyway."

"Randy's voting no," Everett said.

"That was before they announced the shopping center," Ed said. "That makes a big difference."

"He's still voting no."

"I think he should vote yes."

Everett gave up on the screaming. "I don't think I'd believe anything he said anyway." That was interesting, too, being talked about like he wasn't right there listening. "I'm meeting Joe Esterhouse this afternoon. Maybe he'll listen to reason."

Good gravy. That was one meeting Randy was glad to miss.

"Randy McCoy!"

A blue Ford had pulled to the curb beside them, and all four of them, Ed, Everett, Sue Ann, and Randy himself, jerked around to look.

"Well, good evening, Humphrey."

Humphrey King threw his door open and squeezed himself out of the car and came running, as fast as he could, around the car to them.

"Randy! Tell me it isn't true!"

"We're here talking about the new shopping center," Randy said.

"I go on vacation, and they call me in Florida and say a huge new grocery store's coming just a couple miles down the road from mine. Randy, we've got to stop it."

"We're going to," Everett said, and Randy took a deep breath, waiting for Ed to jump back into the fray.

But Humphrey's voice had been loud enough to carry across the street to the other side of Hemlock.

"Stop what?"

Randy still had Sue Ann's hand in his, and he pulled her back a little from the bonfire, and they watched Richard Colony trot over to them.

"Stop the shopping center," Everett said.

"It'll ruin us," Humphrey said.

"It's competition," Ed said. "Most businesses get better when they have to compete."

"It's not fair against a big chain, though," Humphrey said, and turned to Richard. "We have to stop it!"

Randy saw Richard's frown. The knife in his stomach turned again.

"I wouldn't mind that shopping center."

"Wouldn't mind?" Everett about screamed. "Wouldn't mind a highway where your front yard used to be?"

"I've started looking at houses in Gold Valley," Richard said.

That was it.

"Sue Ann, that pot roast of yours!"

Her mouth fell open. "Pot roast? What . . ."

"It'll burn," Randy said, turning and pulling her along, gently but firmly. "I don't think we ever thought we'd be out this long."

"There's nothing in the . . ." she started, but they were already far away enough that the neighbors at the corner couldn't quite hear.

"You all have a nice day," Randy called back to them, and then to Sue Ann in a low voice, "I just said that so we could excuse ourselves."

"Oh." Sue Ann's eyes were open wide. "I see. That was smart, Randy. You're getting good at this."

Wasn't another person in the courthouse. Joe sat in his usual chair in the big room and waited. Rain drumming on the windows.

Just on time. Everett Colony slammed open the main door, still shaking his umbrella. He didn't know where to sit right off. Finally he pulled a chair up to the other side of the table.

"Thank you for meeting me," he said. He didn't sound thankful. "I want to get this road done with. I don't want months more of fighting."

"I think there will be," Joe said.

"Randy McCoy's no help," Colony said. "He's not listening to his own people. I want to get you to listen to reason."

"I've been listening to a lot, but not much reason," Joe said. "You're not the only one in this county, Dr. Colony, and your neighbors aren't the only ones."

"We're the ones affected."

"Nobody's looking past themselves," Joe said. "That's how it's been from the start. They'll do anything to get their way, whoever gets hurt."

There were both hot angry, and there hadn't been much chance at the start they weren't going to be.

"You're accusing me again," Colony said.

"I'm not."

"I know you are. You still think Wade Harris was killed, don't you? I knew this was a waste of time talking to you."

Right then the door opened again.

"Good afternoon, Roger," Joe said.

Roger Gallaudet stared at the two of them sitting, rain dripping off his coat. "What's this about?"

"What is it about?" Dr. Colony said.

"I called him to come," Joe said. "After you called me, Dr. Colony. I'd like a word with the both of you."

Colony was standing. "I'm not putting up with this."

"Sit down," Joe said, "and you, too, Roger. I've had enough of you two tearing on each other, and I want to get to the bottom of it." Nobody had moved, Roger from the door or Colony from his place. "I'll be voting on the road depending on what I find out here."

That was enough. They both took seats, the three of them in a triangle.

"I know you've got a quarrel over Wade Harris." Joe looked to Roger. "You say the doctor didn't do his job. And you say Roger shouldn't be raising trouble."

"It's not the first time," Everett Colony said. "He causes a lot of harm with those accusations."

"I'm doing my job, Dr. Colony."

"We'll leave that," Joe said. "Because there's something else, and I'll ask you to hear me out. Roger, what part do you have with Warrior Land Trust?"

Roger's look was enough.

"Your wife owns that land, doesn't she?" Joe said.

"You have plenty of reason to want Gold River Highway built, don't you?"

"I'd retire, Joe. Yes, I'd like the road built. But that has nothing to do with Wade Harris."

"I think it does," Everett Colony said. "I think you're calling that a murder to ruin me."

"I'm not calling it a murder."

"And to make anybody against the road look like a criminal. You don't have to call it a murder," Colony said. "You just need to whisper around like you've been doing. Ruin my reputation, and once I'm out of your way, no one else will stand up to this road. They'll be afraid to. You'll start calling them murderers behind their backs, too."

"Stop," Joe said. "He's talked to me and Gordon, and no one else."

"What about Steve Carter?"

"Steve Carter has his own ideas, and they're not from Roger," Joe said. "Same with Randy McCoy and Roland Coates. Doesn't that make you think a little harder, Dr. Colony?"

"I know what I think."

"It's not what you think, but what's true?" Joe asked.

But Dr. Colony had had enough and was walking out. "I don't care what's true," he said. "It doesn't concern me."

He and Roger waited for the door to close. "I'm sorry, Roger," he said. "I want to know the truth."

"I'm sorry, too, Joe. I should have told you about Grace."

"Why didn't you?"

"Because you might not have believed me."

"Should I now?" Joe asked.

"I never knew anything very sure in the first place."

"Would you say it's less sure now?"

"Just forget it, Joe. I want the road too much, and it's too much that I do want Everett Colony out of the way of it. I can't trust myself."

"All right. Thank you, Roger. I appreciate it."

Rain had about stopped.

August 15, Tuesday

Byron was coming down the hall from the front door and Louise followed him in to the television room.

"Worst day I can remember!" he said, just dropping into his chair. "And worse than that to come."

She turned her chair so she could see him. "Are you all right?"

"Right as I can be after the day I've had."

"Well what's been happening?"

"Trucks backed up in the parking lot. Half the plant working receiving. We couldn't unload them fast enough." He closed his eyes like he'd fall asleep. "Never seen so much coming in the dock."

"What was it?"

"Everything. Wood, hardware, lacquers, machine parts, everything. A whole month's supplies and more coming in one day."

"Well, why?"

"Just to wear us all out. How should I know? And I was getting all the saws oiled and new blades. Mr. Coates said, 'Byron, I want those saws ready to run two months without stopping.' And I said, 'Do we have some orders in, Mr. Coates?' And he said, 'It doesn't matter. We're going three shifts and Saturdays, and I don't want to lose a minute for a broken-down saw or a drill.' Then when I was done with the saws, I worked on the drills. And when I was done with the drills, I was helping Grady with the overhead crane."

"Will you be working shifts?" Byron didn't like his regular days turned topsy-turvy with evening and night work.

"Might be. Mr. Coates said, 'Byron, I'll need your help, and all the long-timers. I'll be calling in everyone I've ever had here and hiring temporary if I need to, and someone'll need to be watching to make sure the work's being done right."

"There must be a reason," Louise said. "Mr. Coates, of all people. And he hadn't said anything before today?"

"Not a word. Nobody knew until the trucks started pulling in, and then Doris starting handing out everyone's shift hour schedules. I'll get mine tomorrow. And tomorrow we'll get the production schedules. Doris said she'll be there all night working out how to we're supposed to build everything Mr. Coates wants."

"Mr. Coates must have done the ordering at least last week for it to all come in today."

Byron was nodding. "Thought the same thing myself. Doris said Mr. Coates had told her he was doing some ordering himself, which he does sometimes. But she looked in the file cabinet when it was all coming in today, and that's when she saw what a lot of it was. And this is what she told me. Mr. Coates did it all on Tuesday morning last week, first thing when he came in. Then he didn't tell a soul, and not a person in the factory even noticed he was doing it."

"That was right after the board meeting."

"Wonder if that could mean anything," Byron said.

August 16, Wednesday

Jeremy Coates appeared plain uncomfortable, sitting across the desk from Randy, straight and stiff, and as sullen as a two-year-old.

"Thanks so much for coming," Randy said. "It's just a simple question and we could have done it on the telephone."

"I don't trust talking on telephones," Jeremy said. "I don't know who's listening."

"It would just have been me, and it doesn't matter anyway, and it's just a simple question."

"Well what is it?"

"Back a month or two ago—let's see, it would have been in June at the high school graduation—I heard sort of secondhand that you'd been out to see Wade Harris in Gold Valley."

That riled Jeremy. "What about it?" He leaned forward like he might even be ready to throw a punch. Randy eased himself backward in the chair to get a little more out of range.

"Nothing! Nothing at all. It's not about you, Jeremy, it's more I'm curious about Wade. Because it sounded like when you met him that day of his accident, you might have been the last person to see him."

"I didn't see him."

"Didn't you have a meeting set up with him?"

"Who says I did?"

"His wife. She asked me about you."

"His wife." That took some lip chewing, but finally Jeremy decided what to say. "We did have a meeting scheduled, but he never showed up."

"You were waiting for him?"

"There at his office. But he never came. Look, Randy, don't tell that around. I already told Gordon Hite I wasn't even in the county."

"Why would Gordon care where you were?"

"That's something else, and it doesn't matter. I never saw Wade Harris that day."

"Then I don't understand," Randy said, and he didn't. "He was coming over the mountain into town when he went off the road."

Jeremy had put on the most suspicious, skeptical look a person could. "I don't know what he was doing. But he never showed up."

"Gordon's asking you questions? Are you in trouble, Jeremy?"

"Has anybody told you I was?"

"Well, no, nobody's said anything."

Now Jeremy was looking a little more calculating and shrewd. "Is there anything else you want to ask me?"

"That's all. I was just asking about Wade."

"Then that's all I know."

Randy was feeling somewhat confused. "That's fine."

Steve was sure wishing he'd brought his own stepladder. When Patsy had said there was one at the courthouse, he should have known it would be as old as the building itself. But he was at the ceiling and he could see the plywood up close.

It was the same brown as the walls. It was nailed up—lots of nails.

"Oh, man!" he said to the empty room. One-inch plywood! Did they even make that anymore? It was going to weigh a ton!

Calculate—four feet by eight feet by one inch, convert to metric, density about point seven—well, almost a hundred pounds. But that big, it was still going to take two guys and real stepladders. Good grief.

While he was up close, he took the opportunity to appreciate the artwork on the ceiling. What it lacked in subtlety, taste, skill, balance, and artistry, it made up in pure garishness, although maybe a typical Jefferson County native might be better equipped to appreciate it. A person had to be up close, though, to really see the brushwork and facial expressions in detail. Good grief.

"I'll tell you, maybe I should retire."

"If you do, Byron," Louise said, "I'll move out."

"Wouldn't be any peace or quiet here with you anyway. Not that there's any at the factory these days."

She'd made his favorite chicken and cheese casserole. "What was it like today?"

"Still trucks coming in. And twenty new people, but mostly who've been there before. And they're starting shifts tonight."

"Are you working nights?"

"Not the first two weeks."

"Has he said why he's doing it all?"

"Not a word. But Jeremy was in this morning, and they had plenty of words for each other. They were up in the office and I only heard a little when I went up front for some work orders. Jeremy wants to know what all the extra work is about, and Mr. Coates won't tell him. I think that's why he won't tell anybody—so Jeremy won't find out."

August 19, Saturday

"I told Wade I wanted to meet you."

Eliza sat and rocked in the porch shade, and Cornelia Harris rocked beside her. "What did he say?"

Cornelia laughed. "You know Wade. He said, 'Go ahead. I don't think she's contagious.' "

"That is just like him!" They both were laughing. But Cornelia was like the leaves that had opened so joyously before but were now full-grown and drying and tired.

So Eliza led them beneath the leaves, through the trees, and they walked. And they talked. They talked about Wade and his ways, and the girls Meredith and Lauren, and her life now. Both of their lives.

"You were married . . ." Cornelia said.

"Yes," Eliza said. "I was."

"And now?"

"He died."

"Tell me."

"His name was Card." He was old, very old. His wife had died and he wanted someone to keep his house. Eliza had been old herself, past marrying age, and Card talked to her father. That was how it was done back in the mountains, back in time.

297

Her father had been of the old people, the ones who lived there long before houses and roads, and Card had been, too. But also mixed with early white settlers.

"Was that all right?"

"It was very right."

Her husband had wanted more than someone to care for him. He himself had wanted someone to care for.

Then five years later she moved back as a widow to her father's cabin, this cabin, empty by then. She and little Jeanie.

"And I'm still here."

August 26, Saturday

"Well, well, this is all fairly interesting, if I understand it," Randy said, looking at the letter from Asheville.

"What is it?" Sue Ann asked.

"All those letters the lawyers have been sending about the Trinkle farm. I sent them to our own lawyer down in Asheville, and it looks like he speaks the same language that those Trinkle lawyers do. Did you ever know any of those Trinkles, Sue Ann?"

"They were all gone out of the county, weren't they?"

"As far as I remember, they were. There was old Hermann back fifty years ago, and his sons with the German names that were our parents' age, and they were the ones who all moved out, and their children, the ones that are our age, that are the ones that have always been fighting over the farm, I don't think they were even raised here."

"But they owned that big farm in Gold Valley."

"Somehow or other they did, not that they could ever agree on how. But according to this letter, those other letters were saying that they finally had agreed last year, and all their lawsuits were being dropped."

"Then it didn't matter that you never did anything with those letters."

"Well . . . well, maybe we should have. Because it looks like their lawyers were asking us to clear up a few matters on our end about the deed, although I'm not sure we could have, anyway, as they go back to the Civil War or earlier, and I know we don't have any such records."

"The Civil War! That far back?"

"That far. Isn't that something? So we never answered, and I guess they just decided not to worry about it." Randy leaned back into his armchair, grateful as ever for it. "I'll give this letter to Patsy and see if there's anything we want to do with it. And I wonder if it's going to stay warm much longer." He turned on his television to hear the weather.

"Weather Seven!" the weather man was just saying. "Here's the radar, and just a little rain there south, toward Spartanburg. Should be cool tonight. Our first hint of fall! Low sixties in most of the region and maybe fifties high in the mountains. Warmer tomorrow. Let's look at the map."

"We'll close the windows tonight," Randy said to Sue Ann.

"I'll get some extra blankets out," she said.

"And here's the tropics. Let me introduce you to Grant, who just got qualified as a tropical storm. Someone to keep an eye on."

August 28, Monday

Steve stared at the living room floor.

"There was a tornado?"

Natalie looked up at him from the sofa.

"Three tornadoes."

He stepped over the Legos, around the cars, dodged the doll house.

"It was completely clean when I went into my office."

"That was three hours ago."

"Three hours?" He looked at his watch. Five o'clock. "So what's for supper?"

She didn't answer right away.

"Fish sticks," she said, finally. "When are they going to build that new shopping center? Will it have a pizza takeout?"

"A couple years." Five o'clock! "I want to see the weather." He turned the television on. "So where are the tornadoes now?"

"They went thataway." She pointed toward the bedrooms.

". . . and there it is, folks, Hurricane Grant. We're guessing landfall Friday or Saturday, and it could be anywhere between Daytona Beach and Maryland."

August 29, Tuesday

"I don't know how long we can do it!" Byron said. "And I can't believe what it must be costing, all the overtime and the wood and the lacquer and all. And we're just piling furniture up in the warehouse out back."

"Isn't anyone buying it?"

"Oh, they're calling all their customers and trying to get it out the door. Must be offering all kinds of discounts to move it."

"And does anyone know why?"

"I've been thinking."

He didn't real often, so Louise listened close.

"You know," Byron said, "he told us about needing that road and the zoning to sell the factory, so they could expand it. Well—I think he's trying to show that the factory can build as much furniture as anybody would want, just the way it is."

"I think you're right, Byron! That makes perfect sense."

"Wouldn't need another row of saws if the ones there work three shifts a day."

"Would they? For month after month?"

"I'd hate to be part of it," he said.

"But he still doesn't have anyone to buy the furniture."

"And I don't know how he'll pay the bills when they're due."

Byron turned on the television. The weather had just started.

". . . and now, we're looking at it coming ashore about midway between Jacksonville and Savannah and following a track inland northwest from there, probably just missing Atlanta on the east side. And up here in western North Carolina, eastern Tennessee, if it gets caught up in this low-pressure system, it could just stall out for a couple days."

August 30, Wednesday

"Mr. Carter? This is Patsy, at the courthouse. Joe said to call you. There's a man from Asheville who needs to talk with a board member, and Joe thought you should."

"Who is it?"

"Mr. McDonald. He's with the State Department of Emergency Services. He wants to talk about flood emergency plans."

"Okay, I'll call him."

Beautiful day out there. Blue skies, puffy clouds. Life was nice. Who needed a grocery store?

"Emergency Services, Angus McDonald."

Angus?

"Hi. I'm Steve Carter with the Jefferson County Board of Supervisors. I'm supposed to call you?"

"Hi, Steve. Thanks for calling. The subject is Hurricane Grant."

"Okay. Good."

"We're being proactive here. The department is contacting all local governments to coordinate emergency planning."

"I've been following it," Steve said. "What are you forecasting?"

"We're just watching the Weather Channel like you are."

"It sounds like a lot of rain."

"Exactly. I've been looking at hydrology reports for the Gold and Fort Ashe valleys. I don't want to sound too technical. *Hydrology* basically means groundwater."

"I was looking at some of that data this morning, too," Steve said. "We're on a fifty-year high for precipitation since March, and the water tables are probably as high as they can get. The last thunderstorm caused flash floods. I even did some ground conductance testing with my kids— kind of a science project."

"Uh . . . really?"

"Yeah. Way high. Not that it was real precise, but this was the third year we've done it, so we have sort of a baseline."

"I see." Mr. McDonald sounded amused. "Then I guess you don't need me to tell you what a major rain event is going to do."

"I can guess," Steve said. "But I don't have any way to run a real simulation. Do you have some scenarios?"

"We do. Do you want the good news or the bad news first?"

"Try the good news."

"Okay. Hurricane Grant might miss you to the west, and you'll get two inches of rain."

"I'll take that," Steve said. "What's the bad news?"

"Well . . . Grant slides down the low-pressure trough and stalls right over your head. Complete worst-case scenario if that happens: a five-hundred-year flood."

The worst flood in five hundred years.

"But," Angus said, "the planning scenario is a fifty-year flood."

"The last one was twenty-nine years ago."

"Then it's a twenty-nine-year flood."

"What does that translate to for river levels?"

"Hard to say," McDonald said. "Ten to twenty feet I'd guess. What are your flood plains like?"

"Mostly good. Gold River is pretty clear. There are just a few structures in the actual plain, and the main bridge is the interstate, and it's way high up. The Fort Ashe has more buildings. The most vulnerable place is Wardsville itself. The first buildings are about nine feet up."

"Okay. What's your plan?"

Steve smiled to himself, one of those ironic Humphrey Bogart smiles. "Basically cross our fingers and hope it's not too bad."

"That's your flood emergency procedure?"

"I just wrote it this summer. I added the part about crossing our fingers."

"That's probably not going to do."

"This is a really sparse county, Angus. Low population, low budget, on the edge of economically depressed. There's not much we can do."

"I think I need to come up for a visit."

"We'd be honored," Steve said.

"I'll put you on the list. How about Friday night? It's getting real busy around here."

August 31, Thursday

"What a pile of furniture," Byron said. "Desks, hutches, tables, everything. I never saw the like."

Louise was just settling into her chair. At least he'd waited until after supper and the kitchen was clean.

"Is it enough?" she asked. "That he wouldn't need the new road?"

"Road? I don't know. I only know it's about killing us all."

"Because I was reading today about the shopping center. Luke Goddard wrote a big long article in the newspaper about how those new shopping places destroy historic downtowns like ours."

"It says what?"

"And that's why I don't want any road," she said.

"What historic downtown?"

"Wardsville."

"I wouldn't give a nickel for downtown Wardsville. It's the factory that's important, and Mr. Coates sure wants the road."

"It's not his salon that'll get put out of business."

"There's more to this town than your salon."

"There is," she said. "And they'll all be put out of business, too."

"The furniture factory might be out of business without the road."

"I don't believe it."

"And you'd love to shop at those new stores they'd build up there."

She sniffed "Not when they're built over all my friends' graves."

"Graves? What are you talking about?"

"That's what the newspaper called it."

"For crying out loud! That's the most fool thing I've ever heard."

"I don't want to talk about it. And besides, how could I shop there anyway? With the salon closed, I wouldn't have a penny to spend."

"Are you saying I can't take care of my own house and family?"

"But it wouldn't be my money."

"If I'm out of a job at the factory, then what would we do?"

She really was about to cry. "I don't want to talk about it any more. It's the most terrible thing that could ever happen to this county."

"What'll I tell Mr. Coates?"

"Just tell him whatever you want! I said I don't want to talk about it! He can just take his old factory and make it a salon itself, for all I care."

"Turn the factory into a salon? Are you crazy?"

"I don't want to talk about it!"

"You say that and then you keep talking about it!"

"I'm not saying anything else. Except I don't want any road."

"Louise!"

The weather report was just coming on the television.

". . . big storm coming! Batten down the hatches, folks, because it's going to be a monster!"

County landfill. Joe said the sand pile was out here. Steve parked at the end of the dirt road. Yep, landfill. What a smell.

Whoa, right there—that was a pile of sand, all right. He started pacing it off with his wheel measure, estimating angles. Fourteen feet in the center? At least twelve.

He'd do calculations when he got home, but he was already doing them in his head. Pretty much a cone—pi times radius squared times height, divided by three—at least seven hundred cubic meters.

Utility building. He had the key. Stuff, stuff, stuff, there. Burlap bags. Tied bundles. Ten bundles, fifteen, twenty—seventy-five, eighty—a hundred thirty—two hundred fifty bundles. Twenty bags per bundle. Okay.

Driving to Wardsville. How to get all those tons of sand from back there to town? Where to put them?

Take a walk through downtown. Figure out a line—keep the elevation constant, but shortest distance. He had his wheel measure—okay, so here's the geek taking his little wheel for a walk around town.

He'd check his calculations and the topo maps back home, but it was pretty obvious how this was going to work. If it was going to work.

"That was Patsy," Randy said to Sue Ann, setting down the telephone. "There's a man coming up from Asheville tomorrow night, and Joe said we'll have a board meeting to hear him."

Last edge of sunset slipping behind the mountain. Sky was clear except off to the south. Mostly stars. Moon wouldn't be up for hours to come.

Joe focused on the stars.

Sky was full of them. Once in a while he thought about how far away they were. A man could almost feel the earth turning under his feet, looking up at a sky of stars.

Watch them close enough, and he could see them shifting. That was wind high up. It was different than summer twinkling from water in the air, the night before a storm. Autumn shifting was from cold fronts. But it was August, and there were no clouds north or west.

He took a breath, deep in through his nose, testing the quality of the air. Tobacco leaves, the neighbor's cows, forest and mountain smells faint; and a catch to it. A bare sting back of his nostrils. That would mean thunderstorms, but not with winds high up.

At the ground the air was still and not humid. Sound carried. He could hear water in the stream, and a car far off, then an owl.

He stepped inside and blinked in the kitchen light.

"Rain?" Rose said.

"I don't know. Everything's contrary. I don't know what's coming."

Back and forth, Eliza rocked her chair. The dark of the moonless night poured onto the porch, and behind her, into the cabin. She could feel it flowing past her. It was a night where candles and lanterns would only make islands, and the black would crust everything and not be dislodged.

All about in the stillness there was tumult of unstable leanings and balances overmatched. The Warrior spoke apprehension and of war impending.

September

September 1, Friday

Get started! Come on!

Bang!

Finally. Steve straightened his papers for the hundredth time. Of all days to wait for the clock before they could start the meeting.

Angus McDonald was there in the front row, and Gordon Hite was next to him. Not too many other chairs were filled.

"Come to order," Joe said. "Go ahead, Patsy."

At least Joe was being quick. Patsy read the names quick, too.

"Everyone's present, Joe."

"Thank you, Patsy. Jefferson County North Carolina Board of Supervisors is now in session. We are meeting under the emergency provisions of the county regulations, and I'm also serving notice that our meeting next Monday will be canceled. The emergency provisions allow us to do that without the usual two-week notification. The regulations require us to describe the emergency involved, and that is the current forecast by the state Department of Emergency Services that there is a likelihood of heavy rain and possible flooding in Jefferson County. Sheriff Gordon Hite is present, as well as representatives of the volunteer fire department and rescue squads, and the county manager. We will dispense with all other business tonight, and reschedule that for our next regular meeting on the first Monday in October."

Good grief. The guy must have the entire state code memorized. Steve swallowed his impatience. A minute or two wasn't going to make a big difference. What they really needed right now was calm.

Joe was looking around the room. "That takes care of that. Steve Carter will introduce our guest."

"Thanks, Joe."

Show time. Steve did his own looking around the room, mostly to get himself calm. "This is Mr. Angus McDonald of the North Carolina State Department of Emergency Services. Mr. McDonald and I have talked several times over the last couple days, and he's here tonight to make recommendations and to tell us how the state can help us."

"Thank you, Steve. It's a pleasure to meet you all."

Angus McDonald exuded confidence. Blue shirt, yellow tie, just the right amount of gray hair to be young and competent yet experienced and assuring. Right out of central casting.

"Even this afternoon when I was getting ready to come up here, I was still hoping it might not be bad." He shook his head. "But the last forecast just an hour ago is looking real bad." Deep sigh. "Wardsville is in line to get one heck of a flood.

"Grant is right on track to make landfall midnight Saturday night, at Savannah. We'll be getting rain here by Saturday evening—tomorrow. Right now we're forecasting as much as ten inches of rain between Saturday evening and Monday afternoon. The Fort Ashe River will be out of its banks by late Saturday and cresting sometime Monday."

"How high will it be?" Louise asked.

"That's always hard to tell," Angus said. "Ten to twenty feet."

"How high is that?"

"The last flood was twelve and a half feet," Steve said. "I measured some places on Main Street. The floor of your salon is eleven feet above normal high level."

"Now, let's wait a minute." Randy was looking pretty glum. "You're saying this is a forecast. It's not really certain, is it?"

Angus shrugged. "The whole thing might miss completely."

"It just might. I've seen those forecasts be pretty far off the mark."

"You might get lucky," Angus said.

"Or we might not," Steve said. What was Randy's problem? "I think we should be planning for the worst, here."

"That's not what I'm saying," Randy said. "I'm not arguing. I'm just hoping. We're talking about how many feet here and there, and it might not ever get up close to that."

"We're all hoping," Louise said. "We remember the last time."

Randy nodded. "That was a mess, and I don't want any repetition."

"We got it cleaned up," she said. "We'll do it again if we have to."

"Well now, I'm not so sure about that. That's why I'm hoping that this storm would maybe just leave us alone." Randy did his own looking around. "That was a different time, that last flood. Wardsville was different then. There were plenty of people downtown and businesses in every building.

"And it was a lot of work cleaning up, and I remember because I was there. They closed the high school and put us all to work. The whole town worked."

"But I'm not sure I see that happening nowadays. I'm not sure people would think downtown was worth the effort. Mr. McDonald, this town might not recover from another flood. That's why I'm hoping it won't be as bad as you're talking about."

Angus shrugged. "Sorry. I really am sorry, but I can't help you there." What was Randy thinking? That the guy could cancel a hurricane? "I just give my reports to the responsible officials, which would be all of you. Those issues are beyond me."

"Mr. McDonald," Steve, the responsible official, asked. "What kind of help can we expect from the state?"

"If the governor declares the county a disaster area, there are grants and interest-free loans for recovery projects."

"I mean right now." Steve turned to Randy. "I think we need to concentrate on getting ready for this flood."

Angus was frowning. "This is going to be a regional disaster. Communities are supposed to have already prepared. When this thing hits, we're going to be stretched thin."

Randy was sunk in glumnity. "How do you get ready for a flood?"

"Sandbags," Steve said. "The county has a sand pile out by the landfill, and about five thousand burlap bags."

"Five thousand?" Randy said. "That's the Great Wall of China."

"Not quite. Most of Main Street is eight feet above the normal high-water level. I've worked out a perimeter around Main Street that's 540 yards, and the bags are thirty inches long. That's 650 bags for one row. Five thousand bags can build us a wall about six feet tall. Since the perimeter is eight feet above the normal high water level, that brings it up to fourteen feet."

"How are we going to fill five thousand bags?"

Shake out of it, Randy!

"If we start first thing tomorrow morning, filling two hundred an hour, we'll make it."

"Two hundred sand bags in an hour?"

"Thirty people in a shift," Steve said. "Can't we get that?"

"Where will we fill them? Just out at the landfill?"

"We have to keep the sand dry. Could we bring it into the high school?"

"We can't get trucks into the gym," Randy said. "Do we have trucks?"

"We have one dump truck." It was the first Joe had moved. "And there's no shortage of pickup trucks in Jefferson County. Just need a backhoe to fill them."

"Patsy." Louise was alive now, too. "Call Byron. The furniture factory has loading docks. We could fill bags there. And they have plenty of people to fill them."

"Will we have enough people to do everything?" That was Steve's main question. "Can the state help us at all?"

Angus shook his head. "I'm afraid you'll be on your own."

"Now, Steve," Randy said, "you're saying there is a chance, though?"

"Yes, there's a chance. I just don't know how far the river will come up. We can beat it if it doesn't come too far."

"If it's people we need, we'll get the people." Randy had finally given up on giving up. "We'll start with the football team and work from there."

"Here's Byron," Patsy said, holding up her cell phone.

"There's a hundred strong men who work at the factory," Louise said. "Let me talk to Byron and he'll call Mr. Coates."

Randy was sounding hopeful. "All of you out there," he said to the audience, "start calling your friends. Have them call the Sheriff's Department to find out where we need them. Steve, I suppose you should park yourself down there with Gordon."

"Now, Randy," the sheriff said. Steve felt a chill. Gordon Hite theoretically would be the person in charge. "This is a lot effort we're talking about here. On the one hand, we might not have a flood at all, and on the other hand, if it's really as bad as the man says, I don't think we're going to stop it."

"I understand what you're saying," Randy said, "and that's true, but I think we really should make the effort."

Gordon apparently did not. "And somebody might be putting all those numbers into their calculator, but how do we really know whether we have enough sand or bags?"

"Steve said he counted them," Randy said.

"That's a lot of bags to count," Gordon said, "and if it is that many, I don't think that sand pile is going to fill five thousand of them. Like I said, a person can do their figuring, but this isn't a schoolwork problem to do with numbers and figuring. I don't think we've got enough bags or sand. Anybody can look at that pile and know it isn't enough to build a wall six feet high around the whole town."

"Yes it is," Steve said. Who was this oaf, to question an engineer? "We have five thousand bags, 250 bundles of twenty each, and we have 820 cubic yards of sand, which is twenty-five percent more than we need." He was angry. "I measured the pile myself, and I calculated the volume." He looked over to Joe and Randy. "We can do it, but only if we do it right."

Joe knew what that meant.

"Gordon," Joe said. "I think you'll be plenty busy just managing your department. We'll have Steve in charge of the sandbagging."

Gordon scowled. "I think you're wasting a lot of time and work."

"That might be, but we'll try it."

"Of course we will," Randy said. "Steve says there's a chance, and that's good enough for me to at least try. We have to try anyway, don't we? How could we not try?"

"I'm not ready to give up yet," Louise said. "Steve, Byron says for you to call Mr. Coates right after the meeting."

It was like a movie. Steve was picturing Judy Garland and Mickey Rooney, and maybe Jimmy Stewart. We can do it!

Pretty wild. In three months Steve had gone from bit player to leading man.

But there wasn't time to think.

"It just depends how high the river comes up," he said, half to himself.

Eliza answered. "It will come as high as it wishes."

September 2, Saturday

It was raining.

Louise stood at the front door of the salon and watched the drops pittering and pattering on the sidewalk, and on the windows, and on the street. Not very hard yet, but the clouds looked like big gray cotton towels sopping wet just out of the washing machine. Twenty boys and girls from the high school were milling around by the drugstore, and a few other men were on the sidewalks, standing under awnings.

The river looked about normal.

She turned back into the shop. Two long tables from church were spread with chicken and hot dogs and five big coffee urns. Artis Hite and two other ladies were in the back making sandwiches. The rest of the church ladies had gone home to be out of the way, but they'd be taking turns through the night.

Louise was ready.

"Excuse me—can I get a haircut?" a man's voice said.

She spun around. Right in the middle of a hurricane! What kind of ridiculous man would come into her salon . . .

Oh, for goodness' sakes.

"Matt! Oh, Matt, look at you!" She wrapped herself around him in the biggest hug a short grandmother could give a tall grandson.

"I made it, Grandma."

"Look at you! And of all the days for you to get here!"

"I just got home yesterday, and Mom told me what was happening up here. I came up to help."

"Well, we can use it! Oh, I'm so glad you're home safe and sound. What a treat to see you! I was worried every single day you were gone."

"I'm okay, Grandma. I'm worrying about you. Is Grandpa around?"

"He's up at the factory filling sandbags, and everybody down here'll be laying them out."

"I'll go see him. I'm pretty good with sand."

Jeanie seemed satisfied. "As long as the creek doesn't carry the whole house away."

"It won't," Eliza said. "There have been other rains."

"This is a hurricane, Mother."

"There have been other hurricanes."

Zach was already in the car. Eliza pulled her shawl over her head against the rain and flew to join him, and Jeanie with her.

"Where are we going?" he asked.

"To Wardsville. Turn at the stoplight and there will be a building."

He started driving. "The high school?"

"No. But close to it."

"It's an old factory," Jeanie said.

"There will be people there," Eliza said.

"There better be," Zach said. "I'm not filling sandbags by myself."

Good gravy, it was raining. It was surely feeling like a hurricane.

"Now, you'll be safe here," he said to Sue Ann, and she nodded. "The basement will be the safest place."

"Randy—it's you and Kyle I'm worried about."

"We'll be fine."

"Here comes the first truck."

Steve was standing on the bridge with Randy and his son, Kyle, and a dozen county employees, and Gordon Hite. The Fort Ashe was still kind of placid, but it was already right at zero feet flood stage.

And the rains were coming down, and the waters were coming up.

The truck full of sandbags parked at the end of the bridge. "We'll start down there, just past the post office." Steve said. Gregory Peck in command. "Right by that oak. Then across Main Street and back behind that first empty building, and then along the riverbank. I'll show you." They turned the other way. "And then cut back across Main Street at the green building, and up to that hill." The important part was to get the line started in the right places.

"What about Gabe's repair shop?" Gordon Hite asked. "We'll leave him outside the sandbags."

"We can't go that far," Steve said. "We don't have enough bags or sand or people."

"Doesn't seem to me it's that much farther," Gordon said. "Now, let's start back there, past the garage."

The idiot was doing it again. If the sheriff couldn't stop them from trying, he'd make sure they did it wrong. And Joe was nowhere to be seen.

"Do you think I don't want to? But it won't work," Steve said. "See how the road dips, there? The sandbags will have to be twice as high for that whole distance."

"It looks high enough to me. We can't go cutting the town in half and leaving Gabe's and those other buildings to get flooded."

That did it.

"Forget it, Gordon!" Had he ever in his life called a person *Gordon*? "You're not going to wreck this. Now, either do what I say or get out of here." To Randy. "Take the football guys down to the post office and start there with this load of bags, and I'll be back to check."

A second truck had turned onto Main Street.

"The rest of you, come with me down the other way."

"Bunch of useless know-it-alls." Gordon was not leading, following, or getting out of the way. Steve had to walk around him.

The phone on Patsy's desk was ringing. "This is Joe Esterhouse."

"Joe, it's Marty Brannin."

"Thank you for calling back, Marty."

"I don't deserve that. Joe, I'm sorry. I haven't been able to get any help for you at all. The whole state is getting pounded right now."

"I understand."

"Emergency Services doesn't have a candle to spare. You talked to them?"

"Mr. Angus McDonald, here in Asheville."

"He's the one. If he can't help, nobody can."

"That's too bad, Marty. You know what this will mean."

"I know. We'll get you some loans, I promise that."

"Don't know that anyone will want them."

"There's just not much to do at the last minute."

"Never was much we could any time. Thank you for trying."

"I'm sorry."

Joe walked out to the hallway, to a window, rain beating against it.

Randy took a minute to walk over to the bridge. There was still some light through the clouds, enough at least to see that the river was as dark and swirling as the clouds overhead, muddy brown with branches and leaves, and it didn't seem much pleased with the pylons from the bridge, or with its own banks for that matter. The water seemed more solid than the land, maybe because it was stronger, and it had a purpose, just to get by.

The wind was harder than before. It seemed to have a purpose, too, and it had about as much water in it as the river, and at least as many leaves and debris, which out on the bridge here, left Randy feeling like he was under fire.

And the town was under siege. The river was an attacking army and they were trying to fight it off, building a wall. Thinking about it that way, and looking at the determined river, Randy wasn't very sure they'd win.

The bag was coarse burlap, feeling like tree bark, and Eliza held it as Zach shoveled sand. He was so fast. Heap after heap flying in, and the limp bag filling and taking shape. Then a man named Grady lofted it onto his back and it was away, and the next begun.

The factory was bright and frightful! Great machines and a hard blue floor and gray metal boxes and pipes adhered to the white walls, and all much too large. Fifty men and women were working, taking turns shoveling and holding and carrying, as if they were one great beast.

Roland Coates had greeted her, and for his sake she had walked the paths through the building, and he was proud to show it to her. And he had brought her to Byron—Louise's husband. Roland and Byron, they were very much alike.

"Pleased to meet you," Byron had said, and stared at her with narrowed eyes and frowning brow. But then a young man had come and Byron had left her to greet him.

And now, she concentrated on the bag and sand and Zach's shovel.

It was troubling. She was in this hard, bright place, and it was uncomfortable. Her purpose for being there with these other people was to contend with the river and the wind and rain, which were better left to themselves.

Preventing a river! It was contention with the Warrior himself. But she was making a choice, for these people. What would come of it?

That wind howling like a wild animal and more water than the skies could ever have held. Louise stood at the door. She could barely see the men working in the headlights of the cars.

316

"Artis," she said, "can we get more coffee? These pitchers are empty."

"I'm making it."

They still had tables of food, and more coming in, and plenty getting eaten, and six Baptist ladies were making as big a hubbub as the hurricane was.

Gordon Hite stumbled in, just as the whole room went black.

"There it goes," he said. "Lucky it held on as long as it did."

"Light the lanterns!" Louise commanded. And soon the salon was bright, but not near what it had been. And it was so dark outside now.

Gordon was looking down back at his wife. "Artis! Everett Colony wants a plate of sandwiches or something down at the Episcopal church." He turned to Louise. "Everett's at the church treating people."

"Is anyone hurt?"

"Fred Clairmont slipped and broke his arm, and there's been a sprained ankle or two. Just hope nobody ends up in the river."

Seven inches. In thirty minutes the water was up seven inches. Just three feet below the sandbags.

Steve did the calculations again for the hundredth time.

Five hundred forty yards. Every row was 650! Absolute best case, they could do eight courses of bags. Two yards high. The wall would be six feet high, maximum.

The first row was eight feet above the average high-water mark. Eight feet plus six feet. The top of the sandbags would be fourteen feet above flood stage.

Maybe it would be. Everybody must be getting tired. The first row of bags had been fifteen truckloads, one load every five minutes. Now the trucks were ten minutes apart, just finishing the second row. He had no idea what was happening up at the factory. Hopefully Louise's husband had enough people and shovels.

First row, eighty minutes. Second row, two hours. Eighteen inches of wall in over three hours, and slowing down.

The water was up seven inches in thirty minutes. Not slowing down. It would reach the sandbags in three hours.

Calculate.

Constant rate of water rising, constant rate of wall rising . . . the water would crest the wall in four hours. Midnight. And it wasn't a constant rate of water rising, and it wasn't a constant rate of the wall rising, either.

Somehow, through the hurricane, his cell phone was ringing.

"This is Steve."

"Steve Carter? I'm Charlie Ryder. I'm checking. Oh that road—"

Steve hurled the phone into the river.

Randy had to sit down. His arms felt like lead and he could hardly lift them, and the rain was pelting down to soak through anything. It was soaking through everything he had on. It'd be hard to say what was worse, the rain or the wind. He could just see Kyle and his team in the headlights down the next block.

He caught a glimpse of his wristwatch in a moving light. Almost eleven! Had it been that long? How much longer could they go?

But the water kept coming and coming, faster and higher, way up over the bank and the first rows of sandbags.

An empty truck roared off back toward the furniture factory. There wasn't another one yet and everyone at the line had to stop again.

Randy got himself up. "Gordon?"

"Yeah?"

"I think we need people to be ready if that water comes over."

"That's what I've been thinking."

"Might be another hour," Randy said, "but we're not keeping up, and it'll come fast."

"We'll keep an eye on it."

A couple of men headed down toward Louise's, but Randy had to sit down again, even in the wind and rain. They weren't close to keeping up, and he knew what it meant. Somewhere there'd be the first stream over the top, and then more, and the breach would open up, and it would all come pouring in.

He remembered the last time, even thirty years later it was still fresh in his mind, the brown water racing down the street, every business in the town with that torrent running through, waist deep or higher.

Not one of them was going to get over that. Not this time.

It was the end.

Pretty foolish, crying like a baby when the rain's already pouring down and the wind's screaming louder than anything.

They'd close the town. Just empty buildings filled with mud up and down Main Street, and a road over the mountain, and soon why even live in town anyway? Why look at it all run-down and dead?

There wasn't a way to stop the water. Wardsville had put up its best against the river, and the river was the easy winner. They'd be the hard losers.

Finally another truck pulled in, and all he could see was the arms and hands reaching in and pulling bags off. The only light was headlight beams jutting through the rain. And across the river there more head-lights coming up.

A hard wall of wind hit him, filled with water, and he staggered back a little. Then he got his bearings to look back over the river.

It was hard to see. It looked like a line of lights. It would have to be reflections on the wet road, because it looked like headlights and more headlights stretching back down Marker Highway.

Randy got himself up and went staggering toward the bridge as fast as he could through inches of water and pounds of weariness. The river wasn't up to the bridge deck yet, and it wouldn't be before Main Street was already flooded.

But there were men at the other side. He started running toward them.

He couldn't even think, really. What was he even doing? Three men were at the edge of the river looking at the bridge.

"The bridge is fine," he called, not even knowing what he meant. "It's fine. You can come over it." Somehow he knew they needed to. "It'll hold. You can make it. We can make it."

He still didn't even know what it meant, but they were here to help. He knew it.

And one of the men turned back to the first trucks. "Move it!" the man yelled. "Move 'em, move 'em, move 'em! Get 'em over!" The first truck was roaring louder than the rain, blowing past them, then the next, and more. They were big trucks. "Move it!" Someone had a light stick and he was waving trucks past, and someone at the other end of the bridge was sending the trucks in either direction along Main Street.

"Thank you so much," Randy was saying to the one man who'd sent the trucks across the bridge. "Thank you so much."

"Who's in charge?"

"Steve Carter is in charge as much as anybody, and you'll find Sheriff Hite over there," Randy said. "You'll be best off just getting sandbags from the furniture factory and laying them out."

"We brought our own bags," the man said, and Randy finally realized that they were army trucks. He looked back at the town and a big spotlight glared on and the street was filled with its fire and the whole town was crawling with men, and it was like his eyes had been opened to see things he hadn't been able to before.

They weren't going to lose. He could see it all now.

Two hundred bags left, and that was it. Now what? Steve was standing in the loading dock at the factory, looking at the little pile of bags.

Now what? Nothing! No bags.

What else could they use? Nothing. Logs? Bricks? Cinderblocks? Cinderella?

Pumpkins? Mice? He needed a fairy godmother.

"Mr. Carter?"

What? A guy in a big army surplus coat.

"I'm Steve Carter."

"Corporal Ramos, sir. Could you come with me?"

Gordon was having him arrested. "What's happening"

"If you could come, sir. Captain Bednarek can explain."

Who were these people? Where had this Hummer come from? And maybe the coat wasn't surplus.

They pulled out into Hemlock River and through the rapids toward downtown.

What were the lights? Somebody had the power back on Main Street?

Trucks. Big trucks, and lots of people. Lots of people pulling sandbags off big trucks. It was a whole battalion of National Guard! A brigade, at least. Or a couple companies.

"Where's Bednarek?" the driver screamed out his window.

The man pointed.

They pulled up by the command center—three men standing on the corner at Main Street and the bridge.

"Mr. Carter? You're the engineer in charge?"

Huh? Uh . . . "Yes."

"Could you look over the line, sir and see if it's acceptable? Corporal Ramos will go with you."

"Yeah! Let's go. Um . . . I'm just wondering who sent you? We heard there was no help available."

Even in the dark, Steve could see the man's expression. "Somebody pulled some really big strings."

The telephone rang. Nobody else was in the courthouse. He picked up the handset.

"This is Joe Esterhouse."

"Mr. Esterhouse. Please wait for the governor."

He waited.

"Joe?"

"Yes, sir."

"Tommy Johnson."

"Evening, sir."

"I'm calling back to check on you. Did your help get there?"

"Yes, sir, they did. About a half hour ago."

"Did they make it in time?"

"It looks like they did, sir."

"Good. I'm glad you called when you did."

Joe still had the pink notepaper from March in his hand. "You gave me your telephone number, so I thought I'd use it."

"That's why I gave it to you."

"And we appreciate the help. I don't think we would have recovered from a flood this time."

"Let me know if you need anything else."

September 5, Tuesday

The water was still high, but it was down closer to where it was supposed to be.

"Hi, Grandma," Matt said, sitting right down on Becky's chair in the salon. "It's a mess out there."

"It's nothing like the last flood," Louise said. "That was a mess!"

"This is enough."

"So, did you talk to Lyle?"

"He said I could work for the week."

"Then your grandpa can get you that job at the factory, and you can be in the basement as long as you want. Do you really want to stay?"

"Sure! For a while. I need to find a job."

"You won't find one around here," Louise said.

"Grandpa says if the road gets built, they'll be hiring at the factory."

Louise bit her lip. She was not going to pull Matt into all of that.

But right then, the door opened and Randy McCoy and Steve Carter came tromping into the salon.

"We'll need new bags anyway," Steve was saying. "Hi, Louise!"

"Well, look at you two," she said. "I bet you're both feeling pleased. There is not a spot of mud on Main Street."

"Which is different than the last time," Randy said. "But there's still the paper work to be done, just like for anything."

"We're figuring what the county had to spend, and we'll get the state to reimburse us," Steve said. "I hope. Bags and sand. Emergency services. Police overtime. Food. Did you spend anything on all that food?"

"Of course not," Louise said. "Everybody just brought it."

"It'll cost to clean up the sandbags," Steve said.

"Matt's all ready to start on that," Louise said. "Lyle hired him."

"Oh. Good," Steve said. "So what are you doing with them?"

"Sheriff Hite told us to just dump them in the river," Matt said.

A big scowl appeared on Steve's face. "He said what?"

"Dump them in the river."

"What does Lyle say?"

"He says do whatever the sheriff says."

"He would." Steve didn't seem to have gotten off real well with Gordon. "Just throw the bags in whole?"

"No," Matt said. "Cut the ends and dump the sand off the river-bank, then send the bags back to the storage shed at the landfill to use again next time."

"Can we fire Gordon?" Steve said.

"Don't worry about Gordon," Louise said. "He's just never been through a flood before as sheriff."

"Actually," Randy said, "we can't even talk about it. We can't have more than two board members talk official business together except at official meetings."

"Then I won't talk to you," Steve said. "You're Matt?"

"Yes, sir."

"Tell your grandmother, and Mr. McCoy, that guy right there, that I think we should fire the sheriff."

"Grandma . . ." Matt started.

"I heard him," Louise said. "We won't right now, and besides, we can't. He's elected."

"Why is he even involved in this anyway?" Steve said. "The sheriff isn't in charge of cleaning up."

"Now, Steve, we're all involved," Randy said. "Sometimes it's just who's there that makes a decision."

"But that's the wrong decision. Where does all the sand go if you throw it in the river? Somebody should figure that out first. And we're not going to use the bags over. We can do better than this."

"I'm all for that," Randy said. "I just don't think anybody knows how, and there isn't any money to pay for it anyway."

"Look what we did already!" Steve said. He'd gotten so determined in the last week! It made Louise feel determined herself.

"Steve," she said, "just go have a talk with Lyle. And if he or Gordon give you any trouble, we'll put Joe on to them. But I think you're right. Nobody would have thought we could beat a hurricane, and we did."

"We did beat a hurricane, didn't we," Randy said. "Even if it took the National Guard to help. But we beat it."

September 12, Tuesday

Tearing. Ripping. Leaf after leaf. Everywhere was smelling of tobacco.

Joe was walking the fields, tearing leaves but still watching. Fifteen boys, high school and past school, tearing leaves.

Leonard Darlington hired Mexicans. Most of the farmers did. Joe cobbled together a crew from town and around and Rose fed them all, but it was harder each year to find enough, and they cost more.

But he'd got enough for this year. Wouldn't need them next year.

In the computer age, why were so many trees dying? And why did so many of them show up in his mailbox? The physical inbox, the one that brooded on the corner of his desk, usually in lonely solitude but today crushed under the massive weight of . . . Mount RushMail. He wasn't running a civil engineering practice—he was a mere cog in the great life cycle of paper as it went from forestland to landfill.

Time to slay this dragon. Steve took his weapon, Murgatroyd, the purple plastic letter opener with little green race cars, which Max had given him for Christmas, and attacked.

An hour later he was approaching the bottom.

Big manilla envelope. No return address. Asheville postmark, from August. A little curious.

He wielded Murgatroyd—who was actually quite sharp for a thirty-nine-cent piece of plastic.

A contract, some paragraphs blacked out. December 1, a year ago, between . . . Trinkle Land Trust and Regency Atlantic Associates.

Well, how interesting. Jarvis had come through.

But there was still other mail. Set Mr. Jarvis aside for a more opportune moment.

"I'm doing my big article on the flood," Luke said, plopping himself down in Randy's office.

"You're only now getting around to it?" Randy said.

"I'm sure you've been following my ongoing coverage. But this is the inside story with all the investigative details. You know what I mean."

"I don't."

"What I want to know is why the county was so poorly prepared, and all those other backroom deals and decisions."

"Just go, Luke. I don't have any time for this."

"Who was mad at Gabe to leave his garage outside the sandbags?"

"His insurance will get him right back in business. It's your place we should have let flood."

"I love these quotes," Luke said.

"Speaking of quotes—I wanted to ask you something."

"Oh, I don't answer questions. I only ask them."

"Back in April, one of those times you were bugging me about Gold River Highway. You said you were meeting Wade Harris in town here. Did you ever do that?"

That put a cork into Luke for a few seconds at least. "Well, no," he said, finally. "He died before we could."

"Wasn't it going to be that day of the meeting?"

"It was, but he called and canceled it," Luke said. "Said he was meeting a customer and couldn't make it into town."

"Now, what does that mean?" Randy said.

"What does what mean?"

Wade hadn't seen Jeremy, and he hadn't seen Luke, either. Where had he been coming from? "Well, I'm just wondering where Wade had been all afternoon."

"I wish I'd seen him," Luke said. "That would have been a story."

September 18, Monday

"I like this better, Joe." Marty Brannin was at his place at the kitchen table. The morning sun was a flood in the window. "Lots better than dark night meetings. And I don't mind any delay in getting back to Raleigh." Wolfing his eggs and bacon, poor man was always in a hurry. "I'd be hard-pressed to decide between late night pie and a country breakfast. But anything's better than a fast-food egg biscuit."

"You're always welcome, Marty."

"Thank you both. Let's see, anything I need to do for you since your flood? The governor has taken an interest. Wardsville and Jefferson County are magic words in Raleigh right now. The little town that could, you know."

"Steve Carter's been taking care of things."

"And now I'll sing for my supper. Joe, I had a scheduled sit-down meeting with Jack Royce. I said I wanted to ask his advice. I wasn't sure he'd talk to me, except I used my own magic word."

"What word was that?"

"*Trinkle.* I said, 'Jack, I've got an unusual opportunity here, and I just have a feeling you might want to discuss it.' I told him there was a prime slice of real estate in my district, and there were some possible deals, but I'd been given his name to talk to first. And of course he remembered my asking about that Charlie Ryder and West Carolina Development. So he took the bait. I acted like I knew more than I did, and he acted like he knew less than he did. But just dropping that Trinkle name made his eyes get real big. He knew, if I was asking *him* about *them*, I must know enough. So he told me he'd been working with them on some legislation. Then he said we better keep each other informed."

"What does that mean then, Marty?"

"I'd bet one of Rose's apple pies that the Trinkle family paid Jack Royce to get that road built."

"I'd about decided that, too."

"Then it's for sure. A couple other things. He's never heard of that Regency Atlantic. That must be a legitimate business deal. Next, I haven't found anything about who's against the road, and that's what you're looking for, isn't it?"

"Seems to be," Joe said. "But knowing for sure about the Trinkles means a lot. I wonder when anyone here would have heard about any of this."

"It would have been happening by last fall. That's when the Clean Air Act was written. So, what do I do now?"

"I don't know. I suppose we should just keep in touch."

"The Planning Commission of Jefferson County North Carolina is now in session." Either try to sound like Joe, or try to not sound like Joe. Steve would never find his own independent existence as a board chairman. He would always be under the shadow of the master.

Be patient, Grasshopper. Your time will come. In just fifty years, you too will understand the Gavel of Authority.

"Is this a quorum?" he asked.

"Probably not," Ed Fiddler said. They were the only two. Humphrey King was absent. Duane Fowler had not actually been to a meeting yet that year. In fact, Steve hadn't even met him yet. And now that Randy was off the commission—it was getting pretty sparse.

"Okay. We've got one item here, so we can discuss it, but we'll have to pass it on to the Board of Supervisors without any recommendation."

The only other person in the room was Roland Coates.

"Mr. Coates," Steve said. "Do you have any comments?"

"Just what I've said already. I want my zoning changed."

"Can't you tell us anything?"

"It's a business deal, and I'm not telling you my business."

"How can we do anything if we don't know what you want us to do?"

"I don't see that I need to," Mr. Coates said. "You can't vote one way or the other without your quorum, and its Randy's board that counts anyway."

"I guess that's correct," Steve said. So who needed an existence, anyway? "Mr. Coates, could you tell me one thing?"

"Maybe."

"This isn't going to be another grocery store, is it?"

"Where in tarnation did anybody get that idea? No, it isn't any grocery store or any kind of store and it never had been!"

"Okay. Thanks. I was just checking. And thanks for your help in the flood."

"Pleased to be of service."

"I really mean it, thanks. Um . . . anything else?"

"I don't have anything," Ed said.

"Okay. I guess we're adjourned. Thanks for coming, Ed."

"No problem. I was on my way to get some ice cream at the store and just thought I'd stop in."

The last sunset light swept across the porch. And Eliza was also sweeping the porch. The leaves that had opened so jubilantly were now aged, dry, humbled. Their moment of the circle was past, and they would return to the soil.

But not on her porch!

The leaves were like the weeds, only by misfortune appearing where they were not allowed. And like the river waters.

It was still troubling. She had sided against powers of wind and water that had greater right to do as they wished than she had to prevent them. And now she had a bond with the people of the town that she had not before.

She swept the leaves away. And any more that fell would follow!

"You're back early," Natalie said. She smiled. "You can say good-night to everybody!"

"Sure," Steve said. "I rushed through the entire agenda just so I could get here. Gosh, what a waste! Let's see—twenty-five-minute drive to Wardsville, five-minute meeting, twenty-five minutes back. That's nine percent efficiency. Or ninety-one percent inefficiency."

"My whole life is inefficiency."

"It depends how you juggle the numbers. I'll go say good-night."

Which he did, very inefficiently, but to great constituent approval. And then he was at his desk.

A little extra time. What to do? Ah yes, my dear Watson. The Trinkle case. He took the envelope out of the drawer.

There was a big difference between engineering specifications and contracts. They might both *look* like dense, intractable, boring piles of printouts. Well, actually they both were. But at least with engineering, either the sewer system worked or it didn't. With contracts there were always clogs.

Surely a reasonably intelligent person with enough Extra Strength Tylenol Headache Formula could figure it out. And after a while he had a few interesting points highlighted.

Regency would buy the Trinkle farm from the Trinkle Land Trust.

The contract was written August 20 of last year.

The contract was signed December 12 of that year.

The closing would take place within one year of signing.

The sale was contingent on many things, but most had been satisfied between the writing of the contract in August and the signing in December. Some others had still been open.

The contract was contingent on clear title to the land, with no outstanding lawsuits. That had been satisfied.

The contract was contingent on all taxes having been paid. That had been satisfied.

The contract was contingent on the commitment to complete Gold River Highway into Wardsville, and that one hadn't been satisfied.

Add it all together, and it sounded like over a year ago, sometrinkle, somewhere, had high expectations of a complete Gold River Highway.

And Regency had trusted them enough by December to sign a contract—with a contingency. Trust, but verify.

He put the papers back into the envelope.

Mr. Phelps, this tape will self-destruct in five seconds.

September 19, Tuesday

"What's on your mind, Joe?" Gordon said. "Because I hope you've got over all that other."

"I haven't."

"Oh, I wish you had. There's nothing to it, Joe, and you'll be better off to give it up. Nothing's changed since summer."

"I know who's behind the road, and how it got this far," Joe said.

Gordon settled his whole weight into his chair, ready to be aggravated. "There's always tomfoolery when the state does anything, and I don't care much about it. Last time you were claiming someone shot Wade Harris, and that's what I don't want to hear about."

"I came to ask you one thing. I want to know what you and Dr. Colony are so worried about anybody uncovering."

"I'll tell you it's police business, Joe, and not your business."

"Does it have anything to do with the Trinkle family or the new shopping center?"

"No, it doesn't. And don't start quizzing me."

"Then just tell me."

"I'm not going to, Joe. I'm as elected as you are, and you can't come in here and demand me to answer questions."

"I can still call in the State Police if you won't do your job," Joe said.

"You've been saying that for months."

"The reason I haven't is you and Dr. Colony saying I shouldn't. It's time I knew if that's a good enough reason."

"Oh, all right!" Gordon was plenty aggravated. "It's Jeremy Coates."

Joe waited.

"You're making it worse than it has any right to be," Gordon said. "Jeremy went and got himself a gun, and he's been shooting out peoples' car windshields, and that's all there is."

"Why would he be doing that?"

"You'd have to ask him. It was Roland that brought him in here. Jeremy had shot at Randy McCoy's car, and Roland's, too."

"He must have had some reason."

"I guess it was about Roland selling his factory and Jeremy thinking he could stop it. I don't know, it's all mixed up. But I let him off when he said he wouldn't do anything else foolish. Now, Joe, you know what'll happen if outside police come in and look around. They'll be sure Jeremy shot at Wade and hit him, and he won't have any way to prove he didn't."

"Where was Jeremy that night?"

"I asked him and he said he was over in Asheville, where he lives."

"Why are you so worried for him? It sounds like he should be arrested."

"But not for killing Wade Harris. Roland thought right away that he had, and had me out to the factory to arrest the boy, and I had to calm Roland down and tell him that Everett Colony and I had both checked real well and there weren't any bullets in Wade or the car."

"You never did," Joe said. "You or Dr. Colony."

"Because there weren't any, and I didn't have to."

"Why's Dr. Colony part of this anyway?"

"He's the one who's so sure we shouldn't get outsiders involved."

"I wonder why he's so sure."

"I guess you should ask him."

Except he wouldn't give an answer. "Did anybody ever tell Randy any of this?"

"There's no need to. He got his car fixed, and he told Gabe it was just a rock that hit the windshield while he was driving, so that's what he thinks it is."

"While he was driving?" Joe couldn't keep the anger down. "He was in the car when Jeremy shot at it?"

"Nobody got hurt."

"He could have."

"But he didn't."

"But Randy asked you about finding a bullet?"

"He claimed he just found it out in his yard or such."

"You knew where the bullet was from," Joe said. "You should have told him."

"There's no need."

"Gordon, you're acting a fool." Joe said it as hard as he could, slapping him with the words.

"Joe, what good will it do anybody to put Jeremy Coates in jail?"

"Sounds like he should be, and you with him."

"And what would that do? Do you think that does anyone any good? And what happens after, with it in newspapers across the state, that Jeremy Coates murdered Wade Harris? People who've lived here all their lives accused of killing each other? If you try to call in the State Police, I'll fight you. I've asked what happens if you try by yourself to get them in here, without my being part of it. You'll have to get a judge to decide between us, and it might sound just as crazy to him as it does to me and as it would to anybody. I'm no fool. It's you that is. There's not everybody in the county who'd say you're still fit for the job you have."

"I'll do what I have to," Joe said. "Whatever people think."

"Oh, you're home!" Louise ran out into the hall. There was Byron dropping his lunch pail on the chair, and Matt right behind him.

"We're home," Byron said. "What's for supper?"

"Pork chops and rice. You must be famished. Are you hungry, Matt?"

"Sure, Grandma."

"Loading lumber into the saws all day," Byron said. "The boy's working harder than anyone."

"It's okay," Matt said, with his big smile. "It's more fun than patrolling Baghdad. I've never seen such a huge pile of furniture."

"It'll be a lot more," Byron said.

"How will Mr. Coates ever sell it?"

"He's trying, Louise! Let the man alone."

"I just wonder," she said.

"Doris says he was talking about opening his own store, up there in Gold Valley at the new shopping center."

"Don't you start that, Byron." But she didn't feel like arguing. "We've been through too much together to fight."

"Mr. Jarvis? Hi!" Use the happy voice. "This is Steve Carter, up in Jefferson County."

Short pause. "Well, Steve, good to hear from you. How are things going up there?"

"Very well, thank you." Try . . . Paul Newman, in *The Sting*. No, more like Robert Redford. "I had a few questions."

"Oh sure, Steve. I hope you've had some questions answered already?"

"Yes. I have. Thanks very much for asking. All I've got left are a couple of the technical ones I mentioned before."

"Just tell me what you want."

"I think I'm okay now with the traffic projections, and of course that was the big one. I guess just some more on the environmental impact. Oh, and how about the core samples? Just the data. You don't have to send me any dirt!"

Stupid joke.

"Ha! That should be no problem."

Jarvis is laughing at stupid jokes. That would mean he knows he needs to keep his friend on the board happy.

"Great. Now. Just between us. What would be the chance of getting anything changed? It would sure be a lot easier if it didn't have to be such a huge road."

"I understand." Longer pause. "Okay, between us, there is not any chance. We're working with traffic projections that were given to us, and we have to satisfy them. Those numbers require a road that size."

"And, um, just really between us. I mean completely off the record. Those projections are complete fairy tale."

Jarvis didn't pause. "Three bears plus Goldilocks. That's four lanes."

"Okay. Back in the real world. Supposedly, the grant was funded before the project was planned, so there was no telling back then if twenty million would be enough."

"Theoretically, that is true," Jarvis said. "If we hadn't known what the project was, there would have been no telling if that was enough."

So . . . if they had known what the project was, they would have known how much the grant should be. Too twisted.

"What if twenty million isn't enough?"

"We'd just redesign and build what we could. But, strangely enough, twenty million is exactly the right amount."

"Good evening, Ed," Randy said over the hedge, which Ed Fiddler was giving one last trim for the fall, which happened to be the time each year that Ed's homeowner policy came up for renewal. "I'm seeing just a little red and orange out there in the leaves."

"Right on time," Ed said. "Beautiful time of the year."

"It is that, it certainly is. Makes me think of homecoming."

"It'll be Hoarde County this year."

"I still remember that pass you threw at the homecoming game our senior year against Hoarde County," Randy said, nice and jovial.

"I remember it like yesterday! Those were the days, Randy. But I'm looking for a game this year, too. Your Kyle's got an arm."

It was all just a friendly chat between two neighbors, and friends, and if it did happen to leave Ed slightly more disposed to send in that renewal payment, that would be an added bonus. No need to actually mention the insurance—the letter from the underwriter would have already come and be sitting on Ed's desk, and Ed might have even sent in his payment just automatic without thinking about it. It just didn't hurt to be friendly.

"And Ed," Randy said, thinking Ed's promotion at the bank would make light conversation on an agreeable subject, "I guess you've gotten used to being vice-president now?"

"I'd been doing the job for years, working toward it," he said. "It's nice to finally get the title, as well."

"And the paycheck, I hope."

"That's been nice, too. Not that we're a big bank with big salaries, but it was a nice increase. Now, Randy, talk about being a small bank, I've got my eye on Gold Valley."

Randy caught his smile just before it fell right off onto the sidewalk.

"What are you thinking about that, Ed?"

"I'd like to get a branch out there in the new shopping center. Of course the real profit's in mortgages out there. If we had a loan office where people could see us, and got in with the developer—now, that could be some real growth."

"That's good to know. I'll be glad when it's all voted on and done with. I don't know what Everett Colony will do if they do build the road."

"Pack up and leave, probably. I thought he was doing that last spring."

"Leave town?"

"Since we're neighbors," Ed said, lowering his voice, "and I know it won't go any further. I did wonder if he was. He walked into the bank and took fifty thousand dollars out of savings. In cash. They had to call me down to approve it."

"Cash? Fifty thousand?"

"Then the next Monday he put it all back in."

"Of all things," Randy said. "When was that?"

"End of April. It was a Friday. I remember because it was the day they put up the list of starters for the football game and Kenny was listed as a receiver. He sure was excited."

"I remember Kyle telling me he'd made quarterback." He shook his head. "I wonder what Everett Colony was going to do with fifty thousand dollars in cash. And then he didn't do it."

"Next is talking to Dr. Colony," Joe said. "I'm not looking forward to it."

"Just to ask him about Jeremy Coates?"

They were back from their walk and were sitting in the kitchen. He'd made a point of taking walks together. Rose had made a point of sitting with him at night, and not cooking or sewing.

"He might know why Jeremy was doing what he was. But what I'd like to know is why Dr. Colony wants to hide it. He'll have some reason more than protecting the boy."

"There might be something else he wants to hide?"

"That would be my guess."

Then they sat, quiet, thinking their thoughts.

Sixty years side by side.

"Joe. You're being careful, aren't you?"

It was the first time she'd said that.

"Not much I can do." Then he thought better. "I am."

"What would happen if the State Police came?"

"I don't know. They might not find anything. Or they might find everything there is. It'll be opening a door and it can't be shut. I don't know what to do."

"It's a hard choice," she said.

"It's a hard choice."

October

October 2, Monday

Again, it was time. Eliza waited; Joe struck the table; the meeting had begun.

"Come to order. Go ahead, Patsy."

The names were called and answered. The first vote was taken.

Then Joe spoke. "Next is receiving public comment." She prepared herself to listen; there would be much to hear.

She had become familiar with this way of speaking. It was ritual speech, not what was used commonly. Each one spoke as if from their heart, as if what they said was well accepted and apparent, as if everything was one color. The rhythm of the words was ritual, the emotion hopeful or fearful, angry or thoughtful. In the first months Eliza had mistaken that the speaking *was* heartfelt; now she understood it was only ceremonial, for no one truly believed what was said; and everyone listening, and the speaker, understood that the words should not be thought of as truth.

There was some said about *The Factory* and *The Zoning*, and there was much said about *The Shopping Center*, and much more said about *The Road*, and the future and the past and jobs and values and life. Many spoke of *The Mountain*.

Ayawisgi.

Eliza listened, to what the speakers said, and to what was spoken through them. She heard the unheard voices and knew the unseen speakers and felt the conflict rising like a flood.

There would soon be violence.

What was her part? The Warrior said as always, but with increasing strength and anger, *Do not desecrate, do not defile, do not violate.*

Finally she closed her eyes and withdrew. The tempest was too great. She was only pulled back by Joe's voice, like gravel.

"We will continue with our agenda now."

This was the next ritual. Many statements of very obscure meaning, each followed by a few words by Louise or another, then a vote. And as always, she heard nothing.

"Eliza?"

"I vote no."

And she even smiled. Were the words as murky to the Warrior as they were to her? He offered her no guidance on any of them.

But then there was a discussion she did understand, in part.

"Now we have a request from Mr. Roland Coates for a zoning change for his commercial property on Hemlock Street in Wardsville. Could you describe this, Steve?"

"I could try."

There was already a weariness in the room, but those listening came awake.

"Mr. Coates is presently functioning under a special-use permit," Steve Carter said. "It allows him to operate the factory, but it does not allow any substantial changes to the size or use of the structures. Now, Mr. Coates, you'll correct me if I get any of this wrong?"

"I sure will." Roland Coates was watching, very awake.

"Okay. Mr. Coates is involved in some business deals where it might be necessary to make substantial changes. Due to the confidential nature of the deals, he can't specifically tell us what the changes would be. So the request will be to grant a new special-use permit. It would be for any industrial or commercial structure and use, with specifics to be added within twelve months. That's all correct?"

"That's what I want," Roland Coates said.

"Let me get this straight," Randy McCoy said. "We're voting to let Mr. Coates do anything he wants, and he'll tell us later what it is?"

"That's about it," Steven Carter said.

"Is that even legal for us to do?"

"I don't know. It doesn't seem like it should be."

Joe spoke. "This comes from the Planning Commission without a recommendation for or against."

"Right," Steve said. "We only had two members present, so we couldn't vote. By the way, Joe, do you think we could maybe get some new people on the commission? We have one vacancy and it seems like some of the other members aren't that interested."

"We'll put that on the agenda," Joe said. "We'll have to find someone. Now on this special use request, What would you say, Lyle?"

"Well, Joe." Lyle was such a funny man! "It's *special use*. You can kind of do what you want."

"Joe." This was Louise. "I think we should try, at least. I know especially in Mountain View that people are worried what might happen, but Mr. Coates has been here his whole life, and I don't think he'll do anything that would hurt anyone else. I don't think he's trying to fool anyone, either. I think it really is that he can't tell us."

Louise turned to look out at the audience. "And I'll say something else that might make people think twice about rejecting the request. Everybody knows Mr. Coates is all for Gold River Highway, but I just wonder about this zoning. Maybe if he got the zoning he wanted, he wouldn't need the road as much."

"How would that work?" Randy asked.

"I'm just sort of thinking it. It's not that I know."

"Or," Randy said, "maybe you do know but you can't say it, the same way Roland can't say it, either, and since Byron works there you might have heard some of what's supposed to happen."

"Oh, just never mind!" Louise said, with an anger that surprised Eliza. "I just think we should vote."

"Is there a motion?" Joe said.

"I move," Louise said. "Joe? What if it fails?"

"He would have to wait two years before he can apply again, unless there is a substantial change in the application."

"Would approving the road count as a change?"

"That would count," Joe said. "Is there a second?"

"I'll second," Steve said. "If we don't vote tonight, the Planning Commission will get it back."

"Go ahead, Patsy."

"Mrs. Brown?"

"Yes."

"Mr. Carter?"

"No."

"Mr. Esterhouse?"

"No."

"Eliza?"

Of course, it all meant very little. She only knew that for Louise, and for Roland Coates, it meant very much.

"I vote yes."

"Mr. McCoy?"

"Good gravy."

Randy seemed confused; Eliza had come to recognize this in him. Did he ever receive guidance?

"I guess the right thing, not knowing where we stand on the highway itself, is to vote . . . um, no."

It was a struggle for him to say this, but those listening had no struggle. Eliza hadn't seen this type of celebration at a meeting.

"That's two in favor, three opposed," Patsy said.

"Motion fails," Joe said. "And our last item is a report on renovations to this meeting room."

"Oh." Steve said this after a wait. "The plywood. I looked at it before the flood. I think we could take it down. I just didn't want to do it by myself. It's heavy."

"I'll have Kyle help you," Randy said.

"Anything else?" Joe said. "Then this meeting is adjourned."

"Now, Louise," Randy said, finding her there in her big coat at the back door, "I just want to say I do appreciate everything you said up there about Roland and his factory and all, and I just hate having to choose between Mr. Coates, who is such a pillar of our community, and my friends and neighbors, but it seemed like, with the votes we've had all going against Mountain View, they really deserved to have their way for once."

"I was just hoping so much we could get the zoning the way Mr. Coates wanted it," she said. "And then we wouldn't need that road."

"Do you really think it would have worked out that way?"

"It might have. Mr. Coates did say a few things to Byron that we're not supposed to let out. Now I don't know what to do! I don't want that new Regency place, with a big road running right out of town to it, and Byron is beside himself worrying that the factory's going to close down, and he's so worn out working these long shifts."

"I've been hearing about all that," Randy said. "It sounds like they're building the biggest pile of desks and bookshelves there's ever been."

"It's all just going into that warehouse in back," Louise said. "They can't sell it all. I just don't know what's going to happen!"

"I'm expecting Roland to express his disappointment to me," Randy said. "Maybe Everett will have a kind word, to make up for it." Then he noticed something out in the parking lot that took his mind completely off Roland and Everett and even the road. "Well, now, look at that."

Eliza was standing, straight as a telephone pole like she always did, and the young man who'd driven her to the meeting was sitting in his car, and the hood was up.

"She's having trouble?" Louise said. "Let's see if she needs help."

"She's got help. Don't you see who's there under the hood?"

Joe didn't even try fixing new cars. But old cars without all the gadgets, sometimes just the smell could tell what was wrong with them.

And he couldn't just walk past and leave them.

"Try it again," he said.

The boy turned the key.

Joe stood up and came back to lean in the window. "Pump, I'd say."

"Fuel pump?"

"There's no gas even getting to the engine. You got gas in the tank?"

"Yeah." The boy had his hair tied in a long tail. But the car had been taken care of properly.

"Had any trouble with the pump before?"

"No, but it's old. I was going to replace it."

"They go sudden like that," Joe said.

"Is that garage down the block open?"

"Not since the flood. You'd have to go to Marker to get it fixed, or Asheville."

"I can fix it. I just need a new pump."

"Might be that Gabe could get you one. Or the junk yard."

"Yeah. Okay. So I need to figure what to do now."

"Do you need a ride?"

"I can stay in town. I just need a ride for Eliza."

"Thank you," Eliza said. Joe Esterhouse closed the door for her and she watched him walk around to his own door. What hard work this truck had seen! It was written on the seat and the steering wheel and the doors how many miles there had been, and with what effort.

Joe sat beside her and started the engine. "Where do you live?"

"Do you know Cherokee Hollow?"

He only nodded. Then he began his driving.

She sat with him in silence. She could always see something of the interior of a woman or a man, but Joe Esterhouse was only a wall. He had always been that to her, from the moment she had met him. She had assumed there was anger behind the wall, at first, but now she couldn't tell at all.

"Where's Gulotsky from?"

There had been ten minutes of silence as she had tried to understand anything in him. Now he was looking into her!

"At first it was Ganolvsga."

"That's Cherokee."

"Yes. But too hard. A government man changed it so he could write it more easily."

Then he said, "Wind."

She was surprised! Did he really know?

"The wind blows. And I was Ayetsasdi. *Laughter!* No one knows those words anymore."

"There were still people speaking it seventy years ago."

"My parents did, and my husband too."

Then silence again. Dark, also. They turned from the paved road to the old road, and he slowed. There was no sign whether he had driven this road before.

"All the way to the end," she said.

"Not much back there."

"Just me!"

"You aren't with your husband now?"

"He died. Many years ago."

Through the last trees and to the stream, and the truck stopped. Joe got out and came around to her.

"Thank you," she said. "I'll be all right now."

"If you don't mind, I'll check inside for you."

This was an act of courtesy. She led him to the steps and to the door and opened it for him.

He had a flashlight, suddenly very bright, and he searched the whole room. This was more than courtesy.

"I will be all right," she said again.

He stepped forward to see better into corners. He was looking into her—deeply! But she wasn't fearful of him. The flashlight went dark, and it was very dark, and the moonlight filled the room very slowly.

"You're here alone?" he asked.

"Yes. But there isn't danger."

"I don't like that boy's fuel pump breaking."

She didn't understand. "Zach's car?" She lit the kitchen candle.

"You need to be taking care," he said. "At least until this road vote is over."

"The road." She could see Joe's face, for the first time since the meeting. "What power does it have? There is such anger and war over it."

"There's no trouble like there is with a road." He stared into the candle's single light. "Greed and fear and hate. And each one having his own way. Will you be voting no on it?"

"I don't know."

"You'll be safer if you do, and if you let people know it."

"Safer?"

He turned to look outside. The flashlight pushed aside the dark.

"What did you have planted?" His light had found the garden.

"Oh, everything! Here." She lifted the curtain to the pantry closet.

Joe turned back to the room and turned off the light. "Rose cans about that much."

"I've only finished. There is so much."

"Why do you say you're safe here?"

"I am safe." It seemed he would understand. "The Warrior. This is his place."

"Ayawisgi?"

"You . . . know?"

He nodded his head, not in agreement, but in acknowledgment of what surrounded them. "Ayawisgi, Warrior, that's what the word means. The mountain."

"The strength of the mountain. Its spirit. Its purpose. It is the Warrior, the Ayawisgi."

"Is that from your parents? They were Cherokee?"

"My father taught me. Do you know about the ancient spirits?"

"I know of them. They aren't right for churchgoing people."

"You think they don't exist."

"It might be they do." He walked out to the porch, to stare at the peak above them, pale under the moon. "There's evil behind this road."

"The Warrior is against this road."

"There's evil on that side, too."

She accepted Zach's ridicule, and even Jeanie's disapproval. She had never heard a man who understood in this way.

"The ancient powers aren't good or evil, they only *are*."

"No." He said it with certainty. "They'll be one or the other. And what's not good is evil."

"What is good?" She didn't believe him.

"Only the Lord's good."

Which Lord? He had said it simply, as if anyone would know what he meant. She remembered—at the funeral for Wade Harris—how she had felt.

"I don't understand."

"You should be careful, Eliza. Good night."

October 6, Friday

"You're home?" Louise went running into the front hall.

"We're home," Byron said, with Matt right behind him. "Both of us."

"Did Mr. Coates let you out early?"

"Mr. Coates just let us out, period," Byron said. "No Saturday work tomorrow, and half shifts next week, and Matt's laid off."

"Laid off? What's wrong?"

"It's okay, Grandma. The job was only for a few weeks."

"It's not okay." Byron stomped past them toward the television. "Mr. Coates is giving up, and that's what's wrong."

Louise went running after him. "Giving up?"

"That's what he said. Said he's run out of money, and he has a warehouse full he can't sell, and he's not going to make payroll for this last week."

Matt was in the kitchen and Louise was right by Byron. "You're not getting a paycheck?"

"The man's trying as hard as he can! But nothing's working out for him. He thought maybe he'd got one of the store chains to take a shipment, but it fell through. And there's more. He called me up to his office to talk."

"Just you?"

"Just me, except he wanted you to know. He said he talked to the people buying the factory to tell them how high production had been with all the extra shifts, and how that might prove they wouldn't need to expand the factory to get what they wanted out of it."

"What did they say back to him?"

"It just wouldn't make a difference. They want the road and they want the zoning and that's that."

"Oh, Byron!"

"And that's that with the whole shebang. At least we'll all get a rest now. And he says he'll get caught up on payroll as soon as he can."

"We'll make do," Louise said. "But what am I going to do with you?"

Eliza was silent. Zach beside her followed the old roads, circling the mountain. These were roads that had been before roads were driven, or ridden. They climbed: the road, the car, them; through the northern gap, and the vale of swift Galvquodi was beneath them

Now Galvquodi, the sacred, was called Gold River, and with the gold leaves and gold light, it was a good name. The whole world of the valley was gold and black, and the sun was far to the west.

They descended.

The road was never straight, and its distance was never in sight. But it continued and they followed it. When there were turns, Zach knew his way.

Above, the sun descended. The gold became dull and red, and the trees dark silhouettes, and the ridgelines just lines in the mist.

Ahead, a thick, rounded spire was above the trees, and the road curved to it. This crossroads was called Tyrol Church.

They reached it quickly and Zach stopped beside another car.

He opened her door for her and held her hand as she stood. Then they walked together.

Cornelia stood to meet them. All around stood stones.

"Thank you. Eliza."

"Cornelia."

"Thank you for coming."

"Of course!"

They sat on the stone bench, side by side. Zach withdrew, to his car, to wait.

"I don't know why—I needed someone."

"I do know."

"How did you feel?" Cornelia asked.

"How you are feeling now."

"Does it ever end?"

"It changes."

Cornelia led her the few steps to the stone that had Wade's name. "Today is our anniversary. Wade said we'd go on a trip." Then silence and growing dark. "This is as far as we got." Her finger touching the stone. "The end of the road. Why? Where does the road go? Here? Is this all? Does it really go nowhere?"

"Life doesn't end," Eliza said. She felt the cold of the questions and the mist all around her.

"But it has."

"It just becomes different."

"Then it isn't life. Life is talking to him and being with him."

Eliza only knew what she had been told, by her family, by the Warrior. But now it seemed hollow.

It had all become so cold.

She knew these churches and of the people who had built them, who had fought and buried the ancient knowledge. Now she stood in their shadow and fought herself with the knowledge she had.

"I don't know," Eliza said.

October 10, Tuesday

"Sue Ann, does it ever happen to you that you hear something, or see something, or both, and maybe you think there's something strange, or odd, at least, about it, or maybe you don't even, but it's just poking around back there in your brain, and you don't even know it is, and then all of a sudden, just for no reason, you figure it out or have some new idea about it, or just see it different?"

The two of them were cleaning up in the kitchen together after one of Sue Ann's wonderful dinners.

"No," she said.

"Well, I do," Randy said, "and in fact I just have."

"What was it?"

"It's about Everett Colony and Wade Harris." Neither of those was the happiest person to think about, and the combination even less so, but it was strange enough to mention. "And this is from something Ed Fiddler said. Everett Colony took fifty thousand dollars, cash, out of the bank on a Friday back in the spring, went to see Wade Harris that Sunday night, and came back to the bank Monday morning and put the money back in. And Cornelia said Wade didn't have a chance to tell her what they talked about, but it left him real thoughtful. And that Monday night was when he had his accident."

"What does that mean, Randy?"

"I wish I knew. But does seem strange, though, doesn't it?"

October 13, Friday

"Here they come!"

Louise came running up to the front of the salon to look out over Becky's shoulder, but she couldn't see anything over the people all up and down the sidewalk.

Boom, boom, boom.

"I hear them," she said, and pushed out into the crowd.

Oh, they needed something to cheer everyone up. She needed something!

The last week had been a disaster! Byron home at noon every day. He was at such aimless loose ends and grouchy by evening, she knew that wasn't going to work at all. So then she'd just gone to the salon for the mornings and been home with him afternoons, and that was hardly better. And Matt had gone home to Angie's, so it was just the two of them. Too bad he wasn't here to watch.

There they came!

Out from behind the post office, at the front, was Gordon Hite in his sheriff's car with the light flashing.

Whoop! whoop! to break a person's ears. Why did he have to do that?

Then three pickups loaded with hay bales and the homecoming court sitting and standing in them, waving and smiling. They were *so cute!*

After them were the cars and trucks pulling floats, mostly trailers with plywood cutouts of a Cherokee doing something mean to a lion, with students throwing candy from behind signs for Wardsville Drugstore or the Imperial Diner or whoever was sponsoring them.

And all the time the drums and trombones getting louder, and finally there was the band in their red and gold uniforms just like an army! Forty of them playing their hearts out as loud as they could.

Louise's heart was fluttering itself!

She waved her American flag as hard as she could.

Then there were the Boy Scout and Girl Scout troops, and the Future Farmers of America, and the 4-H club, and Grace Gallaudet in a car with the top down representing the founding family of Wardsville. And last was the fire truck with the whole football team sitting along the top and the cheerleading squad in front, and everyone on the sidewalk cheered their loudest.

What could be more exciting?

"I think that was the best ever," she said to Becky as the last of the parade turned the corner and headed up the hill to the high school.

October was going as hard as it could, every tree putting its whole heart into color, and not a cloud in the sky all day. And now it was dark, Randy was sitting on the forty-yard line, four rows up, and there were four big galaxies of stars on telephone poles at the four corners of the field, brighter than it had been at noon, and the sky blacker than midnight.

"There he is," Randy said to Sue Ann, pointing at the players galloping out from the locker rooms, and Kyle right at the head of them all.

"Cherokees, Cherokees, roar!" The crowd was on its feet doing just what the cheerleaders were telling them, and almost every person had on the school colors. Sue Ann had on her blue and yellow sweater he'd bought her when they were still just high school sweethearts.

They called out the names of the starters, and Kelly ran out from the other cheerleaders to give her brother a kiss on the cheek when they called his name, and the crowd thought that was so cute they gave the two of them another big roar, and Gordon Hite topped off the cheering with a whoop from his sheriff's cruiser siren. Then the band was striking up the national anthem and all the hats came off, and everyone was singing, and then there was the biggest roar of all.

"Hoarde hasn't lost yet this year," said a voice behind him.

Even Luke Goddard wasn't going to make a dent in this evening. "They haven't played Jefferson County yet," Randy said to him, and turned back to watch.

Hoarde County won the coin toss, and the Cherokee defense got down to business. They did a fine job of it, too, a good four and out, and then Kyle came pounding out, as confident and assured as an army general, with his troops behind him.

They didn't huddle on that first play. But right as they lined up, Kyle must have seen something he didn't like with the way the other team was set, or something he did like.

"He's calling an audible!" Randy almost couldn't believe it. Here it was the very first time they touched the ball, and the boy was dropping the play the coach had sent him in with and was calling his own. Jimmy Balt took off in motion to the right side.

"Hike!" The whole field heard him, and Jimmy was off like a shot, with half the Hoarde County defense after him, and the other half scrambling in over Kyle's line. It had been a good try, but he'd signaled too strong he was passing, and Jimmy was never going to get clear, and the pocket was crumbling.

Then Kyle swung left and let off with a rocket, and Kenny Fiddler was as wide open as a yawn on the forty-five, and the ball settled into his arms like a baby, and he was gone.

"There he goes, there he goes!" Randy was shouting in Sue Ann's ear, and Kenny was a bullet right down the sideline, and Hoarde County never had a chance in the world of catching him, and there wasn't a man within ten yards of him when he crossed the line.

The crowd went as wild as it should have after that, and Gordon was even whooping his siren again, which seemed a little excessive. The boys had Kyle up on their shoulders and the officials were waiting for the siren to stop.

But the siren kept up and the police car was moving, pulling away from the sidelines and out to the parking lot, and there were more sirens, getting louder as the crowd got quieter, and there were lights coming right up Hemlock. People were climbing up to the top of the stands to see what was happening on the street behind them, and Luke was pushing his way through the middle of them.

"The furniture factory . . . "

The words just came rippling down the stands, part spoken and part felt, and then part smelled, an acid, smoky smell that caught people like a rough branch rubbing their cheek on a dark walk.

"What is it?" Byron hadn't said hardly a thing, just listened, and Louise couldn't stand it.

"I'll be right there," he said finally, to the telephone. "I'm going out," he said to her.

"What is it?"

"Fire at the furniture factory."

"Well, I'm coming, too!"

"Then let's be going," he said, turning off the television, but he still gave her a minute to pull some fried chicken and sandwich supplies from the kitchen.

Luke was back down from the top of the bleachers, and he stopped just a minute next to Randy. "Fire, and a big one, and getting bigger even while I was watching."

Then he was gone and Randy looked over to Sue Ann. "I should probably go over to see, and maybe it'll help Roland for me to be there, as he'll be worrying about insurance as soon as he thinks of it."

"I'll stay here and watch the game," she said.

"That's exactly what you should do, and I'll be back by half time."

Byron had to park a block away from Hemlock, in Mountain View, there were so many cars everywhere, and fire trucks and police cars closer to the factory.

There were lights all around, too, especially at the high school.

"It's the football game," Louise said.

Byron didn't waste a second getting out and trotting off. Louise took her time following after him, a cooler in each hand.

When she got up to the factory, it didn't make sense at first. The red glow was in back. She could see flames spurting up and sparks flying, and spinning red and blue lights from the police cars and fire trucks. There was a big crowd, too, and lots of them in blue and yellow from the high school, and over all a terrible smell of smoke.

But the factory lights were on with people in and out the front door, and it didn't seem hurt at all.

Then Byron came running out the front door and was on his way around, and Louise caught up with him.

"Where's the fire?"

"The warehouse. The whole thing's going up."

She ran with him, her coolers bobbing on either side, to where the firemen had the crowd stopped.

"Oh my goodness!" The flames looked a mile high, throwing chunks and embers way up into the night, and painting the back of the building red. All of that, and the heat on her face and the smoke in her eyes, and Louise was mesmerized.

All three of the county's fire trucks were parked in as close as they could and the fire fighters were squirting water as hard as the hoses could, but the fire had the whole warehouse building covered.

"I think we'll have to let it go." The fire chief just shook his head. "We're going to get someone hurt soon if we stay in too close."

Randy was standing on Roland Coates' other side, and the poor man was jumping one foot to the other, mopping his forehead, going from one fit into a dozen.

"Just keep it from the factory! We can lose the warehouse—it's ruined anyway—just keep it back from the factory."

One corner of the burning walls fell in and launched a geyser of sparks like the Fourth of July, and they rained down on the factory roof.

"Watch those! Get that quick!" Roland went scampering off and had the closest fireman by the shoulder, trying to point his hose up to the roof, before Gordon Hite could pull him back.

"Keep the roof wet," the fire chief shouted, and the hose did turn and dowse the place the sparks had landed, but Roland was still too close and got a dowsing himself. He came back soaked and with his fire put out.

"They'll keep the fire away from the factory," Randy said to him. "It'll be safe."

"That's the whole month of production! Half a million dollars of furniture! And the lumber stock, too! All of it's gone!"

"Now, Mr. Coates, the insurance adjustor will be here first thing in the morning, and everything will be taken care of, and it's all covered."

"I know it's covered!" Roland was as bedraggled and dejected as a puppy having a bath. "It better be covered! I told you I wanted everything I could get for fire!"

"It'll be all right," Randy said.

"No matter who set the fire!"

'Who' was sort of what Randy was thinking himself. Especially with Mr. Coates so determined to have as much fire insurance as he could get.

It was a lot to think about.

"Grady!"

"Oh, hi, Louise." He sure looked exhausted. It would all be especially hard on him, being on the volunteer squad and working at the factory, too.

"How'd it start?"

"I don't know. But it sure did. The whole two months' work up in smoke."

There was a big crash and everybody jumped, and the warehouse roof fell in and the fire exploded out.

That whole inventory! So Mr. Coates wouldn't have to find anybody to buy it after all.

"Now, tell me if I can believe my eyes," Randy said, settling down next to Sue Ann. "That scoreboard says twenty-four to three?"

"And Kyle's doing so well," she said.

The last quarter was just starting, and even if the fire wouldn't be going out until it was good and ready, it was still less exciting than the Cherokees putting the finishing touches on their biggest game of the year.

"It'll be a busy day tomorrow," he said. "The flood, and now this. Fire and water, you could say."

October 14, Saturday

Steve looked around from the computer screen.

A bright yellow plastic wheelbarrow was winding its way across the floor, filled with envelopes. Attached was Josie.

"Here is your mail, Daddy."

"Thank you very much." He spoke as seriously as she had.

After the official transfer, and the exit of the vehicle, Steve took the big NCDOT Asheville envelope and peeked inside. Ah, yes. Environmental statement, nice and thick. And core sample data.

He'd been thinking about this data. They had supposedly drilled 150 feet into the mountain to see what it was made of. Not just any mountain would take a 130-foot cut.

In fact, not many engineers could really evaluate a cut that huge. NCDOT sure didn't do it routinely. And they'd been in such a hurry.

In Chapel Hill, though, was a man who could. Steve still had fond memories of his geology classes. Surely Dr. Lombardi would be pleased to answer a few questions.

It had been a busy day, just like he'd told Sue Ann the night before, with the adjustor coming up from Asheville first thing, and Roland needing all the calming down he could get. Now Randy was finally back in his armchair to get a little calming of his own.

And he needed all the calming he could get.

Most of the time, selling insurance was a straightforward affair, and he enjoyed doing it, and it gave him a heartwarming feeling to know that people had just the right coverage in case something did happen.

And if something should happen, then the check was in the mail right away. And even when there was some question about exactly what was covered and exactly what the loss had been, it usually got resolved, and even if the customer wasn't completely happy, Randy had never really seen the underwriter do anything but the best they reasonably could, under the circumstances.

But once in a blue moon, really, or even less, a case popped up where something wasn't straightforward. He'd even worked with Gordon and his force when the authorities should be involved, where there was fraud or worse involved, because insurance claims could mean a lot of money.

Not that even for a minute did Randy think Roland Coates would ever do anything that wasn't upright and proper. And while it was true that he had specifically asked about fire coverage, that didn't have to mean anything. But it was also true that he had a warehouse full of unsold furniture and a drawer of unpaid bills, as most people in town knew. All of that didn't have to mean anything, either, as coincidental as it had been. Surely anybody seeing poor Roland that night, and today, too, would see how truly torn up and beside himself he was.

And, well, Roland was no actor.

And, hard as it might be to imagine, Roland might be more upset than even just the warehouse burning would explain.

So Randy had had his little talk with the adjustor, the two of them just by themselves, and he'd said what he had, and he certainly hoped he'd done the right thing.

October 18, Wednesday

Steve was getting to like Kyle McCoy. The kid was hyper-courteous, but apparently he still liked to pulverize opposing football teams and basketball teams and anybody else who it was acceptable in polite society to maim.

And now they were on ladders directly under a hundred-pound piece of wood, removing the nails that kept it from falling on them.

"Do you know how long this has been nailed here?" Steve asked.

"No, sir. My father might but I hadn't ever noticed it myself."

355

The opposite corner was Julius Caesar, in a robe, with his hand up and leaves in his hair. That, however, provided no clue to what was in this corner—symmetry of design was conspicuously absent. The two scenes adjoining the plywood were pilgrims at Plymouth Rock, and some other character who was either Charlemagne or possibly Theodore Roosevelt, or even Marilyn Monroe, but probably not.

The last nail was coming out. Steve had his end loose, and then Kyle dropped the hammer and they were holding the whole thing by themselves.

"Here we go," Steve said, and slowly they stepped down the ladders and laid the plywood on the floor. "Wow. Thanks."

Kyle smiled, a pure clone of Randy. "Yes, sir."

Then they looked up.

"What is it?"

"I can't tell," Kyle said.

It was a profusion of jagged green lines and green triangles and other green shapes, squarely in the artistic tradition of the rest of the ceiling. But where the rest was supposedly realistic, in this section the realism overwhelmed itself by the great number of details in its small space. The result was in pure abstraction, accentuated by one straight, bold brown line through the middle.

"Maybe it's a Picasso," Steve said.

"More like Jackson Pollock," Kyle said.

"What?"

"I'm taking Art Appreciation."

"They teach Jackson Pollock at Jefferson County High School?"

"No, sir," Kyle said. "But I've been looking at books on my own at the library."

"It would be hard to throw paint at a ceiling." Steve looked up. "Does it say something?"

"I'll get up and see." At the top of the ladder, Kyle was inches from the ceiling. "It does, but it's hard to tell. 'TS40'? Or something. Way back in the corner. It's kind of scratched up."

"Oh, well. Maybe somebody knows." Steve lifted the edge of the plywood and leaned it against the wall. "I wonder what we should do with this. I'd hate to be arrested for stealing it." He had to laugh. "The sheriff would grab any opportunity."

"Yes, sir. You crossed him back during the flood and he'll remember that."

"I won't forget, either," Steve said.

"Is there anything else I need to do for you, Mr. Carter? Otherwise, I'll be needing to leave, now."

"No. That's fine. I'm meeting someone in a couple minutes anyway."

Joe parked his truck in the courthouse lot and walked in the back door and up the stairs. Steve would be waiting in the main room.

"Thanks for coming," Steve said, and they sat at the tables. "You probably want to just get to business."

"That would be fine."

"Okay. I've been finding a lot of stuff about Gold River Highway and the new shopping center. I think you need to know about it."

Such a young man. And smart, but he had sense, too. "Go ahead. And I'll tell you a few things."

"Okay. I've got a copy of the contract between the Trinkle family and Regency Atlantic. They signed it last year, and Regency says they'll only carry through with buying the land and building on three conditions—the taxes get paid, the deed is settled, and Gold River Highway gets built. The first two were settled, so that means that last year, both parties were expecting Gold River Highway to be approved by this December. You said you knew who had pushed it through the Assembly?"

"Jack Royce. It was the Trinkles that paid him."

"Paid?"

"That's how it usually is."

"Right. So you already knew how it happened?"

"Only some." But he still didn't know the important part. "Who'd be against the road?"

"Against it." Steve shook his head. "I don't know, beside everyone you know. Just that whole gang who've been against it since January. Everett Colony and his friends."

Since January.

"Are you okay, Joe?" Steve asked.

That was likely it. The weight of it came down on him.

"What are you voting on this road?" Joe asked.

"Uh . . . I don't know yet," Steve said. "Everyone wants me to vote yes. I just can't stand thinking what they'll do to the mountain."

"Tell people you don't know. Tell anyone who asks."

"Okay."

"Is there anything else you know?" Joe asked.

"I guess not. I know a lot more now about how NCDOT works, but that doesn't matter for this. Oh, I know. Joe, can you tell me anything about that corner of the ceiling?"

"Oh, that." Joe turned to look. It was about the way he remembered from thirty years back. Somehow, looking at it took some of the weight back off.

"What is it?"

"It's a Bible verse."

"It is?" Steve stood to look at it closer. "Why was it covered?"

"The board decided it wasn't fitting for the courthouse."

"Oh. Because it was religious?"

"That's what they said. I didn't see it was a problem."

"You voted against uncovering it."

"Just so you others wouldn't have the trouble of deciding what to do with it."

"Right. What is it?"

"He knew right off," Steve said to Natalie.

"So what was it?"

"I thought it said *TS40*. But it was Isaiah 40. It was an *I*, not a *T*."

"What does that say?"

"He recited it. From memory." Steve held up Max's Sunday school Bible. "Check this out. 'A voice is calling, "Clear the way for the Lord in the wilderness; Make smooth in the desert a highway for our God. Let every valley be lifted up, And every mountain and hill be made low." ' "

"Why would they have that on the courthouse ceiling?"

"It was supposed to be about founding Wardsville in the wilderness. Isn't it weird, though? We uncover it right before we vote on building a road over Mount Ayawisgi?"

October 20, Friday

"Louise! Louise, come out here!"

She did! She came flying out of the kitchen into the hall, and there was Byron standing at the front door with his eyes wide open and his mouth open even more.

"What is it?"

"You won't believe it!"

By now, she'd believe anything. When he was home, all Byron could talk about was what a frenzy Mr. Coates was being in every minute—up and down, hot and cold, and driving himself to distraction.

"Just tell me!" she said.

"Mr. Coates called us all up to the front, the ones who were there, just when we were finishing up for the day. He looked as bad as I've ever seen him. And he said, 'I've got bad news, terrible news, and I don't even want to tell you, but I will.' It was only a dozen of us there with him—that's all that were working today. And he said, 'The insurance company and the State Police have been asking questions and looking around, looking at the warehouse and how the fire started and who might have thought to do it.' "

" 'Thought to do it'? Oh, Byron. I've been so scared that Mr. Coates had done it."

"I think that's crossed a few minds. But that's not what he said. 'So they just told me,' he said, 'the police want to arrest Jeremy for it.' He couldn't hardly say Jeremy's name."

"Jeremy!"

"Jeremy. And sounds like the boy got wind of it, because he's gone."

"What do you mean, gone?"

"Not at his place in Asheville, not been at his job all week, no sign of him."

"Why did they ever think it was him?"

"It sounds like it was the insurance company asking questions first, and they put the police onto him, by what Grady and Doris are saying."

"Poor Jeremy." It was terrible. Somehow, it didn't seem like a surprise. But it was so terrible. Jeremy running away, and how must Mr. Coates feel?

"And the worst of it," Byron was saying, "is that I think Mr. Coates knew it all along."

And it was because of that terrible road!

"There it is."

Yes, it was. Eliza stood with Steve Carter beneath the strange markings. They confused her.

"I don't understand it," she said.

"Right," Steve said. "I had to ask Joe. He remembered it from before it was covered up."

It had seemed important to uncover it. But now, it was not what she had thought it would be. "Does it have a meaning?"

Zach was leaned back in a chair, waiting for her, but also looking with her at the ceiling.

"Yeah," Steve said. "It's from the Bible. It's actually a verse about making a road. 'Every valley be lifted up and every hill be made low.' "

"What is the road for?" she asked.

"Well, for God. 'Make a way for the Lord' is what it says."

Bring down a mountain. For a road! Two Powers in opposition, in absolute conflict.

"Randy McCoy, good evening."

"Randy? It's Louise."

Randy put his head down on his hands. He'd been expecting the call, not that that meant he was ready for it.

"How are you, Louise?"

"Well, better than I was a little while ago."

"What can I do for you?"

"I'm calling to see what you've already done."

She didn't sound angry. "Only what I had to," he said.

"Did you tell your insurance people that Jeremy started the fire?"

"That's what I had to do."

"Oh, Randy." No, she wasn't angry. Her voice in the telephone sounded just so sad. "Did he?"

"I think he did, Louise."

"And now he's run off?"

"I guess I've heard that, too."

"You could have called me, Randy. If I'd known before Byron did— maybe I could have been more ready. These weeks have already been so hard on him."

"I wanted to call. The police and the insurance investigator told me not to. They didn't want word to get to Jeremy."

"But why did he do it?"

"He was thinking it might break up Roland's deal to sell the factory. I won't say that makes much sense, but it seems more and more people don't use any sense in what they do."

"How do you know what he was thinking?" Then she said, "And how did he know to run off?"

"Maybe somebody talked to him." The week had been hard on Randy, too.

"You two were in school together, weren't you?"

"We were, Louise, and we even played basketball together."

"Then good night, Randy."

"Good night, Louise."

October 23, Monday

"I didn't say that!" Steve had the *Wardsville Guardian* in his hand. "I didn't say it!"

"I know you didn't," Natalie said. " 'People in Gold Valley are mighty worked up about the road, Steve Carter said.' You couldn't talk that way if you tried."

" 'Mighty worked up'? Good grief. He asked how I was planning to vote, and all I said was that I knew most people in Gold Valley were strongly in favor. That's all I said."

"He's translating so people in Wardsville can understand."

"Whatever. So it says I'm voting for it, Joe's voting for it, Randy's voting for it, Louise is undecided, and Eliza could not be reached but might be voting for it." He looked at the headline, *Unpopular Gold River Highway Passage Nearly Certain*. "I didn't say I was voting for it. Natalie— my faith in the press has been shaken."

Then he thought about Joe. "I'm supposed to tell people I haven't decided yet."

"Now, that's not what I said," Randy said, and it had been worth a walk to the newspaper office to say it. "Luke, you know I said that many of my constituents in Wardsville were against the new road, and some were for it, and that I was still listening to their comments."

"That's what you said, but a good reporter goes past what the person says to what he means. Especially if the person's a politician."

"That sounds like a bad reporter to me, if it means putting words in my mouth that I never said."

"I didn't say *you said* you were voting yes; I just said that you were voting yes. You as much as said it anyway. You said many of your *constituents* were against it, so it's obvious you were hinting that you couldn't say *you* were for it, even though you were. And why would you hint that you were if you weren't?"

"I won't even try to understand that." He wouldn't have even if he had tried. Randy was so tired of the road! "Do you know how many calls I've got since this came out?"

"They have a right to call you. Now look, Randy." Luke hadn't even put his feet down off his desk. "After Steve Carter was so upset by the road plans back in July, and Louise Brown was so upset by the shopping center plans back in August, most people are thinking the road's as good as dead. But I don't think it is, and as an unbiased news service, I don't want my readers to be misinformed. They need to be making their voices heard and not be assuming it's all over. Whether they're against it or for it."

"Whether they're against it, is what you mean. And they aren't all against it. And by this article, I'd say you've told the whole county that it'll pass unless someone does something about it."

What an amazing e-mail.

Steve read it, and read it again. He started fishing through the links.

What a great e-mail.

Dr. Lombardi was the smartest man on the planet.

Everything was there. Calculations—elegant, complete, indisputable. It was all perfect.

The man knew these mountains so thoroughly, he hardly even needed the core samples.

Based on this e-mail, the proposed 130-foot cut for Gold River Highway over Mount Ayawisgi was . . . doubtful. Impossible, possibly. The rock structure was fragmented and might not support it. A forty-foot cut was the maximum anyone could be sure of. Deeper than that would take a lot more sampling and analysis.

Forty feet would mean . . . Steve started his own calculations. The grade would have to be more than the allowable maximum. It would be too steep. And that would mean . . .

Steve leaned back in his chair. His first thought was to call Jarvis. But the state was not committed to the project until the Jefferson County Board voted. If he called now, the project could collapse. And the 130-foot cut might actually be possible—it was just no one knew.

If he waited until after the vote, then the state would be committed, within the budget. But they might have to reengineer the whole thing and just build the best thing they could with the money they had. And probably that would be the road they should have planned in the first place.

But they really wouldn't know what they were voting for in December—Big Road or Little Road. Should he tell anyone?

He'd talk to Joe at the November meeting.

October 25, Wednesday

Bright sun, just up to the treetops, burning the mist. Joe breathed the morning in, warm for October.

Rose was feeding the chickens. He watched her from across the garden, mostly stalks and brown but for a few vines. The tree shadows cut black through the haze low by the stream.

Sounds cut through the air, too.

Just the scratch of the feed tossed in the coop and the hens pecking, and the stream behind. Hens sounded put out and bothered.

Not a breath of wind.

Joe took a step toward her.

Sun and shadow striped the ground, dark and light, mixed everywhere. Tricky, and hard to see plain.

The chickens gabbled and clacked and Rose dropped the cup back in the feed bag.

"Step forward," Joe said. "Slow."

She did, not looking back, but just at him.

"Keep on, and slow."

She took five steps and he nodded, and she looked back and saw the copperhead.

"Just let it be and keep an eye on it," he said.

He walked to the barn slow and steady, and then back to where he'd been, and Rose stock still, and the snake close by the chickens, and them fussing all out, skittering around the coop, beside themselves and keeping its attention.

They squawked loud and the snake shuddered, and the echoes died, and Joe set his rifle down from his eye. He went to his wife and took her hand, and they went together back to the house and left the enemy dead, to clean up later. It was still twitching.

October 30, Monday

"Now, what would you think of doing this on a computer?" Randy stared at the tax ledger, which seemed to get bigger every year, and it was already more than big enough.

"I wouldn't complain a bit," Patsy said. "We just have to buy the computers and that special software."

"Which was special expensive. And then type all this into it." Randy opened the book. "Which would take about forever. And no matter what those salesmen say, it doesn't work right the first time, or the second time. Anyway, it's just four times a year. Two times to send out the tax bills, and two times to list the unpaid taxes in the newspaper." At least they had Patsy's computer to type up the newspaper ad, instead of handwriting it like they did not that long ago. "So let's get this show on the road."

He started skimming the pages, checking the balances. The sixth page was the first stop.

"Tax parcel 01-0235, 4260 Coble Highway, Marvin and Hazel Garner, $324.62."

"Six hundred what?"

"Three hundred twenty-four and sixty-two cents." And on they went, page after page.

They kept it up until lunch, which was as far as they were going for the day because Randy had appointments in the afternoon. "We'll finish Tuesday," he said, putting a bookmark in where they'd stopped. "I'll tell Luke we'll have it for him Wednesday morning."

"That'll be a record, Randy. Finishing in two mornings."

"Guess we're just getting good at it. Who needs a computer anyway? You know, I wonder if it's less names than last time. Do you have the last ad somewhere?"

"It's in the back of the book."

"Now isn't that smart, to keep them in there." Randy opened to the back, and there were the last few ads—the one from May and the two from the last year. He took out the November ad from a year ago. It was the whole page, all those names and numbers. He looked at the back of the ad, which was the front of the newspaper.

"Well, look at that." It was the front page story on Mort Walker dying in his barn. "A year ago."

"That's done." Joe put himself in the chair by the door to pull off his boots. Mud an inch thick on them. "Don't think it'll freeze hard."

"Are there apples left?" Rose handed him his house shoes.

"Some."

"I'd be glad for a few more."

"I expect you'll get that." He had his clean shoes on but he stayed in the chair. He just didn't feel like standing up.

"I'd make a pie for the church dinner," Rose said.

"That'd be nice."

Rose was raising a racket washing the pots. Joe thought over tomorrow and what there was to do.

"Might look at the fences in the morning."

"What's that?" She turned back to look at him.

"Might look at the fences," he said. "Leonard's putting his cows down that way next week and they'll be right into the south field if they can be."

She was back to her clatter, and he leaned his head against the wall.

"Are you all right, Joe?"

"Just tired."

He got himself up on his feet to look out the window.

Clouds were coming in over the moon. Thin wisps of them up high, and a haze just thin like steam down closer to the ground. The smell of it had the autumn smoke in it and a small part of roots and pond water.

"Doubt it'll frost at all tonight."

"What about rain?" Rose asked.

"Not tomorrow or next day."

Still a bunch of pots piled by the sink. Always were after she'd been canning. He put his head down to see the thermometer outside the window better.

The window cracked loud in his ear. Then he felt his cheek stinging. There was a big loud clang of pots.

What fool thing was happening?

He straightened up to look at the window. There were just a few pieces of it left in the frame. Most of it was down on the floor in a mess.

"Joe . . ."

He looked around to Rose. Two pots on the floor that she'd dropped. She was staring at him, eyes open big.

Something was wrong.

She was leaned on the counter funny and she started drooping over.

He just started to move and she hit the wood floor, on her side, all bent and haphazard. He got up close to see her looking up at him, eyes wide and red staining her clothes.

"Joe . . ." He could hardly hear her.

"I'll take care of you," he said.

"What happened?"

"Don't know." She was sheet white. "I'll get you to help."

He left her there while he took the phone and called the neighbor. He didn't even know who answered.

"Rose is bad hurt and I'm taking her to the hospital in Asheville." It was all he said and then he hung up.

She was just looking at him and her mouth was open and she was breathing heavy but slow. He picked her up and held her right to him and carried her out the kitchen door.

He set her in the front seat of the truck and put the seat belt on her to hold her up and then started up the dirt road toward the interstate, driving as fast as he could.

It was a road he'd driven all his life. It was hard to think.

Just on the interstate flashing red lights came up behind. He didn't slow down, but the sheriff's car came up beside him. Gordon was on the passenger side with a deputy driving, and he just pointed ahead. Then the sheriff's car pulled on in front with lights still flashing and Joe followed right behind.

Rose wasn't moving, just staring at him, until her eyes closed.

"I'll take care of you, Rose. Don't be worrying." And he followed the red and blue lights, not so sure where he was going.

His own breathing was getting hard. The lights ahead started moving one side to the other, and the steering wheel felt like it was shaking. The truck bucked a minute, then was driving smooth again.

Then there were more flashing lights and a siren. Gordon was back beside him, waving him to the side, and he did go to the side and the truck was bucking again over gravel, and then it slid over more to the side, leaning, and there was a harder buck, and then he picked up his foot off the pedal and sat, suddenly all still but the sirens screaming. The lights were right up around him. Both doors of the truck opened and hands were reaching in, and he stood up out of the door and got pulled over into the back of the ambulance all bright and crowded and with Everett Colony's voice. And Rose laying out straight and wrapped in a white sheet, and hands still holding him, and the sirens and bumping and Rose white as the sheet, and no idea where he was or what was happening.

October 31, Tuesday

"Randy McCoy, can I help you?"

"Hi, Randy. I'm Marty Brannin. I think we've met a few times?"

"Sure, Marty. Sure we have, and I remember you." Randy took a breath. "And I guess I know why you're calling."

"About Rose Esterhouse."

"I'll be glad to tell you everything I know."

"I've read the papers."

"The Raleigh paper?" That would be a surprise, that it had got that far.

"The Asheville newspaper had the most, but it's in the paper here, too."

"Well, then, this is what else I know. Rose is out of danger, but they're not sure how much she'll recover. But I was down in Asheville this morning and you could worry about Joe as much as Rose. He's taking it real hard."

"Did you talk to him?"

"Um, well, not really," Randy said, and it was still very hard to even think about. "I was there in the room with him, but he wouldn't say a thing. Well, to tell the truth, Marty, I'm not sure he knew who I was exactly."

That got a long quiet out of the telephone.

"I'm sorry to hear that."

"He's eighty-one years old, Marty, and it's been a real shock to him."

"Then maybe I'll try seeing him myself."

"Give him a while."

"I will. The papers say the police are looking for a man who set a fire up there last month."

"Jeremy Coates, that's right. Jeremy's been real upset about our new Gold River Highway project, and he's been trying to stop it however he could, and the sheriff here's pretty convinced he's the one they want."

"I see. Well, they'll get him soon, I'm sure. Thanks, Randy."

November

November 6, Monday

It would be time to start soon and they didn't have the first idea what to do. Louise just hated having the meeting tonight, the four of them with an empty chair in the middle!

And Gordon standing guard in uniform by the door.

"I'll go ahead and start," Randy said, next to her. He was probably vice-chairman—she didn't remember. "Come to order. The Jefferson County North Carolina Board of Supervisors is now in session, and I'll be chairman for the evening. We'll approve the minutes."

"Patsy has to call the roll," Steve said.

"Oh, of course. I'm sorry, Patsy. Go ahead."

"No, don't," Louise said. "I can't bear it."

Randy looked up and down the table. "Patsy, let's just say we're all here except Joe is absent."

"Thank you," Patsy said.

"And now the minutes," Randy said.

It didn't seem right to be having the meeting at all. Louise closed her eyes to not see the audience.

"And next," Randy said, "I'll just tell everyone that Joe and Rose's daughter Mary is up from Florida and I talked to her yesterday. She'll be staying with them as long as they need her, and she said they'll be going back from the hospital to the farmhouse this week. And Sheriff Hite wants everyone to know that his office is working real hard to find the person responsible."

He didn't say who that was, but they all knew. Poor Mr. Coates. Byron hadn't seen him in the factory all week, he was so broken up about Jeremy.

"And I guess now we'll listen to public comments."

Louise closed her eyes. She didn't want to see the faces.

"Everett Colony, 712 Hemlock in Wardsville. I've been telling you all year how this road will destroy our neighborhood. Do you see how it has? It's ripped this town apart. Neighbors split, families split. It's set brother against brother and father against son. . . ."

"Roger Gallaudet, 715 Jackson Street in Wardsville. It's not the road that's done all this. It's us. It's only uncovered what we always have been. Build it or don't build it. Just get it over with. . . ."

"Jim Ross, 4500 Eagle's Rest Drive in Gold Valley. Build it. That mountain's been a wall between two halves of the county, and the road will tear it down. . . ."

"Annette van Marten, 2970 Lofty Ridge Road in Gold Valley. I thought I wanted the road. But after all this fighting, I've gotten to where I'd rather have a wall between me and Wardsville. . . ."

It was starting to all run together.

"Eileen Bunn, and I own the Imperial Diner in Marker. There must be so many better things to do with all that money. . . . Ed Fiddler, 713 Washington Street, and I say build that road as fast as you can if this county isn't going to shrivel up and die. . . . I'm Emma Fiddler, and I say just leave us alone and build that road somewhere else. I'll agree with Eileen Bunn, there must be better ways to spend that money. . . . Zachary Minor, Junior. I'm the proprietor of Zach Attack Whitewater Rafting. What gives any of you the right to tear down a mountain or fill a valley with your stupid huge houses and parking lots? . . . Annie Kay Rout, Cherokee Hollow Road. We have everything we need already. We don't need to truck in food from a thousand miles away. I moved to Jefferson County to get away from waste and pollution. Please don't do this!"

It kept going and going.

"Humphrey King. I hope more than anything we don't get that new shopping center. All of you here, if King Food hasn't been good enough for you and you want something else, I promise I'll make it better. I'll even knock out the wall on one side and that'll make room for three more aisles, and I'll get whatever you want in there. Because if a big new store opens, I'll be closed down in six months, and what will I do then? I've lived here my whole life with all of you."

"Richard Colony. Everett was right about splitting families. Well, if they're split, then the damage is already done, and we might as well go ahead and build it. The fire's already been kindled, and not building the road won't put it out."

"Don't talk about fire!" Louise couldn't listen anymore. She had to say what she had to say!

"I didn't want to come tonight because I didn't want to listen to hours of meanness and cutting each other, and I'm not going to put up with any more of it.

"When Wade Harris died, how did everyone act? Terrible. The only thing anyone could think of was what it meant for themselves and Gold River Highway. When we asked Steve to be on the board, people said terrible things about him.

"We've been through too much now! We've been through the flood and we did everything we could to hold this town together and we just barely made it. And that's thanks to Steve, especially, but all of you. Did you see what we can do together? But just the next board meeting, people who were side by side through that were right back to their fighting and being hateful.

"And then the fire! That's put more than a hundred people out of work, and everyone here is affected by it.

"And now this. I don't know why anyone would have shot a gun into Rose's kitchen, no matter what anyone says or thinks. I know it can't be that they wanted to hurt her.

"It's an attack on all of us! It's like all of us have been hurt."

The pain of it was almost too much.

"We have been hurt," she said. She looked right at Richard Colony. "You said the damage is already done. Well, I say we can undo it.

"Now, if this road and shopping center are so important that all you can say is that Gold Valley is selfish and wrong for wanting their road, or Wardsville is selfish and wrong for not wanting it, or anybody is wrong for wanting or not wanting that shopping center . . ." She had to swallow. "Well, it isn't wrong to want those or not, and I'm talking to myself as much as to any of you. What's wrong and selfish is cutting off friendships we've had for years. Now, you look around here before you say something, and think real hard about what you're going to say before you say it."

And then she folded her arms and shut her mouth and stared up at the ceiling and not at anybody else.

"Well," Randy said after about three minutes of silence. "Maybe we should go on, and I'm sorry if any of the rest of you had meant to say something but got scared out of it, and I know it isn't really right for board members to intimidate the audience like we've sort of done here." He waited a few more seconds.

"But we do all know she's right," he said.

November 9, Thursday

"Good afternoon, Gordon, and I'm just stopping in for a minute."

Gordon looked up. "Do you need something, Randy?"

It was assurance, really, that Randy was looking for, but it wouldn't do to ask for that, at least here. "Well, if there was any news about Jeremy, I would be real glad to hear it, and I'm not trying to be a pest, but I had a question or two about the fire at the furniture factory, since I'm still trying to get all the insurance forms finished up, and I thought I'd stroll down here and ask."

Even though the forms actually were all finished up, and had been for a while, but it seemed the best way to ask about Jeremy Coates.

"There's nothing to say."

"Well, even that's something to say, I guess. There really isn't any news at all about Jeremy?"

"Nothing."

"And all that anybody can do about the fire, or the shooting, is to find him, isn't it?"

Gordon hadn't moved a bit, leaning back at his desk, staring at Randy with about the same feeling a person might have for their alarm clock going off at six o'clock in the morning.

"What else would there be?"

It seemed to Randy like that was really Gordon's job, to know what else, but maybe there truly wasn't anything. "Well, I don't know, but the underwriter for Roland's insurance policy is looking at that million-dollar check they had to write, and I expect he'd like to have a word with Jeremy, at least."

"The State Police and the FBI are looking for him," Gordon said. "Nothing I can do. He's probably out of the state now anyway."

"I'm sure they'll find him. Gordon, just putting a few things together, from the newspapers, and Roland, I'd like to ask you a question."

"Well, go ahead."

"It was Jeremy that shot at my car, wasn't it?"

"Oh, why can't that just be let go of? Yes, it was."

"Now, why didn't you tell me?"

"Jeremy was in enough trouble with Roland."

"You should have told me."

Gordon hunched back in his chair. Everett thought we shouldn't."

"Everett Colony?"

"He thought we might cause a lot more trouble if we did."

"I guess I should talk to him. And I'm wondering, too, if you've talked with Joe any this last week."

"I haven't."

"I guess I should do that, too," Randy said.

Steve stepped out of his car. The dirt was soft.

He'd pulled to the side, but on this road, that was still the middle. Nobody would be along here anyway.

This was the curve. There was no sign of the crash anymore, six months later. Just some scars on the big tree. If there was anything else, it was under the leaves.

The trees were bare and the leaves a crunchy foot deep.

Steve walked around the bend and turned to look at the tree. A person coming up the hill would be facing this way, just as he slowed to take the bend. That tree was right in front of him.

It was a tight bend. Wade would have slowed way down to take it, no matter how much of a hurry he was in. Instead he went straight over the edge. Why?

Coming down the hill—if he had taken the bend too fast, maybe he could have rolled and ended up back there. It was hard to see how that would happen.

Gordon Hite said Wade had been coming down the hill. Ergo, Wade had really been going up the hill. That was one thing for sure—if Gordon said something, it was wrong.

Looking at the scene, it was obvious that Wade had gone straight over the edge.

Steve walked to the edge. There was another tree, right by the road. He leaned against it, looking down the winding dirt road. Wade would have come right up there, right at him almost. Then right on by, inches away, straight over.

This was where a person would have stood if he'd wanted to watch the whole thing. A person would be looking right into the car, right at Wade.

No, no, no!

A person could have been behind the tree, so Wade wouldn't have seen him. Steve moved back, behind the tree. Right there.

Why would the person have been there that day? Why was Steve here today?

Because it was all so obvious, only Gordon Hite couldn't see it.

Steve did not shoot guns. He knew how they worked, though. He stood there a minute, put his arms up, and pulled the trigger. He felt the recoil, heard the report. Then he turned to his right—careful, the ground was uneven—and put his hand through the leaves at just where the casing had landed. He patted the ground, back and forth, feeling for it.

It was all just his imagination.

All but the cold, hard cylinder he touched. An inch long and gray.

Randy looked in Everett's office, and Everett was there.

"Excuse me, Everett."

"Randy."

"She said to come on back."

"That's fine. Sit down."

Randy did sit, and he didn't know just how to start. But it wasn't going to be fine. "It's about Joe, of course."

"Of course."

"Everett, I don't know how much you can tell me, and I know it might be a while before any of us would know anyway, but I'm just asking about Joe and the board, and if you have any thoughts about when he might be back to work with us."

"He won't be."

Randy nodded. "Can you tell me how he's doing? Or Rose? How will she be?"

"Rose won't recover. Not at her age and hurt as bad as she was. She'll be in bed a long time. Maybe she'll be walking again eventually. But I told them not to take her home. They need to find a place where she can be cared for. And Joe, too. That farm's no place for either of them."

"That's real bad news, Everett."

"Sometimes it is."

"I guess that's so." It was a feeling like an earthquake, in a way, having someone as absolute and dependable as Joe suddenly taken away from them, and Randy felt himself reeling. And that might have made it easier to blurt out the next question. "And, Everett, excuse me also for asking, but why didn't you let Gordon tell me about Jeremy? Especially about shooting at me?"

"Oh, that."

"It's a serious thing, really, and I had a right to know. He shot Roland's car, too. Gabe told me his windshield got broken just like mine."

"That's why I told Gordon to keep it secret," Everett said. "Because of Joe."

"Now, I don't understand that."

"Joe Esterhouse has had an obsession all summer about the road! He was fantasizing about murders and attacks and saying he'll call in the State Police to investigate."

"Murders? Now, Everett, you aren't talking about Wade Harris, are you?"

"No, I'm not. But Joe was."

"Joe was. . . ."

Of course. Especially since the shooting at Joe's farm, maybe even before that, Randy had had his own thoughts. It wasn't a surprise, really, that Joe had been thinking the same. But hearing Everett say it did make it seem more real, despite that he was meaning the opposite.

"And they would have latched on to Jeremy right away," Everett said. "He wasn't trying to hurt anyone, just scare people into voting against the road."

Randy had to take just a moment to think all that through. But it didn't take long to fill himself up with more questions. "But it might be that Jeremy did shoot at Wade."

"If he did, it wasn't to hurt him."

"And what about Joe and Rose?"

"I don't think he meant to hurt them, either."

Randy was having a hard time continuing the conversation. "Well, maybe," he said, "but that's really up to the police. Now, why are you taking such an interest in Jeremy, anyway?"

"Someone has to. Gordon Hite doesn't have the sense."

"I don't think that's the reason." He took a deep breath. He might not have said it, but Everett was having quite an effect on him. "I think you've been afraid they'd find out that you tried to bribe Wade Harris."

Everett Colony was stock still, and then his mouth dropped a little, and then opened wide, and then narrowed.

"How did you . . . Ed Fiddler. He had no right to tell you anything."

"Well, he did drop a bit of information, but it was Cornelia Harris that really got me started thinking, mentioning you went out to see him that night."

"I thought he didn't say anything to her. No one brought it up."

"It's just my own thinking, and I was even ashamed to have thought such a thing. But, Everett, I'd believe it of you. Especially with the way you're acting right now. I think you've been using Jeremy to scare Gordon into keeping outside police from getting involved, because you didn't want them to find out what you've done."

Everett was just scowling, but looking down and not at Randy. "It doesn't matter anyway," he said.

And that did it.

"It does, Everett."

Randy realized the voice raised in anger was his own. "Jeremy's shot Rose Esterhouse. And a good part of it is your fault."

"I wasn't the one to call and warn him to run."

"I didn't know he'd been shooting at people, and you did." Randy was clean mad. "Once he'd burned down Roland's warehouse, that should have been enough for you to come clean with your secrets."

If he'd had a club, he might have been using it instead of just words. And Everett wasn't looking him in the eye but was just looking down.

"It wouldn't make a difference now," Everett said.

"I'm going to wait until after the December meeting," Randy said. "Because that's already going to be bad enough. But then I'm going to make sure everything comes out."

Everett's head jerked back up. "Do you know what that will do to me?"

"I do, and I'm sorry. But I'm not going to keep a secret like that."

"Here!" Steve held the casing right up in Gordon's face. "Ten feet from where Wade Harris went over the edge."

"That doesn't mean a thing. It could have been there for years. Everyone in the county hunts up on that mountain."

"How many people hunt through Joe Esterhouse's window?"

"We know who that was. It was Jeremy Coates. If you even read the newspaper you'd know it."

Calm down. "So maybe this was Jeremy Coates, too."

"He was in Asheville that night. He told me himself."

"I don't think I'd believe everything Jeremy Coates said."

"You don't even know him." Gordon gave a big angry sigh. "And what if it was Jeremy? We're already looking for him anyway. We can't do anything till we find him."

Steve stared at the expanse of sheriff sprawling in front of him. "Gordon. You are the most stupid man I've ever met. You couldn't find Jeremy Coates if he was hiding under your desk. And so now he's out there with his gun? Whose window is he aiming at right now? Mine?"

"Just stay a moment, Jeanie." The sky was burning with sunset.

Jeanie looked at her watch. "A couple minutes."

They sat on the porch and watched the orange and red and scarlet and violet and indigo and black for many minutes, and Eliza couldn't find words to say anything she wanted to.

"How are you, Mother?"

"I'm troubled."

"I thought so. Do you know why?"

"There is so much I no longer know."

Jeanie looked again at her watch. "Should I try to figure out what you're talking about?"

"Yes, dear. Try to."

"You're asking me for help? I don't believe it."

"I don't know who else to ask," Eliza said.

"What about your spirits? Your voices?" There was sympathy, at least, in Jeanie's voice. Not her normal impatient mocking. "Aren't they saying anything?"

"They are." But that was the trouble.

"What are they saying?"

"It is hard to listen."

"Mother, when you got elected to that board, you were so sure that you were going to be the wise woman and teach everyone else all those secrets you knew. I think it's gone the other way. You've finally come down off this mountain and seen how everyone else lives, and you're the one who's being changed."

Was it true? The plan turned on its head? It had not been her plan but the Warrior's plan for her.

And now she felt so little peace in what the Warrior said.

Whatever had got into Byron, Louise had no idea. He hardly let her out of his sight these days. And here he was standing in the kitchen doorway watching her wash dishes!

"I'd be glad for help if you're not doing anything," she said.

"No, you wouldn't be."

"Well, you're right." What would she do with him anyway? "Isn't there something on the television?"

"It can wait."

"Then at least sit down and be comfortable."

Byron sat on the old chair in the corner, and it was the first time Louise could remember him ever being in it. She only used it for standing on to get into the back of the high cabinets.

"Has Mr. Coates decided on next week's schedule?" she asked.

"Still half days. Probably be back to regular come January, he said this morning."

"That'll be a relief."

"At least there's orders. Just need a place to keep wood."

She was getting finished, but she didn't really want to stop. "Will you go back full time when the factory does?" It just popped out, so she must have been thinking it.

"Been expecting I would, but I'm not looking forward to it."

So Byron had been thinking about it, too.

"When would the new owners take over?"

"Could be in January. Just depends on the road."

"What if there isn't a road?"

"I think he'll just close down. There's no reason for Mr. Coates to keep going."

The water was draining out of the sink, and she watched the last suds twirl and disappear. Just an empty sink and everything over and done and gone.

"What do you want, Byron?"

"Don't know."

"Then that's two of us." She sat down herself at the little table where she did her mixing. Goodness, she'd done a lot of that over the years. "We can't have things the way we've always had them, but we don't want them any different."

"That's the truth. It's us getting old."

That word fired her up. Tired was one thing, but not that! "Sixty-three isn't old, and I know sixty isn't."

"Working one place forty years means you're old."

"I'm not ready to give up the salon."

"You shouldn't," he said.

"You shouldn't give up on the factory, either."

"There's no telling with it. These people buying it say one thing, but there's no telling what they'll really do." He looked so sad in his corner. "When you vote on that road, you do what you think is right. Maybe we should just try to hold on to what we've got. Maybe that's what's most important."

November 17, Friday

Randy knocked on the farmhouse door, almost afraid to. But it opened and a friendly face looked out.

"Mr. McCoy?"

"Yes, here I am."

"I'm Mary Anderson. Come in."

"Now, I think we might have met back in March, at Joe's party."

"That's right. I'm little Joey's grandmother."

"He gave quite a performance, let me tell you."

They'd made it to the back end of the hall, and Randy saw into the bedroom for just a moment.

He'd seen it before, once or twice, but this time he barely noticed the bed or table. He just saw the bedcover itself, plain white and flat, but flat as it was, there was still someone in it.

Just a face. Wrinkled and sunken, with hair indistinct against the pillow of the same color, all just white, and the bedcover rose and fell, and Randy could just imagine hearing the wheezing breath. The eyes were closed.

"How is she?"

"She's resting," Mary said, and despite being closer to his own age and in nice pants and a sweater instead of a farm dress, Randy could tell that she was an Esterhouse and didn't chat or say more than she needed to.

But then she said, "Mother's stronger than they thought."

They turned in to the kitchen, and there was Joe at the table. Or it must have been. He never had looked eighty before—he'd looked more like sixty—and now he looked about a hundred. And he didn't look up. He was staring at the table.

"Well, hi there, Joe," Randy said, trying to sound cheerful.

Joe did look up at him.

"I wanted to stop in to see how you were doing. We're all real concerned for you, and just hoping everything we can."

"Daddy," Mary said. "Randy's come all the way from Wardsville to see you."

Joe only looked back down at the table. There was a Wardsville newspaper opened out on it, but not a recent one.

"He wanted to read about Mort Walker dying," Mary said.

It was that issue from a year ago, but he didn't even have it open to the right page.

"We were wondering if you'd thought about coming in for the board meeting next month," Randy said. Joe still didn't look up.

"He's not talking much," Mary said.

"Then maybe I should go."

"We appreciate you coming."

Randy stepped back to the kitchen door.

"He does hear you," Mary said. "Daddy, Randy's leaving now. And I'm going to fix you lunch. Would you like some lunch?" And Joe still didn't move.

"Joe." Randy had to say something more. This was a man he respected so much. "Joe, we're so sorry. We are so sorry. We'll make it up to you somehow. I know it doesn't help, but we'll find him. We'll stop him. Wherever he is."

Joe turned, slow, and looked him right in the eye.

"Who?"

"Well, Jeremy Coates, of course."

November 20, Monday

Come on, come on. What was the problem? He could do a sewage overlay in his sleep.

Steve stood up. Blueprints everywhere. He rolled up a few. Too much clutter.

No, that wasn't it.

The window. It was too distracting. He pulled the blinds down. He just couldn't concentrate with the black night outside, and no telling what was in it.

Try again. A development in Virginia, ninety houses.

The phone. "Steve Carter," he said.

"Well, good."

Oh. It was Luke Goddard from the newspaper. He'd know that pinched voice anywhere.

"What can I do for you, Mr. Goddard?"

"Well, first, you can call me Luke. All my friends do."

"I didn't know I was a friend." No, cut the chatter. Sewage, sewage, lots of sewage. Gravity feed. No pumping stations.

"Sure you're a friend," Goddard said. "And you can imagine what I'm calling about."

Sizing the pipes would be tricky. It was all on one main line.

"I'm imagining it now, Mr. Goddard."

"Good. Do you have a final decision on Gold River Highway?"

"Same as last time you asked," Steve said. "Undecided. Most people in Gold Valley are very much for the road, but there is concern about the impact on the mountain and the views."

"So no one's concerned about the impact on Wardsville and Mountain View."

"Goddard, everything you write about me is wrong."

"Steve!"

"And I'm really busy right now, so we'll have to talk later."

"But when?"

"December fifth. That's a Tuesday. Bye, bye!"

And he pushed the button to hang up.

Were the blinds down in the kitchen? Yes, he'd put them down himself.

It was too hard to think. He tapped in another number.

"Hello, this is Randy McCoy."

"Hi, Randy, this is Steve Carter."

"Oh, hello, Steve, and how are you doing?"

"Okay. I just hung up on Luke Goddard, and I figured if I called you, he couldn't call either of us."

"Now, I appreciate that, and I suppose he was getting you to say something about Gold River Highway so he could misquote you."

"Did he hound Wade like he's been after me?"

"I suppose he did, not that I heard much about it, and not that Wade would have been real friendly to him, or him to Wade, either. But I think Wade was even going to meet him the day he had his accident."

"Luke came over to Gold Valley? He's never come to see me."

"Wade was going in to Wardsville. But then he didn't because he stayed in Gold Valley instead to meet with Jeremy Coates."

"Wait." The phone call had suddenly become important. "Wade was seeing Jeremy Coates?"

That stupid sheriff. That idiot, stupid, oaf sheriff!

"Well, he didn't," Randy said. "At least Jeremy says he didn't."

"Where was Jeremy, anyway?" Steve asked.

"He was there at Wade's office."

"Not in Asheville?"

"Now, that sounds like you've been talking to Gordon," Randy said, "and that's what Jeremy told him, but I think he was really in Gold Valley, by what he told me."

"What does that mean?" Steve said, to himself and to Randy. Randy answered.

"Well . . ." Only Randy could unroll that into eight syllables. "I've had that on my mind quite a bit lately, and I've had a few conversations with people, and I'm getting very worried about some possibilities."

"So you think Jeremy killed Wade Harris? Or somebody did?"

"Steve . . ."

He settled himself in for some nice, long Randy sentences.

"I do," Randy said.

"Okay," Steve said. "What should we do about it?"

"I don't know. But first, somebody has to find him."

"Right. Man. All this over a road."

"It's just two more weeks until the vote."

"I hope we make it," Steve said. Literally. "Do you close up all your blinds at night so no one can see in?"

"Well, we have been, as a matter of fact. But there couldn't really be any reason, Steve. Jeremy couldn't be anywhere around here.

"Right. He's a thousand miles from here." He must be. Probably two thousand miles. Let's change the subject. "Oh. I should tell you something else. I've looked at some data from the DOT. They were saying they want to make a 130-foot cut through the ridge, but they might not be able to."

"They might not . . . What does that mean?"

"It means maybe they'll build the big road they talked about, or maybe they'll build something completely different."

"When would they know?"

"Probably next summer."

"Then we don't even know what we're voting on. When did you find out?"

"A few weeks ago. I was going to talk to Joe at the last meeting."

"Well, I don't know what to make of that," Randy said, recovering his grammatical prowess, "and I'm not sure we should tell anyone because I don't know if it'll make a difference how any of us vote, and it will make a big difference in how many people are screaming at us the next two weeks."

November 23, Thursday

Oh, goodness. What was she forgetting? Green beans, potatoes, cranberry sauce, rolls, sweet potatoes, stuffing. And the turkey. Pumpkin pie, apple pie, rhubarb pie. There was something . . . There were no marshmallows on the sweet potatoes!

Louise snatched the dish right out of the oven—it wasn't even hot yet. Oh goodness. Angie and her family would be here any minute, and she wasn't near ready. At least the turkey was done. That was a mercy!

"Byron, are the chairs all put out?"

"The chairs are all put out." He was watching football on the television.

"Look out the window and see if they're here."

"If they're here, they'll come in."

She ran out to the front door to look, but there wasn't a sign of them. Back to the dining room to count places again.

Back to the kitchen, and there was Byron standing at the sink!

"Now, what are you doing in here?" she said.

"Checking on you."

"Well, nothing's going right. I almost burned the rolls and now the sweet potatoes won't be ready. Oh, Byron!" She collapsed into her chair. "It's all terrible."

"No it isn't."

"It is." They'd be in the driveway any minute, and starving. "There isn't even enough food for everyone."

"Louise!"

"There isn't."

"There's enough to feed an army!"

"Nothing is right."

"Get ahold of yourself."

She tried. She breathed in and it was almost sobs breathing out.

"Now what's wrong?" Byron asked.

"Everything!"

"It can't be everything."

"It is," she said. "Jeremy and Rose Esterhouse and Wade Harris and the factory and everything. Everybody mad at each other and the shopping center and the road. Isn't that everything? What else is there?"

"There's nothing wrong with me."

That stopped her. "You're still on half days at the factory."

"Mr. Coates came in today, for the first time since the shooting, and that's a start."

"Will he ever get over Jeremy?"

"I don't know." He shook his head. "But you and I, though. We'll see it through. Those other things aren't what's important."

He was right. "We will see it through." She took another breath, and this one came back out easier. "If you're all right," she said, "I guess I am, too."

"Sue Ann, that was about the best dinner I can imagine anyone ever making for Thanksgiving."

"It was just what we usually have," she said.

"That might be true, but you're still only saying the same thing I am."

"Oh, Randy."

"It has left me charitable to all mankind, which is a useful mood to be in when I'm looking through the newspaper. And poor Luke looks like he needs a little sympathy." Randy read through the paragraphs. "This is his final feature article on the upcoming vote, and it doesn't look like he got enough of an answer from anybody to even misquote. Every board member he could talk to said they had no idea how they'd vote, and that was just Steve and Louise and I. And there's no telling about Eliza."

"And what about Joe?"

"No telling about him, either, and whether he'll even come to the meeting."

Must . . . stay . . . awake.

Steve smiled at the three little faces. *They* were all awake. They all smiled back.

"Okay. Turn the page."

"Turn the page!" Two shouts and a giggle.

He turned the page. "The little train started up the big hill. It started out easy. Turn the page."

"Turn the page!"

He turned the page. "But then it got harder. Turn the page."

"Turn the page!"

Even Andy wubbled along. Steve turned the page.

"And then it got harder. Is he going to make it?"

"Yes!" Josie said.

"Daddy," Max said, "he always makes it."

"So why am I reading the book?"

"Because we want you to."

"And then it got so hard he gave up and—"

"Daddy!"

"Don't you want a little tension?"

"That's not what it says," Max said.

"How do you know?" Steve said. "You can't read."

"It's *obvious*."

"The train kept trying and trying. 'I can make it!' he said. 'I won't give up!' Turn the page."

"Turn the page!"

"And then, suddenly space aliens invaded—"

"Daddy!"

"And then he reached the top of the hill! And there, in the sparsely developed valley below, was the perfect spot for a brand-new strip retail center—"

"Daddy!"

"No, really. But the little train realized that it would be much easier to get over the mountain with a four-percent grade, which would require a thirty-five-meter ridgeline cut. And what if the geology won't support it? Then what should the little train do?"

"You're being silly," Josie said.

"It is pretty silly. Max, should the little train vote *for* a new road or *against* it?"

"What does *ridgeline cut* mean?"

"It means you drill really, really deep holes into the top of the mountain and fill them with dynamite and then blow the whole thing up, and it leaves a big hole."

"Do it! Daddy, do it! I want to watch!"

"The poor mountain," Josie said.

"Mountains can't feel anything," Max said.

"Don't hurt the mountain, Daddy," Josie said.

"Would there be digger trucks?" Max asked.

"Lots, except we'd have to wait at least a year. But," Steve said, "the real question is whether the retail center would have a pizza place."

"Where?" Max asked.

"Just down the road. Where we get on the highway."

"Pizza?"

"A whole big shopping center. They'd have a grocery store, too. We could get ice cream whenever we wanted. All we have to do is maybe blow the top off the mountain, build an interstate, tear down all the trees, and put up houses everywhere."

"Oh, Daddy," Josie said, and she put her head down in his lap.

November 30, Thursday

"Well, another year," Randy said, "and I'm sure each one is going by faster." Boxes were piled around the living room, filled with lights and wreaths and angels, and the lights were more tangled each year, despite his best efforts.

"Then that makes Christmas come that much quicker," Sue Ann said. She already had the little carolers on the dining room table, which just by themselves made the whole house festive.

"And this has been a year to remember, that's for sure." It was going to take a while with the lights, and Randy set them down. "Sue Ann, as much as I've dreaded having that vote, I am certainly looking forward to having it now, so that it can be over."

Now the earth had the leaf covering. The trees were dead, or so they seemed.

For the trees, winter death was only an appearance. They would live again and die and live again. The leaves would descend even further, into the soil, and become the tree's new life.

Eliza sat by the window. She had the rocker inside.

And even when the tree did die from age or disease or fire, it would still live again. The earth would take it in, and every root would draw from it.

But what would happen to a woman, or a man?

"Nobody's called so far today," Sue Ann said.

"They don't know I'm home, and I expect the answering machine at the office is already full."

"What have they been saying this week?"

"You know," Randy said, "it's still almost straight even between the people who want a new shopping center and the people who don't want a big road through the neighborhood, at least for the people who've been calling me."

"What will you do, Randy?"

"I guess I'll have to think for myself. But without Joe, it might be over before I even vote, because it'll take three of the four of us to say yes."

"Have you heard from him?"

"No, and since I saw him, I'd be afraid to try calling again myself, for fear Mary would tell me they're not either of them any better. But now, let's see what else we can do before we go out."

"Byron?"

Where had the man gotten to?

He wasn't watching television. Louise looked in the bedrooms and he wasn't anywhere.

His car was in the driveway. "Byron!"

The back door creaked, and she went running back to the television room. There he was.

"What have you been doing out there?"

He didn't even have a coat on.

"Now, why do I have to explain any single thing I do?"

"Well. I just couldn't find you."

"I was just out back."

"It's cold out."

"I was only out for a minute. Looking around."

What would he be looking for? "Was there anything out there?"

He shook his head. "Not that I saw."

Kyle and Kelly were home from school, and they didn't even take off their coats but just waited while Randy and Sue Ann put on theirs, because it was the last day of November and there was a job to do.

"Sunset alert!"

Steve pulled himself away from the computer simulation of 3-D topography to look at the real thing. "Thanks," he said to Natalie. "You know, when you've seen one sunset, you've seen . . . that one sunset."

The four of them trooped out into the yard and down the block and around the corner, on up to the end of the street, talking and remembering about all the other years they'd done this, and into the woods, this part being Roland Coates' property.

Eliza watched the shadows unfurl across the floor. Now the day was dying, but it would come again. The sun would return from its death to break the new day.

What did it mean?

She heard the voice, *Do not question.*

Where was Wade now?

There is no life. There is no death.

Why did he die?
Do not desecrate, do not defile, do not violate.

And up a ways, keeping an eye out, Kelly found a likely white pine, one they'd actually noticed last year but had decided to leave at the time. With all the rain, though, it had been a good year for growing, and it was green and full and just about perfect.

"Well, that looks like the one," Randy said, and Kyle lifted his hatchet.

There they were, staring across the table at each other, her at Byron and Byron at her.

"I guess I'll clean up," she said.

"I'll see if there's a game on."

"Byron, how should I vote about this road?"

"What's most important to you?"

What was? "Right now, just clearing the table is. That's as far as I can think."

The sun was gone and the light was going, and Steve hadn't moved. Somehow Josie had ended up asleep in his lap.

There was something portentous about the night, and it made him feel small. There were so many big things.

What right they had to tear down a mountain? A small and insignificant guy like him.

"What's the weather for tomorrow?" Louise was up to her elbows in hot soapy water, and she could hardly believe fall was over already. It seemed like the cold was earlier every year, and it was so dark outside the kitchen window.

"Haven't seen it."

"Well, if you do, let me know."

How could just two people use so many dishes in a day? There was such a pile. Maybe Angie was right about a dishwasher. To tell the truth, it was silly to wash them all by hand.

It just depended on what was most important to her.

She pulled the casserole dish out from under the other dishes, and they settled with a great big clatter.

"Louise?"

Byron was there in the doorway looking at her.

"Well, what is it?" she asked.

"Just heard something and I thought I'd check on you."

She took a deep breath. "Everything's just fine. Don't get all worried."

"The weather's coming on," he said. "Leave those and come sit in here."

They settled in together and watched.

"I love you," she said.

It was dark outside, but the shadows of the cabin were darker. The forest was lit by the starry sky.

The night had come slowly. The day was bright. The afternoon shadows had grown without notice and finally the twilit sky had led the world into black. And now, because she had accepted the leading, she sat in her own black dark.

She had been drawn into the dark through her whole life.

She stood abruptly and struck a match, and lit a candle, and then the lantern. It was bright. The night had come slowly—but in a moment it was dispelled.

Blazing light! Randy stood up from plugging in the lights, and the tree was a hundred stars right in the living room, and a dozen angels, and wrapped in gold.

"It's what I think heaven is like," Sue Ann said, and she always had such a way with describing things. Randy stepped back to see it better.

"Heaven where trees go," Kyle said.

"Then heaven where we'll go must be that much better," Randy said, and then he had a thought, and he had to laugh. "And the Gold Highways in heaven are already built and we don't have to vote on them."

December

December 4, Monday

Time to start. Bang the fool gavel.

"Come to order." The room was dead quiet anyway. "Go ahead, Patsy."

"Mrs. Brown?"

"I'm . . . here."

"Mr. Carter?"

"Uh, here."

"Mr. Esterhouse?"

It would be the last time. "Here."

"Eliza?"

"I am here."

"Mr. McCoy?"

"I'm here."

Randy was half flabbergasted, or more than half. Everybody in the room—and that was as many as could be in that room, with the rest outside in the hall—had their eyes on Joe, and they had since he'd walked in thirty seconds ago. Nobody had known before if he would even come.

Joe had always reminded him of stone. Now he was more like hard iron. His words cut through the room like a sword.

"Everyone's here, Joe."

"Thank you, Patsy," he said. "Jefferson County North Carolina Board of Supervisors is now in session. Motion to accept last month's minutes?"

"I'll move."

"I'll second."

"Motion and second," Joe said. "Go ahead, Patsy."

"Mrs. Brown?"

"Yes."

Louise was barely getting her thoughts back together. They'd been shattered like a dropped plate when that side door had opened and Joe came in. He looked older, but not more worn or weary. It was his hair. It wasn't cropped short like it always had been. It was just long enough now to show pure white, like bleached wool—or like a mountain in winter.

"Mr. Carter?"

"Yes."

"Mr. Esterhouse?"

"Yes."

"Eliza?"

"I vote no."

"Mr. McCoy?"

"Yes."

"Four in favor, one opposed," Patsy said.

"Motion carries," Joe said. "Minutes are accepted. Next is receiving public comment. I will state the rules I have for this evening."

Steve looked through the faces in the audience. Every one was locked on Joe. It was his voice. There was such absolute authority in it and . . . and power. Inexorable, overriding, like the flood. Like a million tons of water flowing and strong and unstoppable.

"We will be discussing Gold River Highway this evening. Every person will be given their chance to speak, and you can say whatever you want. I won't impose any limits. Just remember your words are being said in front of your neighbors and friends and families, and you'll have to live with them.

"After we've heard everything, this board will make its final judgment."

Eliza had closed her eyes. It was so bright to look at Joe. His face was blazing like the sun.

Then the people came. Joe watched. Listening was hard. Remembering who they all were was hard, too. But he was here for a purpose. That would be hardest.

People kept coming. Joe looked at the faces.

Then he made himself look at the one face, and that was why he was here.

"I'm Roland Coates, and you all know what this has meant to me. I've lost a million dollars of furniture and almost my factory, and had to take insurance money which I never have before. I might still lose the whole business and 150 jobs.

"And I've lost my son. And that's what I came to say.

"Right here in front of everybody, Joe Esterhouse, I'm sorry for what my son did to you and your wife. It's my fault. I'm sorry."

Joe didn't answer. He could only look at the one face, and it was staring back at him.

"Byron Brown. I've worked for Mr. Coates at the furniture factory for forty years. If you don't build the road, the factory's going to close sooner or later. What's been important to me is having a job and putting food on my table. But times are changing, and I don't know what's important anymore."

"Cornelia Harris. I came tonight because Gold River Highway was so important to my husband, Wade. I want to ask all of you on the board to do what you think is right. And I want to ask all of the rest of us to accept whatever they decide."

It was near the end now.

"Mary Anderson. I live in Tampa, Florida. I'm speaking for my mother, Rose Esterhouse. She wants me to say that the decisions you make will last for years to come, after we're all gone. Don't think about just now. Think about the future."

"Kyle McCoy. Dad, I know this has been real hard for you for this whole year, and probably most people here don't know how hard this has been for all the board members. Whatever you decide will be okay."

Then no one else. It was the end, but not yet. Joe waited and finally one more came up.

"Luke Goddard, and I live right here in Wardsville.

"Well, it's been a lot of fun, hasn't it? I can't thank you all enough for the newspapers you've sold for me, and just the grand time I've had writing about you all.

"Steve, I bet you're wishing you'd just stayed over there in Gold Valley and not got mixed up with all this trouble. And, Eliza, people thought you were crazy, and you must think the same about them.

"But you others should know better. It's just whoever yelled at you last that you'll do what they say, isn't it, Randy? Or whoever cried the most, Louise? It wouldn't matter except when something real comes along, which it has now for once.

"And, Joe."

Joe waited, and watched.

"Doesn't eighty years wear a man out?" Luke said. "Shouldn't you be napping in some rest home instead of lording it over people who still have their lives left ahead of them? You won't even live to see that road built. Why are you deciding for people who will?

"You're small little people, and now you have this big road that the big people in Raleigh and Atlanta are pushing and tugging over. The best thing would be to just get out of their way. Because you can get hurt. Can't you, Joe?

"We all know what's going to happen. When it comes right down to it, none of you are really brave enough to vote for something this big and new.

"Now go ahead and get it over with."

That was the end. The other four looked shaken enough by it.

"I'll ask that we have a motion and second, whether members plan to actually vote for it or not," he said.

"I'll move we accept the funding and plans for Gold River Highway," Steve said.

"Second?"

"I'll second," Louise said.

"Any discussion?"

He waited again. He didn't have any doubt now. He hadn't before. But seeing the face through it all was enough by itself.

"Let's just vote," Randy said. "I think just about everything's been said."

"Then we'll vote. Now, I'm going to use my prerogative as chairman to change our voting procedure. I'll have Patsy hand you each a sheet of paper, and I'll ask each member to write their name and their vote on it."

"It this a secret ballot?" Jim Ross asked out loud. "You can't do that."

"I'll read them out, with the names," Joe said. "But I want each person to vote without worrying how anyone else has voted, or whether they're first or last. Go ahead, Patsy."

Patsy was handing out her little pink message papers. Joe took his and wrote his name and vote on it. Then Steve handed him his vote, and Eliza's, and then Randy handed him his and Louise's. Joe glanced through them.

"The vote's unanimous—"

"I knew it!"

Randy had been so glad Joe had let them vote that way with the paper ballots, and then when he said that word, *unanimous*, Randy's brain had overloaded for just a second to where he almost couldn't make out what else was happening.

He knew why he'd finally decided. There were too many opinions and facts and uncertainties to ever make a logical decision, so he'd finally just picked what seemed right, and not even why it seemed right, only that it did.

But just like everybody else, he was turning and staring at the back wall, where Luke Goddard had stood and shouted out before anyone else had time to think.

"I knew it!" Luke said, loud enough to hear in the hall outside. Everybody was sort of shocked, and of course most people had to stretch or even half stand up to see him back there. "I knew when you finally had to vote you'd end up scared to death." And what was more, his voice had gotten high pitched, and that made it all the more startling.

"Come on up here," Joe said, and compared to Luke, those words were as slow and heavy as old trees.

Luke froze a second, but then he stepped right up to the podium, people pulling back to let him by, almost like they were afraid to touch him, and the grin on his face was like it was carved on.

"I think I'd even take those votes," Luke said once he'd got himself planted there, "and keep them in a glass case down at the newspaper. Or we should put the case out in front of the courthouse. Right out there next to Mort Walker's little monument stone. That would be the place. It's a good thing he didn't live to see his road fail like this, without even a single vote!"

"The road passed," Joe said.

Eliza had drawn back from bright, frenzied, fire-lit eyes. When Joe Esterhouse spoke, the flame died almost to black. But then it blazed out, and words were its hot embers.

"You're lying."

She made herself face him. His face was set against Joe. But she had to see him. She had to see that it was his mouth from which the words came.

"I'm not lying," Joe said. "It's true."

"It's a lie!"

She had to see him speak. The shrill voice and its fierce, frantic cry were only a man. She saw the man in front of her! His words were a wild wind, but that broke against the answer to them.

"It's the truth."

Eliza closed her eyes.

"No!" the voice screamed. And she knew the voice. She had known it her whole life, and she had known it tonight.

Louise wasn't even breathing. Something was going on, something terrible. Seeing Joe and Luke faced off like they were, she just couldn't breathe. Luke's eyes were like he was only alive on the outside and dead inside. They were fixed on Joe the way a snake would fix onto a chicken.

And Joe was fixed back on him, and Joe looked almost dead, so old and hard, but all night there'd been something inside him she'd never seen anywhere, strong and alive. It was like a rifle pointed straight at the snake's eyes.

Nobody had moved or anything when Joe said the road had passed. For all everybody was feeling, the lock between Joe and Luke was too strong to do anything but just watch.

"It's the truth," Joe said again and held up the pages, their five yes votes.

Truth. The word filled the room like the smell of something cooking when a person was hungry. It was invisible but it was everything.

"That's what it's all been about," Joe said. "The truth. Knowing what's true."

Luke held on to the podium, a bare tree in a whirlwind, and everything Joe said was whipping against him.

"Luke," Joe said. "Now, you tell the truth. Did you kill Wade Harris?"

The whole world fell apart. Louise heard herself sob out a quiet, "Oh no," and all the rest of the room, too. And while she was just breaking, trying to even start understanding what it meant, she knew from seeing Joe and Luke both that it was true.

"Nobody killed him," Luke said.

"I said to tell the truth," Joe said.

"Then it was Jeremy Coates," Luke said. "Everybody knows it would have been. He's been shooting at people and starting fires. The police are looking for him. He killed Wade."

"It wasn't Jeremy Coates," Joe said. "What will you do when they find him? They will, and then he'll tell the truth. Then we'll know it was you."

"Joe?" Gordon Hite was standing by the door. "You shouldn't be doing this. It's not legal."

"Be quiet." It was a different voice, and it was a knife.

Steve waited a second to make sure Gordon was staying quiet, then he looked back at Luke. And Luke was looking at him, a caged tiger stare.

"You saw him that day," Steve said.

"You be quiet," Luke said. "You don't have any part in this."

"I think I do. You talked with him that afternoon."

"I didn't, and how would you know?" Luke turned back to Joe. "It was Jeremy Coates that saw him last. They had a meeting, and then Jeremy went ahead over the mountain and was waiting for him."

"He never made it to see Jeremy Coates," Steve said, and he had Luke's stare back at him. "He was coming up the mountain from Wardsville. It's obvious, looking at where it happened."

"Now, I wouldn't say that," Gordon Hite said.

"Yeah," Steve said, "exactly. We'll get a real detective to look at it." He put his stare back at Luke. "I'd say Wade Harris told you he had a meeting and he was going over the mountain. You went ahead and were waiting for him."

"You don't know anything," Luke said.

"So how did you know it was Jeremy Coates he was going to see?"

The caged tiger had scented danger. "Well . . . Gordon must have told me."

"That's news to me," Gordon said. "Jeremy told me he was down in Asheville all that day."

"Then he was lying," Luke said.

"He was," Steve said. "But you are, too. You'd only know who Wade was meeting if Wade told you." Steve turned to Joe. "You're right. It's true."

"Luke," Joe said into the dead silence, "did you kill Mort Walker?"

Randy was already staggering, completely astounded at the turn events were taking, and with Cornelia Harris's white face engraved into his memory, and Roland Coates' mouth hanging open, but hearing Mort's name was still the last thing he'd have expected.

"Nobody killed Mort!" Luke said back at Joe, and Luke looked just as amazed, but not surprised, if such a thing was possible. "Why would anybody kill him? Nobody knew anything about the road back then."

"I didn't say anything about the road," Joe said. "Is that why you killed him?"

"Nobody knew about the road!"

"Now, I think you might have," Randy said, because it suddenly occurred to him that Luke could have worked it out. And now Luke was looking right at him, and Randy had to take a deep breath to keep going with that terrible stare. But he knew he had to keep going, because he was part of it all, too, and it was becoming a matter of real life and death, and he wasn't going to back down.

"Because," Randy said, "you would have seen that advertisement back last November, the one with all the unpaid taxes listed in it, and I think you might have noticed that the Trinkles weren't on the list—that they finally paid up after all those years—and that would have gotten you thinking something was happening, and then I think you might have gone out to see Mort, to see if he knew."

"You don't know any of that," Luke said, and he seemed to have gotten a little of his confidence back. "And anybody could have seen that ad."

But Joe answered. "The ad was in the same newspaper that told about Mort dying. You'd have been the only one to have seen it before it came out."

"You don't know any of that," Luke said again.

"It doesn't matter," Joe said. "The only thing that matters is if it's true. Is it true, Luke? Did you go to see Mort Walker?"

"Going to see him doesn't mean anything."

"Well, it might," Randy said. He hadn't even noticed, concentrating so hard, but there was Sue Ann standing beside him, and he looked up at her and saw the fright in her eyes—fright because she was realizing, like he was, that if Mort and Wade had both been killed, then everyone on the board had really been at risk. And Byron Brown looked to have thought the same thing, because he was right beside Louise, and then

Kelly was up to stand with Sue Ann, and Kyle planted with them, football fierce and ready to hard tackle.

"And I know," Randy said, "it does seem farfetched, but it does also make sense, that Mort dying just that week would be the one way to get Eliza elected, and you'd know that as well as anybody, Luke, or even better."

"It is true," Eliza herself said, her first words since her *I am here* and her *I vote no* at the beginning of the meeting.

The eyes gazed in to her and she shuddered. Through all the years, it had only been the voice speaking, commanding, working its purpose. But now she saw the eyes. If only she had seen them long ago.

"It was your purpose," Eliza said to him, "and I was deceived by it."

It had been a lie. Always a lie! The Warrior had been her protector, the power over her, the balance and circle of life, greater than any man. Lies! It was hate, greater than any man's, that she saw now.

And death was not an end? Only part of the circle? That was the lie over all the others. She saw into the eyes and saw what death really was—not a beginning but a blackness and slavery and terror. These were eyes that knew death. They were the eyes of murder.

"I thought I was wise," she said. "That you had taught me. It was always lies."

"What do you mean? Did you know any of this?" Steve Carter asked.

Joe Esterhouse answered for her. "She knew. Just not the way you think."

Joe knew what she meant. She knew it was evil they were looking at. She knew it was where lies were from, and destruction, and murder.

"Luke," he said. "Did you try to kill me?"

"Why should I?" Luke said. Almost a wail. "You should be dead anyway! Why should you even still be alive? Just die, Joe Esterhouse, and get it over with for all of us! You had a chance, but you ducked. You let your wife take the bullet for you. Why would you even want to stay alive after you did that?"

The words hardly meant anything. They were just the twitching after the death blow. It was sad.

He wouldn't feel pity for a snake, but a man was worth pity.

"The road passed anyway," Joe said. "You killed two men to no purpose."

"Why?!"

It came out like steam from a teapot. Louise was hanging on to Byron's hand for dear life. "Why did you do it?" It didn't seem there was any doubt that he had. It was just Luke Goddard in front of them, who she'd known for twenty years, but he'd killed Mort and Wade both. "Oh, Luke! Why?"

"For the land," he said.

"What land? The Trinkles' farm?"

"It's not theirs!"

Byron moved around to her side, close to being between her and Luke. She wanted to hide behind him.

"It never was!" Luke said. "That was Goddard land from two hundred years ago. The Trinkles took it and we couldn't stop them, and it's cursed since, and it's cursed forever."

But that was why she'd voted for the road, because she didn't want curses. She'd decided she wanted things to be new. For the salon, for the town, for the factory. But most for Byron, because he was most important to her.

And it did scare her to death, what changes there might be. But looking at Luke, it was like she knew there were curses they were living under, and this might break them.

It was like a movie. Steve was watching a man exposed as a murderer, except it was real. He could step right into the screen and be part of it. The audience, all watching, too, made it even more surreal.

"So you knew what would happen if the road was built," he said. "That farm would be worth five times as much. It wouldn't make any difference to you—you just hated the Trinkle family that much? It was worth killing people to stop it?"

It had been to Luke. They all knew it. Everyone in the room. It was hard to believe he could be that crazed over a land fight six generations ago, but they could all see he was.

"And where's Jeremy Coates?" Steve said. "You must know. You must be sure he's not going to show up and blow your story. You're hiding him, aren't you? Or did you kill him, too?"

"No," Luke said. "He's alive."

Steve turned to Joe. "So, now what?"

"Come in, Marty," Joe said.

It was finally at an end. A black, evil time since that night in the kitchen, worse than any time he'd ever had. But he'd come through it.

This one evil was finally at an end.

The side door opened and Marty Brannin came in, with a State Police detective and two troopers, and pushing a wheelchair. Joe hadn't wanted her to come, but she'd had her way. They'd all been listening in the hallway.

It was the end. But Luke was worth pity, and worth giving a last chance.

"Luke," Joe said. "In front of everyone here. In front of this board that you've been deadly enemy of, and in front of these people who know you, and in front of me and my wife. In front of God. Say the truth."

He waited.

"Say it, Luke."

He waited.

"I killed them," Luke said. He looked to the policemen. "I killed them both. That's the truth."

Joe closed his eyes. Then he looked over to Rose.

He stood up.

Louise was beside him, and he let her hug him and cry over him. Randy waited and shook his hand, talking. Then Eliza was in front of him and hugged him, too.

"Joe," Steve said, but nothing else.

"Why don't you take this," Joe said, and he handed his gavel to Steve. Then he looked back to Rose.

"Let's go home, Joe," she said.

He went to her.

Marty took hold of the chair to turn it. "I'll walk," she said. She held up a hand, and Joe took it and helped her to stand.

Now all the room was filled in an uproar, but it was behind them. They didn't look back.

In pain and age, but together, they left.

ACKNOWLEDGMENTS

My thanks to the honorable elected officials of the Town of Blacksburg, and Montgomery County, Virginia, who informally answered questions and gave suggestions and advice.

After writing much of *Road to Nowhere*, I searched a map of North Carolina to find my fictional Jefferson County. Just north of Asheville, up the interstate, is the real and strikingly similar Madison County. It was interesting to visit and see the places I'd written about, not knowing they actually existed. But Jefferson came first and is my own invention.

ABOUT THE AUTHOR

PAUL ROBERTSON is a computer programming consultant, part-time high school math and science teacher, and the author of *The Heir*. He is also a former Christian bookstore owner (for 15 years), and lives with his family in Blacksburg, Virginia.

More Exciting Suspense From Paul Robertson

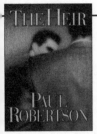

Jason Boyer Just Got an Inheritance to Die for…
When given the throne to his father's corrupt business empire, Jason Boyer only wants to walk away—he saw how it ruined his father. But power-hungry politicians, bloodthirsty media, and shady business partners all try to force his hand. When Jason fights back, the power intoxicates him—and he soon finds himself battling for his soul…and his life.

The Heir by Paul Robertson

Looking for More Good Books to Read?

You can find out what is new and exciting with previews, descriptions, and reviews by signing up for Bethany House newsletters at

www.bethanynewsletters.com

We will send you updates for as many authors or categories as you desire so you get only the information you really want.

Sign up today!